Chimalma's Ultimatum

Raymond Tolman

Chimalma's Ultimatum

Third in
The Serpent Trilogy

SUNSTONE
PRESS

SANTA FE

Sunstone books may be purchased for educational, business, or sales promotional use.
For information please write: Special Markets Department, Sunstone Press,
P.O. Box 2321, Santa Fe, New Mexico 87504-2321.

Cover art by author

Book design › Vicki Ahl
Body typeface › Granjon LT Std
Printed on acid-free paper
∞
eBook 978-1-61139-561-7

Library of Congress Cataloging-in-Publication Data

Names: Tolman, Raymond, 1948- author.
Title: Chimalma's ultimatum / by Raymond Tolman.
Description: Santa Fe : Published by Sunstone Press, [2018] | Series: Serpent
  trilogy ; 3
Identifiers: LCCN 2018032243 (print) | LCCN 2018032974 (ebook) | ISBN
  9781611395617 | ISBN 9781632932372 (softcover : alk. paper)
Subjects: LCSH: Domestic fiction.
Classification: LCC PS3620.O3285 (ebook) | LCC PS3620.O3285 C48 2018 (print)
  | DDC 813/.6--dc23
LC record available at https://lccn.loc.gov/2018032243

WWW.SUNSTONEPRESS.COM
SUNSTONE PRESS / POST OFFICE BOX 2321 / SANTA FE, NM 87504-2321 /USA
(505) 988-4418 / ORDERS ONLY (800) 243-5644 / FAX (505) 988-1025

Dedicated to Paul Flaherty,
a dear friend who shared
many rivers with me.

Preface

We live in a dangerous world. The doomsday clock has been inching closer to midnight, particularly during the last few years. Much of what we humans do plunges us closer to Armageddon. We as a species feel incapable of dealing with an ever more complex world, often we are our own worst enemies unknowingly bringing destruction to ourselves. Overpopulation and resource depletion, climate change, nuclear war, biological and chemical weapons, and endemic terrorism, all produce a gathering concern for our survival. We are fragile creatures that now depend on our science to provide for us cheap energy and resources that are rapidly running out. As our population continues to rise, forcing many of God's creations to become endangered or extinct, we continue to expand our civilizations to every conceivable area of the planet where we can grow food and live. But we continue that population growth at our own peril. In time, cheap and abundant energy will diminish, resources such as fresh water will be unobtainable and polluted. As a species we depend upon science to solve our problems yet many societies are currently rejecting science and turning inward. The wisdom to secure our future is waning. The world seems at odds with itself and sooner or later a mistake may happen. Perhaps a madman will set things in motion that cannot be stopped.

In *Chimalma's Ultimatum* almost two hundred years have passed since a world-wide pandemic occurred on planet earth. A mistake had occurred to conquer the serpents when a pathogen was released which not only killed off most serpents, a mutation occurred that also killed off most of humanity. A tiny number of humans as well as serpents survived the pandemic because they were living in isolated places where they had no contact with the infection. The survivors were able to reproduce, generating tiny pockets of humanity that were unaware of what had happened nor were they aware of other survivors. They all lived in a world devoid of humanity except for the few survivors in their own isolated communities. Humanity had to start all over again.

Humans were not the only survivors of the great pandemic. Five serpents also survived, namely Quetzalcoatl, Kulcukan, Teotihuacan, Tikal and Tsotzil. Quetzalcoatl, Kulcukan, and Teotihuacan decided to work with the humans of Serpiente in an effort to escape earth and return to their home in space. Tikal and Tsozil decided to return to their old ways of using humans to provide them with all their needs, namely the energy that was absorbed by them upon the death of humans.

I am thankful to many people who helped me while writing this book. Paul Flaherty comes to mind. Without his expertise and schooling, I would never have experienced the difficulties and lessons that life has to offer when exploring new rivers. I must give thanks to Judy Tolman, my soul mate, who explored those rivers, caves and climbed mountains with me. Needless to say, I could never have acquired the technology to pursue writing without her assistance. I would like to thank Jim Palmer who photographed my paintings that were used as cover art. I would also like to thank the fine people at Sunstone Press who were patient and kind while this book was being published.

Part 1

An Alaska Adventure

The ultimate weakness of violence is that it is a descending spiral begetting the very thing it seeks to destroy. Instead of diminishing evil, it multiplies it.
—Martin Luther King

And he laid hold of the dragon, the serpent of old, who is the devil and Satan, and bound him for a thousand years.
—Revelation 20:2

Post Pandemic

This is the story of the war that occurred between the human and serpent clans on planet earth after the year 2215 AD. Hindsight is said to be twenty/twenty. Since I lived throughout those years this is also my personal story, my history, but it is far more than that. It is the documentation of human evolution after the great pandemic that destroyed most human and serpent life on this planet. My name is Chato Williams and with the permission of Quetzalcoatl and Kukulcan, and with the documentation provided by the serpent Teotihuacan, as well as the scientists at Los Alamos Laboratories we will share our story with you.

Long ago in a lonely expanse of the Pacific Ocean far to the south of the mainland of what became mainland China a volcano came to life creating an island, one of many that formed and are still forming to this day as a result of the slow but inexorable force of plate tectonics. One particular volcano had rumbled and belched pyroclastic lava, tuff, and a tremendous amount of gases. But more than anything else it ejected enormous quantities of fine pumice. It was a precursor to what was to come in the next few weeks. In the span of a single week the volcano exploded, producing a fine ash that circled the earth many times and blotted out the sunlight that allowed photosynthesis to occur. This destroyed the source of all food on earth.

Within a few days the temperature plummeted all over the planet. Whole continents soon became covered in snow which slowly compacted from its own weight and metamorphosed into ice which covered all land except for a thin band around the equator. The white snow reflected sunlight back into space causing the temperature to continue to plummet, creating even more snow and ice. It was one of many reasons that an ice age was created that lasted for several thousand years. The Ice Age caused a dramatic die off of all forms of life on this planet. But life did survive.

The first time it happened was two million years ago during an age named the Pleistocene when small animals lived that would someday be the seed to all modern life on planet earth. It created a bottleneck whereby only a tiny fraction of the humanoids survived. At one moment the population of hominids who would someday become modern humans dropped to a mere few thousand individuals; some speculate that the number was far less. A precarious start to the human race, but indeed they did survive only to experience the same effect many times again. Based upon direct evidence provided by fossils that were meticulously studied by the people who lived on the earth during the recent interglacial millenniums, a massive death occurred. The volcano erupted several times during the Pleistocene and depending upon the earth's position in space in relation to the sun, created Ice Age after Ice Age resulting in several die offs and then, according to the hominid fossil records, a repopulation occurred. The hominid species that led to modern man was only a fraction of the creatures who suffered during those times but each time a tiny few of most species survived. The human survivors must have been the most aggressive, intelligent and incredibly lucky warriors alive at the time. They survived because they could adapt to a changing environment living a warrior lifestyle. They would kill and eat anything including other humanoids in order to survive.

There is evidence that what was to become the Mediterranean Sea was at one time a series of large lakes, perhaps like the Great Lakes in North America are now. In time the sea levels which had risen due to melting ice; rose, and broke through at the lowest place where the Straits of Gibraltar are located now. It must have been a tumultuous flood that occurred. Equilibrium occurred as the water plummeted from basin to basin until the level of the flooded land became the same as oceans. The last great basin to flood was the area known as the Black Sea. Archeologists have found extensive evidence of houses and settlements and of course newer sunken wooden boats which never decay because there is little oxygen in the great depths that exist there. It was here that the great flood ended and humanity started again.

The early humans, still in the Stone Age, must have experienced a tremendous die-off during those days. But adversities create a stronger human. The lush belt of green which circled the equator began to change. Vast areas such as the Sahara and Arabia dried out becoming deserts, forcing humans to migrate. When the world warmed up some ten thousand years ago the population of hominids exploded. In time they left their homeland of Africa and soon explored and occupied the entire planet. By then many earlier forms of humanoids had died off. Yet there were survivors of intelligent creatures that would be puzzled over and studied such as Neanderthals but in the end only one species survived and thrived, the creatures known as modern humans which in time would conquer and rule the entire planet.

The humans fled to the waterways, those rivers and of course the seas themselves were a source of food and therefore survival. It was at this juncture in time that humans banded together into large clans and the first small settlements became cities. Modern humans created everything from science to religion and built civilizations throughout the world. In time they would use their innate intelligence to create the wheel, build megalithic structures and eventually, ride in automobiles and fly across the skies in aluminum tubes called airplanes. At one time they even developed a terrible device which would split atoms to release tremendous amounts of energy and gave them an insight to whole new worlds of energy that existed deep inside the very atoms that comprise everything.

In other parts of the galaxy other creatures had long ago accomplished this feat. They had mastered the manipulation of energy that existed within the atoms that make up this world. One group of these creatures who had long ago given up war as a way to cope with dramatic environmental change traveled to earth. Those alien creatures looked similar to humans but had evolved millions of years longer than mere humans. The knowledge they possessed would appear to be as magic to any human who encountered them. They visited earth several times, studying, cataloging, and sampling the genetic material of creatures that lived on the beautiful blue planet. Then, after finding many interesting creatures that were studied and cataloged, they decided that there were few creatures here that would be of interest to them for now. Most earthly creatures demonstrated only instinctual reflexes to outside stimuli. Few showed promise of intelligent thought. Most earthly creatures could not plan for future changes in the environment. Only three or four earthly creatures appeared to have the capacity for self-recognition, much less long range planning.

Only one creature, the humanoids, appeared to have the potential for intelligence but they were slow learners and appeared to be absorbed in simple survival. Finding shelter, food and sexual partners was the mainstay of their existence. They spent their days defending their shelters, what food they possessed, and of course those sexual partners from voracious beast and other members of their own kind. The roots of war were inbred into them. On most planets where other creatures had evolved this way they learned too much. In one way or another they had committed suicide as a species. The humans present on earth seemed no different. Only the tiniest fraction of intelligent creatures managed to survive after acquiring great knowledge, particularly knowledge of global warfare.

The star people who visited earth also had their faults and they were certainly capable of making mistakes although usually mistakes only occurred with the interventions of other intelligent life. The star people accidentally brought with them a life form that had also existed for millions of years and had evolved a unique form of intelligence. They were the serpents, appearing to look similar to creatures living on earth known as snakes but they were intelligent creatures who were dangerous because they could enter the minds of other intelligent creatures and manipulate them. When the star people actually discovered serpents living aboard their starship, the star people, who referred to themselves as librarians, quickly decided to rid themselves of the creatures. The serpents were cleaned from the starship and marooned on this desolate and isolated planet in an area which at the time was completely devoid of intelligent creatures. Earth became their jail and their jail sentence was determined to be for all of eternity.

But in time humans explored into what would become America where they were discovered living among ice age animals. It was in the nature of the serpent creatures to enslave intelligent creatures and manipulate and use them. They relished and coveted the life energy that other creatures could provide them, particularly intelligent creatures. Humans fought with them at first but soon found themselves slaves to the wishes of the serpents. Civilizations arose only to find themselves providing sacrifices to the serpents. Those cultures evolved, flourished and then died, leaving only the ruins of their buildings as evidence that they even existed. It had taken thousands of years but finally the humans learned to fight against the serpents. They always lost those battles and their civilizations fell but some humans were able to make peace with the serpents as long as they provided the sacrifices and life energy that the serpents relished. The humans who made war with them never won until finally the most intelligent of these humans acquired new knowledge, a far more refined knowledge known as biological science.

It had taken many years but then the world had dramatically changed again. A pathogen had been created by a mad shaman, a military man who wore stars on his shoulders and who had many scientists who worked for him, who created a spell to rid the world of serpent creatures. He thought that by developing a pathogen that would rid the world of alien serpents, the world would be safe from the evil influences of the serpents. The shaman had long ago gone mad, then died from one of his own inventions, but the pathogens he and his scientists had created lived on. They were diabolical yet simple; a variation of the disease that caused mad cow disease had been genetically mixed with an extremely virulent but harmless disease that was undetectable until it was too late.

After many mutations, each producing an agent with virulent but harmless results, the tiny bundles of life that were benign suddenly mutated once again into a deadly form. Perhaps a different shaman was working this time, a serpent shaman; the pathogen became deadly to the humans. Humans carried the spell with them everywhere they went. Anyone who breathed the air in a room with infected humans would unknowingly become infected. The incubation period following human contact was invariably a slow process. The victims had no idea they were infected. But after many weeks they would inevitably become sick. With the silver birds that the humans flew in, the pathogen became an international virus, weeks before the evil spell was ever suspected. Even after it was detected the hubris of the humans caused them to cling to the belief that nothing could happen to them and of course by then it was too late.

The world only had a few thousand-people remaining alive; creating another genetic bottleneck. It had occurred before but that was many thousands of years ago when humans were just evolving and nature was responsible for the bottleneck. This time it was the humans who created the agent of their own demise. The cycle of life would necessitate starting again.

The Williams Community

I was the youngest boy in the settlement. Given the Indian name of Chato by my father, I started my migration where my great fathers had lived, in a cold and forbidding valley in southern Alaska. My ancestors were trappers who had lived here before the reckoning had occurred, before everyone had vanished from the earth. Living in the backwoods and being so isolated, we were survivors of the great death. We suspected that there may be other tiny pockets of humanity left on the earth. Indeed, there were survivors but most of them were unaware of what had happened and they were unaware of each other. For all practical purposes, each tiny tribe of people was the center of their own world.

Even the fortunate human survivors usually died off, as a result of their isolation. A man alone cannot reproduce and as a result, the total population of the earth dropped for a time to a few thousand-people living in tiny pockets where just by chance the right circumstances occurred that allowed for a continuance of human life. In Alaska, Siberia, and Australia along with some isolated oceanic islands, the pockets of humans that survived were so separated from each other that they were unaware that a plague had even occurred. Most lived as humans had before, in abject isolation unaware of the dramatic kill off.

There were a few people who had actually planned for a world-wide pandemic, war, or natural disaster. They were a group of people called survivalist, who hid away until the pathogen mutated again. When they finally emerged from their silos, caves and hideaways they found themselves in an entirely new world devoid of humans but surrounded by the material culture of the earlier humans. They quickly reverted to a Stone Age existence as soon as their stored supplies of gasoline and bullets ran out. The industrial knowledge to produce and use the earlier technology was quickly lost and barbarism became the norm.

There were other rare instances of survivors; humans who found themselves alive after everyone else had died who knew of the dramatic events that had been leveled upon the humans by the evil shamans. They were people who manned weather stations, military stations, submarine crews and even explorers who were isolated for long periods of time. They usually lived out their lives and then without partners to reproduce with perished. Few lonely souls were left to wonder what had happened.

It took over a year for the plague to mutate again, becoming a harmless and benign virus living among billions of other microscopic creatures. The genetically engineered creatures became like many other creatures in the microbial soup of evolution, totally unaware of the damage they caused. Like most life on earth, they were opportunistic creatures who devoured their host just as the humans had devoured the resources in their environment. Foolish people even insisted that it was God's will that they devoured the resources of the earth. After all, God had provided those resources for humans who foolishly believed that they were the center of the universe. They thought that it had all been placed there just for us, being totally unaware that the human body was itself a collection of millions of creatures that all worked together to form one organism recognized as human.

In time, archeologist would say, that the only humans that were alive after the plague were those that had been isolated from others by both vast distances and time. For example, there were ships that propelled themselves underwater, through the vast oceans of the world, using a nuclear reactor. They were ordered to stay away from the mainland for fear that they would contract the plague. They could stay underwater for years but in time, when the food ran out, they had to go into a port. Most of those ancient mariners died a delayed death but certainly they died, leaving no offspring. Although there were reports of small groups who survived aboard ships, ships that for one reason or another had avoided a port for more than a year. They were people who lived self-contained lives usually aboard fishing ships with all male crews. After the plague ran its course, again, the only true survivors would be those that produced offspring.

The real survivors were humans like my ancestors. I came from a small community of families that lived deep in the wilds of Southern Alaska. My great-great grandfather's family as well as two other families had carved out a small settlement on the banks of a tiny Alaskan river. The river at one time had an Indian name but no one remembered it, they just called it Williams Creek. The patriarchs of the families had been great friends who thought they would spend a year or two there, trapping game and living off the land with their families as best they could. They were doing it just for fun, on a dare taking an extended vacation while they were still young enough to enjoy themselves. They wanted to have an Alaskan adventure. Besides, if it didn't work, if the winters were too cold, the food ran out, or at any time the work became too unpleasant, they could easily return to Colorado where the comforts of civilization awaited them.

It was my great-great grandfather who found out what had happened. In those days, the world was connected by a spider web that allowed humans to talk to each other all over the world. It now all seems like magic to me, the spider web is utterly silent now. We still have the machines that talk to each other but now they are just useless pieces of plastic that house a confusing array of electronics. Generators had originally provided the electrical power to make them work but the generators had long ago run out of fuel. They too, were now just useless relics of a bye gone day.

All of Alaska was that way. It was littered with relics of bye gone gold camps that fueled the imagination as to what it must have been like. Williams Creek had at one time been one of those camps. A place where men dug a soft yellow metal out of the alluvium black sand found in the bends and deepest parts of the creek that ran through their valley. Now all we have to remind us of the old world is a small collection of books that had painstakingly been brought into the cabins at one time or another. The books that I would like the most were two books about Alaska written by an author by the name of Jack London. There was also a small collection of magazines that had accumulated in the house. Family members had worn them out looking at the faded pictures and reading and rereading the articles.

Everything that had to be shipped in or shipped out is moved by airplane in Alaska. In the spring of our last year as the pathogen was running throughout the earth, the family members all loaded their furs into backpacks, and hiked to a flat airstrip for a prearranged meeting. But no one ever showed up. We camped out on the runway for two days with good weather but the airplane failed to show up. Returning to the cabins, my ancestors started up a generator and got on the internet in order to find out what had happened. It was then that they learned of the devastation that had occurred to the human race. In only a few days, the spider web had nothing on the news sites except news of the plague. The entire world was in a complete panic as the infection had been carried everywhere humans congregated. Because it took several weeks before the deadly virus showed, usually by people noticing that they were getting flu like symptoms and getting forgetful, it had traveled throughout the world. In time the news reports became disjointed and vague and then the entire net went silent. The Williams' clan of humans knew what had happened. All the rest of mankind had all died from a disease, some kind of pathogen, a virulent and fast moving disease that caused their brains to become sponge-like. After several weeks, humans who caught the virus quickly lost their ability to remember details, people's names and dates. Then as it progressed they had trouble walking, talking, and then finally breathing. Then, without anyone left alive to be aware of it, within another year the pathogen had mutated again and was harmless, but by then it was too late with only tiny groups of isolated humans who had lived through the extinction event.

By the end of summertime, the citizens of Williams' Creek let their curiosity overcome them, deciding to hike out to the nearest settlement. It was down at the large lake that Williams' Creek and several other rivers flowed into. There was a Bed and Breakfast business there where tourists came to rent boats and fish in the lake. Some supplies could be bought there and arrangements could always be made to get people out of there. But the curious humans realized something was wrong long before they got to the actual lodge. There wasn't a living thing that could be seen. The hikers decided to drop their packs and just watch for a while.

After two hours, not a soul could be seen and by now they were noticing just how run down the building was. The front door was wide open allowing animals to enter at will. They watched as a family of raccoons went into the building. Certainly, if humans were inside one or the other would come running out. Nothing happened. Then they noticed something. A car was parked in the parking lot. Moving closer to it to get a better look they found inside of it, a person, who appeared to be sitting behind the steering wheel. As they crept closer, they suddenly realized that the person in the car was a skeleton wearing clothing. The tiniest of animals had consumed all the flesh. In something of a panic, they turned and ran back for their packs. They quickly returned to their wintery valley and the safety of their cabins.

Being terrified of the outside world, our families didn't believe in leaving the confines of our valley. We could live there indefinitely, but in time we ran out of everything that made living easy, things like gasoline, ammunition and canned food. Fortunately, we had some antique saws that someone had collected as a hobby. One of the long blades still had little cartoonish figurines painted on the long blade. Now, long after the gasoline had run out, the saws provided the tools to cut firewood. We reverted to the use of slings, bolos and bows with arrows when hunting.

My family had another dilemma to deal with, I was the last child born, the extra child, who would never have a mate, because in his small world there was no one of the opposite sex to mate with. I took it all in stride. Despite the fact that there was no one to mate with I was highly respected by everyone. I was, according to my mother and father, smart and obviously very athletic. As a young boy of sixteen years I was an accomplished hunter which took courage because of the crude implements we used. I was especially efficient at disposing of the large bears that constantly plagued the settlement. During the night, I would listen to the sounds around the tiny community which consisted of a dozen cabins, six of them occupied by people. More than once, one of the families would hide in fear inside their log pole cabins while a bear would spend long hours desperately trying to rip it apart in order to gain entry. The bears were after the stores of food inside the cabins and of course the delectable humans hiding inside would be good to also eat.

It was my job to sneak up behind the bear and plant several well placed arrows in it before the bear could turn and find me. Several remarkable experiences with bears were discussed around the hearth on wintry evenings. On a few occasions, I found myself up a tree shooting straight down at the bear to persuade it to leave.

Bears are usually solitary creatures that will attack if threatened or in particular if their cubs are perceived as being threatened. The females, as with most species, are the dangerous ones. But when food becomes hard to find and easy pickings are discovered around humans they can become a problem, often stalking an area in small groups. Once, I had run out of arrows and I found myself hacking at the face of a bear with a tomahawk until it gave up. Then when the bear finally left and I dropped down from the tree branches, another bear which was pierced by several arrows delivered by my father rushed by me. I then pursued the first bear until I could ambush it and finish the job. I do not relish eating bear meat, it is too greasy but that same grease is used for a number of things by us humans. During the long winter months, we would slather grease all over us to avoid the itching that dry skin produces. It also acts as an insulator against the cruel arctic winds that swept into the valley that was our home.

Winters were particularly difficult times for the families that lived along Williams' Creek. The snow would blanket the valley fifteen feet deep and we had to dig tunnels through it in order to go from one cabin to another. The extreme isolation was mind numbing. In the early years, several of us had committed suicide rather than to live in the extreme conditions but slowly the survivors had become accustomed to the deprivations of living in isolation. We had no choice.

Twice we had encountered men from the north, Indians or Inuit's as they were known. But as soon as we revealed ourselves, the Indians secreted away, terrified. They didn't want contact with the stranded people who lived in the Williams Creek community. Once, one of my uncles and I followed one of the Indians into the wilderness but with a snowstorm covering up the Indian's tracks, we had to give up all hope of making contact with outsiders.

Problems in the Williams Community

After the discovery of the great plague that had killed most humans our three families had actually grown in size, but as resources ran out and hope disappeared, fewer and fewer children were being born. It was the last winter that particularly bothered me. Everyone was desperate. One of the small children born to one of the families had died, a little girl. They had run out of the pemmican they processed during the summer months. The mother found that she could not make milk and the baby had starved to death. With nowhere to dig a grave we took the tiny infant and buried it in the snow. They following day we discovered that someone had dug the infant out of the snow and undoubtedly had eaten it. From that moment on there was suspicion among us that one of us would kill the rest of us for food. We had a cannibal among us and none of the fifteen living people were admitting the deed. Fortunately, I soon found a deer that had made the mistake of allowing a mountain lion to kill it. After the mountain lion had eaten its fill, I stole the carcass. It was just enough to keep everyone alive until other game was found, usually by me.

I had become an exceptional archer despite the fact that my arrows were made from willows that grew along the creek and were seldom straight, even when I cured the arrows using all manner of heat treatments as well as drying the shafts in clamps designed to keep the shafts straight. I was also quite accomplished as a thrower of the bolo. If I could get close enough, I could wrap the balls around the legs of a deer on the run and then as long as I avoided the thrashing antlers I could easily kill it.

I was the primary provider for the families of Williams' Creek but I also was very young and idealistic. Deep in my heart I knew that I had a greater calling and was seriously thinking of exploring further and further away from Williams' Creek but since everyone depended upon me I hesitated. But as the days grew longer, the snow disappeared, and summer approached I couldn't keep thoughts of leaving the Williams' Creek Community out of my mind. Then summer finally set in and it was a bountiful spring. Everyone ate flowers and wild onions that popped up in the green fields.

One night, after I had spent a long and arduous day helping the women picking summer berries that were stored for the long months of winter, I went to sleep early. Summer berries were the family's main source of vitamin C; they had to be hid away or processed into pemmican for the long winter. I was the best bear lookout in the family but it had been a good day, no bears. I relished the short summer months with long days that came each year. It was the season when everything thaws out and becomes green. I had no trouble at all falling fast asleep, even though the northern sun was still out.

Immediately upon falling asleep, I began dreaming. I dreamed of hunting a mountain lion that I had seen the winter before but suddenly the dream changed. A new dream had entered my consciousness. It started out as a series of long red filaments forming a geometric pattern followed by colors exploding into my dream with brilliant colors unlike any I had ever experienced before. Then a clarity of thought occurred. The dream was no longer a psychedelic display of colors but rather I felt like I was actually in the dream.

I dreamed that a friend and I were walking out of a series of vast serpentine canyons. The walls of the canyons were of yellow and blood red layers of sandstone and there were indications that a mysterious people lived there a very long time ago. We were intrigued by the intricate inlay work of the banded masonry that seemed so different to us yet for some reason very familiar as if we had seen it before. In my dream, I remembered walking up to the walls of one of the houses and marveling at the incredible amount of work that the structure would require. I had been used to living in a log cabin or in a teepee, while hunting. In my dream, it seemed that I had even camped several times in the homes of the ancient ones, and could only wonder about the people who had lived there and died out so long ago.

Petroglyphs covered many of the canyon walls. It truly was an ancient place. As we walked the final few steps out of a canyon, we realized that soon we would enter a large forest of cottonwood trees followed by a desert. In the distant north, we could see a large rabbit eared mountain surrounded by many lava flows from long ago; extinct volcanoes. We stopped to talk, yet I cannot remember what my companion looked like. We talked of following the waterway north, which was an odd direction we thought, why would the water flow north here? All the dry rivers we had crossed so far in the canyons had flowed to the west, to the big river that drained the entire area to the south. This was the only river that had any water in it at all. It really didn't matter; we realized the tiny trickle was going to disappear in the sand a few miles away. It was time to make a game plan. We walked along the game trail that followed the tiny river down to a field where huge cottonwood trees grew and in the distance, through the brush and trees, we could just make out a hidden house. As we neared the house, we could see a large structure with a huge back yard and a garden. The house amazingly still had a roof; it even had windows and a door. My companion and I had never seen a human house that was in such good shape. I realized when we got close to the house, that behind it were several other houses that were built similar to the ruins we had been camping in but they appeared much larger and newer with doors and windows and even roofs with strange silver panels on top of them. My companion hid away and watched while I explored.

The yard contained several large ovens used for producing ceramics and baking bread. I walked through rows of large pots that were in various stages of production. I looked around to see if anyone was there, then back at my companion who was hidden in the trees. My companion signaled for me to go on so I soon found myself standing in front of a large window with two large clay pots sitting on pedestals on each side of it. Then I walked over to the window and cupped my hands over both sides of my face to see through the glare, and looked in. There sat a young girl, combing cream colored hair in front of a large piece of glass that reflected her image. She was far more beautiful than anyone I had ever seen before. She looked up at me, and ran from the room. Thinking that I was in serious trouble, I ran from the house back into the cottonwood brush and hid there with my companion.

Watching the house, we noticed the young girl come outside and look around. Not seeing anyone and shaking her head she went back into the house. Curiosity overwhelmed me, after a moment I decided to risk another look through the window. I returned, but as I started to look in the window again, two large black snakes that were in the two ceramics next to the window, rose up on either side of me. They arched their backs as if to strike. Just then, the door opened again and the girl stepped back into the yard. Without saying anything she stared at me and the snakes. The snakes appeared to look first at me then the young girl, and then they changed into ravens right before my eyes and flew away, leaving me and the mysterious young girl to ponder each other. I reached up to touch her on the chin then I awoke with a start as I discovered a bug was trying to crawl up my nose.

It was still light outside when I awoke from the dream; the sun wouldn't set until much later. I could remember every detail of the dream. I normally didn't pay any attention to dreams but this dream was particularly vivid, it had literally exploded into my mind far more vivid than any other dream I had ever had. It made me ponder what it was all about. It made me start to think, it gave me ideas. I couldn't get the dream out of my mind.

Seeing the black snakes turn into ravens was quite mysterious to me. It had all seemed so real, what did it mean? I had little experience with snakes in Alaska. All I had ever seen were the tiny slippery snakes that played in the small streams that drained the valley. When it got cold they disappeared.

What were all those pots used for? I couldn't imagine. My people never used pottery. Who lived in the other houses? There were far too many of them to be only out buildings. There were obviously more people who lived there. Where did they come from? How had they escaped the plague? Keeping in mind that

I had never seen any of the objects in the dream and certainly I'd never met a woman outside of Williams' Creek, the only other women I knew were from the pages of ancient manuscripts and books that the family kept.

There was one magazine titled *Arizona Highways* with an article about ladies who were waterskiing on a lake called Lake Powell. I often wondered what their personal lives were like. I could read, actually I could read well and had memorized most of the books and articles still readable in our house. At one time or another, an earlier settler had painstakingly brought in a set of encyclopedias as well as sixty or so other books which made up the largest personal library within hundreds of miles. It was fortunate for those of us in the community. We all learned to read and discover things about the ancient world before the pandemic hit.

Learning to read was a strange experience for me. It only took me a few days after learning to decode the letters before I was reading. My mother had taught me but she was amazed at how easy reading was for me. Naturally, I assumed that everyone could learn to read in a few days. My mother said it could take many people years to learn to read. This all seemed incredible to me, but learning new skills had always been easy for me. My mother said I was a very smart boy and that it would be my responsibility to pass the skill on to my children, but I had no idea how it would be possible for me to have children since there were no mates available. I thought of some of the other people in the community who would have considered me to be a wasted human being. Without a family, you are nothing. Now, more than anything else, I wanted to know who the beautiful girl in the dream was, but for now, I had more pressing matters to take care of.

Two other men who were several years older than me were going to rebuild one of the cabins. It was a most difficult job. All the good trees that grew close to the cabins had long ago been downed for building material and firewood. It was a full-time job lasting all summer long just collecting firewood. It was hauled to the cabins and stacked up in piles that were several times bigger than the cabins. It simply took a lot of wood to survive a long winter in Alaska. A new cabin would require good pine logs that took hours just to process a single log. Each log had to be cut from a tree with all the limbs cut away. The bark was peeled away with a knife with two handles and two of the sides required shaping so they would fit snug together. Then the work would begin. Each pole was set into place with the ends notched to hold them together. Rafters were also built from smaller logs and shingles had to be hand cut by splitting logs into flat board- like sections and lapped over each other to provide a waterproof seal. Even so, the cabins had to be replaced ever few years because the snow would set on them for months at a time. During the summer months, they would rot. Three men working all summer long could rough in one good building. To finish the cabin which had a dirt floor required massive amounts of labor to saw wooden planks in order to fashion windows and doors. Finally, it all had to be bear proofed and put together without nails. Unfortunately, the antique saws we used were worn out before we ever started. Files were nonexistent, so a piece of river rock was used to sharpen the blades.

By the time the work was finished most days I fell into an exhausted and dreamless sleep. Toward the end of the summer I had the chance to take another afternoon off and used my time to sleep. As I drifted off to sleep my thoughts were upon bears. I didn't want to wake up with a bear sniffing at me contemplating a meal, so I pulled my tomahawk close to my side where I could get to it instantly. Then I drifted off into a sound sleep.

The dream exploded into my sleep as the one before had done with streams of red lines forming a geometric pattern followed by a brilliant kaleidoscope of colors with rapidly changing images going through my mind. I had experienced sleep paralysis before and thought for a moment, I was experiencing it again but this was very different.

Suddenly my mind focused upon a feather that was just showing behind a deep ravine. A single feather appeared then it moved. This was alarming to me. I focused upon the feather and noticed it move just a fraction of an inch. Suddenly a head appeared under the single feather and then a warrior leaped up appearing just like the one from a picture in a worn-out book I had seen many times. But unlike the Indians in my book this fellow was light skinned. This Indian had brilliant blue eyes and brown hair with three painted red streaks on each cheek and was rushing toward me with a tomahawk in his hand. Instinctively I wanted to grab my own tomahawk but found I couldn't move. Then, just as the Indian was about to split my head open, another tomahawk appeared in the middle of the warrior's forehead. The Indian fell before me with a large volume of blood rushing out of the deep gash that the tomahawk made. I turned to see where the tomahawk had come from and there was another warrior who I, for some reason, seemed to know.

I then felt someone touch me on the shoulder. Turning, I found the same girl I had seen in my previous dream on the ground next to me. It was as if she was my life partner and had been there all along. Then something disturbing happened. A large black snake crawled between us and then crawled away, disappearing into the brush.

Then I awoke. Looking around I could not find a trace of anything or anyone in my dream but the whole episode made my mind start to wonder again. I went back to sleep lost in those cracked glass blue eyes that sparkled in the light of my dreams. The remainder of the night was uneventful but upon awakening I immediately started thinking about the meaning of the dreams I had been having. They simply were not like regular dreams, they were just too real.

On my own, I decided to take my life in a new direction. I finally decided that I had to find out what the dream was all about. I was going to take a chance that the plague had subsided. More than likely, I would be dead in only a few months, one last victim of the plague. But, if I could avoid the old one's places I might have a better chance of avoiding the plague. There was only one way to find out and that was to travel to those other parts of the world. Maybe the plague had disappeared altogether, and after all, I had seen two other humans but it had been two years ago. I debated the pros and cons of leaving the Williams' Creek Community. I figured that I could always return home if I didn't find anyone, if the plague didn't kill me. But then, I thought to myself, what was I accomplishing here in Alaska? People here needed me but I would never be able to live a full life, not without a mate. For some reason, having a mate seemed paramount to me. After all, I had a right to happiness too.

I started thinking about my options, secretly wanting to leave the Williams' Creek Community and find a life of my own. Maybe even find the girl who visited me in my dreams but then, they were just dreams. Besides how in the whole world could I possibly find her, if she really even existed. I would dismiss the thoughts of her in my mind but invariably she would return in flashes of light, sometimes appearing before me while I was having a dream about something entirely different then she would disappear. For a while I considered that magic spirits were toying with me. Maybe a sorcerer was vexing me and playing with my dreams but I didn't believe in such things. If it was something in my food that was causing the dreams, I could not imagine what it could be; no one else reported visitations in their dreams. Again, I dismissed all thoughts of the dream but they always returned and she was always there, a beautiful illusion. More than beautiful, she was my life mate, there was already a bond there, and I could feel it. I had what was to everyone else an infatuation, a fixation, a delusion that I had created by myself that in time led to teasing by the older men who all had mates.

I normally loved to be teased by the older men as well as the kids. I was mature for my age and knew that their teasing was not meant to be cruel; rather it was a form of play. Only one of the older men teased in a cruel fashion but then he teased everyone in a cruel fashion. The older man had no friends in the tiny community and it was noticed by many that he constantly fought with his mate. The whole affair caused friction in the tiny community.

I just considered the older man a weak individual who had to be worked with, no matter what it took, but it also made me think of planning an escape route in my mind. I would make my way to the lake that was far down the valley, where the Williams' Creek flowed past the cabins and fed into a much larger river just before it fed into the lake. I had, of course, been all the way to the lake and had even been close to the human settlement that was there. I knew that the runoff from the lake, many miles below, in the extreme southernmost part of the lake, where I had never been, would flow over a large dam constructed by the old ones. The spillway always carried water forming a large river that eventually fed into an even larger river that went all the way to the ocean. I knew all that from a yellowed map of Alaska that hung on the wall of one of the old cabins.

Presenting a Plan of Exploration

I finally disclosed my dreams and presented my plan to my mother and father. They talked to others in the Williams' Creek Community and before long I was the center of a raging debate. Several members of the families objected to any thoughts of me leaving, they needed my labor and skills but to my surprise, my own parents decided it would be a good idea. George Williams, my father, was most helpful in my decision making. He would say to others, "Maybe Chato could eventually find out what is happening in the place we used to live called Colorado in a country called America. What did we have to lose? If he stayed, eventually he will just grow old and die and no one will ever know or care."

I had no mate to create a family of my own and in time I would have no one to take care of me as the other children in the Williams' Creek Community did for their ageing elders. I had to think about what I was going to do as the summer dragged on. I hadn't convinced myself that it would be a good idea to leave the community where I knew I was needed. But needed for what? Sure, I provided food for the community and had killed more than my share of bears but what kind of future could I really have here?

Finally, everything changed in the Williams' Creek Community. Despite the fact that they had laid in food for the winter one of the older men and his mate was found dead. Apparently, someone had taken a tomahawk and hacked them to death. It was a useless crime. As a group their chances of survival were now less and it didn't take long until the culprit was detected. It was the older man with the cruel tease who had killed them. Everyone thought the crime was one of passion, maybe he coveted the other man's mate or cabin or maybe he was simply losing his mind. It didn't matter. They caught him in the act of slipping up behind one of the children and attempting to slit the child's throat. Living in extreme isolation had finally created a murderer among us, someone who had no firm contact with reality. Everyone tackled him and the man couldn't explain why he had committed murders, only that he had been dreaming peculiar dreams and that he was being directed to kill everyone. No one believed him, despite his pleading that he had been singled out by someone or something, he was having deep feelings that he needed to kill the rest of them.

Then in a moment when no one was watching the man ran away, running up Williams' Creek and into the deep canyon land that was far from the settlement. It was an insane move for even a madman to make. He took no weapons with him, not a fire making kit, not a scrap of food. His body was found a week later where it had been attacked by wolves. His mate was so depressed over the episode that she committed suicide by wandering off into the woods and cutting deep slashes into her wrist. When wolves caught the smell of the blood they found her before anyone else in the settlement, and she also was lost.

The settlement had lost all the men who could do heavy work except for me. All that remained were children, old people and I. We sat around for some time debating what to do and finally my father began directing everyone to do something. He knew that during the long winter months they would all perish if they did not have something to occupy their time. Everyone was given orders to work on a new project.

Plans were made to construct a boat that I could use to get down the river. It would take all winter to construct it even with everyone's help. Father, who was the leader of the community, truly believed that by giving everyone a goal to work toward, everyone would have less time to get into trouble. It was a desperate ploy that provided everyone hope despite the obvious fact that it might be nothing but a death sentence for me and a slower one for them. After all, even if I did discover a livable world, how could I return? How would it be possible to paddle a boat against the fast river currents I was bound to encounter? The obvious was never spoken, that more than likely I would never be seen again. Everyone took turns getting just the right supplies together to enable my survival. I found myself dreaming about how to construct the sea kayak. It was as if someone was giving me instructions through my dreams but I decided that many great ideas must come from dreams.

We planned to construct a twenty-foot-long sea kayak which began by finding just the right tree. In our world, we knew every tree for miles around, it would take us a long time to travel away from home in search of that perfect tree. We needed a tree that could be split with wood splitters into very long planks which would then be further cut into strips about an inch wide. We spent almost a week looking down river until we found just the right tree with few limbs well up the trunk. After cutting it down we split it on the spot. Carrying the log back whole to the settlement would have been a very difficult job even for many people so instead we cut it into strips to make the load manageable. Once that very difficult job was done everyone took turns spending considerable time with a simple knife rounding the edges of the thin slits of boards until they appeared to be sanded by a machine. The next job was to cut a keel board and cross frame plates which would hold the long wooden slits apart and provide rigidity to the craft. Father took down some plyboard shelves, shelves that normally would hold canned goods in one of the older cabins. We had no canned goods anyway.

The design required much more than just a simple shell. The long ribs were held into place using the shelve wood to provide the compartments that would hold all the gear I would take. It took several weeks to cut the compartment separators for the ends of the boat which would guarantee the boat would float even if submerged under a wave. Finally, each storage compartment was sealed with bear grease. The keel, which would bundle and hold all the strips together, would prove to be the hardest to carve. We found a few metal screws from the shelving boards but decided not to use them as the salt water would cause them to rust and eventually fail. We built the keel from a curved triangular board which would cut though the water. The inside of the keel had to be wide enough to allow holes to be drilled in which the wooden slits could be pegged in side by side and yet still strong enough to function as a keel. After mounting the strips to the hull the ends were wrapped with leather strips and then the whole thing was glued together with tree resin. As the hull was constructed the women worked in the long and cold evenings sewing cured deerskins together, in the shape of the boat and sealing them with bear grease.

When camping on a beach the sea kayak would double as a shelter that I could crawl into during rain, snow or even to avoid pesky mosquitoes. The paddler's compartment was just long enough to allow a sleeping person to comfortably slide between tied in dry bags. We built several models of boats so that when we built the real thing it fitted together exactly. I was unaware that thousands of years before, people had explored and conquered an entire continent called North America traveling in just such water crafts.

Two parts of the kayak had to be improvised. First of all, real kayaks that are made by hand require lots of marine grade plyboard held together with glue and screws. Yet throughout ancient history people have constructed sea kayaks that were not only water proof, they were flexible. That flexibility came from lacing the wooden compartments into place rather than gluing and screwing them into place. The Vikings, for example, had long ago figured that a flexible boat will last far longer than a stiff boat and do far better with waves pounding down on it.

We took our time and really designed it well. The end compartments had sealed air bottles that would keep the kayak afloat, even if completely submerged. I knew that soon I would be living in a completely different way. I spent hours every day finding and testing equipment that I might need and use, usually deciding I could live without it. Then as the boat began to take shape, I had the funny feeling that we were inventing something that had already been invented long ago. We packed it and unpacked it many times, each time eliminating those things that we decided would be too heavy or too cumbersome to portage. Having less to carry around a rapid was definitely better.

We decided the things that I could not live without was a fire making kit, bow and arrows, two knives, one small and one large, my best tomahawk, a bolo and a small triangular saw which could be used in an emergency. Using a river stone, I could keep it sharp. I included an old iron Dutch oven which weighed a lot but considering how much I believed I would use it, I decided it must go with me. I would also have to have fresh water containers that would act as floatation when empty. Then there were packs to consider. Waterproof packs were made from animal skins that fit into the waterproof compartments and could easily be taken out and portaged over what was bound to be difficult terrain around impassable rapids.

Early one spring morning, the entire community helped me carry my packs and the kayak down Williams' Creek until the creek was large enough for us to line it using ropes. We were able to load the kayak and line it down several miles of the creek until another major creek joined Williams' Creek with enough water for me to actually float down the remainder of the way to the lake. There I departed from the only family and people that I knew in the entire world. It was a very freighting and lonely feeling knowing that I might never see a human being again. I didn't expect to find any human beings, yet I had a nagging feeling that the whole community was depending upon me. But there was hope, an impossible hope that only the most desperate of people retain. People who live in a death camp and lose hope soon die. But with me searching for answers which might provide an unforeseen intervention, the families had something to hope for.

For a few days, I saw no evidence of the old ones at all, just glimpses of the trail which followed the stream until it finally dropped into the lake. Paddling the short trip up the lake I arrived at the Bed and Breakfast. Tying off my boat I walked over to the rock where two years previously we had all stared at the skeleton in the car. It was still there, somehow balanced behind the steering wheel. The jaw had dropped away and the hat was over to one side exposing long strands of brown hair. The skeleton had belonged to a woman, I thought to myself. I knew that sooner or later, I would see many more skeletons. The door to the lodge was still open and a major portion of the roof had caved in. I thought about going into the old structure to see what was inside. There likely were things there that would be useful but I felt the fear I had felt before. Besides, I thought to myself, if I contracted the disease that killed humans, I would have less time to explore and if nothing else, I wanted to see as much of the world as I could before I died.

It took me three days of hard paddling to get to the other end of the lake. The shorelines were completely overgrown with trees and brush. Walking along the shore it would have taken me two weeks of hard hiking to get to the dam, assuming I did not run into bears or wolves and have to deal with them. I had already developed a deep appreciation for the kayak and was pretty proud of myself. After all, I could be the first person in a new era to explore the world. I was a later day Christopher Columbus.

The dam was a huge earthen and cement structure that held the waters of the lake in place taking me three days to portage around. Over the cement spillway of the ancient construction, a large volume of water spilled over a curved concrete spillway down to huge man made blocks which broke up the tremendous flow. Below the spillway, a large raging river flowed into what I believed would flow into an even larger river, a river so large that at one time it had small ships that went up and down it; originally paddle wheelers that pounded the water during the gold rush delivering everything imaginable. Years later it was traveled by tourist boats loaded with people who wanted to see firsthand the deprivations that the early miners had experienced.

The question was, could I paddle the sea kayak to the large river? The river below the dam was imbedded by rock beds forming huge rapids that churned the water into a frothy white for as far as I could see. It would take me a full week to portage, line, and paddle my boat past the rapids on the river. It would have taken even longer but the roaring river had at one time jerked the kayak out of my grasp while I was attempting to lead it past one particularly bad place. All I could do was watch as the kayak raced away from me far faster than I could possibly keep up. Fortunately, I found the kayak pushed up and trapped by a small tree that had fallen into the river. After spending a day cutting the tree away, releasing the boat, I was pleasantly surprised to discover that the river finally settled out after only a couple of more long miles. The rapids were a real chore to get past, but then maybe it worked both ways. Maybe it kept people from going up the river. Who would want to go up the river, I wondered to myself? As far as I knew, there was nobody left down there to go up the river.

Below the rapids, I could just sit in my seat and float along enjoying the view the river afforded me. Immediately the world changed. There were long sections of the river in which only an occasional ripple occurred along the bank, usually where a tree had toppled into the current forming another sweeper that I could easily paddle around. I had time to myself and found myself thinking about my place in the world. I was exploring a land that at one time was occupied by many people. I could not imagine how many but I knew that there was at one time millions of people who had disappeared. I considered the prospect that they may have left ghosts and I might need to deal with them, but it really didn't bother me too much, after all, I was a living ghost myself, from a bygone era.

Exploring an Alaskan River

I knew it might take me most of the summer to reach the coast, I took my time, ever so stealthy, not making a sound and truly enjoying the new views that the river afforded. It was certainly a very different world than the tight confines of Williams' Creek Community, yet I was careful to avoid possible contact with the old people who left every sort of ramshackle house and mineral workings. I discovered that there were many different animals and plants here on the river that I had never seen before. Instinctually I knew that some were edible and some like mushrooms were to be avoided. What really amazed me was the multitude of berry producing plants that were along the river. I recognized blueberries like the ones that grew along Williams' Creek. But here I discovered great fields, overgrown and forested but still showing distinct rows of plants. A few I recognized and many that were new to me. If the ladies from Williams' Creek knew of the abundance of the berry plants I was seeing, they would be very envious.

My body craved berries, the only type of food that was sweet. Unfortunately, at his time of year they are only tiny buds of bitter green. After collecting a small bag of them that I could boil in water to make a tea, I began to think that maybe the rest of my companions at Williams' Creek, had been fools to stay there.

I was in control of my own fate, free and in perfect health, my teeth are perfect. Long ago, my ancestors made a practice of cleaning our teeth after eating, particularly after eating meat. On the other hand, I wondered if I had already exposed myself to the deadly pathogen that had killed so many, I could already be dead. Perhaps just being here was all it took to get sick. No, I will be ok as long as I don't touch anything that belongs to the old ones. Just thinking about it all seemed useless, besides every bend of the river seemed to provide a new mystery to solve. Traveling slowly, along the edge of the river, was dangerous but I wanted to know things, to explore. I pulled into naturally occurring places along the river that I thought other humans might have visited in the recent past but I found no trace or other humans. Not a cut down tree stump, or single track. No fire pits. It was obvious that humans had not lived here along the river for many generations.

Camping provided needed rest from the river. After settling the canoe along the sandy shore, I would tie off the boat first up river then down river. Unpacking just what I needed for a place to sleep and cooking gear. This way, if I had to return to the boat and disappear downriver in a hurry, I could. I experienced only one difficult moment. While camping on an island that was actually a spur connected to the bank, I discovered that wolves had found me one evening. As I sat eating my rabbit stew I first heard them making their distinctive howls in the distance but shortly they all became very quiet. I knew what this meant; they had found me. Gathering up my bow and arrows as well as a tomahawk always carried in a belt I climbed a nearby tree that afforded good branches where I could brace myself, and silently waited. Shortly I could see shadows running through the trees behind my camp but I remained motionless as they zeroed in on my camp. Finally, the largest of them trotted out to my campfire and cautiously sniffed around. I placed a well-aimed arrow directly behind the ears of the wolf. Two other wolves then followed the alpha male out of curiosity and I placed well aimed arrows into them before they knew where the arrows were coming from. With three of them mortally wounded, the rest of them turned on the still struggling wolves. I watched as they tore each other up then just as mysteriously as they had arrived, they left, leaving tuffs of fir and blood everywhere. I repacked my boat as the night slowly arrived and slid off down the river to find a real island where I might be a safer.

Dropping closer to the coast, I floated past several rusting old hulls that had at one time been large boats that carried people and goods up and down the river. I avoided them, swinging to the opposite side of the river. Here was even more evidence of the ancient ones' houses. I took the precaution of camping where I knew I would not be seen. If an enemy sees you take off the river you are a dead man. They know exactly where to find you. If the enemy does not see you take off the river it is almost impossible for them to find you. There is too much brush for them to put up any kind of search, as long as you don't build too large a fire and create smoke. I was careful, just in case my theories about a planet devoid of people were wrong. I usually camped on small islands to avoid wolves, bears and ghost.

Several days later I come upon the confluence of the much larger river. I could not remember its name from the cabin map and was amazed at how large it was. I never paddled at all down the river. I simply floated, enjoying the trip. It was a terribly lonesome trip and I missed my family and all the other humans I had known. I wondered why I called those people 'humans.' Recently I had found myself placing objects in categories. It was a game I played in order to occupy my mind. I realized that I represented the only human here. Was there even a category called human anymore? Certainly, I knew that if I made a mistake and had an accident there was no other humans to call for help.

As I paddled my way to the ocean, I saw more and more evidence of the old human settlements that existed along the river. Evidence of the old ones could be seen like ghosts, flowing up and down the hillsides. Sometimes the paint still showed on the sides of old structures, making me wonder what kind of a building it was and who had once lived there. Many of them were not really buildings used as a place to live at all; they were the remains of ancient mines used to extract the yellow metal that brought humans to the area in the first place. As a child, we had panned gold out of Williams' Creek. The old ones heated up the flakes of gold and let them cool into tiny beads which became jewelry and fishing line weights. Being soft, the gold was useless for anything else. My grandfather had once said that most of the humans who dug in the earth for the yellow metal only managed to dig their own graves.

I had never realized just how many people there used to be. I certainly could not imagine personally knowing that many people. I wondered how they all got along. How did they all manage to live? Certainly, they could not all be living off the land, with that many people the wildlife would quickly disappear. Most of the buildings they had lived in were nothing but foundations, cement rock squares. Some of the better built and larger houses were still standing but all the wooden structures had rotted and even the brick ones had fallen in. Obviously, there had been massive earthquakes sometime in the past. My great grandfather once described an earthquake that had occurred on Williams' Creek. Large rock falls and landslides had occurred well up the valley. Those places, now overgrown, all looked natural to me. Just like here on the river, everything was overgrown with trees and brush. But I could still see the old buildings or at least where they had been. Some of the buildings appeared to have been dragged from their foundations for a considerable distance. This puzzled me, how could an earthquake do all that to houses? With their collapsed roofs and walls and trees growing out of what had one time been homes and the streets where humans drove around in moving masses of metal were completely overgrown with small trees. The cars and trucks that once carried a multitude of humans around were all just hunks of metal sitting around in all manner of positions. Again, it all seemed like magic to me. Nothing lived here now but wild animals. I could imagine, in the restraints of the overgrown cities were many hidden dangers, easy places to get hurt or eaten. But I was curious; paddling close to the shore to see what I could safely see.

I didn't go into the old places for one good reason. They were places of death and whatever had taken the lives of the old people could still be around. I wasn't sure what the disease was or even what a disease was, I had never experienced any disease other than a tooth that I accidentally cracked and which had become infected. It had occurred when I was a very small child. It was pulled and within a few days I was fine. As I grew into mature teeth, my problem of the missing tooth corrected itself when a new one grew in its place.

The Red Warrior

Eventually the buildings suddenly stopped altogether and the river continued to flow several hundred more yards down to a pristine beach formed where the river dumped its ice-cold water into a vast ocean that contained salt water. I had never seen an ocean before and was mesmerized by what I was seeing. Then I heard a strange sound, and in the river water something leaped into the air. It was an arrow, ricocheting off the water and harmlessly disappearing into the deep water. Then I heard a thud. I had been around enough close calls with errant arrows to know that I was in danger. I paddled as hard as I could away from the flight of the arrows and out to the other side of the river and finally into the sea. Turning to see who had shot at me, I could see a large and very wild looking warrior standing atop a large rock. The man appeared to have been painted bright red at one time, but the color was crumbling off where he moved his muscles. He was wearing protective sheets of metal like armor over his overly developed muscles. Having missed with the arrows, he grabbed and jabbed a large ax into the air. A challenge, the apparition was screaming. I couldn't make out what the man was saying, but the meaning was clear. I plunged my paddle into the water and ventured into a whole new world.

I was thankful that I had avoided the warrior. I realized that if I had been just a few feet closer to the shore I would be dead. I was blessed to be alive, but the apparition also opened up a whole new set of problems and possibilities. Maybe the plague hadn't lasted long. Maybe there were others like him and of course, the Williams' family that had survived. I thought about the two Indians I had sighted just before they saw him and then darted away into the forest. But his father had said that the Indians had always lived far to the north away from other people.

It would be understandable that a few of them existed, but here the plague obviously had run its course. I could not wrap my mind around a simple question; how could people possibly live where the old humans lived? What kept them from getting sick? I had only seen one warrior, but I wondered if there were not others. Was he a lookout for a whole family of warriors? I instinctively knew that in the mind of the warrior, he was protecting his property; it was his town, even if it was built by a vanished race. Was it full of treasures that made living more bearable? There was no way for me to know it but, the warrior owned a female woman who was with child, his child. He was like all creatures that protect their young.

I decided that the warrior that shot at me was defending his territory like many animals do. He was scared that he would be challenged. Challenge him? Who else had challenged him? Why was he so scared, I asked himself? Perhaps the warrior thought that I carried the plague with me. I thought about the arrow and thought to myself that I would like to take those arrows away from him. I could discover secrets to the warrior's survival. Then I brushed it off, laughing at myself. I had never thought about the idea of stealing something from another person. Where I had come from, stealing had been unheard of until just recently. Now even in Williams' Creek there was someone who had stolen food. That food had been stored by another human to use as food. The world of Williams Creek had suddenly changed.

I was surprised at the thought, undoubtedly, I would discover more about myself. I decided that it would be smart to be invisible for the rest of his trip. I ventured far out into the sea where I would appear only as small speck on the horizon. Besides, the waves were not so high there. Then I turned and paddled south along the coast. Who knows, I thought to myself, maybe I would find people there that were friendly. I pulled myself along thinking about it all, wondering about the future. It would be several hours later before I would venture a landing. I had to find a beach with no human habitation at all, not a single track; I didn't want to deal with warriors, wolves, ghost, or unknown perils.

Upon landing I discovered an arrow stuck in the stern of my kayak. Studying it, I was confused. It was a perfect arrow made of a lightweight metal with a razor tip, not at all like the crude ones my family made from willow branches. Then it dawned on me. It had probably been an arrow the old humans had made. I carefully removed the arrow embedded in the stern of the kayak, and added it into my own quill of arrows. Then after scouting the area and finding nothing but small animal tracks I made camp.

Coastal Geological Changes

After leaving the ancient city I found that the safest route down the coast was by camping on tiny islands well out in the ocean. For a way, they were everywhere, tiny islands with young, juniper and pine trees. They were covered with new forest growth; the floor of the forest could hardly hide the ancient sea beds. Either the oceans had dropped here or the land arose. I could not imagine a force that could cause that. In other places, the islands' ancient trees continued right out into the water, only there, they were dead, covered in crystalline salt. It was obvious that sometime in the past the land had sunk there, leaving only the mountaintops still above the waterline.

Then I ran out of islands. For several days I hadn't found a place that would accommodate a camp. The ocean crashed onto a rocky shore with steep and barren hills as far as I could see. Few beaches presented themselves and there had been no fresh water for days. The only time I had come ashore was to fix an occasional meal. I often had to sleep in the kayak. I couldn't risk trying to land the kayak on a rocky shore. I could swim well but I knew that the waves could catch the boat and plunge me onto the shore, crashing me on the rocks, destroying the kayak and probably losing all my most important gear. I needed a flat sandy beach.

Where I was, the rocks of the shoreline jutted well out into the sea. Then I rounded a corner of a large hill that careened large boulders far out into the sea. Rounding the boulders, I discovered a river valley that had cut through the mountainous terrain, a river that carried fresh cold water from far away, and deposited it here in the salt water. The harbor where the river dumped its load was huge. It would take me two hours just to paddle across it.

It looked very inviting. I could see white beaches where water lapped up on a flat shore. Fifty or so paces past the crashing waters of the surf, the valley had a rich forest growing, extending up the side of a valley as far as I could see. I would carefully line my boat up so that I was perpendicular with the shoreline, then start paddling at just the right speed so that the wave would carry me along and deposit me on the beach. The wave landed the kayak perfectly.

As soon as the water started its cyclic run back to the ocean where it would gather energy for another run at the beach, I quickly unlaced the skirt that kept the water out and waited until the next wave came in and gently lifted the kayak for another short distance onto the sandy beach. As soon as the water started to recede again I leaned over and rolled out of the boat. I had been in the kayak for three days now; it would take me a few moments to walk correctly so I crawled and as soon as I could, stretching a rope in order to tie off the kayak. I immediately began unloading the boat, making a portage run to the tree line carrying leather bound packs containing everything I owned. Later I would return and drag the boat into the trees and retie it, a habit I had picked up after the wind blew my kayak out to sea one late evening and I had to swim for it. It could have been a disaster.

After taking several loads I dragged the empty kayak to where I could disappear into the forest. A short exploratory walk up and I found a platform of earth that was absolutely flat. On it, small trees were growing but there was a natural clearing that would accommodate a desperately hoped for camp. Again, I carried the heavy loads and kayak to the clearing. It was a routine that I did without even thinking and each time I had to apply additional bear grease to the keel before putting it back into the water.

By removing some of the structure inside the boat I was able to relieve the stress on it when I turned it up on its side and tied the ends down. After cutting and placing some short branches against the hull of the kayak, I plunged the cut end of the branches as deep as I could into the sand and then tied the boughs over the open side of the canoe. Then I covered the branches and hull with layers of leather that was sewn together and functioned as a tent. Finally, inside the tent, I covered the ground with rolls of leather, laid my bedding on top of it, and finding myself totally exhausted, rolled on top of it and fell sound asleep.

The following morning, I awoke to a new world. Hungry and thirsty, I walked over to the river. Realizing that it was full of fish, I knew it would be easy to noodle a fish out of the banks and I knew I could easily find food in the sea. When I returned to the camp, I started rounding up sticks to start a fire.

Feeling better, after a fish breakfast, I started cutting many of the smaller pole trees down, a laborious job done with the small saw that I carried with me. I would push the small trees over as far as I could and then put the teeth of the saw where it was bending. The cuts were easy with the small saw. With the kayak resting against the back wall, I rigged a cabin frame directly over the entire kayak, as much to protect it as to hide myself. The kayak was my home, on and off the water. Without it, I would have no means of escape.

I was content with this camp but had not ventured far, I hadn't had time to. Now I was wondering if I should have made such a permanent camp. With all the trees in the valley, everything was hidden, my camp was invisible but so was everything else. I had no idea what might be just up the river, and I had made a small fire that could give me away, but then I had to eat, I had been starving but now my mind wondered to the red warrior I had seen. I gathered up a small pack, a possible bag, a bag that contained everything I would need in a possibly bad situation along with my bow and arrows and ventured a short walk from camp. I followed the natural route which was along the river until after only a hundred yards or so I discovered a rock walkway. There on the bank above my head was a cement platform with rusting pipes that once served as a handrail which held humans or something back from falling into the river. Climbing up to it I could clearly see a path leading to a rock wall connected to a rock house that was connected to other houses for as far as I could see through the trees. A hidden city awaited exploration.

It was obvious that it must have been a ruined city long before the death of humans. In most places only the foundations, made of rock survived. In one small section of the city the roofs were still in place on the houses and they were bone dry except for scat that animals had left. There was nothing in the houses, they appeared to be picked clean and then deserted. One structure was very different however. It was a house in use when the plague hit. I didn't like the idea of exploring the homes of the old humans, although they contained many useful items, they also contained the remains of the families that once lived there. After they realized they had the plague, it took the occupants several weeks to actually die from the pathogen and in a few houses, something else had happened. They took their own lives rather than face an agonizing end.

After opening the front door and walking slowly though the house, I found three skeletons where they died, in their beds. Next to one, on the floor was a hand gun, along with several boxes of ammunition. Being careful to look but not to touch anything I examined the damage the bullets had done to the craniums. I had never used a gun before but I knew that they made a loud noise revealing the shooter and decided to leave it and the ammunition lying on the floor.

Hugging the Coast

After three days of exploration without finding a trace of any recent human occupation, I was rested and left the camp. I was still afraid of what might be out there. I had gotten my packing and unpacking routine down to a fine science. I was also still discovering that I was lugging things around with me that I didn't need. My load was getting lighter by the month. But it was only a matter of time until the weather would change. I discovered that I couldn't push the kayak into a hard wind and expect to go anywhere. Several times I strained to go somewhere only to discover the wind had pushed me back to where I had started. Sometimes the wind blew for days on end. On windy days, I would take care of chores like hunting game, gathering berries and tubers and gathering wood, and then I would crawl into bed. I had one magazine with me. The one that had my favorite article about the waterskiing ladies, it also had many articles with pictures that looked a lot like my dream; a desert area with lots of yellow and red rock. I thought if I could find this place in *Arizona Highways*, I would be closer to the source of my dream. After the wind subsided, I continued my trek south.

I had learned to use the islands as a windbreak from the ocean, camping on the east side of the islands not only provided a wind break from the cold wind, snow and rain that fell, the east beaches seemed gentle. Sometimes the snow fell sideways rather than falling down. On those days, I rarely came out of my shelter. There also seemed to be more wildlife that provided food on the east side of islands. I had to find my way through a maze of newly formed islands that seemed to parallel the coast. It seemed to me that the entire land mass had risen out of the sea creating new islands. There was no ancient habitation on the islands, and the ancient settlements that hugged the coast were always well up, shelved on a former coastline. This was fortunate as far as I was concerned; it meant that any monsters like the one I had seen before would be hidden in the old buildings much too far for them to be able to get to me, but I never saw any humans along the coast, just deer, bears and elk. Once I thought I saw a mountain lion, but wasn't sure. I had seen few mountain lions in the wild but it had all happened too quickly for me to be sure.

Hugging the coast did have its disadvantages. More than once, I found myself paddling down a long harbor only to discover that the island was connected to the mainland. When this happened, I had to turn around and paddle several miles back to find a new route. It was a dangerous maneuver, once I had exposed my existence I knew someone or something might be waiting for me, it could be a trap.

The confusing labyrinth of islands I paddled though caused me to make many mistakes. But I was learning. Making mistakes; and solving the problem was how I learned. I clearly understood that I was totally responsible for my own actions. In most situations, I had figured out that it was easier to go south by not hugging the shore. I taught myself how to use the stars for navigation. I had no idea of the names of the constellations that rose and set at specific places on the horizon but I knew about one in particular that rotated around the North Pole. I would look for the Big Dipper and then find the faint star just above the cup in the dipper. Then looking in the opposite direction I memorized the constellations and figured out true south. At night, I would paddle toward those stars. Wondering about the ancient ones, I was beginning to understand how it all worked wondering about the ancient ones. Was celestial navigation a skill they used? Surely, I thought, seafaring tribes of humans used those skills. I wondered about people that once lived in the place called America. Did they drive in caravans that traded across great expanses of land? Did they use the stars to navigate or their spider webs to find their way around?

I found himself studying something interesting when I realized that there was an ancient shoreline, mostly covered up by trees and brush, but in places it was plainly visible, well up, above the current shoreline. In places, it glistened in the sunlight. The original shoreline, it would mark the way for me, but only if I could avoid the numberless side canyons. I discovered that instead of paddling up the side canyons, I would simply keep my southerly route and after a long paddle sooner or later I would spot the ancient shoreline. But eventually curiosity overtook me and I decided to camp and explore it.

A Visit from a Bear

After finding a sandy beach to let the waves carry me in, I unloaded my boat and carried my gear only a few feet before I found a long but narrow spot in the sand. I took two narrow forked supports out of the kayak. I sat the boat against the supports, and began tying off the sheets of leather that made up the tent. I still had food with me. A seal I had shot with a willow arrow gave me food for many days. I wouldn't risk using the metal arrow to kill a seal; I would save it for a life or death situation.

I built myself a fire and cooked a fine meal. A stew made of seal meat, wild onions, pine nuts and some cat tail bulbs. I cooked it in river water with some salt water thrown in for taste. Everywhere I walked when off the water, I looked for food, food that I could store in the dry packs, deep inside my kayak. Sometimes I hunted from the kayak. I would store the boat paddle and use my hands to quietly paddle up to an animal that was grazing next to the shore. The last twenty feet or so I was careful not to move a muscle. Then, as the boat's momentum carried me, sometimes I could get close enough to reach out and touch the animal. I would then pick up the bow and a willow arrow and dispatch the unfortunate thing. I would eat well that night and try to work up as much of the meat as possible which usually involved smoking and drying the meat over a fire. I hadn't seen any other humans. It had been many, many days of hard paddling since I had seen that one human, the red warrior. I felt safe and slept well at night.

The next morning, I finished off my stew, drank some cold water, picked up my bow and a quiver of arrows and my customary possible sack full of emergency gear, and walked up the hill stopping every few steps to listen to what was happening around me. Everything seemed fine so I continued my hike to the ancient shoreline. I didn't know it at the time but I had to walk up exactly eighty vertical feet.

Taking considerable time, I was in for a surprise. There was an ancient shore up to a white sandy beach that was under plant growth followed by a hundred yards or so of trash. Containers of every size, color and shape were there. The plastic bottles had begun to decompose in the sun, and would crumble when touched, but there were also glass bottles in every color. There were large barrels, barrels that looked tiny from the ocean. There were empty, rusting cans that at one time probably held agricultural or oil products. What a mess and what a waste. It dawned upon me that the ancient ones were not good caretakers of the world. In the end, they just left a big mess. I had been following a line made up of an incredible amount of trash. I wondered if the ancient ones had not cared about their oceans.

Upon returning to the camp, I experienced my first truly bad luck. A bear was tearing through my tent which was also my kayak. Fortunately, it had entered the kayak through the tent flaps rather than through the bottom skin of the kayak. But it had managed to tear the seat out of the boat in order to access the compartment where I still had a small amount of seal meat stored. The bear got the meat but I got the bear. It was a large one, requiring several arrows. I knew I would need the grease from the animal to repair the kayak. Bears store fat in their bodies to get them through winter hibernation. As far as the meat from the animal was concerned, I did not relish it, but I wouldn't let it go to waste either. I boiled all the meat until I could render as much fat as I could out of it. I then stored the grease in a leather bag kept just for that purpose. Some of the meat I dried and smoked over the fire, and the rest I left for scavengers. It was always a waste, but until winter finally set in earnest, I could not keep the meat edible for long.

Using the boat as much as I did, I would inevitably snag the hull on a sharp rock or submerged tree branch, and, tiny leaks would appear. I had brought with me needles and string, used to sew the leather that made up all the covering of the boat frame. It took a lot of grease to seal the scratches that dragging the kayak only a short way created. Often, I turned my kayak over in shallow water and let the hull dry in the air. I applied a thin layer of melted grease to the whole thing. Then, after the fat congealed, I turned the boat right side up again and I reloaded it, continuing my adventure.

The bear skin could provide two things for me; after tying the compartment back into the boat and replacing the broken backrest the bear had gone through, I had to decide what to make out of the bearskin. The easiest thing to make would be a simple tube. Something to keep my legs warm, under the boat canopy which would help to keep it dry, and turned so the fur was on the inside, I could use it like a giant sock over my legs and lap on cold days and as a sleeping bag at night. I also thought of making a winter coat out of the fur. By folding it over so the fur was on the inside, I could fashion a poncho, cutting a slit to allow my head to come through, and then sewing it up along the sides, all the way to the arm pits. I could then sew on a hood. For the sake of paddling, I could sew sleeves on the coat despite the fact that I had no idea how to make the sleeves. Could I figure out how to get them past the elbow and leave my lower arms free to paddle the kayak? I stored the skin in the boat knowing that sooner or later I would need to make a decision. Besides, I was aware that I had another coat painstakingly made, packed by the women, and carried all the way from my home in Alaska. I decided I would build a warming tube for my legs, in my spare time around the camp. It was one more job to do. It was one of the best decisions that I have ever made. I thought that Alaska was far behind me but actually, I had much of it still to travel.

Vancouver Island

I entered a channel that was for all purposes a funnel, a trap. Sooner or later I would have to turn around and back track, a task that would take me weeks to do. Then I realized that the channel I was in had a current to it. The water actually seemed to be slowly moving south, carrying the kayak along. It was obvious that I had a clear channel to paddle though.

To my left the coastline was new with an ancient beach well up the rise. The ancient humans had lived above that line. To my right the coastline of a huge land appeared to have risen out of the sea in places but drowned in most places. The island itself, turned out to be a land unto itself. It was huge but the dead trees made it a dangerous place to land; an easy place to puncture the hull of the kayak or experience entrapment, but I believed it was still safer than being near the ancient one's homes.

At one time, huge ships had floundered though the passageway, but I found them lying on their sides, sticking out of the water and mud. I wondered, had the humans come down with the plague and just let their ships go or had some kind of natural catastrophe occurred or both? I slowly paddled past them looking at the decks of the ships. At one time, they were obviously colorful objects, but now they were all turning rust red. Everything had obeyed gravity and was falling into the ocean. They formed their own massive line around the harbors, where the rising land mass found equilibrium for the sinking gigantic vessels. Most of the wooden objects on board those ships were long ago rotted out but the basic metallic ships were still intact. It always bothered me when I could see bones; the bones of the people who could be my ancestral humans.

I found myself paddling south, between the older continent and a huge island which appeared through a narrow channel of water. The channel seemed to have at one time been much bigger, probably many miles across. It was obvious that either the land had risen or the sea had dropped. There were vast areas of coastline that still had very young trees growing on them. It was clear that something besides time had happened to the ancient ones' homes and communities. They were in complete disarray. Many appeared to have been shaken to pieces.

I hadn't seen any signs of bear tracks when I arrived at a landing spot so I ventured a short hike up to the old beach. There, it was a steep climb to get to, through the new trees, until suddenly there was the trash littered old beach with old growth forest behind it.

I realized that there was an entire town behind the beach. Smaller boats, all much larger than my kayak and made out of what appeared to be some kind of metal could still be seen scattered all over the place. Many of them appeared to have been tied up at some kind of dock looking somewhat like a string of fish that someone had caught. It occurred to me, that there must have been boats out in the ocean that carried people in them. Some of them might have escaped the plague. But it had been over a month now since I had seen the warrior. There obviously were people but where were they? Surely, I thought to myself, there must be more survivors. Carefully, I examined the dusty ground that the ancients walked on and could see and identify many animal tracks but no human tracks.

It was time to overcome a fear. I decided to explore a short way into the ancient settlement. Maybe I would look at a few houses that still had not totally collapsed. I had handled many of the ancient one's objects and even carried one of their arrows in my quiver, and still had felt no ill effects. I would be brave and explore but would be ultimately stealthy and careful.

The first house I entered was not a house. It was a business of some sort with broken tables and chairs scattered about. I looked at the garish clown face on the wall along with photos that all had a large yellow M on them. There were also pictures of food on a wall behind a counter. I looked carefully at the pictures of numbered food items not recognizing what most of them were. I had better luck with the drinks. I had seen glasses like those in the kitchens in my home in Alaska. I walked behind the counter, exploring the mysterious clown place. In the back, I saw what I determined was a large kitchen and then an empty store room. Whatever the ancient people were eating there had disappeared long ago. Then I began to realize something. There were no cooking utensils. I couldn't understand why there were no knives or pancake turners, as they were called in Alaska. Looking around, I could not find a single metal implement. Not a thing I could use.

In the next building, the roof had collapsed and everything inside had been exposed to the rain. It too had been ransacked leaving what appeared to be many piles of clothes, all of them rotted and full of insects. The metal shelves that had at one time held the clothes were oddly torn apart. There was nothing in this building that I could use.

I slid along the walls to the next building. It was a two-story structure that looked as if the upper story had been lifted off and set on its side against the back wall of the first floor. I walked up to a glass door and peered inside. A desk that appeared to have melted lay on the floor. The pressed wood the desk had been made of began to dissolve the second water got on it. Behind it, against the wall was another desk made of metal. It appeared to be two metal cabinets with drawers. A thick piece of plastic looking material formed a table over the top of the metal cabinets making another table that had old and useless objects on it. Under the table and between the metal cabinets were the skeletons of two people that appeared to be embracing each other. I came to a start when I realized what I was looking at through the thick glass doors.

Just then I thought I saw movement. Probably a bird or even possibly a raccoon, I wasn't at all sure what I had seen. Making a mental note about it I wandered into the next store. Although badly damaged, with walls falling down in places, the next building that provided a door to the world of the old ones was still standing. It also had glass doors but one of them was partially open. Looking again to where I had seen movement and seeing nothing I ventured inside.

Inside the store I found many machines, all laying on their sides in rows. Looking around I could see pictures of them, standing up and balancing a human on top of them. The humans appeared to be wearing some sort of protective hat. I didn't understand the picture. Why would humans want to sit on two wheels? Then it dawned on me as I spelled out the markings under the pictures; *Harley Davidson Motorcycles*. I remembered that long ago in Alaska, they used a flammable liquid to make the chain saws and ski mobiles work. I had never seen anything work with the liquid and had no idea what the liquid was or where it came from. The only flammable liquid I ever used was seal oil, which I rarely used.

The store had undoubtedly sold these machines that carried people on them. How foolish I thought, where would someone go? It then dawned on me that maybe the ancient ones had trails over which they traveled; maybe they had flat ground to ride on. Maybe the machines carried them between the openings between the buildings. Maybe the machines carried the humans to entirely new places? After setting a couple of them back upright, I admired the machines but I knew that they were worthless. Without the liquid that made them go, they were just useless chunks of metal. Something was starting to nag and bother me. I had been away too long from the kayak. I had bad experiences leaving the kayak unwatched; besides there was nothing in the store that really interested me.

Stepping out of the door I took one step then stopped. Turning, I walked over to where I had seen the movement. There was nothing there, nothing was moving. I started to leave when I looked down on the ground. There, was a human footprint.

With my bow and arrow instantly ready, I explored around the corners of the adjacent buildings but could not see any more movement or tracks. I returned to the one track I had seen and looked at it again. It was not a large person, perhaps even a female or a child, I thought to himself, but there may be others. Returning to the kayak, I looked back once more, and seeing nothing, set out to sea. I paddled through the evening and into the night, camping the next day on the opposite side of the channel.

I felt safe on the other side of the channel, despite the fact that finding a place to land was more problematic. Sometimes I would have to roll out of the boat into the water. The cold splash in the water did not feel good at this time of year but I would do it to protect my boat. I would then drag the kayak to shore and tie it up. If I found something to eat I would stay at the camp. If not, I might float a little and try again. After walking only a few yards I realized that there were ancient houses on this side too. The early humans appeared to have lived almost everywhere. Where had all of those souls gone?

An Erupting Volcano

I was amazed by the number of human homes I encountered. I found disarticulated skeletons in almost every house. Some houses looked just like the owners just disappeared one day, but in a few of them there were stories that could be read. When the last humans began to die, they did strange things. Maybe it was the disease that caused them to engage in strange behavior, or perhaps it was just plain desperation. I would never know. But my fear of the ancient houses had disappeared as I realized I wasn't getting sick from anything and I certainly never saw any people who might attack me. But I was still cautious. Every once and a while I would take out the metal arrow and just look at it. Mute testimony as to what could happen if I let my guard down.

The channel I had been floating down became huge again. I couldn't see the island that had been to the west for over a week. Instead a huge harbor opened up to the east, and I could see, far away, on the mainland, a volcano that appeared to be erupting. The ash cloud from it was drifting to places unknown, far to the east.

After paddling for a full day, I could still see the mainland with the erupting volcano in the distance. After paddling for two full days I slumped down in the boat and tried to get a little sleep. Suddenly I found myself being lifted into the air. When I came back down there was a massive splash and I realized that I was not the one causing it. A pair of whales played with my craft for a moment and then submerged into the inky depths.

Now being wide awake, I paddled the rest of the night, coming ashore on a sandy beach on the mainland, just as the sun was coming up. There were few trees along the beach to offer seclusion. As the sun came up, I took an exploratory walk realizing that I was at the base of a small rise with an entire city, just on the other side. When I first realized it, I almost froze in fear. I could not explore the entire city in a lifetime. Some of the buildings, despite the fact that they had all been knocked down by some cataclysmic force, were still buildings that were at least six stories high. I had read of such things but couldn't imagine what they really looked like. The city was huge. I wondered how the humans who had managed to build such wonderful buildings could out think themselves.

Looking further down the coastline there were human buildings for as far as I could see. I watched as the rumbling volcano coughed up several large rocks, let off a lot of black smoke, and then finally settled down. If the wind changed direction, I could find myself under a black cloud with large rocks falling from it. I had seen many volcanoes before, Alaska is dotted with them. But I had never seen a volcano that was erupting.

Charlie

Dog tired and weary, but full of curiosity, I followed the shoreline as best that I could. I was lost, and would remain lost because the coast was fogged in nearly all of the time. The coast played with me because many land obstacles protruded into the ocean for a considerable distance. They would just appear in front of me, jagged black rock walls covered with trash that extended well into the ocean, perfect places to launch an arrow. In many places, there were rocks just at water level causing strange patterns in the waves. Each time I encountered one, it caused me to make a sharp turn paddling further out to sea. After several attempts, I floated far enough out so that an arrow couldn't find me, yet I could hear the waves lapping up on the shore.

I also made an effort not to allow the paddle to bang on the gunnels of the kayak. A warrior could hear it and possibly find me. It took all day, paddling south until I came to a heavily forested area shrouded in fog. After exploring the area and finding no fresh tracks other than small game and deer, I set myself up a good camp where I could hide. The next day, the fog lifted for a while and I climbed the hill directly behind my camp and discovered a parking lot full of rusting cars and a large, partially collapsed building. I realized that my camp was only a hundred yards from the homes of the old ones. That bothered me, I imagined warriors inside, watching me approach through the windows, waiting for me to get close. On the other hand, I hadn't seen any sign of humans. I couldn't see any smoke other than from the volcano. I returned to camp and stayed for a while. As the fog returned, giving me a false sense of security, I planned to explore just a few of the buildings and then return to the ocean.

I explored large houses which turned out to be homes for the ancient ones.

The houses had not been picked clean like the ones I had visited before. They appeared to have been deserted one day, making me wonder who had picked through those other houses, the ancient ones during their final days, or more recent warriors and of course I would have to deal with the bones of the old ones. I was beginning to think about ghosts.

In one house, I found an entire family who had committed suicide by hanging themselves from a large beam inside their house. The bones were now just heaps of white bones on the floor. It must have been horrible to know you were going to die an agonizing death. Maybe they were the smart ones.

I followed the overgrown roads into a busy part of the suburb, where I found all manner of wonderful things I could use but I didn't collect them because of weight and space. The only thing I decided to keep was a large knife called a machete. It was getting harder and harder to keep the flimsy blade on my triangular saw from bending and the teeth had all but worn away. The big knife would work like an ax. I was now enjoying my explorations, learning things from the old ones. It had become somewhat of a compulsion.

One day I was in a house that still had a roof on it. It was filled with furniture, books and the kitchen was full of cooking utensils including a pair of scissors that I picked up and then set back down. I knew how to use them, but I didn't need them, just something else to load and unload. Then I saw movement and realized that I was seeing my reflection in a large mirror. Walking around a large table with chairs and across the room I approached an oval mirror mounted on the wall. I looked into the mirror at myself.

I had never seen myself except as a reflection in water. I stared at my long hair, tied with a piece of cloth long ago stained beyond repair. The ends of the hair were ragged because I had cut it with my small knife. My blue eyes looked at a face that was shiny black with a reptilian pattern formed from the way the skin protection was flaking off. I reminded myself of the red warrior I had encountered many moons ago. Long ago I had learned to make a mixture of bear grease and charcoal with a slip of clay, to keep my hands and face covered. It kept me from sunburns on nice days as well as being a protection from the cold wind. In all, I appeared to be a completely wild man, a warrior. I stared at the refection and wondered what I looked like without the skin protection, what would I look like if I were clean?

Then I noticed a movement, ever so slow, where the scissors had been discarded. Standing behind the table where I had just been, stood a warrior, staring at me. I instinctively ducked down and loaded an arrow onto my bow bringing it up to shoot. Then I heard a voice. "Who are you? I'm not trying to hurt you! Please don't shoot that arrow; I don't want to have to defend myself."

I gasped, understanding exactly what the man was saying despite the fact that I had not heard another human speak in several months.

I called out to him, "Who are you?"

The warrior answered, "I am Charlie Elkins of the Seattle tribe. We are peaceful people."

I feared that it could be a trick; that he would lunge at me as soon as he got close.

"How is it, that you found me here," I asked?

Without a pause he says, "My ancestors found this place. We came from the sea aboard a large ship that traveled under the water; they were called submarines back then. We found this place after the plague had gone away."

I thought for a moment about that last statement. It further reinforced my theory that the plague had long ago passed. I realized that my fears of the plague may have been unfounded.

I said, "If you will come out I will put my arrow down."

With that, the warrior came out from behind the large table. He was about the same size as me, with large feathers adorning his head arranged to keep the sun off of his face. For clothing, he wore some kind of thick cloth that had been darkly stained with something so it would be hard to see. The warrior held a tomahawk in his hand which he gingerly placed on top of a table, and then he held his hands up and palms out.

"Really, all I want to do is talk to you. I have questions, too. Where did you come from?"

I answered him, "Williams' Creek, Alaska."

Leaving the tomahawk behind, the warrior walked over to me and pushed his hand forward. I didn't know what to do, but the warrior grabbed my hand, and shook it. I reached back and grabbed the stranger's hand and reciprocated the motions. I had just made friends with the first friendly human other than my family that I had seen in all my seventeen years.

Part 2

Into the Land of the Tall Trees

Only a true best friend can protect you from your immortal enemies.

—Rachael Mead

I would rather walk with a friend in the dark than alone in the light.

—Helen Keller

Charlie's Story

*C*harlie turned out to be a descendant of a nuclear submarine crew who had come to port in this large city after food ran out on their ship. They came into a deserted city expecting to die from the plague but they hadn't. Instead they survived by hunting and living off the food left by the old ones.

"Let me show you something," Charlie says. He reached up in a cabinet and picked up a silver object with a fading label on it. He examined it closely, and then using his belt knife he opened the can of tomatoes. Using two fingers he reached in and ate one then handed the can to me. I gingerly reached in and pulled out a canned tomato, having absolutely no idea what it was. I tasted it, decided that it wasn't so bad and swallowed it. Charlie rubbed his stomach in a circular motion. "There is food all around in these old houses, but you need to be careful. Make sure that the can is not leaking or rusted." I looked up at the shelf where the can of food had been, there were several more cans there. Suddenly I realized that I might be eating a more interesting diet. I was tired of sea kelp and wild onions, fish and seal meat, as well as venison and bear meat.

Charlie then asked, "Where is Williams' Creek located? I know where Alaska is but I never heard of Williams' Creek."

"I'm really not sure I can explain how to get there." I wasn't sure I should tell him where my family lived or even how to return to the community.

"Can you show me on a map?" Charlie asked.

The only map that I had ever seen was the tiny map of Alaska that hung on a cabin wall. Let me show you something. He walked over to a large table that had some rolls of paper on it. Charlie looked through them and finding the right map he spread it out on the table so I could look at it. It was a map of the west coast of the United States. I could follow the route I had taken until it went off the top of the map around the huge island called Vancouver Island by the old ones. I was immediately drawn to the fact that for me to continue in an overall southerly direction, I would have to cross a large body of water and paddle back north and then west for a considerable distance. That tiny bit of knowledge saved much time from my journey.

"How long did it take you to walk here?" asked Charlie.

"I left Alaska at the beginning of the summer months."

"No, that can't be right," replied Charlie, with a frown on his face. "There is no way you could walk that far that fast."

"Actually, I didn't walk, I came in a boat."

Charlie gingerly sat down on one of the old rickety chairs and asked with a grin on his face, "You wouldn't happen to have some lady friends with you, maybe hid out someplace?"

I was confused, "Why would you want to meet more people?"

"Just listen carefully," Charlie answered. As they became very still, a rumbling could be heard off in the far distance. "We used to live in the city, where the old ones lived but when the volcano came alive, much of the city was buried under an ocean of hot mud. At one time, there were many of us but most of my people died when the mud buried them. Only a few of us survived. We are all trying to get away from here."

"Where are your women and children," asked Chato?

"They all perished in the hot mud. As far as I know there are only four of us left. With no women, there is not likely to be too many more of us. I was hoping, when I found you, that you were a female. I don't suppose you have a sister with you or a couple of women traveling with you tucked away in your boat?"

Laughing, which was something I hadn't experienced in years, I answered, "I have seen no women at all, although I may have seen a footprint that belonged to a woman."

"Well, a footprint won't do me no good, but it is hope," Charlie sighed in resignation.

"I too am looking for a woman, I saw her in a dream."

Charlie looked at me with an incredulous look on his face. Then he said hesitantly, "Describe that dream to me, for someone coming all the way down here to find her, she must really be a dream. Just how good looking is she?"

I described my entire dream to Charlie who seemed honestly interested. Afterwards I asked Charlie if he had ever been to such a place that had yellow and red rocks in a desert canyon.

"Well it sounds like the Southwest. Utah or Colorado, maybe New Mexico or Arizona, they all have canyons like you have described, but that is a huge place. You could spend a lifetime just wondering around looking for one specific place. As for finding a girl in a dream, well, talk about finding a needle in a haystack."

I didn't understand what a haystack was, much less what it had to do with needles.

We spent the next hour studying maps. I could see several routes into the southwest but they all called for crossing vast distances by foot, walking through high cold deserts. I then saw a place on a map, in a state labeled New Mexico, marked with the word "Serpiente" that immediately intrigued me. I could not take my eyes off the word on the map; it seemed like an old friend. I was not certain why that particular place had such interest to me but it did. It was a gut feeling brought about by the dream which was confusing because I didn't remember the name being mentioned in the dream. I even guessed the meaning of the word; the place of the serpents. It was located in a vast desert area in an ancient place called New Mexico.

Deserts were mysteries to me. I understood the concept but of course I had never actually seen anything like one. We examined every map that was in the old house and soon had a general idea how to get into the desert southwest. I would hug the coast until I found the place marked San Francisco or Los Angeles on the map, then walk toward the rising sun. San Francisco would be the easiest place to find because of the distinct harbor with its iconic Golden Gate Bridge. Serpiente played with my imagination and I found myself debating with myself as to why it had such special significance for me, but I could not answer my own questions.

We searched the house for implements that we could use, always watching the other person, just in case one of them was pretending to be friendly but had ulterior motives. After a while when Charlie noticed me watching him closely, he says, "Look if we are going to accomplish anything we are going to have to trust each other. We need each other to survive, and you are right, there are people about who are dangerous but sooner or later you have to trust someone."

We searched the house for another few minutes then I decided it was time for me to return to camp. After shaking hands again, I went one way and Charlie went another. After we went our separate ways I spent the entire evening wondering if I had done the right thing by letting Charlie leave. Would I ever see him again?

Tsunamis

When I woke up the next day I was surprised to see Charlie down at the beach casting something into the water. Whatever it was must have been something pretty special because within just a moment he was reeling in a fish. Looking carefully, I noticed that he already had one, hanging from a branch through the gills.

"How did you find me," I asked.

"You were easy to track down here, besides I thought you might enjoy some breakfast." Charlie carried the two fish, as well as a metal grill he brought with him. I sparked a fire and Charlie placed four rocks around the fire to balance the grated metal on. I realized that it was used at one time by the ancient ones, possibly for the same purpose. It made an exceptional platform to cook fish or anything else on. Charlie opened up a very large can of something called clam chowder and placed it on the grill to heat.

With the freshly grilled fish and clam chowder it was a great breakfast. Then Charlie opened up a can of something called "Fresh Peaches in Heavy Syrup." It was the first time I had ever tasted anything sweet in my life and I relished it like all young humans do. We were so absorbed in our food that we hadn't realized the thin layer of gray dust that had settled on everything. Then an occasional tiny piece of pumice would fall and bounce on the ground. Looking toward the volcano we realized that the wind was not blowing the smoke away from us.

Charlie watched as I began my normal routine of burping the air out of the bags. I then untied the leather flaps that made up my tent, setting the kayak down on a piece of leather. Charlie realized that I was leaving and conjectured, "Wouldn't it be better if the two of us traveled together? We could teach each other and help protect each other."

I stopped what I was doing and listened, finally saying, to him, "First of all, I remember a companion in my dream but I don't remember what he looked like. But that is not the problem; this is a one-man kayak. It would be impossible to take you with me."

Charlie countered my argument with, "All right, but what if I told you that I know where there are boats just like your boat built by the old people?"

"You do mean a covered boat that you can take out in the ocean?"

"Yes," answered Charlie. "Look, my ancestors were mariners who came from the ocean, I know I can do this, just give me some time to get some things together."

"I will tell you what, I will stay as long as I can, but if the volcano throws fire our way, I will leave." With that all said we both carried the kayak and packs including the metal grill the short walk to the ocean's edge. We also cut green branches to cover it up in case hot ashes from the volcano started to rain down.

Away we went with Charlie in the lead. We would run to a place where there was cover, then stop and look around, and then we would run to the next stop repeating the process over and over. It took me a few moments to get used to the experience of running. I would normally slowly creep everywhere, trying to remain invisible. All hunters and warriors look for movement. Standing still or moving very slowly is hard to see, just watch any wild animal. Charlie's way of running was erratic. I was surprised several times due to the route he took but to my surprise we quickly came upon a shopping area for the ancient people. Following the main road leading into the business district, we finally got there, but we were kicking up small clouds of ash as we ran through an inch of extremely fine gray ash which covered everything. It looked unreal to me, everything was dead.

Although the store looked locked up, many glass windows had been broken and a side door was easily opened into a store that seemed to specialize in camping gear, canoes and sea kayaks. Charlie picked out the best one he could find, the color seemed important to Charlie, he didn't want a red one. Stored out of sunlight and rain, the blue sea kayak he found was essentially just like a brand new one. We gathered up as much gear as we could possibly carry, stuffing it inside and on the kayak. Just as we started to leave, the entire building shock. I wasn't sure if it was a concussive wave from the volcano or an earthquake. At the same moment, Charlie spotted the room that displayed paddles that were strong but incredibly light. I wanted to leave but Charlie insisted we take the time to gather the two largest double paddles. In our panic, we gathered up things that we didn't need nor did we even know what they were used for. Almost immediately we began dropping things off the hull leaving a trail of articles behind us. It didn't matter, in time the entire city would soon disappear forever under a deep blanket of volcanic ash.

As we were returning to the parking lot, the volcano exploded again, belching more enormous black clouds into the air. Even though it was still early in the morning, it was ominously dark and everything was now carrying large amounts of hot ash on it. Breathing was hard and we could see enormous fires ablaze in the city where we had just been. It was obvious that we had only minutes to launch. Charlie and I tied our boats in the surf and loaded both boats as fast as we possibly could. Charlie then offered to help me pack my kayak but I simply said, "No thank you, pack yours!"

It took only moments to pack my boat, knowing I was the only one who knew where everything went, the same way I had always packed it. The kayak had to be balanced with the weight distributed. Just getting into it required a precise balancing act. Everything had its place.

Charlie's boat was stuffed haphazardly with all the gear we had managed to obtain from the old ones, but at least the lids to the boats storage compartments were functioning well. Charlie didn't have a spray skirt that we knew of, and even if we had one, we didn't have time to figure out how it worked. By the time we were loaded, hot rocks were falling all around us. Suddenly Charlie says "Wait," and makes a mad dash back to the camp disappearing in the ash fall. In a moment, he reappeared with the metal grill. Tying it behind me, we pushed off into seawater that was covered with floating chucks of steaming volcanic pumice.

Two hours later we found the opposite shore that we knew would be there because of the maps we had examined. Several times, waves of water appeared which formed huge waves on the shoreline keeping us from approaching the shore. Besides, the shoreline was only visible where the water crashed upon the shore in tumultuous walls of water that were higher than the fully-grown trees that grew there. The shoreline was a death trap for anyone approaching it.

With the volcano erupting to our right, and waves crashing on the shoreline to our left all we could do was to blindly continue in a northern direction hoping to find open sea. There was no horizon line, only dark grey ash which fell everywhere, making our efforts to paddle out of the bay a surrealistic experience. Occasionally we could hear the volcano roar and the waves crashing through the trees along the shore which created a particularly ominous sound. At times, we could not see the front of our boats through the thick ash fall. Everything was just an angry grey darkness with no way to orient ourselves because of the gritty layer of ash turning everything into a dark mysterious gray color, but we continued paddling knowing that we had several miles of paddling until we could escape the fury of the volcano. Several hours later we could see the volcano fully erupting with an angry spray of bright red and yellow liquid rock pouring from the mouth. Earthquakes were constantly occurring as swells of water, tsunamis raced in route to the distant shore where they uprooted fully grown trees. Shorelines were dangerous places especially for flimsy humans in tiny boats.

Staying well away from the shore in order to avoid the tumultuous waves, we were exploring in a northwest direction, paddling all day and well into the evening until a western breeze began to blow directly in our faces. We couldn't go forward without pushing hard against the wind and it was obvious that Charlie's strength was fading fast. He was not used to paddling yet. I couldn't keep up with him while running but here in my element, I was at an advantage.

The sky cleared, carrying the ominous black cloud back to where it had come from. The wind slowed our progress but it also erased all traces of the volcano far behind us. Even though it was still night, we could now see beyond the shoreline, past the crashing waves and the sandy beach to small hills in deep forest. We ferried over to the shore and came upon a deep cove which like so many others I had seen before, would have a small river running from somewhere. It took us many minutes to paddle up the cove so we used the time to make a game plan.

We knew that the further we went up the cove the smaller the waves would be. At least the cove would help erase giant waves produced from the volcano. It had sandy beaches and even a forest we could hide in. The first thing we noticed after touching a sandy bottom and rolling out of our kayaks was that high waves had been here. Water had deposited all manner of stuff in the trees well above our heads. It would be a race to see if we could get everything high enough so the waves didn't wash things away. Even tied off, a large wave could easily crash over the kayak tearing the tie off ropes out of a smashed kayak. As the wave backed out to sea, it would take the kayaks and leave them floating, somewhere out in the cove.

As soon as we landed I decided it would be better to tie off only one end of the boats. If a huge wave hit us maybe the boat would stay attached to the tree and simply float in the direction of the water. I also decided to unpack one item at a time and immediately tie it to a tree. This time I let Charlie help me all he could. After unloading and grabbing as much loose stuff as we could we made the first exploratory search for a flat area well above the crashing waves. It wouldn't have to serve as a camp, merely a place to stash things so the ocean wouldn't steal our homes. Fortunately, we found a place on the first attempt.

We began carrying packs as fast as we could to our high place but as we returned on our last trip to get the blue kayak the entire cove appeared to be draining out to the main ocean. We untied the kayak and started to walk through the trees to the trail that led up the hill as fast as we could. Of course, the kayak was still fully loaded making it heavy and cumbersome to carry. After a short walk, we had to set it down, and catch our breaths.

I was the first to hear it, a far-off roar as the main coastline was hit. In only a few seconds, another wave, smaller yet still very powerful would be upon us. Each of us held on to our end of the kayak as a wall of water many feet over our heads blasted over us. The force of the water was tremendous as it bent trees over. Suddenly I was flying along the trail we were too tired to climb. In the swirling water, we were in a maelstrom of forces, being scoured by everything that had been on the shore or was in the water such as seaweed. The kayak, of course, popped right up to the surface despite the cargo, open cockpit and two dead weights. For a second that seemed like an eternity, we floated on top of foam, elevated well above the beach. Then everything changed direction and we started to fall towards the sea. We grabbed and held on to tree branches to not rush back into the sea where the waves would bounce back and forth across the bay several times, each time smaller than the previous one.

It took a Herculean effort to drag the blue kayak up to where the packs were stored under the branches of a large tree. The final steps were agony. The last thing I remember doing was unpacking a couple of rolls of leather, tossing one of them to Charlie. Charlie was already on his knees, tossing pine cones, rocks and twigs out of his sleeping place. Charlie whispered a "thanks," for the pad and he collapsed on it fast asleep.

Revelations

That afternoon we were awakened as another tsunami came crashing onto the shore, the first one since early this morning that caught us walking up the trail. I couldn't wake up. We just laid on our backs quietly talking to each other. It had all been such a tumultuous experience. Looking back, it all seemed a little unreal. It was as if I had been dreaming all along, taking several minutes to clear my head. We were still tired. Finally, we hit upon a plan where Charlie would go hunting and I would organize a camp. We had already decided that it would be futile to attempt to move anywhere else until the ocean finally settled down. Our real concern was just how well hidden we were. Would we run into hostile warriors? We certainly couldn't pack and leave again. Charlie rose up to his elbows and looked over at me. Returning the look I was amazed. Charlie was spotlessly clean with light skin with freckles and red hair.

Charlie didn't say anything, acting very strange. Then he asked me a simple question.

"Do you have any idea what you look like?" Evidentially the ocean had scoured all the skin protection from my face and arms, leaving my real face exposed. Charlie propped up for a second and walked over to the blue kayak and opened one of the storage compartments. Reaching in, he pulled an object out of his personal gear and brought it over to me. It was a small mirror like the one that was mounted on the wall in the house that we had visited but much smaller. I was amazed at what I saw in the reflection. Looking back at me was a clear skinned seventeen-year-old boy with long, light brown hair. Gone was the reptilian looking monster with the black hair that seemed to stick straight out from his head.

Camping Along the Olympic Mountains

I decided to set up a camp while Charlie explored for traces of anything that could hurt us, namely wolves, bears, and in particular other living humans. Storm clouds were starting to gather so the first thing I did was change my ocean-going kayak into a comfortable tent. Rocks and some flat boards even provided chairs to sit on. A fast walk around the camp disclosed firewood in abundance which I gathered up in order to cook anything Charlie might come across. Charlie returned after an hour carrying a large white bag full of heavy objects and his arms full of mysterious objects. He had discovered as usual, that we were only a short distance from the old one's homes. Most homes had damaged roofs that had rotted and fallen in, but some ancient homes had functional roofs, usually of colored metal or a rock like material. Entering them was like traveling into the past.

While I watched, Charlie opened his sack full of canned goods. I was also fascinated by something else he carried; a bow made by the old ones. It appeared to be made out of some kind of mysterious glass looking material and was strung in a way I had never seen before or even imagined. The string was actually held in place by tiny wheels. Charlie also brought along a dozen arrows made of perfectly rounded wood with the same razor blade points as the metal arrow I had dug out of my kayak. The only problem with them was the feathers that guided the arrows though the air had to be replaced. They would be far superior to my supply of willow arrows. I only had five arrows left anyway including the metal arrow I dug out of the kayak.

While cooking something called Spam, and small potatoes out of a can, we made an inventory of the equipment we had acquired at the boat store. There were dry bags, still in their original clear plastic bags that covered them with price tags as well as two small cooking stoves. We discarded the two stoves as we had none of the liquid that made them work. We decided the most valuable thing we had gotten away with was a huge roll of rope. The rope fascinated me; it was soft yet incredibly strong. I didn't know what to think when Charlie stuck the frazzled end of it into the fire where it melted into a hard knot.

Charlie unpacked a tent. Set it up and we both just stood there looking at it. The tent was bright red in color, something that could be spotted by others from a long distance; it wouldn't work for what we needed but being frugal we decided to use it at this fog shrouded camp and then pack it away for emergencies. He also unrolled sleeping bags that didn't look like they could keep anyone warm. I covered myself with one and was pleasantly surprised when I discovered just how warm the slick material kept me. Charlie explained that the bags were made from a material that would dry out very quickly, making earlier morning launches easier. I had long ago learned the hard way what happens when wet sleeping gear is packed away; it rots, eventually turning into a heavy green mass that stinks. I would always spend many hours during the day, airing and drying the bedding anytime the sun shown.

We still feared the monster waves that periodically appeared and we were dog tired from the ordeal we had just been through. Taking it easy was the order of the day, spending the evening in camp and enjoying the new flavors of food that Charlie had found. Opening each one would be a grand experience. The Spam was more flavorful than I expected and the tiny potatoes were great, and then Charlie unloaded three cans of the sweet peaches that I relished. A deep fog finally settled in around us and we spent the evening telling each other about our life experiences, while we repaired the arrows in front of a warming fire.

Charlie explained that his ancestors had made port in Seattle after running out of food. In desperation, they explored into the city, found it livable and thrived there as a growing, comfortable community for many generations in complete isolation. I was amazed and impressed when Charlie told me things about how easy living had been in the city, before the volcano had erupted. The Seattle tribe of mariners grew more food than the community needed. They even had a flock of sheep which provided them with wool to make clothes out of as well as meat and fine skins.

Charlie also told tales of an earthquake that had occurred during his father's time in which the entire coast of America had risen out of the ocean. When the earthquake occurred, many people died as a result of buildings falling in on them. Charlie's Grandparents had been some of those that perished in the earthquake. The isolated Seattle Clan had at one time, a population of almost three hundred people. Then after a long series of earthquakes, a huge bulge appeared on the side of what had been a distant snow covered mountain. Covered in deep ice and snow, the volcano instantly melted vast amounts snow beds into billions of tons of muddy water that mixed with older layers of ash from the volcano and suddenly the boiling hot slurry of quicksand began a fast decent down the mountain. Traveling for many miles and gaining mass and speed downward, it swept through the portion of the city where Charlie's people lived. The boiling hot mud that swept through the city killed everyone but those who were away hunting. Charlie was one of those men who was away hunting and as a result survived.

As we worked together I relished the feeling of having a good friend outside of my immediate family. I had never had a friend before, only the ones in my imagination, usually based upon a passage or character from the pages of a book. I would imagine them just for fun. We spent considerable time just sorting out and discovering what was stored away in the blue kayak. We had three sleeping bags, three large blue dry bags with carry straps attached to them, several good ropes, a campstool, two camp stoves, two paddles, several knives, and one spray skirt that Charlie had grabbed at the last minute. It took us a while to figure out how everything worked. What we couldn't use we discarded. It was a joy to be alive and have a friend to experience life with. Finally, the ocean and weather began to calm. We carried our kayaks back down to the beach and loaded them with all our treasures and paddled out to see what awaited us.

It would take us several days before the coastline would turn to the south again. Here as elsewhere, the coast appeared to have risen out of the water many feet. It was difficult for us to find camping spots, without dragging equipment up a steep slope, to sea caves that were at one time at sea level. Little vegetation grew along this section of seacoast except for very young saplings. Fire wood however was not a problem because of driftwood that piled up in great twisted logjams along the high-water mark. Charlie had learned quickly how to handle his kayak. While not on the open water we spent our time exchanging stories about growing up in Alaska and in an ancient city called Seattle.

When the plague hit, the crew of Charlie's ship was told not to come ashore. They had drifted around the Pacific Ocean for over a year constantly trying to acquire radio contact with someone; anyone. They found no one was listening to their calls. When they eventually ran out of food they came ashore cautiously and found a building that still had an intact roof and began gathering all manner of food and equipment to live there comfortably. As the city was reclaimed by nature, animals moved back into the city where they were easily shot by the sail.

I had ever used a gun before, and at the Williams settlement, we had no idea how they worked. In Alaska, we had long ago run out of ammunition and used the guns for other purposes. The metal pipes made great clubs for disposing of larger game that thrashed around after being shot with several arrows in them or the guns were fashioned into a handle for another tool.

Charlie's people had used guns much longer but as of recently had run low on ammunition. They could always find more but instead resorted to using hand tools such as tomahawks and bows with arrows, saving the guns for encounters with bears and large cats. Charlie had never shot one of them, but he certainly knew how they worked. He personally preferred the use of the tomahawk, of which he had become an expert.

We used the red tent but the old fabric quickly began to give away and was useless. The short poles that supported the tent did however make fine arrows with a little work. The hard part was fashioning metal tips, used as arrowheads. Feathers were everywhere. The birds that supplied them were easily captured with a bolo that I had brought along and the birds made a fine grilled meat that we relished. With no trace of other humans, we felt very comfortable until one day we spied a large shape out in the ocean. We'd watched it slowly drift toward us over a couple of days and then realized it was a small ship. Cautiously, we paddled out to it to see what it was carrying.

Tying off our sea kayaks, we climbed aboard by using the metal rungs that hung over the side of the ship. The ship turned out to be some kind of fishing ship with rotten nets still hanging in the water. On board, we found the remains of ten crew members, all who had apparently died many years ago. It appeared that they had shot each other with handguns that were still clutched in boney hands. While exploring the pantry area where food was prepared the truth became evident. They had run out of food and were apparently boiling water in a large pot and condensing it to drink. They had run out of provisions and killed each other over the scraps of food and water that were left.

We found the bones of one individual who had apparently been hacked apart and cooked in a large silver kettle. Not a trace of flesh could be found on any of the bones. Evidently there were rats on board that after feasting on the fish on board, had then turned on the men leaving thousands of tiny tooth marks on the bones. Now the rats themselves had starved to death. When Charlie explored the holds he found thousands of fish skeletons. The crew obviously had all the fish they could eat but nothing else. Not a living creature could be found anywhere. It would, in a couple of days, be just another derelict ship that the ocean would wash up on the shore. As the waves crushed it against the rocks in time it would rust and fall apart. Eventually, it would disappear altogether.

It rained every day, sometimes raining all day long. The rain or fog kept us from the water for days on end. During the down time, we would explore the ancient ones' buildings finding all manner of knives, bows and arrows, and canned food. But I always knew I wanted to explore south, and eventually we would need to leave our beloved kayaks behind and explore inland, searching for a serpentine canyon that opens to a cottonwood forest. Hidden, among the trees was a house that held the most beautiful girl in the world. I preferred to believe the dream was real; it was not a dream but a vision. But for now, we would venture to the land of the giant trees.

Portland

I looked down at my hands, they were forming blisters again. When the blisters broke the salty seawater would make them sting. I was tired. The sea kayak was starting to leak again, drops of water added up after long periods of time and added weight to the boat. I needed to kill a seal or a bear to fix the leaks and I had seen plenty of them on the shore but hadn't taken the time, now I was paying for it. Next time we camped I would find a seal to kill, render the oil and reseal my kayak. I thought to myself, maybe we could camp for a few days; perhaps I could find a bear to kill. Bears produced better grease, killing a bear was no easy matter, if I couldn't ambush it and quickly place enough arrows in it, I could be mauled to death.

I looked over at Charlie's sea kayak. It appeared to glide through the water effortlessly compared to my sea kayak. I now wished I had grabbed a manufactured sea kayak for himself but I knew I couldn't carry anywhere near the amount of camping gear and food that I did in my kayak. Charlie's kayak never needed grease or oil to waterproof it but then it would not double as a tent. Fortunately, we both had machine made paddles to work with, the blades sat in opposite positions so that the raised end of the paddle would not cup air and act like a sail, instead it cut into the air. It was a pleasure to use them because they were so light. It was a much easier to paddle with than the one I had started with; made from a single plank of hickory that had begun to cause stinging pains in my wrist.

This was a wonderful time for me and although I missed my Alaskan family I knew exploration was the right thing to do. I was proud of my accomplishments having ventured into the homes and buildings of the old ones, learned to use their food and found many of their implements very useful. Charlie had brought me up to speed on many things that concerned the ancient ones. For one thing, they lived everywhere. They lived in relative comfort and ease and had no idea how fortunate they were. Charlie guessed that it wasn't the people themselves that caused their demise, it was their leaders. Perhaps it was their greed which is a basic part of animal nature. Wolves had taught him about greed. In a flock of sheep for example, they would keep killing long after they had killed enough for food. If they couldn't kill any more sheep, they would turn on each other. Growing old is not an option for wolves.

For a long section of coast, we were having trouble finding camping spots. There were many sandy beaches available but they would all be underwater at high tide, and the rocky bluffs that overlooked those beaches were uninviting. It would be an easy place to fall and break an arm or leg. The one thing we had in abundance was fresh water. It continued to rain all the time with rivulets of water cascading off of the rocky moss-covered bluffs.

A large river finally appeared meandering out of the mountains to our east with many human buildings scattered along the river banks. One in particular seemed interesting. It was a place where the ancient ones would pay to have a place to play, a resort; and the roof was still in place. What Charlie and I were interested in was the kitchen. What kinds of things would reveal themselves that we could use?

What we found was a kitchen in complete disarray but there were wonderful things there. We found canned food in a storage area along with a multitude of kitchen tools including many small knives which I immediately grabbed up. Big knives were of little use to us, little knives were used in food preparation and to make arrow heads. The problem was that I was finding too many good things to use. I couldn't carry everything. That evening, after hiding our kayaks away, for the first time in my life I slept in a real bed only to discover that I couldn't sleep on something so soft. During the night, I decided to sleep on a carpeted floor.

Charlie had no trouble at all sleeping on an ancient bed; in fact, he didn't want to get out of the bed until shattered glass followed by a loud noise got him out. Someone had used one of the ancient one's guns and had taken a shot at us. Taking a quick glance at where the shot had come from we could see a single man wearing what appeared to be military fatigues staring down at us. Another shot, and more glass shattered all over the room. We got down on our stomachs and crawled, then as soon as we were around a corner we ran to the opposite side of the building where we exited into a parking lot filled with derelict cars. Just as we reached the forest a third shot rang out hitting a branch just inches above Charlie's head.

Instantly, everything had changed, we fled to the kayaks and took to sea without bothering to tie on our spray skirts. I almost immediately took on water as we tried to paddle down the coast having to deal with the waves that kept trying to turn us over. Within a hundred yards or so I found a tiny hidden inlet with a beach where there was a place to take out. I bailed as fast as I could with a plastic pitcher we had acquired just for that job. Fortunately, we were hidden. If we had stayed on the open water we would easily have been shot. We determined that we had invaded someone else's private place, a storehouse of food that had jealously been guarded by someone who had survived the plague. This person had obviously shot first and would ask questions later. Charlie and I would be much stealthier from now on.

Several days later we came to another huge river that flowed out of a deep canyon that cut though a forest. I had a decision to make; should we continue down the coast or should we paddle up the river. The problem was, this certainly didn't look anything at all like the country in my dream; in fact, it couldn't have been more different. I could not imagine a place with more rain and fog. The trees here were the biggest trees I had ever seen in my life. We wondered what kind of creatures lived in the forest of giant trees. Were there giants here? We decided to continue down the coast.

The Story of Jonathan Sinclair

We experienced a paradigm shift, feeling lucky because we had not experienced any more living humans. We knew that humans were the most dangerous creatures we could encounter, but it was the only way to make allies. One evening after preparing and then eating a scavenged dinner, Charlie shared a story that was a traditional part of his tribe's oral memories, the story of Jonathan Sinclair.

"Many years after the Seattle tribe settled into the city, the tribe sent scouts out in different directions to explore the land and search for other humans. Jonathan Sinclair had lived through, and experienced a horrendous ordeal in the completion of his exploration and returned to report his experiences. This scout had taken the hard route; the one through the mountains that everyone imagined would be impossible, not easy like the other two scouts who would explore the coast. Instead, Jonathan Sinclair decided to turn to the morning sun. He wondered how the ancient ones had passed through the mountains into the ancient city. It was easy for him to find the huge overgrown road that at one time served the ancient ones who used rolling chunks of metal, called cars, to get around. Finding no trace of living human beings, he continued his exploration, walking down the surefooted roads that the ancients had built deep into the country. He walked through and explored many of the ancient cities that all appeared vacant, until he found footprints in the sand going from house to house and now he worried that his footprints would tell a story for others to read for a long time. He decided to flee the city until he discovered more footprints. He turned south, off the huge road he had been on, along a much smaller ancient road. The road seemed to follow the canyon he was close to but then went off across a vast flat plain. He had decided to continue, following the canyon rim where there would be endless places to hide, and magnificent views of the canyon. Then early one morning he awoke with a jolt after hearing a human voice. It seemed far away to him, yet distinct from the sounds animals make. It seemed to come from far below, down in the canyon from where he was camped.

"Jonathan Sinclair came upon the land of the desert canyons by follow-ing the game trails that always pointed the route through the maze of canyons without wasting time exploring around each one. The animals always knew the best way to get somewhere. He camped that evening just under the top of the canyon wall. There was a small rock overhang that was hidden from above, and provided a panoramic view of the canyon. He could see in the distance on his side of the canyon, an ancient road cut that made sharp turns and finally played out at the bottom near a small pool. The stream that flowed at the bottom of the canyon was tiny. It would appear for a short while then would disappear into the brush or under the rocks and sand. The water then reappeared as it finally cascaded down a rock into a crystal-clear pool on the canyon floor which is why the ancients had built a road down to the floor of the canyon. It was a natural gathering place for humans.

"Sinclair made camp simply by roiling out a leather pad, under the overhead rocks. He wouldn't need the leather blanket he pulled over himself on cold and wet evenings. In the summertime, he often made a tiny one person tent by using tree branches for supports tied together with short ropes. It was all he needed, he could exist out in the hot sun, summer rain and even in winter snow. But now he was tired and wanted to return to his people, his home. He would rest for at least a day before he started the long trip from where he had come and report the footprints. He felt a little silly about the foot prints. He really should know more about what he had seen, after all, he had come this far. But he was worried about hostile humans. He had no idea what he would say if he actually ran into another human. His dreams tormented him over and over with visions of warriors trying to hunt him down.

"Jonathan Sinclair awoke hard the next day. Raising his head off of his mat, he immediately froze. To his astonishment, he could see about twenty creatures, most of them looking like warriors, all well-armed and alien looking. They were walking, single file up the trail toward one of the small pools wearing nothing but moccasins and a waist band that acted as a tool belt with suspenders, and leather flaps over the lap and down the back. They all carried small leather pads on their backs that they reclined on. They were all painted a base of pure white, with colorful drawings and garish black geometric designs that covered their entire bodies.

"Sinclair was astonished to discover this group of aliens walking up the floor of the canyon below his perch. In that instant, he began slowly gathering up brush that was just within reach, brush to hide under if one of them walked up to the overhang. Highly unlikely he thought. It would take a lot of climbing to get all the way up to the overhang but anything was possible. After packing and hiding everything he could in the few seconds he had before the creatures arrived, he pulled a water bottle close and then committed himself to total silence.

"They had several slaves who were actually very young boys, and what appeared to be two captive females. The females appeared to be tied together with a chain of some kind with one of the warriors pushing them along. Everyone did just as the warriors directed them to do. The slaves carried all manner of bags filled with whatever the creatures wanted them to carry. They all worked together to set up a crude camp for the polychromatic warriors. Logs and rocks were arranged so each and every one of the warriors would have his personal seat carefully prearranged around what would be a huge fire. The warriors milled around, and the young boys spent the entire afternoon gathering all kinds of firewood, eventually gathering a great pile of brush.

"Fortunately, there were only rocks, where he was hiding. None of young boys climbed up the trail to the overhang, they just scoured the canyon floor for anything that would burn. Finally, they began arranging their sleeping gear, which was the only gear the warriors had carried other than their weapons. Early in the evening, the warriors all got together and ate something out of a leather bag they had carried up. They then set the bag on a tree stump and every few minutes each of them would get another pinch out of the bag. I guessed mushrooms, or some other mind altering substance, I could only venture a guess. They then all appeared to settle down to sleep but within an hour they were up and nervously walking around, anxiously and aimlessly milling until finally a signal was issued by one of the oldest of the warriors. The warriors gathered around, forming a large circle inclosing the fire pit and the nearby pole construction. The young boys crowded around every available place where they could enjoy the show. Besides, they would need to be available to do all the actual work.

"They were very motivated youth, someday they too hoped to be fully fledged warriors, but only a few of them would survive to become real warriors. It was then that Sinclair realized that most of the warriors were women. Young and arrogant, they bragged about themselves and their experiences until the warriors began singing a low hum that escalated into what the ancient ones would have called a fugue. A repeating and interesting chant, always in unison and in harmony, and the youths immediately joined them in the singing and beating sticks together that mimicked drums. Everybody was humming or singing this strange song with no words, just sounds. It was as if they were being directed by a single mind, yet I never heard a warrior issue an order, or give directions. Then slowly the leader began singing a lyrical song which followed along with the chant, making it all sound interesting and bringing the dancers to a loud crescendo then a sudden stop. For a second, there was not a sound or a movement then they started the song again. They spent a couple of hours just gathered into the circle dancing, and singing, always the same song and dance. They danced in rhythmic unison, all of them doing exactly the same intricate movements, in a circle around the fire. Sinclair noticed a frame with thin poles set directly in front of the fire.

"Then as the evening seriously set in, they built up the fire until it was too hot to stand close by and then untied one of the young girls. She was led, struggling and fighting the entire distance, to the pole structure where she was bent over a thin pole with her arms tied to a pole straight ahead of her. She watched as they fed the fire which was directly in front of her causing the poles to begin to smoke. They seemed to enjoy cutting her clothing off and running their hands over her body. They then left her alone while a large glowing serpent appeared and slowly crawled around her trembling body. After several minutes while everyone watched, the serpent explored the girl's body then crawled away, and waited. The warriors spent the next several hours of the evening taking turns beating and abusing the unfortunate girl in front of everyone. They acted as if they wanted to create as much pain as possible for the girl. She had to have water splashed on her burned face to keep her conscience. After each warrior took her turn with the girl there was a scene of arrogant bragging over who had hurt the bleeding girl the most. Then the serpent again crawled all over her, undoubtedly enjoying the terror and pain that the girl was experiencing.

"Finally, after all the warriors had tired themselves out on the unfortunate girl, they pulled a mean trick on her. They had tied the rope holding her face to the flames of the fire which they now continually fed with brush. She could obviously feel the intense heat as it consumed the rope that held her hands in place and suddenly she imagined that she was going to fall, face first onto the fire. At the last second, they dragged her limp body back from the flames. She was immediately carried over to a large flat rock, hog tied into a fetal position, then completely wrapped in a thick layer of cold and wet plants. She actually was revived for a moment. Sinclair could hear her rasping breath even from where he was hiding. A small breathing tube was pushed into the mouth of the girl and she was completely covered with plants followed by a thick layer of red mud. They then carried her over and tossed her into the fire. They all seemed to quiver as the exhausted human girl screamed pathetically. A warrior reached in and turned the girl over, and a few groans later, the girl finally died. They seemed to enjoy and rejoice in the death. Two of them, using flat implements, quickly covered the fire with a layer of thick wet soil sealing in the body and turning the liquids into steam, cooking everything.

There was more dancing around the fire until finally exhaustion began to send them to their bed rolls and chairs. They lounged around, drinking something that the slaves had lugged there for the warrior's comfort. The older warriors did most of the talking and drinking. Sinclair could not make out what they were saying. They actually seemed to be talking but it was in whispers, they didn't talk out loud at all.

"After a time, they dug the unfortunate girl out of the fire, and broke away the fired mud, exposing the cooked meat underneath. The oldest female warrior, the one that sang above what the others had sung, cut out the liver which two of them shared, followed by the next oldest eating the kidneys, the brain and so forth. Using their hands to eat with, they applied a small amount of white material, probably salt, to the meat and the warriors all seemed to casually eat on the organs from the carcass of the girl until there was none left. Everyone got a good chunk of flesh; soon not a trace of her remained. Even the bones were crushed and the marrows eaten by the young slaves. It was all as if she were eaten by some ravenous animals. Perhaps to the warriors, humans were just another animal, they certainly did not seem humans themselves. The young boys fought over morsels of the girl which they ate, playing around like dogs; begging attention for the bone scraps. The serpent settled in by curling up in the lap of the remaining captive girl, evidentially enjoying the sheer terror that it generated. Terror that became greater as the end neared and all hope was lost."

We took care of a couple of camp chores, checking on a deadfall trap that was still set and gathering some firewood. I was mesmerized by Charlie's story and as soon as we got back to camp I made him tell me more.

Charlie finished his story of Jonathan Sinclair, "That night, clouds came up hiding the moonlight and allowing Sinclair to ever so slowly crawl up the rim trail, a distance of thirty or so feet but in clear view of the warrior's camp. Any sudden movement would immediately catch their attention but by slowing crawling on the ground under his leather blanket which was close to the same color as the nearby rocks, he slowly moved just one limb at a time, as slow as he could and still manage to make forward progress. To a warrior, he would appear to be just another rock. Reaching the top of the rim, Sinclair stole away in the dark, putting as much distance between him and the creatures as he could. The realization immediately occurred that he would never be able to convince the family elders of what he had seen.

"Sinclair discovered that he made the best progress by simply walking fast each day. He applied layers of grease between his legs to keep them from chaffing. In his panic driven journey, he made much better progress than when he had come out but experienced the most terrible dreams he could ever imagine. After just a little longer than a month of the fastest pace his body would allow, he arrived and reported to the tribe of Seattle that he had discovered a race of degenerate people. He described in every detail what he had seen.

The elders didn't know what to believe, most of them decided that Sinclair had gone insane, that he must have made up the story and must have had ulterior motives. Perhaps he wanted the riches he found there for himself and was attempting to scare them away. The other explorers had never returned and in the end, they never would return adding more mystery to the story. But the elders couldn't imagine the creatures like Sinclair had described. They expected to find humans like themselves. They hoped to find humans looking for contact with other humans, certainly not the repugnant creatures Sinclair described.

"Sinclair only lived for a short time after his return, telling his story to us, many times," Charlie sadly finished.

"Always the same way. He saw what he saw and he tried to report what he saw. Unfortunately, others turned his story into a myth and sometimes the butt of jokes, Sinclair was believed by only a few. But I," Charlie muttered while thumping his chest with his thumb, "I actually knew Jonathan Sinclair. I knew him well and was there when he died. On his deathbed, he told the same story about discovering the serpent and colorful humans but now he was having encounters with serpents in his dreams, his dreams killed him. I believe the serpents reached out to him, somehow."

Charlie had been away, exploring when the volcano appeared and then a mudslide occurred and suddenly the Seattle Tribe of Mariners, simply disappeared under a layer of hot mud. After giving up, trying to find survivors, he began to wander around, just living off the canned food he found in the houses of the ancients, and then after only a couple of weeks, along comes a fellow by the name of Chato who was searching for the most beautiful women in the world in the most dangerous place he knew of.

An Archeological Search for Living People

I was amazed by Charlie's story of Jonathan Sinclair. As he told it the hair on the back of my neck raised up, much like when encountering large bears or mountain lions. I had seen strange people in my visions. I already suspected that they were out there but only had disjointed glimpses of them in my dreams. The story left me a little shaken but still our main concern was encounters with creatures that automatically go into attack mode, attempting to crush our skulls, stealing everything we had, and possibly eating us.

We more than suspected that other humans were out there and we found ourselves playing a very serious game. The adventure of exploring a vast coast requires long days filled with tedious paddling followed by a frantic search to find a logical landing and camping site before it gets dark. All camping sites are different but they all have some common features. Preferably a place that provides all the amenities a camp should, such as a nearby freshwater stream and seclusion under a canopy of trees that allows you to see everything on the ocean but keeps the camper well hidden. The camp always required beaches that allowed plenty of room for loading and unloading the boats.

At one of those rare, but perfect campsites, we found a large mound of charcoal close to the shoreline. Charcoal that I discovered while digging a hole to relieve myself. At some time in the not so distant past, someone or something had burned a large amount of wood leaving a circular deposit of black charcoal. It was now overgrown with weeds but still unmistakable. The fire could have been burned in as little as a year before. We would now consciously search for sites where evidence of earlier explorers such as ourselves existed.

We explored places where anyone who was skirting the coast in a boat would logically gravitate to. We knew that others, making their way down the coast would naturally seek resources they could acquire from the houses of the ancients. We explored inland to the nearest house and checked it out to see if it had been broken into and looted. In fact, we discovered the houses that were closest to the best camps were already looted. All the canned goods were long ago eaten. Often there would still be a pile of rusting empty cans, with angry teeth produced from a knife used to open them. The ancient ones used a can opener which made a neat circular cut around the can. Those cans were later very useful as camp pots and containers.

The empty cans we examined looked to be very old, opened many years ago. But we also discovered piles of cans that could have been eaten by someone as recently as a few days ago. Someone had quite recently opened cans, eaten the contents, and casually tossed the empties on the floor. They then gathered up all the remaining can goods to eat in a safe camp. They had been doing exactly the same thing we were doing. We were investigative archeologist searching for evidence of previous people. We were wondering who else was out there? I, of course, knew of other humans who were out there; they had visited me in my dreams.

I wondered to myself; where had the peaceful people, like Charlie who had escaped the plague gone? Long ago I had seen the red warrior, as well as the man dressed in camouflage gear who fired a rifle at us. All but one of my encounters involved some creature who wanted to kill me. Even in my dreams, I seemed to be fixated on creatures who wanted to kill me.

Then of course, there was my friend Charlie. I grew great strength from our friendship. The only problem was where would we find the women who would complete our future dreams?

We had basic questions. Why were there so few people now living along the sea coast? Did the earthquakes and volcanoes drive human survivors away from the coast as they had in Seattle? Would we find more people further inland?

What was the serpent in Sinclair's story and finally, what would we find at a place named after serpents?

We studied houses in the small communities close to where we camped. In hard to reach campsites we found only one house that had apparently been broken into. In large ideal campsites, we found many houses that had been broken into and the canned goods consumed. In all cases, it appeared to have happened long ago. Sometime, long ago, others had paddled down this coast exploring land to the south, land that would be much warmer, and where life would be easier to live.

Arrival in San Francisco

Charlie and I paddled for days on end down a coastline that had continuous ancient human occupation. We lived well, not seeing another living human being but in time I began to wonder if continuing south would be a good idea. We had hoped to find a place called San Francisco which seemed to provide the most direct route to the ancient place called New Mexico on the map. The volcano above Seattle had closed any hopes of crossing into the interior of the country there. A month later we found a huge harbor with a large partially collapsed bridge spanning it, the bridge we had been looking for, a landmark impossible to miss. The bridge appeared to be built high in the sky. After the coast had risen, the harbor had shrunk in size but still was incredibly large to someone in a kayak. Now the bridge truly appeared to be built high in the sky.

We decided to camp on what had at one time been an island that was in the middle of the harbor. Now it was a large island with a shallow harbor over to the city. A huge city awaited us full of unknowns and we felt we would be safer, hidden away on the island. Apparently, the place was at one time a prison facility. The sign over the entryway of the main door was Alcatraz. We found nothing but empty cement rooms with rusted iron bars on them. The place looked like no one had actually lived there except for the ghosts who were locked behind the great iron doors. I wondered what the people who were imprisoned there had done to deserve such a cruel place to live. Certainly, the ancient ones had their fair share of ruthless people who lived among them. The kitchen was devoid of anything.

The following day we paddled over to the city finding nothing but a raised coastline, with miles of down and burned buildings. In places where the buildings had been built on sand, they looked as if they had actually sunk into the ground. Neither Charlie nor I could imagine the liquefaction whereby the ground turns into quicksand during earthquakes. It was a strange place for us, although it was early winter the surrounding hills were green and the air was warm.

We had to make major decisions about how to find our way to Serpiente. This was rather straightforward and fortunately, we could find maps in the stores that catered to the rusting cars that were everywhere. The cars themselves often had maps hidden away in tiny compartments that were apparently built into the car just for carrying them. We needed to locate maps to help us to estimate what the distances would be and color coded representations of the terrain we were required to cross. Neither of us had any idea how to survive in a desert, we had much to learn. According to the best maps we could find, we would be required to cross vast distances without water or food.

In the cities, the streets had become impassable due to the debris that had fallen from the once tall buildings. The city was overgrown with tall trees which grew between the buildings turning them into confusing three dimensional mazes that we had to climb through. We decided to continue paddling south until we came to a narrow inlet cutting through mudflats under a fallen bridge. In the distance, we could see a huge, but swampy lake with thousands of birds flying around it. Paddling across the waterway which was a different color than the ocean salt water, we finally came upon a flat sandy area where we could step out of the kayaks. We explored up a hill made of large rocks by the ancients. Reaching the top, we discovered a vast flat area and the remains of a wire fence with a sign that read, Moffett Federal Airfield, no trespassing. We were at the end of a large vacant road called a runway where the ancients flew in aluminum tubes, magically through the air.

Charlie had seen parked airplanes before in Seattle but it was all a revelation to me. I had never really understood the concept of airplanes other than the story my father told me about the Williams' Creek community. Tiny planes came regularly to service the early trappers. But I had not seen them for myself.

We had immediate problems. How would we travel without the aid of sea kayaks? It would be impossible to carry all the equipment we had accumulated.

We spent a full day, sorting through the contents of our boats and then dragging them up to the fence where we tied them off. There was no place to hide them, besides we wanted to be able to find them if things did not go well. We spent an evening figuring out how we could carry the bare essentials on our backs. Basically, it was a matter of tying several dry bags together to a wooden frame cut to fit each of our backs. Our journey began by walking down a long cement road that was overgrown along the edges. Ahead of us was a large building with huge airplanes parked haphazardly around it. We were concerned about the fences. We did not know if we could find a way out of the airport. We walked through the large building into a parking lot filled with hundreds of chunks of metal left by the ancients. The inside of the building told a story. Skeletons could be found lying along the walls where they died, leaning against it. There was no escape in the airplanes for those people; the pilots had also been infected. In the end, they leaned upon the wall staring into nothingness and death.

Following the roadways which at first seemed to go around in circles, we found our way to a road going south. We followed it until we could turn due west. Even though the days were warm, the nights were bitterly cold and as we walked further inland we figured the situation would become much worse.

We decided to head to a place marked on the map as Gilroy where there should be another roadway over to a major road marked Route 5 on the map. After a long day walking I came to the conclusion that we should have traveled further down the coast in our sea kayaks to a huge city marked Los Angeles. Our destination would have been due west. But then, the entire coast appeared to look like a city was always hiding just behind the sea waves. While in Seattle, where I first met Charlie, I had seen pictures of the bridge in the huge harbor and I knew we would be able to spot the landmark from the sea. Instead of taking the time to double back, we decided to continue our southerly destination until we could find a route over to the area marked as Arizona and finally New Mexico.

The immediate problem was whether or not to walk down the large roads the ancients used. They were the obvious and shortest routes between the ancient towns but they might also be an easy place for us to be spotted. We wanted to avoid warriors at all cost. We thought about skirting the main roads by staying out in the country where there was more cover to hid behind, but instead we discovered absolutely no evidence that any roads had ever been used by any living humans. It was all a mystery to us; we expected to find faint trails made by other people but all we found was animal trails, not a trace of humans.

Our journey was not difficult hiking despite the long stretches of space that we saw on the map. Humans had built houses and businesses all along the sides of the roads where we found shelter, food and water.

After reaching each destination marked on the map, we made a point to investigate the nearby houses to see if they had been looted. Finding no trace of others, we enjoyed the available resources by looting houses ourselves and we journeyed on. We decided to follow the biggest roadway we could find, marked Route 5 on the paper maps we had. According to our maps there was little ahead but long stretches of empty road. But we were worried about crossing the deserts ahead, like the one marked Mojave Desert, which would be another challenge altogether.

Brooks Horse Stables

Deep in my heart I knew there were others out there who might discover us, and without the kayaks, escape would be much more difficult. In spite of the obstacles, Charlie and I knew that walking across vast stretches of land was the only way we were going to get to the land labeled New Mexico on the maps. We had no idea how long it would take us but carrying what we could on our backs, we followed alongside the overgrown roads, roads that often-had trees growing up through the cracks in them. The only roads that had survived the time span of two hundred years since they were last maintained were the cement roads, and they were crumbling from the edges inward. We knew cities could be interesting places to explore with the possibility of canned food in the ancient houses. Now I wished I had one of those motorcycles I had seen in one of the ancient cities. I of course, found several of them lying about where they ran out of fuel, but had no idea how they worked and certainly had no idea how to find the liquid that made them go. The biggest problem we encountered was how to carry enough water. Water is heavy. We found it difficult to carry enough water until one day we passed an ancient walled structure with animals roaming around a huge pasture behind it.

Brooks Horse Stables, the sign said, was a large ranch that at one time took care of horses and animals for the wealthy. Inside the standing walls of the fields, were four horses and one last cow that had escaped starvation and predation because their ancestors had stayed within the walls of the ranch. Originally built as a curiosity for tourist; a way to show them how water was obtained long before electricity and liquid fuels, a large tower with metal fins pumped water out of the ground into a large holding tank. After all the years, it was still producing a tiny trickle of water that the animals depended upon for survival. There was usually at least one animal at a time licking the water from the pipe or from the tiny pool it formed on the floor of the tank. The actual water tank had long ago been pushed over by desperate thirsty animals, only a tiny pool now formed on the floor of the tank. It would obviously not pump water forever. Charlie suggested that we could open the main gate so they could escape their tiny world. But, I argued, they had lived in that pasture, protected from coyotes and dog packs, for many generations now. They know no other home and with an open gate other creatures would explode upon their world.

Charlie, raising his shoulders says, "I have another idea. I have read many stories in books about the ancient American West." Then lowering his shoulders, he added, "We can use those animals to carry our water and gear."

I couldn't help but argue with him. "Being completely wild it could take a long time to train them to carry our stuff. Being completely wild, they will run away every time we try to get near one of them." I tried to argue, thinking about how long it would take. "We don't really need them."

Charlie explained, "We don't have to go after the horses, if they want to drink, they will come to us. For now, let's fill our water bottles and keep the horses away from that water pipe. Let's see what happens when they get thirsty."

"So, you really think you can calm them?"

"Sure, well I think I have an idea how the ancients did it, the hard part will be teaching them to carry us, how good of a bronco rider, are you?"

I had no idea what he was talking about but I reflected upon a Jack London book I had once read. The ancient people described in the book used boats and railways, but mostly they used pack animals to carry gear into the wilds of Alaska in search of gold. Could we do the same, use pack animals to travel across the country, into the land of Serpents?

Anything could be possible, if not improbable. But we were compelled to do the impossible. I was amused and amazed when I finally came to understand that Charlie was seriously thinking about using the horses, even riding the horses. I had never imagined an occasion in which I would ride a horse.

We took a long length of rope with us and the water jugs, placing the water jugs, one at a time, under the pipe. Then we sat quietly as we allowed the jugs to slowly fill. For a long time, the pipe produced a slow but steady stream of water droplets, and after a while several drops would come together to produce a tiny splash on the floor of the tank that ran away to a tiny pool then disappeared. After first filling a bucket with water and then carefully lining up the water storage canteens and bottles, and long before the first vessel was full, the horses had walked up to the edge of the broken tank, poking their heads over the metal to study us. Charlie had tied one end of the rope to the metal pipe and a loop on the other end of a rope and just the right moment, he simply tossed the loop of rope over the nearest horse's head. She started to bolt away but discovered that she was caught. The horse stubbornly fought the rope but only for a short while. She was weak from thirst. The other three of them all bolted away, but ran only a short distance and then turned to see what we were going to do. The stallion seemed defiant. After all, we had just captured a member of his harem.

Charlie, who had found a small bucket inside one of the sheds, lifted it up and put it under the horse's nose. She immediately began drinking out of the bucket until all the water was gone. Charlie petted the head of the horse while she drank which seemed to settle her down. Then he made another loop in the rope and pulled it tight over the horse's face, he could now lead the horse. The interesting part was watching Charley trying to lead the horse over to a stable where we could lock them in with water to drink. Charlie spent considerable time being dragged around the pasture instead of actually heading toward the stable. He finally figured out that if he just walked away while leading the horse it would usually follow him. By the evening, we had managed to catch another thirsty horse the same way, but the last two were determined not to allow us to catch them.

We camped out on the floor of the tank, the weather had held, no rain, only dry western winds.

So, I demonstrated my expertise with a bolo by gingerly flinging it through the air and then wrapping it around the rear legs of the stallion. While it stumbled around, Charlie ran up and tossed a lariat rope over the horse's head. I then tossed Charlie's bolo around the front legs. The great horse finally fell over and while Charlie held the head down, I tied hobbles on the legs and unwound my bolo strings. Lastly, we tied a halter to the horse, so we could lead it around until the fear of the us subsided. It would take time, but the horses could be worth it. The final horse, another female, simply walked up to the stallion then went into the stall next to him. Giving them water to drink calmed them for a while but we knew we had a larger problem. How were we going to feed them? The hay that had been stored in the barns had long ago rotted into a grey mass. Without them being able to free range they would starve unless we solved that problem.

We solved the problem by leading them to good grass and putting hobbles on them. They were easily recaptured that way. We went to work at what was at one time a working blacksmith shop. Fortunately, both Charlie and I were pretty good at working leather which was suddenly in abundance. The old cow had provided us with leather as well as much needed meat. It took considerable time until we figured out how to tame the horses so we could ride them or load them with packs filled with water and cooking goods.

We found many old saddles but they had all rotted and been torn up by mice. However, we were able to use the hardware from two old saddles in order to build new saddles. We also took some parts off of the best two saddles, saddles that had been in a metal box and after enough grease was applied to soften them up, the result was two functional saddles. I wondered if I would ever sit in one.

It took us considerable time to figure out how to make and use bridles. First, inside the main house we found a picture of a horse wearing a bridle. We could at least see where all the straps went on the horse. All the bridles had been, hanging from nails along a wall, now they were nothing but some metallic parts and leather that had long ago been chewed up and decomposed. It took considerable time until we figured out how to tame the horses down so we could easily lead them with a bridal. Charlie was never mean to the horses, never raising his voice while working with them.

After several days, we were ready to go on our voyage, not knowing whether we would be able to ride the horses or not. Then the day came and after saddling up the stallion, I placed my foot in the stirrup while Charlie held the horses head down. Once on top, he let go and away I went flying into the air and landing on the ground. Fortunately, Charlie was able to grab the lead line and I climbed back up. This time I stayed on for several seconds before I went over the head of the horse and then had to roll on the ground in order to escape the thunderous hooves of the stallion. It took eight tries before I finally managed to stay on top of him, then instead of bucking he took off as fast as he could and ran to the other end of the pasture. The exhausted, tired, and thirsty horse walked back to the stable where there was water waiting.

Then, after several failed attempts one morning we decided that we were ready. We loaded the horses and headed down the overgrown road in front of

Brooks Stables. After only a few miles it was obvious we had made the right decision. If nothing else, we might be able to outrun any warriors we might encounter.

Finding food was not really a problem. We discovered that as long as we stayed close to the ancient roads, there were always houses that could be found with untouched can goods. If it had been summer time, fields would have been full of food growing in them but at this time of year, there was little natural food. Occasionally we would identify the dead remains of a plant that was a tuber called a potato. Sometimes we would find whole fields of them but we would have to compete with the wild pigs who also wanted to grub up the potatoes. They usually kept their distance from us but the curious ones sometimes got just a little too close. This made food easy to find. I decided that I relished wild pig meat, cooked slowly over a fire. Charlie preferred the much harder to kill antelope that seemed plentiful. He would prepare a stew by boiling cut up meat with an ever-changing combination of what vegetables we could find. We always used wild plants to season our food but we enjoyed such delicacies as canned potatoes and green beans and corn. But what we enjoyed more than anything else, was a young calf we found with a leg caught up in some wire. It was killed and roasted over the grill that we carried with us everywhere, despite its ungainly shape.

It was not an easy trek across the desert. Finding water was always a problem but we found small amounts of it in containers inside of the wreaked and derelict cars. In the small settlements that dotted the highway we usually could find water stored in tanks that were at one time used to heat the water. But there was long stretches of road where water was scarce and the horses suffered. We quickly realized that the trip would have been impossible without the aid of the horses that carried the bulky packs that contained bottles of water.

On several occasions, we ran into packs of wild dogs that attempted to attack and overcome us. They followed us for many miles then waited until we camped. However, after several of them was shot with arrows the rest of the pack would usually turn on the wounded animals and forget the two travelers and our horses. They were much like their ancestors, the wolves.

Sometimes it was not that simple however. One morning we woke up to the horses making a terrible noise. Although they were hobbled, the animals were desperately attempting to escape. They were surrounded by a pack of dogs of every description that was slowly moving in on them. One of them clamped down on Charlie's left arm as he rose from his bed. Charlie immediately brought his tomahawk across the dog's skull knocking him out instantly. I watched in amazement as several other dogs attempted to get to Charlie but he instantly dispatched them one at a time. It was all it took; the remaining dogs took off to a safe distance growling and barking but fearing to attack. Several willow arrows from my bow set them on the run to get much further away. After the event was over we had our choice of thirteen dogs to choose from for breakfast.

The events of my life caused me to constantly reinvent myself. I had been a clan protector in Alaska, then I turned explorer living out of a kayak. After meeting Charlie I had become a scientist, investigating the past and now I was a cowboy. I wondered what I would become in time.

After reaching a place marked on the map as Bakersfield we decided to turn due west across a desert marked as the Mojave Desert. With the horses to carry water bottles and gear it was getting much easier as the days dragged on. We learned to care for those horses better and better. The hoofs of the horses were obviously not designed to travel long distances carrying heavy loads and since we had to trim them with a knife, we actually rode the horses for only short periods during the day, always staying off the harder ancient roads, leading them instead. We traveled along a route marked ninety-five on our maps finding ourselves crossing vast distances with nothing but flat land that stretched to every horizon. But all along the way we found ancient buildings where water could be found and sometimes we were lucky enough to find canned food in the kitchens that had been used to feed many people. Our destination was a place marked Barstow, where a Route 40 could be found that would lead us all the way west, to a place marked on the map as Albuquerque.

NASA Dryden Flight Research Center

We were concerned that we would run out of water and become desperate. In our continuous search for water and food, each day was a hunt for our next meal, usually made up of whatever we happened to find, usually a rabbit which we would use a bolo to catch. This was hard because many of them got away because they changed direction after the bolo was thrown. We needed to constantly find water because the horses required so much. But then, they could carry large amounts of water for us all. We climbed a large metal tower that we happened upon and saw another vast military facility with many huge buildings that all seemed to be made out of some kind of metal. The outlines of the facility were easy to spot with the huge metal fences that always enclosed them. Inside the miles of wires were post that were erected with small boxes mounted on top of them. They all pointed down at the ground. We had no idea what they were. After several fenceposts there was always a sign that was wired to the fence. The sign read, Keep Out, NASA Dryden Flight Research Center. It looked like a particularly scary place with several huge airplanes with drooping wings.

These airplanes looked different than the ones we had seen before, they were all dull grey in color and they appeared to be carrying objects under the wings. Beyond the center were ancient towns that extended as far as we could see. In the crystal-clear air, we could see that people had lived in wooden houses well into the far away mountains. We knew that according to our maps, the city of Los Angeles would be on the other side of those mountains. Actually, it most likely would be an immense ghost city. It would be surrounded by numerous miles of downed houses where the roofs had eventually failed and the houses melted away as vegetation grew up around them. Then in the center of it all, close to the coast, would be a city with tall buildings. We wondered if the huge buildings had survived the earthquakes that occurred along the entire coast. They would be full of the scattered skeletal remains of the ancient people that lived there but my mind wandered to the possibility of living people. Did the mariners we discovered settle in Los Angeles, or continue south, following the coast to parts unknown.

It was apparent that a group of people had paddled on to the south past where we took out. Possibly many waves of humans had paddled along the coast. Perhaps they settled in the city, existing in isolation like Charlie's family had in Seattle. We knew that at one time, living humans had made it down the coast, living out of what was some kind of boats, most likely kayaks similar to Charlie's blue kayak. It was all splendid speculation, thinking about Los Angeles. Built from the ruins of the ancients, there could be a whole new civilization there, blossoming behind the distant mountains using technology from the remains of the ancient ones, but more than likely we would find nothing but the rubble of old buildings.

We came upon and climbed a high metallic tower that seemed to be well built, with welded metal steps for ancient workmen to climb. From the metal basket on the top we couldn't see a trace of smoke carried from distant winds. Our added weight made the tower sway slightly in the breeze. It was a scary place to climb to but like all young boys we had begun to be somewhat competitive. We had not really expected to see any smoke. Fires would have been easier to spot at night but we could only do the best we could. Occasionally fires were started naturally. We had no way of knowing whether or not humans had started them.

As we began descending the metal steps, Charlie hesitated and asked, "What do you think of going to the city over there, the city of Los Angeles? It may be worthwhile to explore the city."

I simply answered, "No, I have a personal purpose in going on to Serpiente!"

Charlie laughed and said, "Yeah, if I was looking for the girl of my dreams, and she was at least half as beautiful as you have described her, I suppose I could turn down exploring the largest ancient city on the map, a place where humans likely live! A place where there might be women! Instead, you want to cross hundreds of miles into a vast territory where I seriously suspect there are evil warriors under the command of serpents, and once we get there we are going to a place marked Serpiente or 'serpent' on the map, which for some strange reason, you seem mysteriously drawn to. We could die trying to find that girl, if she even exists."

For some reason, Charlie's voice had a note of sarcasm in it, and it bothered me. I had never experienced sarcasm before, not even in the William's Creek Community. Climbing a few more steps down the tower I said to him, "Well, it sounds like you have made up your mind to go to Los Angeles. I will truly miss you."

Not another word about exploring Los Angeles was uttered. After returning to the horses and getting a drink of water, we began our search for a small town marked as Barstow where the road marked Route 40 could be found. It would require a long tedious walk made possible only because of the horses. I thought back to the rapids on the river below the dam in Alaska. Did it keep people out? Maybe the desert had kept people out of the ancient coastal communities in the same way; after all, the only way we could cross the desert was by using horses.

We stayed in Barstow a couple of days, mostly looking for food and traces of humans. We found plenty of stored food and water, but not a trace of post pandemic humans. We even found a store that had all kinds of colorful bottled liquids. I picked one up labeled Dad's Root Beer, twisted off the cap and enjoyed a drink of hot and sickly sweet woody liquid. I could not swallow it. The majority of the beverages that were stacked up were in boxes of cans containing something called Bud Ice, Millers and Coors, all a kind of Beer; they were stacked several layers high on the metal shelves. I picked up one packages of the bound beer to examine later and found it tasted terrible. I assumed that whatever it was that the ancients had relished had long ago spoiled, and I tossed them away.

We realized very shortly how small the town was. Although it had only taken us a couple of hours to casually walk through it, we were faced with the problem of outfitting ourselves for a longer walk across a blank area on the map. As usual, after a good night of sleep, followed by a full day to hunt, eat and clean ourselves up, we would feel much better about leaving on our next long journey, just as the sun was setting. The fast walking was much cooler at night and we felt much safer, walking at night like all desert animals do. Dangerous animals were much easier to spot while on the move and we avoided them at night.

We rode and walked to a placed marked Needles on the map. To us, Needles was just a name and a small dot on a map. Just beyond Needles the road we were following would hopefully take us to a large dam that had our road, Route 40 going right over it. The river marked the Colorado didn't look large on the map, but we had been surprised before. Some things that were marked on the maps turned out to be nothing, just dry stream beds and other tiny streams turned out to be raging rivers. From Needles, it should be a direct walk, all the way to Albuquerque.

After a full night of fast walking, and with the sun coming up, we looked for a shady camp. If we couldn't find it, we would make one. Usually we would hobble the horses where there was food growing for them, anything we could find, or even put the horses inside of a building, in the shade where we would ration water for them to drink. Wherever we stopped, we made an attempt to find a house with one of the hot water tanks in it and replenish our water supplies and canned food, which we found to be very scarce. We then slept during the heat of the day conforming to the ways of all desert animals. That evening, we lead our horses in a fast trot again, following our habitual pattern. We walked until we had to stop and doctor ourselves or make a new pair of moccasins. Each foot required a skin from a rabbit.

When we got to Needles, we were shocked by what we saw. It turned out to be small city indeed, but there was hardly a town there. The road sign clearly read Needles, California. But only the foundations to the ancient buildings remained.

At some time in the past, something had completely destroyed the town. We guessed that maybe the wind had blown it away. There was nothing there for us, but fortunately we still had some water with us. We figured on resupplying our water at the river.

A Red Face Ambush

We continued along the roadway until we could see a very wide river forming a lake above the dam. The roadway was still in place, built over the massive spillways which carried a huge volume of water through them. It was a natural bottleneck; anyone or anything that wanted to cross for a hundred miles would have to cross the river here. The only other crossings that we were aware of was to the north near a town named by the ancients as Henderson, Nevada that backed up a huge lake by the name of Lake Mead. Above Lake Mead the river cut through most of a State called Arizona through a deep canyon and was not crossed again until a place named Marble Canyon, well to the north of our chosen route.

We rode the horses slowly towards the dam but as we approached the massive structure, we became nervous, allowing the horses to advance only a few steps at a time. Then I caught a glimpse of black feathers slowly rising over a cement embankment. Suddenly a face appeared under those feathers with three red stripes on each cheek. Then, several warriors appeared, all standing behind the cement embankments. Unfortunately, we had walked right into a perfect place for an ambush. Only a second after we saw them, a flurry of arrows landed around us as we ducked for cover against a concrete abutment that had, at one time, channeled the ancient one's cars across the dam.

It was a poor excuse for cover. One arrow actually imbedded itself in the saddle that I had been sitting on just a second ago. We immediately turned and as fast as we could, before the next volley of arrows fell, started to leap up to the saddles and motion for the horses to move, but instead, one of the warriors ran out and began screaming at his fellow warriors. The second volley of arrows didn't come. The warrior was screaming something that we couldn't understand while jabbing his finger at us. Charlie leaped on his horse and as soon as I could dislodge the arrow embedded in my saddle, I leaped on my stallion and we rode them as fast as we dared, retreating back into the tiny site of the town of Needles we had just walked through. Dropping off the horses to let them breath, we found an ancient adobe wall that Charlie could easily climb so he could see what the warriors were doing.

They seemed to be gathering up things and then returning to the group. Then suddenly, about fifteen of them turned and began running directly toward us. We immediately gathered the leather straps and lead ropes and began running, while leading our horses. A short time later we came to an intersection of the roads and a dilemma presented itself. We knew we would run out of water, well before we could return to Barstow. We had already looted the few sources of water there. We assumed that the warriors would know this as well. The desert was the reason they did not travel there. It was impossible without horses. We remembered another route that went directly north so we cut across the land until we intersected with it and headed due north into the unknown. We would find one of the other bridges that crossed the river.

In an attempt to put space between us and the warriors, we constantly ran while leading the horses. We wanted to keep them fresh. We would ride them only if we couldn't walk fast anymore. We thought we would easily outpace the warriors but they seemed to have gathered up a group of men who could run and they were keeping up with us. We could see them appearing in the distance, all of them carrying weapons, running in a monotonous gate after us. They seemed to be after our blood. It never dawned on us, at the time, that the real pursuit of the warriors was the horses that we were leading. The lead warrior had realized that the horses might get hurt from an arrow. Horses were extremely rare and valuable, giving the warrior instant advantages over a mere foot soldier. They wanted the horses; Charlie and I were just fast food.

The Red Face People

The Red Face, one of the serpent tribes, had warred for years against other tribes that had horses, and they had always lost. Even horses that they had stolen were always stolen back, leaving them impoverished, afoot and without means to truly wage war against other tribes. Yet they needed to support their families. They adapted by becoming nomadic, constantly foraging for food and at war with anyone that didn't wear the three red stripes. It took only a short time until the Red Face people had looted all the ancient resources they had control over. They were like termites, eating through all the ancient houses, tearing many of them down for firewood, a valuable commodity in the desert.

Everyone who existed worked to support a warrior class who protected them from everything, but mostly themselves. Few of them made it into the warrior class. Only the strongest and most arrogant were chosen by the serpent. The serpent invaded their dreams, changing them forever, they were no longer human. They were armed monsters, who were greedy and could exact a reasonable living by being cruel. They reveled in their cruelty, cruelty that would feed the serpent. The serpent was treated as royalty and absorbed the energy produced by the cruelty.

The serpent chose who would become a warrior and during formal ceremonies the serpent would take functional control over the initiate's brain. In a short time, the warrior would become an extension of what the serpent could see; a human spy. The serpent was the computer behind the warrior's eyes, and of course his brain making the warrior a complete slave to the wishes of the serpent.

The community of individuals that made up the families of the Red Face People, were a desperately poor group of people. Their only purpose was to support the warriors and tend to all of their needs. Anyone not working for the warriors would be killed and eaten. It all had become a natural way of living, the warriors being the apex of a natural facet of serpent creation. The real purpose of the warriors was to inflict terror in other tribes, which provided life energy for the serpent as well as retribution for the great dying that had occurred.

The Serpent's Clan

In the beginning, only a handful of serpents survived the great dying. Quetzalcoatl, Kukulcan and three other serpents survived in splendid isolation, during the pandemics. They lived deep in the canyons, just upstream from the human settlement of Serpiente, close to an ancestral nest. Their ancestors had experienced a mutigenerational human family in Serpiente who had learned to communicate with the serpents. The serpents didn't control the humans, they taught them to communicate with them. It was a unique experiment, a symbiotic relationship in which two species complemented and worked for each other. Now Quetzalcoatl and Kukulcan were making gestures to make peace with the other remaining humans. They had made a royal decree to farm the surviving humans, as if they were farming animals, which to them, they were. The serpents would teach them how and what to build and humans would supply the labor. The humans would maintain their freedom to live as humans do as long as they served the serpents. The difference was, humans who lived in Serpiente were really free from the mind probes of the serpents. They were a scientific people who acquired the hieroglyphic resources of the serpents. The humans were working with, and not for, the serpents.

The Anderson Family had always worked for the serpents and they had learned much from them over time. A mutual respect existed. They had no reason to fear each other. But, Serpiente was an isolated community. The humans who lived there were unaware of what was happening in the remainder of the world. They were unaware of the cruelty of other serpents who maintained the old ways.

After the pandemic was over Quetzalcoatl and Kukulcan had decided to incorporate humans into their culture. Serpents desperately needed humans to work with and for them. A serpent could never build a fire, a shelter, a spaceship or split an atom by itself, but it could easily teach a human how to build them. In this one place, humans and serpents served each other in a symbiotic relationship. Humans can manipulate anything with their hands whereas serpents must always change into another form. Humans are ready-made workers who are easily manipulated and pliable creatures, saving the serpents tremendous amounts of energy. Energy used in such activities as serpent teleportation, which consumed a lot of energy.

It was in the serpents' nature to break away and live separately creating their empires. It was how they had always survived. Quetzalcoatl and Kukulcan thought differently, they wanted the male serpents to stay close, for their mutual protection, but instead the male serpents were hopelessly addicted to the sensations they felt when they absorbed energy which could only be obtained when released upon a human's death. They loved the old ways, and were against making peace with the humans. Leaving the nest, they decided to conquer and use the humans, leading them into warfare with other tribes. The two serpents who left each cultivated a different tribe of humans who would all work under the serpent, who would completely rule them. All serpents communicate through a hieroglyphic, telepathic language with Quetzalcoatl and Kukulcan being at the center of awareness but now the two rebellious serpents would no longer communicate with Quetzalcoatl and Kukulcan.

Each tribe adopted the personality of the serpent who controlled them. The Red Face People, named for the three stripes they all wore on each of their cheeks, became a lazy and indolent people living in a highly structured, male dominated world. There, females are considered subservient, relegated by a common law yet they cared for huge fields of corn and other crops grown alongside the rivers that flowed through their territory. All women did the bidding of the men, even juvenile men. They are considered and treated as subservient beggars, the lowest a creature could get and still be alive. The women were required to go through a ritual of begging for scrapes of food along with the dogs at meal time. Women and their children were owned and shared by all men in the tribe. There was no such thing as family, but when in private, some families did exist. Some of them only pretended to be completely crazy. They just wanted to live.

It was all done the way the serpent wanted it. He did not trust females, particularly Kulculcan who as the queen was not trusted by the rebellious serpents. Throughout history Kulculcan had given away far too many gifts of knowledge to the humans. Knowledge that made the humans stronger and the leverage of the serpents less, she acted as if she had been programmed to actually care about the humans, particularly the females.

Red Face human females lived in absolute fear of the men and the men lived in absolute fear and obedience to the warriors, who were slaves to the serpent. The men in the tribe were cruel to women as it was the only world that they knew. The women were absolute slaves living on the edge of existence. The men rarely, did anything for them or cared for the small children that ran around looking for scraps of food. Men didn't have time for women, they were busy assisting the warriors in making arms, gathering and transporting water and food; they provided all the muscle power needed to carry everything which was required for future raids. Much of what they did was carry supplies which they would hide in order to leave caches for future raids.

It had been done this way for so long that they knew no better. It took a massive amount of planning to conduct a raid into the far north. To find a family living in an isolated place, kill any of them that resisted, and take as many hostages as possible. Binding the hostages and putting them in a forced retreat after a raid, was the usual escape method used by the warriors, particularly if hostages were taken. Someone was bound to be coming after them in order to rescue the hostages. Plans were always made to intercept as many of those people as possible, adding to the hostages already taken. Then they would all disappear, running to the far south as fast as possible. Once they entered the canyons, it would be easy to hide away along a small waterway. Canyons also provided many interesting features like rock overhangs and large trees that provide interesting campsites, and some had running water in them. If they got away with the raid, they could spend a week or so playing with the captives, enjoying their torment. Finally, they would ceremonially kill a couple of the hostages, and then cook and eat them. When they ran out of food and hostages they would return to their homes, to the tin roofs, dogs and women. The fun would be over and now the men would expect the women to serve them again, as they had always done before. It was always the same, the women wanted to avoid the whippings and beatings of the men. If word got out about a woman who was resisting, she and the women she lived with could all receive beatings from any number of men.

Far to the north of the Red Face territory, humans had begun to reclaim tiny plots of land that had water resources. They raised sheep and cattle on those tiny estates. The real power centers of the humans were farther to the east where there was more rain. There, huge cattle ranches were operated by human families. Those territories were well guarded by humans who rode horses and killed anyone who entered their territory unannounced. The cattle barons ruled their empires with absolute power. They had experienced the Red Face warriors and were constantly at war with them.

Usually the Red Face warriors just laid around and did nothing but gossip, but when an opportunity for plunder arose, they all thought alike and could be ruthlessly persistent. The character and nature of the serpent actually determined the character and nature of the humans who served them. It was in their character for humans to serve the serpent. The serpent would enter their dreams and reward the warriors by activating the pleasure centers of their brains. As soon as the human allowed this to happen, he was instantly under the control of the serpent who would invade his mind and reprogram it, leaving the humans in complete compliance to the serpent. The new warriors would spend much time dancing in circles around fires while the serpent controlled their movements. These humans had long ago been conquered by the serpents, becoming serpentine themselves. They learned to absorb life energy like the serpents. They enjoyed the terror of a hostage as much as the serpents did. They lived to create terror. Then satiated, they returned to their dirt villages where they would hide and live like lizards under a crude shelter consisting of a sheet of roofing metal or cloth tied over walls of tied brush. They were nomadic. The only permanent thing about them was the scattered cornfields, which the women obediently worked. All attempts to make peace with the Red Face People had failed.

I later learned that in this land, once called America, there were many tribes, always consisting of a hundred or so people, who were the prodigy of the original survivalist who hid away during the pandemic. Most survivalist died when they came out of their shelters too soon. The few survivors that did live, each lived entirely different lifestyles. Some were actually friendly but most were extremely cruel, a reaction to the hardships they suffered from dealing with tribes like the Red Face People. The Red Face People and others like them were hated by all. When encountered, the Red Face would fight as if they had no fear of death. Whatever it is in the human mind that fears dying was turned off by the serpent. They fought as if they were insane, broken arms or legs did not stop them, they seemed to not feel pain from their injuries. The only way to stop them was to kill them. Yet, they were not insane, only the serpent was insane. They were a pariah to all humans

Only certain tribes had the privilege of using horses. Considered wealthy because they lived a totally different life style, they were powerful and they protected large areas of land with their own armed warriors, who rode horses. Rewarded for their allegiance to their tribe, they were dangerous men who would kill you at the faintest sign of a provocation.

Hoover Dam and on to Las Vegas

Each morning before we went to sleep, we would examine the maps we had, and make our plans for the following night's destination. We had seen no trace of the Red Face People as we rode and then ran with our horses, putting great distance between us and them. We figured they would give up the chase after a few miles and return to their bridge. Maybe, we just didn't understand them. We did not know that we were entering the heart of the Red Face people. They knew where all the water was. All we had was maps that showed rivers that were usually bone dry. The number of ancient structures we expected to encounter came to an abrupt end, leaving us with nothing but the roadbed and desert.

This roadway had a faint trail going down the middle of it. Obviously, others had at one time or another traveled down this road but the traces were few and in places, questionable. We certainly knew how to read the road signs that directed the traffic for the ancient ones who had built these roads. With their maps, we were able to read the road signs and even the mile markers that were clearly readable, each one representing a mile. As we traveled down those ancient roads, we could not see a trace of our pursuers and felt that surely, they had given up.

We finally came upon a tiny place at the intersection of two ancient roads, where we actually found some water in an old metal tank. The tank had been beaten up for some reason, but there was still water inside. We cut a hole into the metal and drained it into our empty water jugs. Looking once again for our pursuers, and not seeing them, we continued north on Route 95. As we trudged along we could read more and more signs about places in Las Vegas, but decided to ignore them because our route would take us to the edge of a place marked as Henderson where we would turn and cross the river at a place called Hoover Dam.

Upon arrival, we discovered that Hoover dam no longer existed. It appeared as if the canyon wall on the far side of the river had moved, shearing the dam in half and draining the huge lake that at one time had been above it. We could only imagine an earthquake had occurred here. Or maybe someone had destroyed it on purpose but we had no way to imagine how humans could have done it, unless the ancient ones had destroyed it, but why would they do that? We had to decide what to do next, and in a hurry. We had allowed ourselves to enter another trap; we knew that we would have to return the same way we had come, unless we could find another route where we could disappear.

Now, to the north of the missing dam, the bottom of the lakebed was a vast swampland with a huge river full of quicksand that slowly flowed through it. To the south, the Colorado River was large, cold and moving fast. We undoubtedly had to get to the other side of the great river but it would be impossible to get the horses across. We figured that there were many bridges that crossed the river; there should even be pipelines and private bridges, to the other side. Somewhere, there must be a place where we could finally lose the Red Face warriors. Unfortunately, the map that we had, only listed a place called Glen Canyon Dam which was far to the northwest as the next possible crossing. However, there might be a possibility at a place labeled as Lee's Ferry at Marble Canyon where we might be able to cross by swimming across the river.

Our warriors from Needles finally showed up tracking us on the road from Boulder city through the remains of Henderson over to what was left of Hoover dam. If we had stayed there only a few minutes more they would have had us in a worse ambush than at Needles. Fortunately, we had many old structures to hide behind so they wouldn't stop until they found our trail returning from the dam, and then they would be on it. We were very worried, guessing that where you find one group of warriors, there is likely to be more and this group of fifteen Red Face warriors didn't seem to want to give up the chase. We wondered how it was possible for them to travel so fast and without food or water. We were unaware that the Red Face people had long ago left hidden supplies of water and food for raids.

We played cat and mouse with them for several miles and then we seemed to lose them. We finally came upon a sign that said, 'Welcome to Las Vegas.' It was a large, spread out city in the desert that looked completely out of place, it completely mystified us. How did the people who lived there in the past get their water? At first glance the city simply had no reason for existing but it was a welcome respite for us wanderers. Water, as usual, was found in the tanks that every house had. The water that was found in those tanks was often brown from rust or simply tasted bad, and sometimes had to be filtered through layers of cloth and boiled in order to be drinkable.

We wandered down the main street looking at the rows of large businesses that seemed to cater to some mysterious pursuit of the ancient ones. We found shops with plastic mannequins that still had fragments of clothing on them. But usually the buildings were just large buildings that seemed to store the ancient humans in them. In several of the large buildings the ancient ones appeared to have gathered before they died of the plague. They seemed to be preoccupied with funny machines that played some kind of game. We could not understand what they did. Obviously, no food was involved and if they provided a service it was a mystery to us. We finally decided that it must have something to do with the peculiar pieces of faded paper found with pictures of people and numbers on them. Perhaps it was something they used for trading. There were rows of machines that had handles on them. The human skeletons were packed around them in piles as if it was the last thing the humans wanted to do before they died. Charlie suggested that maybe we were in a place of worship.

We walked past buildings that must have, at one time, been a huge playground for the ancient ones. Everywhere were pictures of scantily clad women who appeared to be dancing. Charlie made a point that he would settle for just one live woman, but as far as we could tell, not a living soul was to be found in the entire city. We finally came to a large structure marked Smith's which turned out to be a supermarket. It was empty of canned goods until we explored the back of the store and discovered a locked storage room. It had enough food in it to last Charlie and me for years to come. I was in heaven. We found entire boxes filled with cans of peaches, cherries, and pears and many other mysterious things all stored in heavy sweet syrup. After making ourselves almost sick eating three cans of peaches, we decided to pack away only enough for an occasional treat. Then, after looking at a map of the Southwest, we decided on another route to a place labeled Albuquerque but we encountered a problem as we traveled. The further we traveled into the city the more evidence of looting we found. We concluded that people in the direction we were going had systematically been devouring the usable goods left by the old ones. Then everything came to a halt. We found, inside of one dusty store, footprints of moccasin clad humans; many of them. We were worried about running into other warriors so we left the main roads that had obviously been traveled by post plague humans and decided to hide as much as possible while pursuing a northern route around the city.

Using the sprawling city to our advantage, we ducked around buildings that hid us until the warriors finally got a glimpse of us and would not give up their pursuit. Finally, we came to an immense intersection of roads and turning north we followed what was marked on the map as route fifteen. We rode our horses fast for a short distance then we slowed as we hoped to be out of sight. We got off our horses, and ran while leading the horses. At a hurried pace, we ran for many miles until we couldn't see the warriors behind us. On horses, we easily outdistanced them but every time we stopped to rest, we would get a glimpse of them in the far distance. We knew they were going to follow us until they could arrange for another ambush. They would track us down no matter how far we went and the group was getting larger. They had found another group of Red Face warriors in the city who joined them in their pursuit. Now we had fresh runners after us. Without the horses, we would have long ago been captured and killed.

After many miles, we spotted a small stream that was conducted under the road through huge pipes and by carefully leading the horses down a sharp embankment, we finally found fresh water for our poor animals. We knew that they would know that we had walked the horses down to the stream. Charley started to return to the top of the hill to erase all our tracks with a piece of brush, being careful not to leave any extra horse or human footprints behind. But I suggested that instead, we need to leave a trail away from us. So, while Charlie filled water jugs, I led the horses across the stream making a point to leave an obvious trail up the other bank. Then, after finding a convenient place to lead the horses off the road, I dropped down a trail on the opposite side of the bridge. Tied off the horses, and running back to the edge of the road with a piece of brush, I hid my trail. Fortunately, crossing to the other side was easy with brush growing everywhere hiding my trail, then after again hiding my obvious trail I led the horses in a wide loop back down to the original trail. After reloading the water containers, Charlie and I turned and splashed our way down the small river into a whole new world.

After walking a mile or so in the water and knowing that the water would erase our tracks, we left the creek bed but followed its general flow anyway. We were in hope that the warriors would not discover our deception. Fortunately for us, the twenty-five or so warriors took the bait and followed the main road. We finally found ourselves camped at a small river marked as Virgin River on the map and then we headed toward the mountains ahead of us where we could find cover and finally escape the warriors.

Crossing the Kaibab Plateau

The following days were spent climbing up and down large canyons, with flat places in between them. The entire countryside drained into a large river somewhere to the south of us, the river we had to cross in order to find a new way to our destination. Finally, after climbing up and down several canyons we decided to take a chance and travel out to where roads were built by the ancient ones. It was much easier traveling but far more dangerous. We could see sign that others were living in this country. Here the ground was flat and we could see for miles but others could also see us. Whenever possible, we would climb to a high place and in the middle of the night we could see campfires in the far distance; probably the camps of the Red Face people. During the daytime, we would find a side canyon, wandering into it until we could disappear altogether. About dusk we would build a fire and cook a rattlesnake or rabbit and eat some canned fruit with it. We knew that at daybreak and dusk a campfire would be a difficult to spot. Finally, after several days of this routine we decided to ride out to the edge of the canyon and get our bearings. It took us several days to reach the rim of the canyon.

Charlie and I had no real idea where we were but we suspected that we were in a place called Arizona when we arrived at the giant canyon that all the side canyons had been draining into. It was obvious that we could not cross it. We could see, what appeared at first glance; a tiny stream at the bottom of a vast canyon. Leaving the horses behind and climbing down an old trail that appeared to have not been used for at least two hundred years we climbed down as far as we could, realizing that there was no way to cross to the other side, particularly with the horses. In time, we realized that the river was simply so far away at the bottom of the canyon that it only appeared to be small; in actuality it proved to be a very large river, particularly for a desert. It didn't matter, even though it was an extremely large and Grand Canyon, we decided to simply enjoy the views, which were magnificent. We were in a heavily forested area with what appeared to be camping places that were custom built by the ancient ones so they could enjoy the views of the canyon. We seemed to have lost our pursuers.

We ate rabbits, one small deer which lasted several days, pine nuts and wild onions but little else in the way of food was available to us. Our canned supplies were running low. In places the problem we encountered was a lack of fresh water. There were small banks of dirty snow that we melted down for water but as we traveled out of the forest, we just about ran completely out of water. Then we stumbled upon a small creek where we replenished our water supplies and feasted upon the water cress that grew in the shallows. It was maddening; we could see a river flowing far below us but had no access to it until we finally found on the map one of the ancient roads that crossed the river at a place marked on the map as Marble Canyon.

It took many days of careful travel along the edge of the large canyon. We then ran across more ancient roads that could take us into several small towns but we suspected that the Red Face people were in those towns because at night we could see scattered fires in the distance.

We traveled for many days picking our way toward Marble Canyon. There were roads on the map that ended there but we didn't know if a nearby bridge would allow a crossing. One thing we were sure of was that the bridge that was north of us, marked Glen Canyon dam, was probably patrolled by the Red Face people and they would lay another ambush for us. Due to our rambling across the northern rim of the canyon we figured that our earlier pursuers would be waiting there for us.

After many days of travel which was difficult because of the fear of running into Red Face Warriors we finally came to a place where we had access to the big river and camped to prepare a meal. We could see that it might be possible to lead the horses across the river but it would be an incredibly difficult task. The place was labeled on the map as Lee's Ferry. Unfortunately, the opposite side of the canyon had bluffs that seemed to drop precipitously down to the river and would be impossible to climb, particularly for the horses. We scouted north just long enough to see many campfires so we returned to the only possible crossing available; Lee's Ferry. We camped next to the crossing at a place where the road actually dropped down to the water level on our side. There were many sheer cliffs on the opposite shore but there also appeared to be a slit in the bluffs that might allow us to escape. The horses had become our sea kayaks, and I surely didn't want to return to carrying all our water and food. But how were we going to get the horses across the river?

In fact, my whole life had changed as a result of leaving my sea kayak far behind. The horses quickly became accustomed to the same routine everyday becoming tamer and tamer. Charlie and I talked while crossing the long distances. We would ride for an hour then we would lead our horses, walking and talking, exchanging ideas and knowledge about everything.

I had adopted Charlie's use of feathers to shade my eyes. In the desert, I used them no matter what the weather, tied into my hair with a headband. Charlie explained to me that if I didn't shade my eyes, when I grew older, growths would occur in my eyes and I might even grow blind. I believed him; my grandfather had growths in his eyes, eventually becoming blind and before he died everyone had to take care of him.

Winter was passing and the days were getting longer and slowly starting to warm. For safety, we continued traveling at night and slept in the shade during the day. After studying the maps, we decided we could search for a river called the San Juan that flowed into the river we had just crossed then turn south in search of another river called the Rio Grande. Based upon the best map we carried ever since we found a display of them in a building that catered to the metal cars that the ancients traveled in, this river would lead us to Albuquerque. Now I knew how the ancient ones found their way around. They used maps. Now the maps were useful as far as the roads and towns were, but we were concerned that they did not show where rivers were. They were very useful in finding ancient cities where canned food could usually be found. But first we had to cross the hundred feet of water that plummeted down the vast canyon below us.

That evening we settled down to sleep as soon as the sun began to add color to the brilliant red bluffs to our north. I had another dream in which I could see myself walking up a large sandy mesa from a river and looking to a large mountain which stood by itself in the direction of the setting sun. A raven dropped down to the ground in front of me and morphed into a large black snake. The scales of the snake shimmered into a rainbow of colors, then the snake rose up and undulated back and forth a couple of times then turned back into a raven. The raven then flew to the south of the mountain to our west. This seemed strange to me but I was figuring that there was a reason for everything in life, including my visions. The remainder of the day I slept soundly but when the sun was just setting to the far west I awoke to the sound of the horses making a commotion. I turned back over to sleep thinking it was probably a dog or coyote disturbing them.

Suddenly I awoke again with a start as I heard the slightest twig being stepped on. Looking out of the cover I was under I could just make out a feather behind a rock outcrop just a few yards from me. I ignored it, thinking that it was undoubtedly Charlie doing something. Then I turned my head back down on my arm to sleep for just a little longer when I realized that something was wrong. The feathers that Charlie wore were white. The feather I had seen was black which brought me up for another look. As I rose up the feather moved ever so slightly then a head appeared below it as a warrior with brilliant blue eyes and three red stripes on each of his cheeks appeared.

Suddenly the warrior let out a war cry and charged me. I was totally unprepared. Tomahawk in hand the warrior ran as fast as he could until he was over me raising his tomahawk to bring it down on my head. Then, as if by magic a tomahawk appeared in the middle of his face. It was exactly as it had been in my dream vision. Immediately he slumped to the ground but several more warriors appeared all apparently determined to kill both of us.

Charlie had already thrown his main tool for defense, his tomahawk which saved my life, and before he could grab anything else the warriors tackled him. Two of them held his arms behind his back, pulled up as high as Charlie could stand it, without actually dislocating his arms. I never made it out of my bed before two warriors captured me, holding knifes to both sides of my throat. The leader of the warriors walked over to us. He stood there with his hands on his hips and a look of disgust in his face while looking at his dead companion. Turning, he simply said, "Tie them." Then he walked down to admire the horses.

We were hog tied with leather straps from our saddles and could do nothing but lie on the ground, face down as the warriors gathered up every bit of our camping gear and weapons including our bow and arrows. All we could do is watch, while the warriors all adorned with black feathers and three gaudy red streaks of paint on each cheek, admired the horses. They argued at length over the horses until the leader and another warrior squared off against each other. They were definitely having an argument over the horses. Perhaps a squabble over who would get which of our horses. Suddenly the leader plunged a knife into the other warrior he was arguing with, the warrior was tackled by several of the other warriors who seemed to understand exactly what they were doing. They held him down on the ground while two of the warriors began twisting the arms until there were multiple spiral breaks on the bones. The victim screamed in agony which seemed to delight all the other warriors who jumped around as if dancing without any rhyme. After twisting the arms, the ankles were grabbed and twisted first one way then to an impossible position the other way. More screams in agony, the warriors continued to appear to be in some kind of rapture, enjoying the unfortunate warrior's pain and even his last gasp of air. The leader then cut three deep gashes, making sure he cut to the bone directly over the red paint on the warrior's face.

Afterwards the warriors just hung around the camp all day while Charlie and I lay in the sand wondering what our fate would be. The warriors were all men who were evil reincarnations of the plains Indians who roamed the west several hundred years ago. Their ancestors had been survivalist who had hid away until the plague had subsided. Although they spoke to each other in broken English, they refused to talk to Charlie and me; in fact, they seemed to ignore us but after a full day of lying in the sun without any water of any kind, the leader finally walked up to us and started asking questions about horses. He certainly seemed to understand the idea of horses, to have seen them before, but he obviously had no experience in dealing with them.

Turning us over so we could see him, he stood in front of us with his arms on his hips, he looked down on us and says, "Horses are good animals, having one makes you very strong."

He waited as if the thought had to sink in to us and then says, "How long have you had horses?"

"All this last winter," I answered him. I found that talking was extremely difficult, I was so thirsty. Charlie croaked "Can we please have some water?"

"I will think about it, tell me more about the horses."

Charlie and I both said nothing while turning our heads from side to side. The warrior turned and walked back to his camp returning with a couple of the other warriors and a jug of water. He held it in place for us while Charlie and I each took deep drinks until suddenly he wouldn't let us have anymore. Instead he poured it out on the ground.

"If you want more water, you will have to answer my questions," the warrior said. "If you are hungry, I'll have them bring you the testicles and eyeballs of our dead friend and you can chew on them. If you don't help me, we will make you enjoy your own testicles."

The idea was revolting to Charlie and me. We were not cannibals; I couldn't imagine chewing on something so raw and hideous. Then one of warriors walked away. Nothing happened for several minutes until he returned carrying two packages wrapped in large leaves. Placing them down on the ground in front of us, he carefully unrolled the leaves to expose the dead man's eyeballs and testicles. The testicles had been separated so each of us could enjoy one apiece as well as the two bloody eyeballs. The other warrior punched both of us in the gut. He then muttered something under his breath about improving our appetite.

The leader had won and for the next while we talked about horses. It became obvious that the warrior needed to know how to take care of the horses because they would provide him great status in his tribe.

"What are you going to do with us," asks Charlie?

"Let's talk about that after, you tell me all about the horses."

"We can take care of your horses," I suggested.

The leader thought about that for a moment, looking right past us, as if he was calculating his next move. Then his answer finally rolled out, every word was articulate.

"You are lying to me. You plan to take control of the horses again, and then escape on them."

Charlie answered cautiously, "We would rather live as your slaves and take care of the horses for you, than to die."

The leader rubbed his forehead and then said, "You are outsiders. It is impossible for you to live among us and we don't take prisoners, we eat prisoners." He had a strange, matter of fact way in which he talked, yet was always studying us and analyzing our reactions.

I talked for a while about some experiences we had with the horses but they had nothing to do about the practical side of taking care of horses. After a while, the leader became impatient with my story and simply took a step and then delivered a sharp kick to my groin. Tied as I was, I was defenseless and instantly in extreme pain. The leader enjoyed his position of authority which allowed him to be the one who usually hurt others; he was very good at it.

"Now let's get back to what we were talking about, how to take care of horses."

I couldn't talk but I jerked my head up and down giving Charlie permission to save himself from experiencing a lot of pain. Charlie explained as best he could. He was stretching out his answers in order to stall for time. As the morning passed into afternoon, Charlie passed on knowledge that we had worked long and hard to learn, little things, such as how the stallion should always be the lead horse or how sometimes a horse must release gas before the cinch could be tightened. Finally, the leader ran out of questions and started to leave, as if by a second thought the leader turned and asked, "What were you going to do with the horses?"

I answered now that I had recovered from the pain with a calculated lie, "Tomorrow we were going to travel down the canyon rim; we know where there are more horses like the ones we brought."

The leader looked at me in surprise and reflected, "If you had more horses you would have them with you. Besides, we have been watching you for weeks now. You have no other horses."

But, Charlie implored him, "What are you going to do with us?"

"Tomorrow when the sun comes up we will cut three deep cuts on each of your faces, you will bear the mark of the Red Face people. Then we are going play with your bones and finally cut out your hearts and feast on your livers. We even know where there are wild onions to eat with your livers." The warrior made a grimacing look as he brought his thumb across his throat then he rubbed his stomach in circular motions. The answer we got was unnerving.

"But why," asked Charlie? "We have never harmed any of you until you attacked us. All we want to do is leave this place."

The warrior answered him. "The fellow you put that tomahawk into was very important to us. Trust me, you are going to die, but we want you to think about what is going to happen to you. We want you to consider what the death of my friend has caused. Tomorrow morning you will die as surely as the sun rises" With that said he turned and started to walk away, then he turned and asked, "Where did you get the horses from?"

"Far to the south of the Needles Bridge," answered Charlie with a lie.

"They are our horses now!" With that said he pompously showed his butt to us and rejoined the other warriors that had built a large fire and were roasting steaks cut from the legs of the butchered warrior. We also watched as they ate what remained of the peaches in heavy syrup that Charlie and I had so carefully saved back.

Escape

*D*uring the night, it started to rain again, which was fortunate for us because of the tiny amount we could capture with our open mouths. It tasted very good to us. Except for what the warrior had given us we hadn't had anything to drink for two days. That night we watched as the Red Face warriors consumed more meat from their friend and the sugary fruit juice until several of them became sick. They would vomit and then after a while they would begin eating again. The leader seemed intelligent yet they seemed to lack the most basic amenities of being human. For example, instead of walking away from the camp to urinate they simply would stand up, turn and pee. That just didn't seem right. They were very dirty and apparently, they didn't care. During the night, they would get up and pee right next to their beds then lay back down. We just had to lay there unable to move a muscle with the dead man's eyes and testicles staring up at us.

The next day the warriors didn't kill us. Instead the warriors decided to take us back to their village so all could enjoy our deaths and the father of the dead warrior could exact his vindictiveness upon us. He would get the honor of cutting the three deep cuts on our faces. The symbolism was certainly clear. In death, we too would join them with the three red marks. It was their calling card, a way to show off their kills. The warriors found the ropes that we had carried with us all the way from the ocean and tied them around our necks. They then cut the rawhide away, except on our hands. They then lead us the eight miles over to their village. The village consisted of three small teepees along with several small shelters built with brush and covered with scraps of metal and leather.

Our arrival was greeted with awe as the villagers discovered the horses as well as us. Once there, we were each tied to a post that was used for the purpose of cruelty. We were left out in the cruel sun. Occasionally the father of the dead warrior would come by and hit each of us in the stomach or groin with a stick, or a child would throw a rock at us. Within only a few hours, Charlie and I were clinging on to life by a tiny thread. We were fed nothing nor were we allowed to drink anything. Even the dogs would come up to us occasionally and growl, and then realizing we were still alive they would walk away. I wondered what dogs were doing around the camp but I was sure they were used for food.

Everyone was desperately poor and the camp stunk. The one leader who had spoken to us about the horses was indeed the leader of the village and a true warrior. He was the only person who had actually spoken to us at all. He would point to something and the Red Face men would seem to naturally know what he wanted them to do. The humans under his control seemed to communicate by speaking.

The Red Face warriors were the descendants of survivors of the plague who lived in large underground silos that at one time housed nuclear tipped missiles. They had survived but the world they now lived in was remarkably different and so were these people. They lived unlike any of the other survivalist who lived through the pandemic.

Most survivalist in this area lived wild like the Indians who lived there many centuries ago. But these people lived for more than the glory of war; they lived for the opportunity to cause pain in others of this land. It was a mystery to Charlie and me, how had these people sunken so low? It wasn't that no others were allowed to exist, because they did not hold the political inclinations that the Red Face People held. They had long ago forgotten such principles as democracy or social justice. This tribe of humans was now less than human; they were demonic, somehow manipulated and directed. These warriors lived for war, stealing anything they could from anyone they could find. We were only their latest victims.

Looking around I could see several children running around naked and a couple of women who seemed to live in terror of the men who owned them. The only wealth that could be seen was in our horses and weapons. A man walked past us and was crying like a small child. A few minutes later another warrior walked by laughing at something unknown. They didn't seem to have any interest in bragging about battles that had been fought, it was as if they lived only in the present.

The leader was the only one who made plans and anyone who argued with him would become food for everyone else. It seemed to Charlie and me that the two women we had seen were probably stolen from another place, another family of survivors. They did all the menial chores such as preparing food and gathering firewood. The children seemed to have no self-control what so ever; they just ran around pretending to be warriors like their fathers.

That night we couldn't sleep. The old man who was the father of the warrior that Charlie had killed came up to us and instead of punching us he started a conversation with us through a toothless mouth. "I am going to kill you tomorrow morning," he said.

I asked him, "Why?" He answered with a matter of fact statement. "We own all of this land." He pointed to the four directions. "We own everything that walks or lives here or has ever lived here. We own you and it is my right to do with you as I wish. Tomorrow we will build a large fire and roast you alive; you will make many fine meals for us and your death will provide great satisfaction for our warriors and the serpent. I will have your hearts boiled until they are soft and eat them." At that he walked away with a look of satisfaction on his face.

Our arms were tied behind us with a rope going from our hands to the top of a post so that if we started to slump down it would cause a searing pain in our shoulders. In that position, we couldn't allow our legs to relax. All we could do was stand, and wait for our imminent death, and wonder what the old man was talking about when he said, "All we are waiting for is our friends and the serpent to arrive. When the serpent arrives, we will torture you and then feast upon you."

At that time, serpent or Serpiente was only a name on a map, and of course, part of a story that Charlie told. I really had no idea what a serpent was, but I knew I didn't want to be the main course. I had assumed that a serpent was some kind of snake, I was obviously uninformed about the powers these creatures had. At the time, I simply couldn't grasp it all. As the dreadful evening dragged on, heavy rain clouds moved in on us and what started out as a gentle rain, turned into a full-fledged storm with lightning all around us. The rain came down in icy cold sheets causing us to shiver uncontrollably. We were to endure another icy cold rain, for a second night. Again, we found ourselves looking to the sky with our heads tilted back and our mouths wide open, trying to capture every raindrop we could. The warriors, of course, all hid inside their make-shift shelters.

My body was in agony, when suddenly I realized the leather straps that held my hands so securely that they had long ago turned blue, were slowly loosening up, the leather was stretching due to the rain-water. Despite the pain, I jerked my hands back and forth until, an hour before daybreak I had pulled one hand loose and then quickly untied myself and then Charlie.

We didn't dare attempt to retrieve our weapons but at least we had our freedom, if we were lucky and could get away from the warriors by putting some distance between us. We looked around to see if the warriors had posted a look out. They had, one of them was leaning against a rock in a sitting position with his legs crossed and a piece of cloth over his head to keep the rain out. The lookout had fallen fast asleep. I could see my bow across his lap, but I would need to kill him to retrieve it I didn't want to risk a commotion. Besides, I had never killed anyone, yet. I knew I could if it was the only way to survive. Suddenly my eyes locked on the two women who were forced to sit outside of a shelter where, their masters, was snug and warm. They watched us with eyes that were sad and forlorn but never making a sound, never doing anything but shivering while they sat and watched us. I felt sorry for them but knew we were in far worse shape ourselves.

We were in a quandary as to where to escape too, until we realized our bodies had already taken control, in a mad dash through the rocks and brush we ran as fast as our limp bodies would carry us, toward the river. It was the only natural barrier we could possibly put between us and the Red Face. We were returning to where we had been captured, knowing the warriors could easily out run us, especially if they used the horses. But then, we had never actually seen one of the warriors get on a horse, they had only led the horses and seemed scared when doing that. We knew we could swim to the other side of the river and there was also a trail that led down the bank until the cliffs began.

The further we got away from the warrior camp, the faster we ran, running as fast as we could, which was painfully slow, due to our exhausted state. We were lucky, the Red Face camp had slept in late because of the rain and when finally, one of the men got up to look around, he was captured in a brawl with the women. It then took a second more before someone discovered our disappearance. It only took a few seconds more before they found the footprints, pointing out to them what we were going to do.

We had hardly got to the river when we saw Red Face running toward us. The river ran fast and was at a high volume because of the spring snowmelt in the mountains. It was cold and dangerous water. We retreated down the trail that led alongside the river until the bluffs began to form. The trail ended there, with a small pool of circulating water that joined the river and went to places unknown.

As we descended the trail as fast as we could, we could hear the war cry of the warriors who had discovered our escape. The war cries carried in the air above the thundering tumult the river made. We were out of options. We dived into the tumultuous water as arrows began to cascade down through the air around us. Swimming as hard as we could for several hundred yards, we swam until we couldn't anymore and then we got out in order to get warm. After another turn of the canyon we came upon another place where the ancient ones had access to the river. A Red Face was there, waiting to pick us off as we floated by. But we saw him first, and spent our evening hidden in the rocks. The Red Face didn't seem to be hiding. Maybe they were there to collect our drowned bodies, for food. After shivering most of the evening while hiding in rocks, we wanted to pick just the right time, when the bottom of the canyon was deep in shadows, but the moon would highlight everything up high. We then painfully slipped back into the icy water and quietly floated past them. The Red Face never noticed us. Another curve in the canyon and we would never see them again.

The Grand Canyon

Separated by the sheer cliff walls of Marble Canyon, we had escaped the Red Face. We knew there was no way the Red Face could pursue us without actually getting into the icy cold water, and we suspected they could not swim, after all; where would they have learned?

We swam on and off most of the remainder of the night until we found a small beach where we could get out of the river and sit on a rock as the sun just cleared above the canyon rim providing the only warmth we felt that day. We were in a panic as to what to do but the truth was ever so apparent. The only way we could go was down the river. We walked along the edge of the river whenever possible, looking for anything edible. Snakes, lizards, earthworms, a stray crustacean in a tiny pool of water, several minnows, several frogs, several turtles, a rotten log with grubs, flower bulbs, and cacti was our diet. Every morsel of food tasted great but it took so much work just to find something.

Utterly trapped, we spent the entire day swimming down sections of the icy cold river where we couldn't walk. We swam until we couldn't stand it anymore and we got out to warm ourselves, reluctantly returning to the water over and over. Before the sun went down we climbed out of the water and dried ourselves in the last rays of the warming sun. When the sun finally went down we were dry but very cold and hungry. We hadn't eaten anything substantial for several days now and could find little to eat. All we had was the shreds of cloths on our backs and questions about how we were going to climb out of the canyon. This seemed more impossible the further we went. As the river cut down through the rocks, escape was becoming more and more treacherous and the rapids more dangerous by the mile. Usually there was nothing but sheer bluffs of limestone on either side of the river making escape unthinkable.

We slept fitfully that evening under a tiny ledge of rock that sheltered us from the rain that seemed to come every evening. Instead we experienced a new sensation as the sun appeared over the rim of the canyon the following morning, but we were sick. We had picked up a sickness from the Red Face people and Charlie in particular was finding himself as weak as he had ever been. I explored the crevasses of the rock we had been sleeping under and discovered that we had shared our rock ledge with a coiled-up rattlesnake. I pulled the angry hissing snake out of the rocks with a stick and dispatched it with a rock. Not having a knife to clean it with, or a fire to cook it on didn't matter, we carefully beat the head with a sharp rock until it was disarticulated and using a thumb we pulled the skin off and gutted the animal. Eating the snake raw it was the first food we had consumed for four days and it tasted utterly marvelous to us.

That evening we ate raw cat tail bulbs and a raw catfish that made the mistake of swimming too close to us. It all tasted terrible but it didn't matter, we were famished and now we were becoming terribly sunburned from swimming in the river all day. Charlie's fever was getting worse and his swims in the cold river were getting shorter and shorter. But late in the afternoon our luck dramatically changed as we came to a large beach with the remains of one of the ancient ones' camps hidden in the brush. We discovered six skeletons including one that belonged to a small child but the important thing we found was camping equipment, left by the plague-ridden humans who thought they could escape if only they could get far enough away from other people.

We discovered a large raft that had rotted into the ground and traces of pitched tents. After a little looking, we also found two whitewater kayaks with paddles that had fortunately been stored under a rocky overhang perpetually in the shade. It took Charlie and me several hours just to clean the rats nest out of the kayaks and inventory the tiny stores of canned food that we found and dug out from under the sand. We also discovered several utensils that would aid in our survival.

Charlie even discovered a small plastic device hidden in a bag. He handed it to me to look at, I was mystified until Charlie took it back and by running his thumb across the wheel produced a tiny flame. I was amazed that I could actually look through the clear plastic and see the magic liquid that was used by the ancients for all manner of things. We also found a small plastic box that was buried in one of the rotting bags under the sand, it contained fish hooks along with clear line that still seemed strong after all these years. Hidden away in a bag buried under the sand we also discovered many other items that we played with for several minutes trying to discover what they were used for. We finally figured out that one of the implements was used for making fire. Our last discovery was a small rusty metal grill that looked very similar to the one stolen by the warriors we had escaped from.

Most of the canned goods had rusted through and were ruined. Plastic containers that normally would hold flour or sugar were empty. The contents long ago had gotten wet and had been devoured by insects but we did find a metal can full of salt which would flavor our food.

That evening we had cooked fish for dinner along with a small pile of wild onions that Charlie collected along the river and a can of Spam which we also used for fish bait. The best discovery for me was one can of peaches in heavy syrup which brought a huge feeling of satisfaction to me. It was a feast and afterwards we were very satisfied with ourselves. The pickings had been slim but we now believed we had a fighting chance of getting down the river. Charlie immediately began to feel better. We had hope.

Finding Resources at Phantom Ranch

The following day was a new experience. After sharing another catfish over a fire, we paddled the much smaller and tippy crafts which were very different from our original kayaks which never tipped over on in the flat ocean. Now we were paddling tiny kayaks down a whitewater river through many rapids without the benefit of spray skirts which had long ago rotted away. The paddles were similar to the ones we discovered in the city with the volcano but now we had to learn a whole new way of paddling the smaller boats that reacted to our every move.

After taking several swims in the icy cold water we decided to carry the boats around the larger rapids, at least the ones that allowed a portage around them. Most of the rapids only allowed one path and that was through a frothy whitewater world often swamping our boats. We hung on to everything and swam over to the shore where we would dump the water out of the kayaks. Still, it was far better than swimming down the icy river.

Eventually we found another camp site but this campsite had few things we could use. However, it did have one thing that might prove invaluable in the near future. We discovered a knife in a rusting metal box along with several small knives that could be fashioned into arrow heads if we could find the right material to make a bow. The wood around us made great firewood but was worthless for making bows. Still we had hope, we even found a dead bird along the way and refurnished our headbands in order to keep the sun out of our eyes and hid away the extra feathers just in case we could find something to make arrows out of.

Eventually the canyon opened up and took a long turn to the setting sun. In places, we found relatively flat areas at the bottom of the canyon where remains of very ancient houses that were inhabited by a people that Charlie called Indians. They were not as well made as the ruins in my dreams but they obviously were much older than the homes the ancient people lived in just before the plague.

Charlie said, "You realize that we are the Indians now."

I answered him, "Well maybe so, but I don't think they lived very well, who could live in this isolated and desolate country?" There was nothing but rocks piled up in layers that were beautiful in their own way but surely didn't lend themselves to a place for human habitation.

"Well," Charlie answered me, "I suspect they knew things that we don't. They lived here for thousands of years and they knew where every water hole was, where it was safe to live, and they ate a much different food than we do."

"I wonder what happened to them," I asked.

"Probably the same thing that happened to all most of the more recent people, some kind of plague."

Each day we floated down the river and Charlie and I slowly grew stronger. We could stay on the river for longer and longer times before having to take off and warm ourselves in the sun or by building a fire. The canyon provided monolithic isolation from other people, namely the Red Face people. After many days of carefully drifting down the river, living on catfish and onion shoots that sprang up along the edge of the river where there was soil, we found ourselves in an extremely wide part of the canyon.

Everywhere we looked we could see towering cliffs that supported bands of growth supporting tiny worlds, which were completely inaccessible. Occasionally we would come upon an obvious place which would allow good camping. After exploring several obvious camping places, we discovered several fortified sites. The ancient ones had carried everything imaginable and made a circle around the most secure places well above the high-water line. Their remains all told stories of desperation. Anyway, they failed to isolate themselves. Perhaps the last ones that came through carried the plague with them. Unfortunately, too many people had the same idea. It didn't matter; the pandemic and time had found all these people, despite their futile attempts to hide. In places, there were great rock piles which were obviously not natural. At one time, it could have been a wall.

These people lived their final days in abject fear of something. Were the rocks piled up to protect a family or isolate themselves from the pandemic? Even if the plague had only lasted a few months, what were all those people planning to do if they did survive? Surely, they would run out of food and I doubt if the local wildlife would last long. Besides a couple of hiking trails, they would have to float all the way back to the bridge where long ago an ambush had occurred, where we first encountered the Red Face.

Then, after many miles of travel, everything suddenly changed. To our right a large canyon opened up and we discovered a village of the ancient ones with houses that were still standing. The sign, which was still readable, identified the place as Phantom Ranch. I was uncomfortable; it was located on the side of the river controlled by the Red Face. Could there be a way down from the top for the Red Face to get down here? It would take a monumental hike for anyone coming down from the top but maybe there were other Red Face people already here. After carefully looking for any signs of other living humans, and finding none, we pulled over and tied off our kayaks.

Along the bank, a fence had been constructed at one time, probably for the same reasons the campers built rude barricades. The wire had rusted away for the most part and in one section, the bank had eroded away leaving several missing fence posts. Taking out there and looking over the open fields we could see houses and trees but nothing appeared to be moving. Looking up we were curious about a metal device that crossed the river. It appeared to be a device with a large cage suspended from it used to ferry objects back and forth across the river.

Phantom Ranch was located at the conjunction of a large side canyon draining a huge area. It was in an old canyon with a deep slit carved through the rock which went for many miles to the north. The immediate canyon walls went straight up on either side of the canyon floor until they reached the deep layers of the lava beds. Beyond that, where we couldn't see, there was another series of steep climbs to reach the actual rim, all assuming that there was a trail there at all. But with our recent luck, I was expecting Red Face warriors to be walking in single file down that trail as we rolled out of our kayaks to explore.

The floor of the side canyon was indeed unique and very large. A small family could have actually lived here. I wondered where the creek was that flowed down the canyon and how much, if any water flowed down it, but we hadn't seen it yet. Without much water, it might be easily climbed by a human. But then, more than likely there would be sheer cliffs where waterfalls would form. It all played with my mind for some reason. I truly wanted to avoid the Red Face at all cost.

We ventured into one of the buildings, in what turned out to be a lifesaving exploration. It indeed looked somewhat like a ranch house, many small rock buildings all connected with metal roofs. Most of the glass in the windows was still intact. There had been several outbuildings, all long ago rotted to the ground. The main house was what we wanted to explore. Inside, there was evidence that the ancient ones used canned goods but we only found one can of something known as Purina Dog Chow. Since we had had our fill of dog meat, we passed on opening it up. The place looked like a Bed and Breakfast where meals were served. It would take a little exploring outside in another small rock house before we found a cache of canned goods that the ancient ones had somehow managed to carry all the way down here into the canyon. In that one small building we found shelves with several cans of food, including large cans of peaches in heavy syrup that were still setting on a shelf as if someone had left them there just for Charlie and me. We concluded that only a tiny few people had actually lived here, we found few remains of the ancient ones. The remains of the last people we found were evidentially guarding the fence with their rifles, fences now rusted and dissolving like the very bones of the ancient ones. These ancients were terrified of the plague victims. How many panic-stricken people had begged to be let in only to be shot? We concluded that if the Red Face People had found this place then they would have used up all the supplies here long ago. In fact, we were the first humans to step foot in the place in over two hundred years. Then, looking at the opposite bluffs on the other side of the river we discovered what we had wanted to discover all along, there was a visible trail that was leading up the vast labyrinth of canyon walls to the other rim of the canyon. It was our way out of the canyon but first we had to rest.

We also discovered, in one of the fields, a single creature that looked like a degenerated horse. It was running wild and at one point started up the canyon trail but Charlie blocked its passage and soon the animal went back to grazing on green grass that grew in the tiny fields. We also discovered a garden that had been planted by the ancient ones. Volunteer tomato plants were just starting to turn into tiny green bulbs, but still provided an unexpected food for us when the tiny buds were sliced and cooked in a metal pan we found. Adding salt to the mixture along with a rabbit provided a great meal for us.

We found everything we needed to construct some packs we could use to carry bedrolls, cooking gear, and supplies across the river and on to the trail on the other side of the river. We decided we could take several kayak trips if necessary to get everything to the trail across the river. Once there, we would hide the kayaks then attempt to hike to the canyon's south rim. After four days of recuperating by simply resting and eating we were able to cure a thousand hurts. Then slowly we began transporting our supplies to the opposite side of the river but instead of using kayaks, we figured out how to use the large metal ferry that made crossing the river easy.

Hiking up the well-developed trail, we discovered that it was far longer than we had anticipated and we were out of drinking water well before we reached the top. But after several hours of walking, always up a sharp incline, we reached the rim where it was perfectly flat except for some distant volcano cones that appeared to be very old.

After finding water, we explored many rock buildings, usually with the roofs having fallen in, allowing rains to destroy all the contents. However, we did find one intact place that reminded me of the Bed and Breakfast at the lake I had traveled to when I first started my journey. It was much more massive than the place in Alaska and when we found the kitchen, the roof was still intact but we found nothing in the way of useful things. It appeared that someone had long ago picked through the remains removing all the small knives that made such wonderful arrowheads. Usually we could find at least some of the tools left by the ancient ones; a shovel with a metal handle, a hammer, a hatchet which could be turned into a good tomahawk, but here, there were no tools to be found anywhere. Someone had picked the place clean, which made us worry and wonder; would we be facing more warriors without a way to defend ourselves? Were their Red Face People here?

We had another decision to make. We had, of course, lost the crumbling maps that showed the way to a mythical place called New Mexico, but on one of the walls of the largest building hung a huge three-dimensional map which was mounted to the wall. It still hung as a map for the ancient ones who evidently were curious about the canyon. We could trace our route down the canyon where we had been, but were in a quandary as to where to go next. If we retraced the canyon wall to the east, which is where we wanted to go, it was obvious we would have to deal with several side canyons that dropped into the much larger Grand Canyon. By studying the river on the map, we realized that, where the smaller canyons opened up into the larger canyon there were large rapids. We had already swum those rapids hanging on to our paddles and kayaks. At each major rapid the kayak would fill with water and we would be thrown out of them to experience each rapid the hard way.

Looking at the map and considering our route, we followed the rim of the canyon that ran due east and then curled to the north. We would need to somehow cross several canyons that drained into the larger river behind us. We considered going south toward a place marked Flagstaff on the map but then again, we would be forced into walking over vast distances of desert on a road that appeared to be used by someone. It was true that we could possibly resupply in the ancient town of Flagstaff, but then again, we might run into more Red Face, after all, someone had obviously stripped the useful implements from where we were now.

Our thoughts drifted back to dealing with the Red Face. We dreaded any idea of dealing with them. We were defenseless and the Red Face appeared to be crazy. When we first encountered the Red Face, we could not understand why they followed us so far after the bridge ambush. We could understand it if they were protecting the bridge but instead they ran after us. Only a group of madmen would attempt to catch up and capture men on horses. They ran as if they did not feel pain, how was it possible for them to have run so far? We had hardly escaped down the small river before they arrived. Then later, after we were captured, why had most of them refused to converse with us? Charlie and I traded questions. Charlie would point out, "The lead warrior seemed very intelligent, yet he did incredibly bizarre things." I answered, "He certainly enjoyed inflicting pain and watching others suffer. He is a monster."

After our ordeal, we contemplated our experiences. The Red Face acted very differently than any humans we had ever encountered. Charlie, who had known at one time, many humans, was as mystified as I was. We had never imagined that humans could be so cruel. Then, there was the conversation with the father of the man Charlie had killed. What did he mean when he said, "All we are waiting for is the serpent to arrive, whereupon you will learn about pain. We will all feast upon you."

There was another route that was marked on the map to a place called Tuba city where the route again divided, but one of those routes appeared to go directly into the region we were seeking. Unfortunately, it crossed a vast desert area that was marked as the Navajo and Hopi Indian Reservations. Charlie and I had no idea what a reservation was or if we would find anyone there. Much more importantly, we wondered if we could find water there. But the route into Flagstaff also promised a long walk through endless miles of desert with no promise of water.

Part 3

An Encounter with the Hopi Shaman

Don't be afraid to cry. It will free your mind of sorrowful thoughts.

—Hopi Proverb

The Hopi

*I*n the end, we decided to travel to a place marked Tuba on the map. It was a smaller place but we had learned long ago that even a single house could sometimes supply us with some water and food. After loading our packs with as much water as we could carry, we headed down the tiny trail that was in the middle of one of the ancients' roads. Someone else had been making the long journey here. We turned due east following the path, always searching the horizon for movement but seeing no one, until we reached the last canyon marked Little Colorado River Gorge Overlook. The overlook allowed someone to walk out to the very edge of the trail, and look down at the tiny river, the Little Colorado, far below. The canyon walls were vertical, dropping straight down to the river and providing no way down. We turned northeast from the overlook as a shortcut appeared but immediately we discovered that the small trail we had been following was still there with us. Others had figured out the same shortcut long ago. We knew, deep in our hearts that we would meet other people where we were going, every new view was intimidating. Who was hiding there?

Tuba turned out to be a desperately ruined city even for a city of the ancients. Few of the homes were still standing but we could still sometimes find the tanks located inside of the rubble. Tanks that at one time heated water for the convenience of the ancient humans. We could not find any canned food in any of the homes. The houses appeared to have been picked clean long ago by some unknown and mysterious people. We smelled something rotting in one of the houses. Inside we found a decomposing Red Face Warrior who had somehow been killed then deserted some time ago.

We were able to find one of the stores that the ancient ones used to store their food. The shelves were stripped clean and all was gone except a few cans that had long ago ruined. Then, just as we had given up on finding food, we started to leave the building and discovered a large group of strange warriors standing just outside the entrance watching us.

They didn't seem to know what to do. The men just stood there in a non-threatening way. They had tomahawks and even bows and arrows but only one of them had an arrow notched and ready to use. It was as if they were just standing there waiting for us. There was only one door into the store that I could see. We were trapped.

We ran back to the store entrance expecting to engage in a life or death fight but instead nothing happened. We immediately noticed that they did not have the red markings on their faces and so we slowly stepped out into the sun. The warriors all focused on us but still made no threatening gestures. We both raised our hands to show our palms and that we were carrying no weapons. We then got down on our knees and waited. The warriors all set their weapons on the ground and showed their palms the same way. Looking at each other, Charlie and I were mystified and I called out to them, "Hello, my name is Chato and this is my friend Charlie."

They spoke to each other in a language that I had never heard before, then an old man who was dressed slightly differently with what appeared to be a blue stone necklace around his neck came forward. In imperfect English he says to me, "We are Hopi, and you must be Chato," pointing to me and then to Charlie as he said his name. "Why are you here?"

I answered him, "Right now we were looking for something to eat. We are on our way to a place called Serpiente, New Mexico."

This seemed to intrigue the old man who asked, "Why do you seek a council with serpents?"

This question intrigued us. I had never thought of talking to serpents, I had only experienced dreams with something like serpents in them. Finally, the old man stuck his hand out and said, "I am *Catori* which in your language means peaceful one and we," pointing to the other younger men who were gathering around us, "are members of the Hopi tribe. We are a peaceful people."

Charlie answered, "We wish you no harm, and we are only passing through. We are looking for a place that my friend Chato experienced in his dreams. He is seeking to meet a girl he dreamed about. According to what he told me, she is a very beautiful and special girl."

The old man asked with a grin on his face, "A girl?"

"There were serpents in the dream that somehow changed into ravens and flew away," I added.

The old man seemed very interested in that statement and said, "We have watched you ever since we discovered you at the bottom of the canyon. We watched you for three days before you walked up the long trial that served the ranch at the bottom of the canyon and long before you got here. We had to be careful. You could have been of the Red Face people. Up till now, the canyon has always separated us from the Red Face people. They cannot swim. They are a terrible people who not only have no honor or personal dignity, they have no souls. They are survivors of the plague that killed most of mankind. But they did not learn the lessons. They came out of the plague and after emerging from their holes they had built, immediately began to multiply and became warlike. They would attack us but we are separated by the great river that flows down the canyon of creation. The only red face people we do encounter come from the south but there is only a few of them and we kill them as soon as we discover them. They will kill you for anything of value that you have. But we had to be very careful because you too are descendants of the ancient ones who used to live in all these houses. The people who used to live here came to this land hundreds of years ago offering us little more than their religion. It is true that they also brought with them horses and many foods that we now grow in our gardens but then they took all that was ours; even our great *Kachinas* were stolen and sold. We have only regained a few of them. At one time, we had over five hundred *Kachinas*, now we have but a few. My people have lived in this land for thousands of years and away from the white men who invaded our lands. That is why we did not come down with the sickness that their shaman created."

I inquired, "Well, we knew that they came down with a sickness but that is really all we know. My family was far to the north in a place called Alaska when it all happened and Charlie's people were in a boat that traveled under the water. Our families escaped the sickness because we were hidden so far away."

The old man asked, "So you are of the Alaska Tribe and Charlie is of the...?" he stopped talking to let Charlie explain what tribe he was from.

Charlie volunteered that he was from the "Seattle Tribe of Mariners."

Finally, the old man says, "Come with us, I want to learn more of your experiences and in particular I want to understand your stories of serpents, we will give you food and water and show you how to get to your place called Serpiente. We owe the Anderson family a favor."

Charlie and I could not imagine what favor that the people of Serpiente had done for the Hopi, nor did we have any idea who the Andersons were, but we were thankful for their cooperation and help. We followed the Hopi people to a camp alongside a small arroyo where a tiny flow of water was providing the camp with the water everyone needed. There was more living people here than I had ever seen in my entire life.

Everyone appeared to be peaceful and showed no animosity, only curiosity to Charlie and me as we walked into the Hopi camp. They were entirely different from the red cheeked warriors we had encountered before on the other side of the canyon. They were clean and appeared to be curious rather than warlike. We were directed to sit down on a bench made of wooden planks and several giggling young girls brought steaming bowls of what appeared to be rabbit stew made with several vegetables that we had only tasted cold, out of cans.

The food was the best tasting that Charlie and I had ever experienced. We realized that fresh food was far superior to the ancient ones' food because over many years it had lost its nourishing energy. As I poked around the steaming bowl of food, I even discovered things in it that we had never seen before. The old man called *Catori* says to us, "Rest for now, tonight we are going to talk to you about your journey to discover the meaning of your dreams. You may discover that we know far more than you realize."

Hopi Wisdom and History

That evening the Hopi built a large bonfire and more food, which was plentiful, was shared by all twenty or so people including Charlie and me. Afterwards as the evening became dark the people performed several ritual dances that amazed both of us. Charlie even got out of his seat and joined them which seemed to please everyone. Charlie was particularly thrilled when one of the young Indian girls came over to him and flirted with him. She was far too young for Charlie but the experience made him as giddy as a small child who had as my mother used to say, "Had stolen cookies from the cookie jar, and gotten away with it." Then the women all left for their teepees and all but a few of the men broke up and settled into their beds. The remaining men, the oldest, then settled down for some serious talking. The old man began by telling a most interesting story.

"There is a belief, maybe it is a just a legend, that we Hopi came from a planet near a Blue Star in the constellation called the Seven Sisters." At that statement, he pointed to a point in the night sky where there were six bright stars, making both Charlie and me wonder why he called it the Seven Sisters. "Our history tells us how the earth was first explored by our ancestors who returned to the Blue Star to report their findings, eventually our ancestors made the decision to migrate to the earth. We Hopi believe that the earth is alive and has its own spirit. This earth is physically and spiritually connected though vibratory centers. Both humans and the earth have an axis around which the body and mind function and which must be kept in equilibrium for everything to act and function properly. The ancient scientist who lived in New Mexico even determined that the smallest of all things, the atoms as they called them, vibrate in their tiny spaces, and they are all interconnected depending upon their weight and character. The earth vibrates and spins on an axis which spins around the sun along with many other worlds. They all spin around, along with many other suns around the galaxy which vibrates in place and which spins around the entire sphere that is called by those people, the universe, and it all vibrates in a vast void."

"There is also a belief that before creation there was only the infinite Taiowa, the creator. Then, long ago it is said that our people reemerged from a hole in the earth, deep in the Grand Canyon where we found you, but that is what the white man said, not us. But the white men, those who studied such things say that we came to this world from across the ocean in small boats that carried us all the way to South America where we founded this world. In time, we traveled all the way back to what used to be called America and became many different nations of tribes. In time, we settled here."

"There is also a belief that at one time, after the earth was destroyed, we emerged from a *sipapauni*, a deep hole in the earth that connects to another world. It is represented in our daily life by a small hole, covered in the floor of our *kivas*. It is where we hold our religious ceremonies that are secret from outsiders and those who have not been initiated. According to our own history when human beings arrived in the New World it was through a *Sipapauni* which was somewhere in what was called southern Mexico, Guatemala or further south, and of course others say it was in the Grand Canyon close to where we found you."

"Our home community, *Oraibi* which means 'High on Rocks,' has always been regarded as the center of the vibrations of the earth. Originally, our home was aligned with the stars and other communities such as here in *Oraibi*. Our earliest ancestors lived along the south rim of the Grand Canyon, a place where it would take all of our energy and ingenuity to survive, leaving us no time to engage in frivolous or evil ways. We chose that place because of the energy that is present there. Some white historians date the beginning of our original *Oraibi* as around 1300 A.D. They studied the trees that we built our homes out of and decided upon that date. It is frequently referred to by them as the oldest continuously inhabited community in the United States. However, we believe that we have lived here much longer than that. There are reasons why we have lived here for many years, obviously, where one is in relation to the earth and the solar axes has a physical, emotional and spiritual affect. We have eyes that see into the future and gain truth from those energies and because of that we can make prophecies that are very true."

"The earth has been created and destroyed many times. The sickness that killed all the white men except for a tiny few was not the first time this world was created and then destroyed. The first world was very different from the world we live in now. The first people lived in a place called *Tokpela* which means endless space. The people were innocent of all evil thoughts and there was no sickness. The people multiplied and spread across the earth despite their different colors and languages. They remained peaceful and in harmony with all the other creatures of the earth. Eventually, however, an evil force entered the First World. An outside force took control over them and soon men armed themselves and became skilled in fighting and destroying. They made war upon each other and even practiced human sacrifices. *Sotunang* told the good people to leave their homes, take nothing with them and follow a cloud and a star which could be seen only by those still righteous. The people were told to do that in order to save themselves. They were told to work hard and save food like ants, then live with the ants underground. The Gods then caused volcanoes all over the earth to erupt, setting fires that destroyed all living things on the surface of the planet. The earth was then destroyed by fire and all of creation died except for the ones who did as they were told."

"When the world was destroyed, *Sotuknang* rearranged the land of the earth and the great oceans of the world so that when it was time for the chosen people to emerge from their underground homes, all would be new and they would not recognize where they had lived before. In time humans began to live again but soon again, humans began to lust after material things more and more causing them to fight among themselves again. They made war again and practiced human sacrifice. Spider Woman, the mother of the First Man and the First Women who had watched over humanity, despaired at what she saw. The world was destroyed again as the earth shifted on its axis. Earthquakes occurred and mountains arose and tore the land apart and most humans again died."

"Once again, all of those that had ignored the path set out for them by the Creator were destroyed in upheaval. Only the few righteous humans who had been forewarned of the coming disaster took refuge in the underground chambers and survived the disaster. They prospered again until they were manipulated and began their evil ways again. It seems that it is in the nature of humans to become corrupt and wicked."

I interrupted his conversation by asking, "What was it that caused the humans to become evil and destroy all that had been created by the righteous humans? Humans must have been righteous and creative creatures who lived in peace and then along came something that changed everything. War occurred." Again, I asked, "What was it that caused the humans to become evil?"

The elderly Hopi frowned and scratched his head through the thin grey hair. Finally, after holding his breath, deep in thought, he let out a long breath of air and says, "We are not sure, but we believe it has something to do with an alien race of serpents that was cast off among us."

"Please tell us more," Charley pleaded.

The old man finally said, "Many of us consider *Kokopelli*, who was one of our *Kachinas* to be a serpent. *Kokopelli* was a trickster God. He would tell you three truths, and then the fourth thing he would tell you would be a lie that could trap you. It could lead to your death. It was said that Kokopelli liked girls." He looked over at Charlie with a grin that appeared on his face and says, "Like your friend, Charlie who seeks the company of women."

Charlie started to say something but the old man stopped him. "It is understood why you seek the company of women, when I was young, I pursued the company of women. Now I have only one woman that is the life and center of my family."

The old Hopi man reflected a while and says, "That is why, when you see him in rock pictures, he always has a huge phallus which he is proud of. He loved to seduce the young girls, he was a trickster God. Actually, *Kokopelli* was a serpent that played a flute, seduced young girls, and used our good nature against us."

The old Hopi stood up for a moment, stretched his legs, and then sat down again, talking as he sat. "That is why we are so interested in your pursuit of a place called Serpiente. Why did they seek you out? What is your connection to Penny Anderson's descendants? You see, the serpents lived in the canyons of Serpiente for a thousand years but they then moved along the river named by the Spanish, the San Juan River. The Navajo who were our enemies fought with them many times. They called them Skin Walkers. The White Men who encountered them, called them Shape Shifters. They are very evil creatures who have been the cause of war since people arrived on this continent. We do not allow them among us. Anyway..." He paused to collect his thoughts returning to his creation stories.

"When Spider Woman asked how she could save the few people who had not forgotten the sacred ways she instructed them to create boats made of reeds so that when a great flood came they would be saved. In time, all but the humans who had built boats of reeds perished and humans lived well for many years. The world was destroyed again by a flood and nearly all of the people drowned under the water. The ones who survived then experienced a great Ice Age and people traveled all over the world. Then the survivors prospered for a while but as they learned and made technological advances they forgot their origins and their obligations to the Creator. As the humans before them had done they began to covet riches and material things. They became greedy and argued among themselves, stealing resources from those who could not defend themselves, and then wasting those resources. They polluted the very waters of the land and ruined the forest and deserts alike. In time, some societies developed flying devices and used them to make war in order to attack their neighbors and even distant peoples. There was so much corruption and greed in the world that the Gods feared for the survival of the few who remained righteous, and decided to destroy the earth for a fourth time."

"Then again, all of creation changed again. Two hundred years ago we experienced a forth purging of humans on this earth when an evil human Shaman, a white man, who wore stars on his shoulders, but was as evil as serpents, was casting spells. Flinging bundles of energy, cast like invisible fireballs that plunged into the hearts of the unknowing receivers. He wanted to kill all the serpents who were living in this world but that was impossible. Many of them also lived in isolation and escaped the great plague. Instead, his evil spell came back upon himself and nearly all humans died out. We are now living in the fifth period for humans to learn to live in peace. I do not believe we are going to make it. The serpents make living in peace impossible, but there is one more time after that when we may learn to live in peace. If we do not learn by then it will be over for we humans and we will cease to exist. But there are many stories and nobody knows for sure what will happen or how it will happen. That is why we are interested in you two. We Hopi are particularly interested in what you have experienced in your visions. Let me be honest with you, you need to understand that many of our people, including myself, have experienced visions, sometimes visions of the future. Our visions are pure, they come from us in our oldest traditions, in the Hopi way. But recently we have experienced a new kind of vision, visions that come to us, we did not invite them."

"We were confused because traditionally the serpents have always left us alone. We live a great distance from them in a place that has a special relationship to the energy of the earth which generates energy field lines that create a focal point of natural energy at our home in *Oraibi*. It has a positive effect on humans and a negative effect on serpents. It drains energy from them, and the serpents avoid it."

Charlie ventured a question, "So they would need to expend a lot of energy to manipulate your dreams? Do they have to be close by when they inter your dreams? Why would they even bother?"

The old man slowly answered the question, but it seemed painful for him to do it, it was as if his life energy was draining away as he answered. "We have eyes that see into the future and we have gained great truths, we have made many prophecies that have come true. But now we worry about the influence of the serpents. How can we trust our visions, if the serpents have entered our minds? What are their ultimate motives?"

"How many of you are experiencing visions?" I asked.

"Only three of us, but we are the chiefs of our people. How did they know which of us were the Governors of our people?"

The old Hopi was struggling to put his words together. He had not spoken English for over twenty years. "Besides, we used spells which should have protected us against the serpents."

Charlie and I locked eyes when thoughts of spells were brought up. We didn't believe in spells. The problem was, after the vast earthquakes which occurred along the western coast line of the country known at one time as America, it changed the earth's energy lines. New energy patterns appeared in different places. The energy force that protected the Hopi people vanished.

"Now the elders were the first to experience the serpents. It was only a few months ago that the visions began to occur. We all saw you in our vision, we knew you would venture into our country and we would meet. Chato, for some reason, you and Charlie are very important to the people of Serpiente and that means dealing with the serpents that live there. The serpents that live near Serpiente are different than the ones that enslaved the Red Face People. They are concerned for your safety and want us to assist you."

Speculations Around a Hopi Campfire

The Hopi people had known of Serpiente for over two thousand years. They were one of the first to send delegations to the Indian Gathering Place in the canyons below what would be Serpiente, where delegations from tribes all over the land would meet and exchange gifts and ideas. Peace broke out as they declared a policy of mutual aid. If any individual village was attacked, everyone would send soldiers to assist, creating a massive show of force. Everyone protected his neighbor, and the people lived well.

The old Hopi said, "Many years ago we met with many tribes from all over the world, even tribes from what some call the Old World. Now there are new people who live in the place called Serpiente. There, the people are still using many of the machines that the ancient ones built. But those of us that are here today have never been there. We stay to ourselves as we always have. We have forgotten the way there but we can get you close to it. I'm sure someone or something will help you find it."

"Why me?" I asked. "I have no idea why they are visiting me in my dreams. All I know is that when it happens it clearly is more than just a dream. The images seem to explode onto my consciousness, they are extremely colorful and sometimes I get a slight headache from them but the pain always goes away as soon as I get up and move around. But why me, there is nothing special about me that I know of?"

The old man looked away for a moment then says, "We are all special in our own ways no matter who we are. I suspect that the serpents believe when you and the girl mate, your children will be different somehow. I suspect that the girl in your dreams is already different somehow. Have you considered the fact that in all the people in the world you were chosen? I realize that there are fewer of us humans around now but there are still many of us who survived. It is like when the white man's diseases came to this world. It was said that ninety-nine percent of the people died but not all of us. The people who survived were changed in many ways. For one thing, they no longer needed to worry about disease such as smallpox. They became immune. But they also saw the world in a different way. Besides to us, not all white men are evil nor are all the serpents evil."

"What do you mean," I asked?

"There are great tribes of white men who are not infected by the serpents. They live to the north and east of us. But there are others." He paused in his conversation when he realized he was saying so much, but he continued anyway.

"American Indians believe that they were visited in the distant past by a race of white people who had long flowing beards and mustaches. Their leader, known as Viracocha, taught the humans many marvelous things including how to protect themselves from the influence of the serpents. Then after a long stay, he left us, returning to the stars. He promised to return someday. Maybe he will return and protect us from the evil influence of the serpents. Maybe he will teach us new things and make our lives easier, maybe you are Viracocha!"

Grinning, I rubbed the stubble on my chin that I had just recently begun to grow, and asked him, "Do I look like someone with a long flowing beard that came from the stars? I don't think so. I got here by paddling in a sea kayak for a thousand miles then walking all the way from a place called San Francisco, and I was almost killed by the Red Face People, the people who wear the three red stripes on their faces. Look, you people probably saved our lives. This is the first place we have been where we feel safe, feel at peace. I am certainly no Viracocha nor am I special in any way that I know of."

The old man thought for a minute then answered, "I can already tell that you are a righteous man or you would have eagerly accepted the honor of being Viracocha. Perhaps it is not you that will save the world. Have you considered the possibility that it will be one of your children, or even their children that will become that special person, and that is why you are so important? As I said before, not all serpents are evil. You may be needed to correct a great wrong. It is said that the leader of the serpents is not evil but defends its 'self when attacked. One of the serpents even helped the people by teaching us many useful things. It is the degenerate ones that we worry about."

"Do you really believe that someone can see into the future," I countered.

"I know what is true" the old man said. "I suspect that if you look into the history of our people you will see the truth in my words. We have made many prophecies over many lifetimes and they have all come true. Chato, you and the girl in your dream are the key to the future of us all. It is very important that you find your way to your dreams. We cannot protect you on your journey but we will watch after you as best we can as you cross our land. When you reach the other edge of our land, from there on you will need to find your own way. We are leaving in the morning, and will travel toward the rising sun for many days. You should follow us and then go on until you come to a great river that flows from high mountains and then enters the desert after flowing through a great chasm. Be very careful there. At one time, many tribes of Native Americans used to live there. Most of them were peaceful people like us, but many others came into the desert lands before the Spanish or White Anglos arrived here. Many of them were not peaceful. We have had to defend ourselves from them for several thousands of years now. I feel certain that some of them survived the great plague that ravaged this land."

Finally turning to go to bed he turned his head back and says, "I hope you do not trust the serpents. They will teach you many wonderful things but in the end, they will lie to you. The serpents that we knew of long ago are not the same ones that live now. They will take control and conquer your mind. If they ever gain complete control over you, your descendants will be just like the Red Face warriors. The serpents relish human death; they gain life energy from our deaths. Beware, I suspect that you have never experienced the Painted Warriors. They are far more dangerous than the Red Face Warriors." At saying that, the old man turned and went into his lodge leaving us in a quandary as to what he was talking about.

Hopi Thoughts

I was very confused by the stories that the old man told us. But then, I had come to the same truth for myself. I was tired and still a little sick. My body had not recovered from the flight from the Red Warriors and I guessed correctly that they wanted our horses and would have killed or done anything for them. But what was constant on my mind was what the old Hopi man had told me. It was all too much to consider. I laid in my bed for several hours thinking about the Hopi prophecies but could not understand my own role in it all.

The following day as if someone had given a signal, everyone packed up their gear and took down their crude lodges in order to return to their home at Oraibi. As Charlie and I watched, they loaded up everything into packs except for the poles and started to walk in the direction we were going.

Just before they left the old man came back for one last visit, offering advice. With his finger pointing he warned, "Don't forget, follow the rising sun until you come to a river that flows from the north to the south. It is the biggest river there. Follow it south past a large city that was once at the base of a mountain that looks like a slice of watermelon. Then follow it south until you come to another large mountain that stands out on the mesas to the west, in the direction of the setting sun. Serpiente is located in the canyons to the south of that mountain. Getting there will require that you venture into country that my people have not visited since the pandemic. We do not know anything about what is beyond the desert that separates us."

The old man then immediately turned and left. For a moment, he almost had to run to catch up to the tail of the line and the tribe then disappeared around a bend in the canyon. In ten minutes, they had all vanished into the juniper and cedar trees and over the small hill leaving Charlie and me completely alone. We wondered if it had all been a dream. But it had not been a dream. As we walked over to where the fire had been the previous night there were still burning coals in it and setting around it were four clay pots. One had dry corn in it, one had dried beans in it and two which were setting next to the fire to keep the contents warm, appeared to be more of the stew we had enjoyed the previous evening. The mysterious Hopi people had provided them with an excellent breakfast but they had also left them with many unanswered questions.

I had to ask, "Charlie, exactly what does a slice of watermelon look like?"

Charlie of course had no idea; he had never eaten watermelon and had no idea if it was vegetable or mineral. We did have a general memory of the maps we had processed before our swim down the Colorado River and we both remembered a river that divided the state known as New Mexico down the middle. But that was down the middle of a piece of faded paper that we had hardly been able to be open without tearing it apart. We did remember however, that there was a large city located almost in the center of the state by the name of Albuquerque. If we could find that place there would be a large river there and that was the river we were looking for. We felt safe next to the tiny creek even though we knew that the Hopi had left the area. After another night to recover we put on our packs and immediately fled the area in search of a place called New Mexico.

Following the general direction down a road that was marked by signs that lay along the crumbling road as route two sixty-four, we discovered again that walking across a desert in summer is not a pleasant thing to do. As we traveled each day it got hotter and hotter until we finally gave up traveling during the day altogether. We walked at night burning energy that kept us warm. Then, during the day we would hide in one of the ancient houses that always seemed to appear after a day or two of walking. Even though we were used to finding water there was little in the way of food. These houses were picked absolutely clean by the tribes of people who lived here now.

We followed the same trail the Hopi Indians were traveling eventually discovering their homelands. It was early in the morning and the men were working in the fields to prepare them for cultivation. We had hoped to rejoin them but the Hopi seemed to be a very secretive people. They would stand and wave, but when we tried to approach them, they politely but firmly walked away. Most of them lived on the mesa tops which were easily defended. We decided that all that needed to be said, had been said and we continued our journey past the ruined villages of the Hopi.

Encounters with the Painted People

We were in a quandary as to how to find the city of Albuquerque, which was supposedly a city below a slice of watermelon with a river running through the middle of it. We knew what the printed word looked like, but we had no idea where the city actually was. The real problem we were dealing with was the fires that we could see burning, in the far distance while traveling at night. We had long ago left the Hopi area and were pretty sure those fires didn't belong to those gentle people who would have no reason to light signal fires anyway. People, who would build a large fire at night, are not afraid of others for a good reason. There was probably many of them camped there. In large numbers, there is strength.

We found ourselves constantly searching for fires on the horizon as we walked during the evenings and on through the night, if we came upon one, we would change our direction to avoid it. We soon learned that every time we tried to change direction to the south, we eventually ran into more fires at night. We worried about whose territory we were entering. Someone was clinging to life out on those sandy mesas. Then we began to find evidence of recent use of a campsite by someone. The fire pit was still there with black charcoal still piled on the pit. In circles rocks and logs were piled for people to sit on. They all seemed to be rather strange and dangerous places.

One day we experienced a band of people walking right past us where we were sleeping. We awoke to a conversation overheard between the leader and another soldier. We were hidden well off the trail, under blankets made from sewing several buckskins together. On the ground we were protected by plants that hid us. We raised our heads, ever so slightly and watched them walk past us. They were all dressed in black deer skins, as one might expect. But some of them were completely painted white and their bodies were covered with colorful geometric illustrations, designs highlighted in black. Only a few of them had hair, and those that did, had dyed their hair various colors, working it into their personal geometric designs. As we watched them pass, we realized that most of the warriors were actually women. They seemed to be escorting a different young woman who was wearing something that looked like a cloth bag. All of them were well armed and they appeared to be very warlike. As they were walking in the same general direction we were going, we decided to roll our beds up, and follow them at a distance.

Hiding away in the rocks well above them we watched as the warriors tied the captive young girl to a small tree. The spectacle sickened both Charlie and me. We remembered our close encounter with the red people and knew what would have happened to us if we had not escaped. Fortunately for us, the warriors were in a hurry for some reason and left with the captive girl the following day, again, going in the same direction that we had planned on traveling.

It was obvious that there were many small groups of people who had survived the plague not only by living in very isolated areas but also by living in deep underground bunkers that their ancestors had designed for just such a situation as a national disaster. After the plague, they had multiplied by living off the land and using the creations of the old people. Sometimes they raided other tiny groups of survivors until only small tribes of the most war like people resulted. It was a dangerous world we were entering.

It was tedious work traveling at night with only the aide of the moon, but it was the only way we felt safe. Food had become a problem because we were afraid to cook anything. During the day, a fire produced smoke and at night it was like a beacon to anyone who was in the area. We had to cook our meals in deep ravines where the light couldn't be seen or in areas where trees would hide the light. In most stretches of our journey, trees were almost nonexistent. I could never have imagined that just finding firewood to cook a meal could become a major problem. We had to decide whether to follow the route we had planned across old roads that dropped through a long and desolate desert crossing over to what had appeared on one of the maps, as the Rio Grande River or find a new route. But the further we traveled the more people we seemed to run into. Furthermore, the old houses that we encountered were not only stripped clean of any food, but they were also devoid of any sources of water. Everything of any value had been stripped out of them, leaving only shells. Some of them appeared to have been recently lived in but were now empty. We had never experienced anything like it in our entire collective lives. There simply was no water to be found and preparing any food was out of the question.

We finally arrived at a place just north of what was, in another time known as Gallup, New Mexico. There we witnessed an event that would forever change our lives. It started early in the morning, after a long uneventful night hiking several miles we found ourselves walking along a trail that gradually climbed a rocky ridge top. We walked the rocky trail looking for a place where we had a clear view of both sides of the canyons that trailed below us, as well as a place to sleep. Soon, the canyon on our right opened into a small green meadow where we located a spring and there was a small rock house built right into the side of the mountain. That house was being attacked by a band of painted warriors. They looked like the same creatures that passed us on the trail, all dressed in black, with brilliant colors covering their skin and with feathers that were black.

We lay down on the ground so as to not to reveal ourselves and watched as several warriors slowly forced their way past the rock walls that surrounded the pitiful house. Inside of the house was a family who were doing all they could do to defend themselves with spear-like weapons, jabbing at the attackers through the tiny windows the rock house afforded. We had no weapons or we might have charged down the hill to assist the family but it was impossible to get down from where we were. All we could do was watch as the lopsided battle was waged.

A warrior aimed an arrow and within a moment the battle turned in favor of the attackers. First, the father was dragged through the door out into the yard, with an arrow imbedded through his lungs. We could hear his rasping sounds even from where we were as a warrior held him up. Another warrior took aim and with a tomahawk he split the man's skull wide open, killing him instantly. The body was then dragged over to the shade of a spreading cottonwood tree to be prepared.

Then his mate, a younger, good looking young lady, was dragged out of the house by four warriors. She was tied up and once more the warriors returned into the small house where they found two small children who were also dragged out screaming at the top of their lungs. The children were bound and after examining the inside of the house, bringing some items out into the yard, the warriors picked through them and examined them but only kept a couple of items. The few male warriors all took turns torturing the young mother, as the terrorized children were forced to watch. Afterwards, they unceremoniously dragged her naked and bleeding body to a small juniper tree, tying her hands behind her to the small tree. She was tied tightly to the tree so it would hurt more. She sat there bleeding, in a state of total shock and exhaustion. The warriors then turned on the small children, leaving the mother screaming in desperation. A boy of perhaps eight and a little girl of perhaps six were both tightly bound into a fetal position. Then for some unknown reason, the warriors began forcing them to drink water.

Charlie wanted to leave right then and there but I whispered to him that there may be scouts in the area. It would be better if we remained motionless, not drawing attention to ourselves. So, laying as close to the ground as we could and not moving our heads but in the tiniest of increments, we watched as the warriors again untied the mother, and taking turns, held the mother down, torturing her. After everyone was satisfied, the mother was retied to the tree. All but one of the warriors laid down in small groups under the shade of trees and appeared to go to sleep.

We were in a quandary as to what we could do and decided it would be a hopeless gesture or simple madness to attempt to rescue the woman. What we really had was a perfect opportunity to escape, but we both wanted to learn more about the creatures we had been watching. As we began to quietly argue about the situation I saw movement out of the side of my eye. Far below us, on the same trail we were, someone or something was slowly making its way up the trail.

Now, in order to escape we would need to wait until the creature disappeared behind one of the piles of large rock, and then we could make a mad dash. The only way out was continuing up the ridge trail which was getting more and more difficult. We would be exposed and easily seen until we reached the top of the mesa. Instead, the creature didn't reappear at all. It was as if, whoever or whatever it was just sat down behind one of the large rocks and was waiting for some reason. Maybe it hadn't seen us at all, maybe it turned around. But certainly, we had left footprints, it certainly was aware of us, but to return to the group it would have to walk all the way back down the ridge and then up the floor of the canyon to the rock house. But then, there was no way down to the rock house from where we were without descending back down the trail below the bluffs and then returning by coming back up the floor of the main canyon. It would take some time for that to happen so we continued to hide there as quietly as possible. Maybe the intruder had decided to take a nap just like the other creatures we were watching.

Except for a look out, all of the warriors were fast asleep, curled up around each other. Then, just as the sun was setting, the warriors began to become active. After taking care of bodily functions, which they did in private, away from where a large pile of wood was piled up, they walked around, revisiting the small house and then walking down to the spring. They wanted to know what was growing there. Evidently, they found what they were looking for. They put wet green plants that they gathered into a large clay vessel taken from the house. They also brought back a bucket of thick mud. They sat around talking for a long time until it was truly dark again. Then they lit the huge pile of wood that had been heaped up, letting it burn down into a glowing bed of deep coals. Next, they carried the naked children over to the bed of coals, sitting them up; they again forced them to drink all the water they could possibly force down them. They were then soaked in water and a thick wet layer of wet plants were wrapped around them followed by a thick layer of mud which was applied all over the small children. Afterwards the warrior poured a small amount of water around the edge of the coals, followed by actually pouring a small amount of water directly on the coals so they wouldn't burn so fast. Then the children were unceremoniously tossed into the steaming coals. Instantly the children began to scream. The warriors then started rolling them around in the coals, never letting them stay in one place for too long as they wanted them to experience the fire as long as possible. The little girl died almost instantly. The boy hung on for several minutes as first one side of him was roasted and then another. All the warriors gathered around as the children screamed, seemingly relishing in the terrible pain that the children were experiencing. After a short period of screaming by the children, which was matched by screaming from the warriors, the children finally died. The leader and another warrior then took a large leather robe that had been soaked in water and threw it over the two pitiful victims to 'steam' the bodies. If the warriors acted like it was just another deer or antelope that had been put on the fire to cook, it would be one thing, but these creatures seemed to relish the pain they produced. They seemed to be in some kind of rapture when death finally occurred.

An hour later they dragged the bodies out of the coals, dissected them by making a cut from the bottom of the belly and up to the rib cage. Taking a knife, one female leader carefully removed the steaming liver, heart, and kidneys which she placed on a large flat piece of wood where they were further cut up and the warriors lined up to pick out the choice parts to be devoured. The female, the mother of the two children simply stared blankly off into space during all this. After a while, a fellow walked over and jabbed her with his hand without getting a response, so he pulled out his knife and slit her throat. That produced a response, she died. The warrior held out his arms, holding them over the dead woman in what appeared to be an undulating dance as she bled out. Then he abruptly turned, and returned to the others who were picking meat off the children's carcasses.

We watched as another warrior arrived from the trail that was in the valley, dressed in black leather but without all the geometric shapes painted on his skin. His skin was covered with what appeared to be clumps of paint, what was understood to be camouflage. When he stopped moving, he seemed to disappear into the background. He walked directly up to the leader and began pointing a knife blade directly at us.

A deep darkness came upon us despite the brilliant sunlight, the incident changed our atmosphere and mood, and the warriors began gathering up weapons. We crept away from the rim of the hill slowly at first but as we finally put a mile behind us and the tragic scene we had just witnessed, we began to jog, and then sprint until we couldn't run anymore. We topped the rim of the canyon as the group of the warriors began running up the canyon into a dead end with high bluffs that blocked their progress.

We ran north, into a waterless desert, just wanting to get away from the creatures. We finally settled into a dry ravine, covered with our deerskins, curled up against a wall of dirt where we would be invisible to anyone in the area, and slowly went into a troubled sleep. We would both experience nightmares that night. We simply couldn't get the sight of what we had witnessed out of our minds. It made us wonder just how far the human race had regressed. Now we were dealing with another tribe of crazy sub-humans that we knew nothing about. We both had serious thoughts about returning to our homes but after thinking about it a while we decided that we had come too far to turn back.

Both of us were suffering from a lack of both of water and food, but we continued walking slowly in a northwest direction. We were afraid of turning southeast, our true route because of the fear of running into more dangerous warriors like the ones we had just encountered. We had purposely made a change in our course, heading out across the desert where we expected to see no other people. For water jugs, we still had several of the small containers called canteens, we had acquired at Phantom Ranch. We carried them in our packs, but only a couple of them still had water in them. Having little water and certainly no canned goods with us, all we had was our small packs in which we carried the deer skins, fire starting equipment, and a container where we kept an occasional bulb plant or bird egg that we might run across. Going into the desert may have been a mistake, the further we traveled the dryer it got, yet we knew it was possible to survive there. We even found ruins of a truly ancient people who had lived there well before the civilization that died because of the pandemic. Most of them reminded me of the houses I had experienced in my visions of Serpiente. Somehow, people here had been able to acquire water and food.

Walking down a ravine which had a moist, sandy bottom gave Charlie an idea. He found a sharp turn in the ravine which stayed in the shade most of the day and began digging a hole in the sand. Within a few minutes the hole filled with water which we sucked into our mouths as fast as it appeared.

Walking into Chaco Canyon

After a day of walking, I fashioned for myself a bolo, the only weapon of sorts that we could make without tools and within another mile of walking we had managed to capture a cottontail rabbit, then another after another few minutes of walking. That evening we finally had food and water returning our bodies as well as our dispositions to a better state of being. The rabbit skins could be used to make moccasins or great gloves against the night cold. The following day we found an ancient road that traveled due north without a trace of habitation. It could be an easy way for us to travel but we decided against following it because it appeared to get more and more desert like, without a trace of human habitation.

The dry ravine we were following finally played out and became shallow as the water that it would carry after rains would have soaked into the ground and all we had before us was a flat plane with only a few volcanic hills to break up the monotonous scenery. The good thing was, we stopped finding any trace of people other than the remains of the much earlier civilization. Finding ancient ruins meant we could usually find desperately needed water nearby.

By the fifth day since we had left the site where the family had been killed, we began to feel much better about ourselves. We knew that we hadn't been followed. If they were determined to catch us they could have done it long ago. Instead, we hadn't seen any other humans except the remains of truly ancient Indians who had long ago disappeared.

We found another large wash which had its source to the east and appeared to turn north where we found it. We knew that if we continued to follow the dry stream north it would sooner or later enter a wet river but it would not be the river we wanted, it would probably be the San Juan, a river we had seen on one of the ancient maps. Instead we plodded up the wash stopping whenever we found a wet area where we could dig into the sand and find water. It was easy, evidently the ravine had carried water from a thunderstorm recently and even though we found little standing water, just below the surface was plenty of water. Then we discovered a place that amazed us. As we walked up the sandy soil of an arroyo which was enclosed by canyon walls that cut through miles of monotonous flatland, we came upon exquisite ruins made with the same banded masonry style that I remembered in my dream.

As we explored up the canyon we found ruin after ruin. They appeared to have been reconstructed at one time or another and they were part of some kind of park where the ancient ones came to examine the work of the old ones. After several hours of exploration, we came to a recent construction marked 'Park Superintendent.' It was an entirely different construction with the roof mostly intact. The thing that intrigued us the most was the complete lack of the looting that had occurred at other houses we had passed by weeks before.

The kitchen was still full of implements which we eagerly rounded up, mostly pots and pans and sharp knives that could be fashioned into arrow heads. Then I noticed something while looking out of the kitchen window. At some time or another someone had planted a small garden behind the house where it was unusually moist because water flowed down a small ravine into it. There appeared to be all manner of volunteer vegetables just for the picking. Famished and deathly tired of eating cottontail rabbits that wandered into range of our bolos, we looked at tomatoes turning red on the vines; okra also grew there with squash and two peculiar types of vegetables we had never encountered before. We later found out that these were cantaloupes and small watermelons. We immediately left the structure and began gathering up vegetables and fruit out of the ancient garden.

Taking some of the squash, tomatoes, onions, corn, carrots and okra which seemed to grow in abundance we made a stew out of chunks of rabbit in a large pot we found in the kitchen and when it was done we feasted. Because we had eaten only rabbit roasted over a small fire for several days we were famished and in dire need of real food. We even found a container on one of the selves in the kitchen labeled salt. It had turned rock hard but when a chunk of it hit the water it quickly dissolved, allowing us to flavor our meal even more.

We ate until we thought we would burst but an hour later we were trying to figure out what the large green melons were. Upon cutting one open we found it full of black seeds and water. After only one bite we knew we were in for a treat. The flesh of the melon was bright red and sweet and it was while cutting a slice of it to eat that Charlie realized something. "Look at this, do you remember what the Hopi Indian told us about looking for a mountain that looked like a slice of watermelon?"

"Sure, I remember," I answered.

"We are looking for a mountain that looks like this." He held up a slice of melon that was green on top with a creamy white rind and the red fruit below it. "This is what the mountain is supposed to look like above the ancient city of Albuquerque."

Having not seen a trace of another human in the small desert canyon we decided to camp there for a couple of days until we could process some of the vegetables by drying them, making them portable. We already knew the onions would last for several days but the other things would require painstaking drying which we accomplished by putting the cut-up vegetables on flat cooking pans we found in the house and placing them in the seat of an ancient truck that was parked there. As the sun arose in the morning the heat trapped inside the cab of the truck would dry the vegetables out. The food would lose some of its life energy but still be edible and portable.

For Charlie and me, we felt at ease for the first time in a long time despite the fact that we were surrounded by ancient structures. On our third day, everything changed. Late in the evening a huge flock of black ravens arrived which literally devoured everything that was left in the tiny garden, leaving us in a quandary as to the timing of the invasion. Where had they come from? The birds then settled on the rock cliffs above us as if just watching to see what we were going to do next. We made another meal out of rabbit and vegetables, ate it and decided we would move on after eating the remainder in the morning, then we settled down to sleep under the stars, not wanting to sleep inside the old house where the ancient ones had died and left their bones.

The vision started as always, with a series of red filaments appearing, turning into brilliant geometric patterns against a colorful background. Then it exploded onto my dreams and pushed them out of the way as had happened many times before. I could see myself looking at the ravens that had been flying around us. The ravens would land and change into what appeared to be ancient Indians who were living in the ruins as they may have been several thousand years ago. They reminded me of the Hopi people industriously working their fields. I saw many small garden plots, everywhere there was a flat piece of land without an Indian house on it, there seemed to be people taking care of bundles of corn and carrying jars of water to tiny mounds in which something grew. I guessed it was bean plants that grew out of the tiny mounds. In my vision, I walked down the tiny creek which had a small stream of water running down it and the water appeared to be on top of the ground instead of deep in a ravine as it was now. I looked up to the canyon rim and could see small trees growing there.

Continuing my dream walk, I came to a group of Indians who were absorbed in what a shaman was doing. The shaman appeared to be shaking a rattle covered with feathers. I stopped to watch the shaman for a moment. The shaman's face had been covered in charcoal to make it appear black except for three bright red stripes on each cheek. It took me back for a second, remembering our encounters with the Red Face people.

Soon the crowd of silent Indians parted and a pair of large and well-armed men dragged a very unwilling man up to the shaman. Two other men grabbed the legs of the unwilling Indian and he was spread eagled over a large stone. Then as I watched the shaman plunged an obsidian blade into the man's chest. The unfortunate Indian quivered and groaned while the shaman reached into the gaping hole created by the blade and with a few quick moves inside the body cavity, he then reached in with the other hand and pulled the man's heart out. The shaman held it over his head showing that it was still beating. He then took a bite out of it causing it to stop beating. In astonishment, I looked over the shoulder of the shaman and could see a single raven that had an expression on its face, like I had never seen on a bird before. The raven seemed to relish what had happened. Then the shaman turned to me and pointed a bony finger, still dripping with blood. Then all the people who were gathered there seemed to turn in unison and stare at me.

I experienced pure terror, but it only lasted for a second. I remember thinking that I was only having a vision, it couldn't be real. Someone was playing with my dreams. After a moment, I saw the curiosity in the eyes of the people there, an expressionless look as if they too were just waking from a dream, not blind fury, as if I was going to be the next victim.

I awoke in a cold sweat. I couldn't believe what I had dreamed. Then, looking over at Charlie I noticed that he was sitting up and shivering despite the hot weather we had been experiencing. Locking our eyes, we sat and stared at each other for a full minute. Then Charlie slowly says, "I have just had the worst dream of my life."

"Tell me about it," I asked.

"I dreamed I was walking around looking at things, only it was a long time ago when people were still here. The first thing I remember was looking at all the tiny garden plots which appeared to be everywhere. Women were carrying water in pots and watering some of the plants that were in small mounds. I remember them getting water that was flowing down the creek. It was much higher than it is now and it carried a small stream of water down it. I even remember looking at the canyon rim and seeing small trees growing on top of it. Then..."

I stopped him. "Let me guess, you saw a crowd of people gathering and so you walked over to see what was going on and discovered a shaman, shaking a rattle with feathers on it."

"Did we have the same dream?" asked Charlie.

"Did the shaman in your dream plunge a stone knife into the chest of a victim and then carve out his heart which he held over his head while it was still beating?"

"Yup," Charlie exclaimed. "He then took a bite out of the beating heart then looked directly at me and pointed to me. Everyone in the crowd turned and stared at me. At that, I awoke with a dull headache."

We both got up and walked around to see if we could find anything unusual going on around us but, we could find nothing out of the ordinary. Finally, I asked Charlie, "Do you notice anything different?"

"No I don't see anything. We are the only ones here."

"That's right," I said, "Where did all those birds go that were all over the place when we went to sleep?"

"That's right!" exclaimed Charlie. "They are gone. But why would they disappear after sunset? Wouldn't they normally just hang around until it started to get light again?"

"I just don't know," I answered. "But one thing is for sure. It wasn't just another dream we had, it was a vision. Someone is trying to tell us something. Besides, have you ever heard of two people having exactly the same dream?"

Charlie simply nodded his head back and forth.

After a while, Charlie whispered, "I have a theory. Maybe we are dealing with several serpents, one who controls the Red Face people, and one who controls the Painted people. Each tribe dresses differently and behaves differently, because each tribe is a reflection of the serpent that controls it. One serpent seems to distain women and the other makes warriors out of them. But both tribes still do the same thing; they live by terror. The real mystery is what were we going to find when we encounter the tribe known as Serpiente? Are they as bloodthirsty as those we had seen?"

We built a small fire, heated up the remaining stew we had prepared the night before, and forced ourselves to eat it. We then picked up our small packs which now had several metal objects such as cooking pots hanging from them and with our walking sticks, we carefully continued walking up the canyon being very careful where we placed each step as to avoid a common serpent known as the rattlesnake.

At the Base of Jemez

As we traveled east, slowly gaining elevation, the nights became colder and the days became unbearably hot. The desert terrain seemed to last forever. We could see mountains in the distant east where we expected to see a long valley descending to a river. We finally came upon the remains of an ancient road where a large truck was parked. After climbing into the cab, we found a water cooler with a jug in it that was half full of water. It saved our lives. We knew that within another mile or two without water we would have perished.

Looking into the back of the trailer the truck was pulling was thousands of cages that at one time contained birds of some kind. Now there was nothing in the small cages but tiny bones and a few matted feathers. Upon careful examination of the cab of the truck we also found a gun but no bullets and two knives. The knives were immediately pocketed for use. We wondered where the road went but could not remember it from the ancient maps we had examined. The terrain on the other side of the road quickly became more mountainous as we ascended the flanks of the mountain and finally we discovered another ancient roadbed that seemed to be going in the same general direction we were traveling, mostly up. But now it would be much easier. The distant fires that we had avoided were now all but gone.

Both food and water were easier to find in the mountains and we knew that the river we were seeking was still to the east, so we decided to climb the gently sloping roadbed to see if we could find the top. There we hoped we might spy the river and eventually, the city with a mountain towering over it that looked like a slice of watermelon. The roadbed made for easy walking. While looking along a stream for food, we discovered we were actually climbing up the flanks of a massive volcano. Fortunately for us it didn't seem to be showing any signs of recent activity. We discovered large scraps of obsidian laying everywhere, some of which Charlie and I collected. We had found traces of it as far away as the Hopi settlements. We knew this black obsidian would make perfect implements like arrow heads and hand axes. We both knew very well how to shape the volcanic glass into arrowheads. Unfortunately, the obsidian was worthless to us without willows to make arrows or even a bow to shoot them with. Surely, we thought others: a long time ago, would have cherished the black glassy rock and used it for all manner of tools. Those ancient people would also know where to find willows, probably growing alongside a river, and bows which could be made from working just the right small tree. Unfortunately, we still hadn't found the right materials to make our best means of defense.

We put a few choice chunks of obsidian into each of our packs for later use and continued plodding up the mountain. As we ascended following the bed of the old road we discovered more and more wild game as well as many small creeks that carried water, usually in tiny streams that trickled down the mountainside and then disappeared into the dusty sand of the desert below. The water would disappear between tiny grains of sand and follow the sloping rock bed until in time it would pool behind an impervious rock. Far below the ground were lakes of water if one only knew how to find them.

Upon reaching the top of the mountain we indeed discovered that we were on a huge volcano. The caldera formed an immense bowl with several small peaks where it had erupted eons ago. Soon the road bed we had been following intersected with a somewhat larger roadbed which seemed to skirt the mouth of the volcano and then disappear to the east. Walking on the ancient roadway was infinitely easier than cutting through the woods, even though the roadway had in places, dropped off, leaving huge gaps in it where it had cascaded down into the valley.

The Fence

Soon we came upon a fence that had been constructed by the ancient ones that appeared to be many feet high over our heads. On top of the fence was razor wire that would still be deadly to any person attempting to climb over it. At the bottom of the fence was a single strand of wire that seemed to have no practical use until Charlie touched it. As Charlie touched the wire with his fingertip, his entire body convulsed because of a shock. There was something magical about that wire. Looking through the wires, just inside the fence, and on top of a metal post we saw a small box that followed us, wherever we walked. I thought that it must be some kind of magic box because no matter where we walked it seemed to point a tiny round glass tube directly at us. Furthermore, looking inside the perimeter of the fence we could see a distinct trail that had human footprints in it. Obviously, we were not alone on top of the mountain. We were perplexed. Why would people want to live on top of a mountain when there should be far more livable areas along the river that was somewhere to the east of us? As we explored the perimeter of the fence we found deep chasms that dropped off and in the rock faces were tiny caves with rock walls in them. We decided that a race of people had lived here who were far more ancient than the humans who had died during the plague and certainly more ancient than anyone who would be living here now.

We found ourselves in both a panic and a quandary. Someone obviously lived on the other side of that fence and they obviously were well defended. Just recently someone had walked along the trail, just inside the fence leaving footprints of someone wearing some kind of shoes rather than moccasins. The prints appeared to make small squares that dug into the soil. Obviously, they were not making any attempt at trying to hide their trail. Whoever they were, behind the fence they had no fear. The questions we bantered about were many. What kind of creatures had we discovered? Were the people we might discover friendly or were they more like the warriors we encountered before? We suspected the later to be the case.

We decided that we would disappear back into the forest and skirt the fence until we could learn more. Little did we know that the box on the fence was actually a working live camera and we were being observed. Even when hiding deep in the forest, our bodies produced a thermal image that made us stand out as if there were no trees to hide us. Unknowing to us, eyes watched every move that we made.

Charlie and I decided to skirt around the fence, in an attempt to find a natural opening through it. As we hid in the forest, we could spy upon all manner of strange buildings, mostly made of metal, without windows. Some of them were as large as the buildings we had seen in some of the larger cities we had traveled through. The fence itself was built right up to the deep canyons that plummeted away to places unknown. But the strange buildings didn't really seem to have been built for humans to occupy, perhaps we thought, they were built to manufacture something that the humans used.

We camped that evening well below the fence not wanting to experience visitors. We found a beautiful and flat place where unfortunately, we couldn't see much around us but we felt that no one could possibly find us. As we had been walking along, all we could gather to eat in quantity was a mushroom that I had learned about from the Hopi stews. I later learned that it was called a morel. We were trying to figure out what to do without a fresh rabbit to cook. I still had a small amount of rabbit jerky that would have to provide flavor. We added a little salt and I set the pan on the heat in a fire pan we had carried all the way from the house in Chaco Canyon. The mushrooms turned out to be exceptionally good, and best of all, we didn't get sick from eating them. After our dinner, we cleaned and repacked everything, just in case we had to move in a hurry. We finally settled down to hide and sleep under our deerskins

Charlie says to me, "You know something? There must be water around here. I just saw a big dragonfly fly past. I could hear its tiny wings buzzing though the air."

I couldn't imagine how there could possibly be river or swamp water up here on top of the mountain. But then, I supposed, there could be some water from old snowdrifts back in the shade of trees that might still be wet. Then, as I settled into another attempt to sleep, I also heard a dragonfly.

Both of us rose up on our elbows to see three tiny insects flying high in the air directly over us, suspended in the air, well out of our reach. Maybe they thought we had something they could eat, or they were drawn by some smell. We watched them for a second more then we disappeared under our deerskin. All was quiet for a moment until we could hear them flying, just over our heads. Again, we rose up out of our beds, sitting fully up this time. Again, they just seemed to fly up well above us in the air where they hovered. Then, suddenly, all three of them went different directions, flying away from us. We dropped back down trying to take one last chance of actually going to sleep when we heard them again. As the last time, they seemed to be like all pesky insects, studying us, very close. Charlie readjusted himself, pretending to sleep, and at just the right moment, he snatched one out of the air.

It instantly stopped buzzing and waited for imminent death, as all insects do, but as we looked at it closely, we realized that it was not an insect, at all. It was a tiny machine that carried a tiny tube under it. It followed us, like the box that was on the metal post. When Charlie said something, it looked at him, and when I said something the tiny eyepiece looked at me. Someone had created a machine that could spy for them without having to be here in person. With that realization, we began to suspect that someone was looking directly at us. We were being watched by the creatures behind the fence. They knew everything about us and we knew absolutely nothing about them. Charlie tossed it back into the air and the buzzing sound returned. It hovered just above us, for another few seconds, and then took off through the woods. If they returned later that evening, we didn't know it. We were sound asleep, besides, what harm could a dragonfly cause?

The next morning, I awoke to something actually tugging at the deerskin that covered Charlie and me. We arose to face a large grey coyote with red eyes that had found us. It had tasted the deerskin and found it edible. Seeing us emerge from under the deerskin sent him in a mad dash to get away. At least there weren't any dragonflies buzzing around us, at least none that we could see.

We would need to go without any food again this morning. We had nothing left to eat. We decided to collect pine nuts and mushrooms as we slowly traveled. But after only a short walk, we found ourselves approaching a small settlement that was hidden in the forest. As we walked an entire small city appeared before us. Although no one appeared, the streets were not overgrown with brush and small trees as all the other roads we had previously walked down. I was mystified and terrified. The only friendly people I had encountered on my entire voyage of discovery was the Hopi Indians and of course my friend Charlie.

We explored a couple of residential houses and discovered that there was nothing in them. In fact, they appeared to have been completely stripped of any useful articles. Continuing our exploration, we looked around the fence being careful not to expose ourselves to any people who might still be around. Finally, after examining the strange and perplexing array of buildings that was clearly visible beyond the fence, we came to a large closed gate with a sign that read 'Los Alamos National Laboratories.'

Part 4

Los Alamos National Laboratories

*Any sufficiently advanced technology is indistinguish-
able from magic.*

—Arthur C. Clark

Capture

As we looked up to read the sign, we became aware that there was motion behind us. A shadow fell across us. Turning in terror and not knowing what to expect, we saw four men standing in military fatigues, armed with rifles with scopes on them. We had never seen anything like them before. One of the soldiers motioned for us to put our hands up.

Immediately the solders removed our packs from us and after gathering up our stuff they motioned for us to walk toward the gate. To our amazement, the gate opened up without anyone touching anything. It simply opened as if by magic. Inside the gates were a small group of people in white clothes wearing gloves and mask over their faces. The leader of the men who had stopped us, forced us to lay on our stomachs as they put metal handcuffs on our hands, behind our backs. We were then lifted up and directed inside one of the large buildings located nearby. After walking through a long interior hall, while being watched by people who were hiding behind small partitions and furniture, we were dumped inside a large metal box. We quickly discovered the function of the metal box, every time we touched the wall or door or anything except the bare floor, we received a sharp electric shock. All we could do is sit down and wait. I decided that I might starve to death before they made up their minds what they were going to do with us.

Angie Wilkerson

*F*inally, the door opened and a group of people appeared in front of us. A lady walked over close to us, signaling for us to step out of the small metal building. She was elderly, with deep wrinkles in her skin and disheveled grey hair and a hawkish look to her face. She appeared to be totally defenseless but judging by the strange devices held in several of the men's hands, she was completely protected. I didn't want to learn what those devices could do. Stopping only a few feet from us she asked us, "What do you two think you are doing here?"

I answered her, "We are working our way to a big river to the east of here. We are looking for a special place."

One of the soldiers cut into the conversation by saying, "We need to just get rid of these barbarians. They are up to no good, trying to steal our food and take captives."

Charlie asked, "What exactly is a barbarian? Isn't what you are proposing barbaric?"

The soldier replied, "We have dealt with many of your kind before. Your ancestors were people who lived through the plague and then reverted to killing and raiding, in other words, barbarism. We have encountered your kind many times and we know how to deal with you. All you know is warfare and death. You serve the serpents and they have control over you. They have long ago changed your very brains. You are not human anymore. All you want to do is hurt and steal."

He stopped talking when he realized that the elderly lady was patting him on the shoulder. Looking back at her, then at us again, he continued his speech, "Well let me tell you something, you have run into some civilized people here. We are scientists and we know how to defend ourselves, believe me. We know how to protect ourselves against the likes of you two. We watched you all the way from old highway four. Watched every move you made. Now we have to dispose of you, you are not the first we have had to contend with." With that he pushed both of us down to the ground and started to hit us with the butt of his gun, but instead the elderly lady shuffled her fingers, signaling the man to back off.

The elderly lady who obviously was in charge turned to us and added, "All right, let's get something straight. Indeed, we have had to deal with your type before, but we are also willing to give you a chance to explain yourselves. But your story had better make sense or you will be escorted far from here and then released. Sergeant Armijo was right, we are civilized, and we don't intend to kill you, we just don't want to have to deal with you, we have far more important things to attend to."

Charlie managed to step forward so he could face his adversaries, and answered curtly, "Believe us, we wish you no harm. All we wanted to do is find the big river that flows through this place and journey down it. We have business there."

"What kind of business could you possibly have south of here? There is nothing but scattered tribes of warriors who prey upon each other south of here."

One of the younger girls took one step forward and asked. "Why did you release our drone, the dragonfly? Every other creature we have ever encountered has smashed it. It was a test to see what you would do, but instead, you released it. Why?"

Charlie didn't know quite what to say, "I am at a disadvantage, I don't know exactly what the machine does but I didn't want it buzzing around me while I was trying to sleep. What exactly does a dragonfly do?" Charlie asked, directing the question to the same young lady.

"Oh my," the young lady says, appearing to blush a little, "We were watching you on a computer screen. We could see you, as if we were actually there. We could even hear your conversations if you would only speak more. Actually, I was directing the dragonfly that we allowed you to capture. We have conducted the experiment many times before, and this is the first time something unexpected happened. Charlie, you turned my little drone loose, giving back its freedom. The dragonfly could have been a weapon. After all, you knew very little about it. Again, how come you didn't take a rock and smash it into a thousand pieces?"

"Because it is not in my nature to hurt other creatures, well, except for food."

One of the other men asked in a sarcastic voice, "How many people have you eaten?"

I looked at him and said, "We have never before eaten human flesh, but then, we could make an exception for you."

The man stared at us for a moment then says, "Well, I never have encountered one of them that could understand or make a joke." He then said, "The Red Face and Painted tribes are simply a degenerate form of humans, even the serpents, have little to do with them. The painted warriors all receive their information from their leader who thinks for them. It is a dangerous creature to deal with, highly intelligent and ruthless."

After a pause, the man who just a moment ago was questioning how many people we had eaten, was now very sympathetic. But it was in the best interest of the scientist to be very careful, particularly of strangers who could be spies. The elderly lady asked us again what we were doing at Los Alamos National Laboratories.

"I have traveled from Alaska down into Seattle where Charlie and I met," I answered. "We teamed up and are searching for a place south of here where I understood there is a tribe of people who live there. They have sent us visions." While looking at Charlie I said, "They have called us to their place. I experienced a vision of a beautiful girl who lives there who has visited me many times in my dreams. She lives in a place called Serpiente."

The sound of the word Serpiente suddenly grabbed everyone's attention.

"What was that word again," the elderly lady asked?

I repeated, "Serpiente." We were profoundly hungry and we desperately needed water, Charlie and I had run out of everything, the night of the dragon-flies. We must have looked rather pathetic.

Finally, the elderly lady asked, "When was the last time you had something to drink. When was your last meal?"

I answered her "It has been many days since we have eaten more than a few pine nuts, mushrooms, or dried rabbit. The last time we had something to drink was last night."

"Clean them up. Feed them, and then bring them to my office." At saying that, she turned, stopped, and then turning again she says, "Just give them something to drink, I'll feed them at my office." She left, leaving the soldiers to care for us.

"Just one thing," the soldier says to me. "How many of you are out there?" I held up two fingers first at Charlie and then me, bringing a laugh to the soldier. He gingerly lifted us up and took off the handcuffs, then escorted both of us into a very different building.

We couldn't believe what we were seeing and experiencing. The inside of this building looked entirely different from the first building. The very first thing we noticed as we walked inside the building was that the air inside was cool. Until I became used to it, I actually shivered, for the first time since winter. Inside was a vast laboratory complex with many rooms and curious people milling around, leaving Charlie and I perplexed. Along the shelves and covering many of the desks were computers. I had examined the useless computer that my great-great grandfather had used in Alaska but these computers had images of all manner of words, diagrams, and moving people on them. It all seemed like magic to me.

Inside the Laboratory

After what seemed like a journey through another world we were directed into a room with couches and lamps which were producing light and we were seated at a table with chairs around it. As soon as we sat down the elderly lady says, "My name is Angie Wilkerson, my great-great grandfather was a scientist who worked with the people in Serpiente and recognized that a plague was about to occur on earth. There was absolutely nothing he could do to stop it so in desperation my great-great grandfather gathered the ancestors of everyone you see here. Everyone that he could convince of the upcoming plague was isolated in this facility. We of course, are all descendants of those first brave people who shut ourselves off from the outside world. Let's start our conversation all over. This time, tell me all you know about Serpiente."

I began to explain, "There is actually very little that I can tell you about Serpiente. All we know is from my visions. It is a small community with old houses that look like the houses in the canyon far to the west of here and new houses made of similar stones but with metal roofs on them."

"Do you mean Chaco Canyon?" Wilkerson could only think of the ancient ruins that at one time was the center of the Anasazi world. The conversation instantly made her wonder about the connection between the ancient ruins and modern day serpents.

"There was also what the Hopi people told us about the place and what they had experienced in their visions." The scientist seemed to know about the Hopi tribe although they apparently had never actually encountered any of them in recent history.

We spent the next several hours telling Angie Wilkerson our life histories and about all the visions we had experienced and of course what the Hopi Shaman had shared with us. This left the elderly lady looking perplexed. She wanted details about the Red Face and the tribe we called the Painted People. We told her everything we knew as the little lady who called herself Angie Wilkerson, patiently listened to us while ordering new and wonderful foods for us to sample.

"You need to be brought up to what is really going on in this world," continued Angie Wilkerson.

Food was brought in to us by a young lady pushing a cart with steaming dishes on it. She seemed very friendly, especially to Charlie. Charlie watched her every move, expressing a sincere gratitude for the delicious hot food that she was serving. The young lady simply laughed and ignored him.

Angie Wilkerson finally began to talk while Charlie and I stuffed ourselves with strange morsels of food that truly tasted great to us. I watched her and Charlie watched the young girl. We hadn't eaten since the previous evening and although we were used to going for long periods of time without regular food, we were slowly starving. I was even more intrigued when the young girl served me fresh peaches with a cream on top for desert. I had never eaten a real peach before, except the canned peaches in heavy syrup. I decided I liked the fresh fruit better.

Angie Wilkerson began a long conversation beginning with the fact that we needed to receive a quick education about the world we were living in, but there was obviously much more to it than that. She had important items on her mind but wasn't willing to share her most secret thoughts with us until we were ready.

Angie Wilkerson began her conversation with, "We are fully aware of the Anderson family that lives in Serpiente."

Charlie and I remembered hearing the name, 'Anderson' before. We remembered hearing the elderly Hopi man use that name.

"In fact, we knew them well," Angie continued. "They are one of the few clans of people who we have had relations with, however we have very different way of dealing with the world than they do. We are human beings, a scientific people. We use scientific methods in order to solve problems and enrich our lives. All our ancestors were scientists, and all who live, and work here are considered scientists, in one capacity or another. Even those guards that arrested you two, work in the greenhouses where we grow that food you are eating. We are completely self-sufficient here, not asking anything from outsiders. We are also, in effect, librarians who are attempting to save the knowledge that the human race has accumulated over the thousands of years of its existence. The Andersons were originally also scientifically oriented; unfortunately, they have allowed themselves to be assimilated by the serpents."

When she said that, it all started to make sense to me. I looked at Charlie and he was also looking at Angie Wilkerson, instead of the young girl, who was leaving anyway.

"Is she like the Red Face or the Painted People who decorate themselves and wear black leather?" I asked. She did not look like them in my visions.

Angie Wilkerson poured herself a cup of water, added some powder to it, and placed it inside a small box then punched a tiny keyboard. After a moment, she stirred a brown liquid that steamed hot in a cup. Adding a little white powder to it, she stirred it again and handed it to me.

It was the first coffee I had tasted in my life. It was good and as I sipped the hot coffee, she continued her production of coffee in her little box. When she finished, she says, "Let me explain. First of all, I have always preferred my coffee black, without sugar. You might want to try it that way sometime. Perhaps tomorrow morning, before your breakfast, it is best early in the morning."

My mind was exploding with possibilities. Obviously, these were humans like ourselves, rather than the creatures we had encountered. But the thought of the girl in my dreams being under the influence of the same serpents who had produced the creatures we were fleeing, was a terrifying thought.

Angie Wilkerson continued her conversation, "We believe the serpents have their own agendas. You see, we think the serpents have split up with one serpent ruling over the Red Face and a different serpent ruling over the Painted People. Each human tribe has a serpent ruling over them. But we think that Quetzalcoatl and Kukulcan, the ancestral serpent royalty, still live in Serpiente. There are bound to be many more serpents out there but we don't know where they are. Furthermore, we don't know how many of them lived after the pathogen was released by General Armstrong. We do know that there were survivors or there would be no Red Face or Painted people. We also know that the serpents living in Serpiente seem to have changed the way they deal with humans."

"We have not contacted the Andersons in many years. They simply preferred to live in their isolated sanctuary. That is the way it is here in this land. Many tribes live here but are unaware of each other. But what is happening at Serpiente is a mystery to us now. They have absolutely existed in a state of peace, not causing trouble to anyone as far as we know. We do believe that the serpents trained the human children who live in Serpiente in their own way of communicating. Those people are now part serpent themselves. They can communicate with the serpents through a telepathic method that only they can use."

Angie Wilkerson seemed to get serious about her description of their dealings with the Red Face. "At this juncture in history, we know far more about Red Face and Painted People, than we know of the Andersons, in Serpiente. What we do know is, long ago we captured and attempted to question two warriors of the tribe who wears red paint on their faces. They spoke in an undecipherable language and never for a moment stopped fighting against the restraints. Once they were put into the box, they fought and pounded on the walls until they could not move. Then they simply died. We learned very little from them. What we do know, is they live in small groups that mimic families but they are not really families as we think of them. They exist in absolute poverty, with only warfare and tribal ceremonies to bind them together. Hunting for outsiders, other humans to capture, they are headhunters. They are under the direct leadership of a serpent who controls several warriors and those warriors control everyone else. It is the warriors who communicate directly with the serpents; they all do the bidding of the serpent which is to conduct war on other humans. The serpent appears during the ceremonies, when it is safe for them to relish the energy released when humans are terrorized or die. It is like a drug to them."

I stopped her and asked, "What is a drug?"

Angie Wilkerson explained, "It is a thing that makes you feel better when you are sick, however, there are some drugs that when used wrongly can kill you. There are some drugs that cause an addiction, and then your body requires more and more of it to achieve the same effect. Someone who gets hooked on one of these addictive drugs becomes a slave to it."

It all made sense to me now, why the warriors had seemed to tremble as a death occurred. But I couldn't understand how the serpents had manipulated the humans. Then I reflected upon my own interactions with serpents. I realized that my visions had occurred while a serpent in some form was close by, even while I was in Alaska. How had they found me? How much control did the serpents already have over me? I wondered. Was I about to be simply absorbed into another serpent clan? I was feeling rather uncomfortable as I learned more from Angie Wilkerson yet she already seemed like an old friend.

Angie Wilkerson continued, "Actually we are aware of many human tribes that emerged after the pandemic. Most of them live to the north and east. They control huge areas that are feudal estates. Usually, the oldest persons who live among them are the absolute rulers. They use horses in order to raise cows and agricultural crops which they trade among themselves. They live in communities that are constantly moving, following the grass, all inside a distinct territory that is patrolled and defended by human men on horses. Between us and them are thousands of places where a human can live in complete isolation, which is what many of them wanted to do."

Angie Wilkerson continued, "Unfortunately they are in constant war with the Red Face and Painted People and do not have the resources to protect themselves. They live in fear, spending as much energy protecting the ranches and the people who live there, as they do actually working the ranches. With common enemies, the Red Face and Painted People, they seldom argue among themselves but because of the vast distances and inability to communicate quickly, they cannot come to their mutual aid. Raids are spread out over a huge geographical area. Raids are few but when they do occur, they are well scouted and planned excursions with warriors doing the actual killing and hostage taking. Horses are not allowed to exist out of the territory of the land barons. Few of the settlers actually have horses. Those settlers, settled in what isolation they could, sometimes reclaiming homes that had been deserted for thousands of years.

"Raids have proved to be devastating to the area ranchers. They found themselves fighting well-armed creatures that were highly trained and had no fear of death. Hostages were always taken. They would then utterly vanish into the deep canyons of the desert countries, never to be seen again."

Angie Wilkerson continued her discussion and she was offering new and exciting ways of looking at the world, as well as satisfying our curiosities. She also made a point that she earnestly wanted to help us with our vision quest. But we still had a long way to go before we were ready and we were still prisoners of the scientist at Los Alamos. We really didn't care, we were being treated like royalty and Charlie was meeting new young ladies every day.

Angie Wilkerson asked, "Based upon what you two have told me, you managed to cross the desert between a vast ocean and the huge canyon. The desert is a natural barrier. We have no knowledge of what happened to the people along the west coast of America, but we certainly knew that at one time, there were many large cities there. We also knew that many years ago, the entire coast of Western America experienced a massive geological event. The coastline broke apart in many places, particularly along the San Andres Fault. Many volcanoes became active. We were worried for a long time whether or not the city we live in would be safe from the volcano that is located here in Jemez. This entire mountain is a volcano, and if it were to erupt, undoubtedly our world would end.

"We understand that most of what you claim to have crossed to get here was nothing but desert land, land that is very difficult to survive in. Yet you traveled thought some of the most dangerous country we know of, the land of the Red Face and then the Painted People and survived to tell us about it."

"Well yes," I answered.

Angie was thinking out loud, "The land beyond the Hopi lands, across the

Colorado River, our scouts used to venture to that river, but no one ever crossed it. The Hopi wouldn't let us. We don't go there in person, at all anymore, we use drones; you remember the dragonflies?"

I thought about that capability, to fly far away and see what others were doing. They could observe anything, like a bird.

Angie continued, "The warriors wearing the bizarre paint and black leather, they appeared about twenty years ago, cutting our relationship with the Hopi. The warriors with the paint and feathers visited us occasionally; they would walk over to the fence and touch it. The fence would shock them, and they would run away."

I thought back to what Charlie and I had experienced with the fence, we had touched only the small wire that ran around the base of the fence. It produced a small spark which convulsed his entire body. It took him several minutes to calm his nerves after that. We had not touched the actual fence, which carried a far greater charge. Perhaps the small wire warned smaller animals from encountering the much more electrified, fence: small curious animals, like us.

I decided to test Angie Wilkerson so I asked her, "Where are these serpents you are telling us about? All we have ever seen were humans who were acting as if they were insane. Only an insane person does the things that the Red Face people do, but I have seen no serpents. Where are they?"

Angie Wilkerson stood up and walked over to me, placing her hands on my knees, and asked me, "Have you ever had a dream that seemed to explode into your dreams, have you seen strange things there?"

I had to admit that I had.

"Did a black snake turn into a raven and fly away?"

"No," I answered, "In my dream two black snakes came out of some large clay pots on either side of me. They arose as if they were going to strike me then a young lady, a beautiful young lady, looked at the snakes and they turned into ravens and flew away."

"Oh yes, the young lady is a problem but let's talk about you first. You may be under the influence of the serpents right now. You may be one of their spies. Do you know what we do with spies?" She waited for a response, not getting one, she said, "Remember the box you were put in?"

Still, we did not give her a reaction. Then she replied, "We can also electrify the floor."

I understood the threat.

"All I can tell you is the truth, it is our story. We certainly are not in contact with the serpents as far as we know. We have no real idea why the serpents have singled Charlie and me out. But we want to learn more."

"Consider this," Angie Wilkerson says, "Our best theory as to what is going on, is the serpents have divided up. There are at least three groups of them, one that lives close to the Red Face People, one that manipulates the Painted people, and a nest of them live with the descendants of the Anderson family. Your girl, the one in your dreams is probably one of the Anderson family. The Anderson family is the mystery. We used to have relationships with them but because of the warriors, those creatures that roam the countryside, we haven't communicated with them in many years. We have no idea what they are up to but they don't seem to bother anyone. They certainly are not a war-like people. They used to be scientists. I don't know what they are now."

Thinking about it all made my head hurt. "Why did they send for me," I asked?

Angie answered, "I don't know, but we sure want to know ourselves before we let you go there."

I felt a little better when she said "let you go there." At least there was hope, but Charlie and I had much to learn.

A little exasperated I finally asked, "Where did these creatures come from and is there a way to stop them?"

Angie responded, "Our best theory is that the serpents have been using humans throughout all of history. From the beginning, they set us against each other and taught us to make war on each other. In time, war became normalized and, according to the archeological records, we began ceremonial sacrifices. Sacrifices were originally performed to appease a god, usually to insure good weather and crops. But actually, humans were being manipulated into offering sacrifices for the lust of an uninvited and invisible guest. The serpents had no control over the weather or agriculture, but the foolish humans didn't know this. The early humans had no idea they were appeasing the needs of serpents rather than any real god. The serpents are almost invisible in their natural state. They blended in among us and manipulated us, playing on our natural emotions of greed, envy, and lust. In time, someone killed someone, and somehow the serpents were always close by. They actually preyed upon us, exploiting us through our dreams, where our most personal and sensitive emotions were laid bare to them. They could easily explore and then manipulate our very brains."

I asked her, "How do they take control over us humans?"

She answered, "You see, humans have pleasure centers that are easy to control. Deep within our brains we have pain and pleasure centers. If we do what the serpents want, our pleasure centers are activated. If we don't, we become victims. We believe that in time the serpents take over the human brain and a person actually begins to act like a serpent. Everything they do is pleasure centered. Serpents live not by consuming food like we do; they live by manipulating energy in ways we are just beginning to understand. One thing we are painfully aware of, they relish the energy generated by humans who are experiencing pain."

Charlie asked, "So that is why they are so cruel. They receive pleasure by absorbing the energy released by the human who is in pain. But we never saw any serpents, or snakes or any other strange creatures other than the humans. They were the ones that were twisting bones until they splintered."

Angie Wilkerson answered his point with, "They may have been humans at one time, but now they are more serpent than human. They were incorporated into serpent culture; they also relish the death of their fellow humans. They somehow farm the energy of humans for the serpents. They have in effect become tools for the serpents."

Charlie says, "So, if left to the serpents' whelms, they would lead us all down a long path of building communities, then as our population rises, we are manipulated to make war with the nearest other tribe or if no one is available we fight among ourselves. In time, the civilization turns to ruin and then it all happens again, somewhere else. That is the history of this land, isn't it?"

Angie Wilkerson could see the pain in Charlie's eyes, those gateways to the soul, "I'm afraid you are right," she says.

I asked, "The using of humans to create pain and destruction is a fairly new thing that the serpents do?"

Angie Wilkerson answered, "Do you remember that canyon you traveled, the one with the ruins in them? It is called Chaco Canyon and at one time it was the center of the local Indians world that they called Aztlán. The serpents have been manipulating bands of humans to do their bidding for thousands of years. Now you know why there is nothing but ruins there. After Aztlán fell, we believe the serpents followed the survivors south. There they enjoyed the human sacrifices that were performed by the Aztecs but after Europeans began to arrive, the serpents were struck by the same diseases that the humans died from. During that time, some ninety-eight percent of the Native Americans died from disease introduced by the newcomers. Some ninety eight percent of the serpents also died. It took many years until both the human and serpent population rose again in order to start the whole bloody process all over again. The problem of serpent manipulation arose again as the last pandemic occurred. Now as we humans slowly repopulate we are dealing with not only the serpents but we also need to deal with their head hunters; those humans who have been changed by the serpents. But now there is a huge difference."

"What is that," I asked.

The Anderson Family Mystery

"We know about them," Angie answered. "But what we don't understand is the current situation with the Anderson family. It all intrigues me. We have never heard of a report of head hunting among them. They seem to live in absolute peace. They were a scientific people at one time, of course they have been known to kill outsiders, but then, all families in this land will kill in order to maintain their homelands. Because of the pandemic, everyone is suspicious of everyone else and of course, having insane warriors or what we call head hunters, roaming the countryside looking for humans to sacrifice, seems to seal the point. But why have there never been any attacks by warriors from Serpiente? How is the relationship of the Anderson family and the serpents, so fundamentally different than from the serpents and the Red Faces or Painted People? The warriors from the two tribes of head hunters seem so different. Why does one group paint their entire bodies white with black geometric designs, yet the other group only wears the three red strips on their face? Why are the leaders of one group all male warriors, and the other group all female warriors? They seem so different, yet I suspect that they are simply representations of different serpents. Yet there is the Anderson family. They seem so different; I wonder what they are up too?"

Charlie asked, "When was the last time you encountered anyone from the Anderson family?"

"It has been many, many years since we have communicated," answered Angie Wilkerson. "Certainly, well before the arrival of the Painted People which made it impossible to physically journey there."

"What do you know about the Andersons?" I asked.

"The serpents seem to be using the Anderson family and their descendants that survived the pandemic in a very different way than the other serpents both past and present. We think they are seeking a way to use the humans so they can render revenge on the star people who left them here on this planet, thousands of years ago. The star people left them here for a reason; they are unscrupulous creatures, parasites, creatures that use others in order to fulfill their own diabolical needs.

"Thousands of years ago, when they were imprisoned here on this planet there were few humans that they could use but now they have incorporated humans into their sphere of influence to satisfy their craving for the energy that leaves people at their deaths. Perhaps many of our fellow humans are now being manipulated by the serpents for their own reasons. All of human history is a record of that use."

Wilkerson stopped talking for a moment to see if what she was saying was making any sense to Charlie and me, then she said the last sentence again, with emphasis. "All of human history is a record of that use!"

I asked, knowing what the answer would be, "So the visions that Charlie and I have been experiencing have been planted in our dreams by serpents?"

"Yes," Wilkerson answered, "They can read your minds and shape your thinking while you sleep. Everyone who experiences them sooner or later is seduced by them. They can make you do anything they want you to do including killing other humans. We are afraid that if you go there without knowing what you are up against, it would only be a short matter of time until you become another one of their slaves."

Charlie asked, "Why is it then, that all of you have escaped them?"

Angie Wilkerson reached inside the lapel of her blouse and dragged out a tiny owl-like amulet that dangled from a tiny gold chain. "Many years ago, we discovered that there was a way to protect ourselves from their mind probes. The star people left an amulet like this one many thousands of years ago. They themselves had to devise a way to protect themselves from the serpents and they all wore these tiny amulets. Somehow, or for some reason, they left one of them behind when they returned to their home in the stars.

"Many years after that, the original Penny Andersons was given one by a Native American shaman to protect her from the serpents and she took it to the University of New Mexico to have it examined. We acquired it soon after that. It is not just an amulet; it is a highly-integrated circuit which produces a tiny field around the wearer which blocks the intrusions of the serpents. It took us many years just to figure out how it works then many more years to replicate what it does and now we all wear them."

Charlie and I looked around the room and one by one everyone there slipped their hands under their shirts and blouses and revealed a tiny owl-like amulet that hung around their necks. Charlie says, "So the only way we can escape the serpents is by wearing that amulet around our necks."

I added, "I don't understand. How can they hurt you by entering your dreams?"

Wilkerson answered, "Have you ever been lied to?"

"Well not very often, we have only experienced a few people since Charlie and I found each other and left Seattle with me. The only friendly people we encountered were the Hopi people, everyone else wanted to steal our horses, our weapons..."

Charlie interrupted my answer with, "Or to eat us."

"The only way you will ever learn to deal with the serpents is to understand how they have manipulated humans. They relish the energy they receive upon the death of a human and they actually create situations whereby we war on each other so they can receive the energy that is created for them. That energy is like a drug to serpents; they can live without it but prefer to absorb it on a regular basis. Believe me, saying it for a third time; all of our history has been affected by them," continued Wilkerson.

"We here at Los Alamos Labs are the only people who have really figured out a way to be safe from the serpents or their warriors. Throughout time, they have taught humans wonderful things only to have us use our own technology against ourselves to create wars which produced death. They cultivated us by teaching us wonderful things and then they had us destroy each other. The best way to tell a lie is to sandwich it between two truths. The serpents are experts at that. We humans unfortunately are slow to learn that the wonderful gifts the serpents provide for us are actually only a trap. In the end we always kill each other, providing them with the life energy they relish."

Understanding the enormity of what was being said; Charlie and I stopped eating and set our forks down. "How can we help you?" Charlie asked.

I was sitting on the edge of my chair and couldn't help myself. I blurted out the obvious question. "Why in the world do they need me? Why did they come into my dreams? How in the world did they find me, I lived in Alaska which is far from here and what possible use could I be to them?"

Angie Wilkerson looked at me for a minute, took a deep breath and then said, "You are a very special person. I suspect that you are far more intelligent than you realize."

"Okay, I have always learned how to do things very quickly but that doesn't make me special. Charlie here knows a lot of things that I don't."

"Well, to be blunt with you," Wilkerson says, "I suspect that they need you to mate with one of the girls there. Inbreeding becomes a problem when you live in a small community. They have studied your genetics and have discovered that you can correct a genetic problem for them. Who knows, maybe the queen that resides there has a 'thing' for you. If I was forty years younger, I might have a thing for you."

It was the first time in forty years that Angie Wilkerson had flirted with someone. "One thing is for sure, they need you for some reason or the queen would never have summoned you to come to them."

"The queen has summoned me?" I asked out loud, afraid of what the answer might be.

"Yes, we knew of the Andersons, well back in time when the problem of the serpents first became public knowledge. They were the first to make contact with the serpents and one of the first to develop a relationship with them. The first queen was a young lady by the name of Penny Anderson. She was an intelligent girl who first learned to work with them. Her child learned to communicate with them and now they communicate with the serpents as well as each other in the telepathic language of the serpents. It has become their way of life. As time has progressed the descendants of Penny Anderson have become royalty in the serpent community. The problem is, the Andersons have learned to work with the serpents as a shaman would. For now, it seems very helpful to the humans who live in Serpiente, but in the end, it will result in the death of all the humans who live there as well as untold others, and we still do not know exactly what the serpents are doing. In Serpiente they seem to be working with the humans, incorporating them into their society rather than just using them for an energy source."

"So, what do you want of us?" I asked.

"We want to learn what it is, exactly what they want of you. To be perfectly honest with you, we need to know what they are up to. They have obviously turned many of the local peoples into head hunters, which is why we treated you the way we did when we first discovered you approaching the fence. The serpents have tried many times to eliminate us because we know many of their secrets and can defend ourselves against them. Put simply, they fear us. They know that if it came to a war we could eliminate them once and for all. After all, it almost happened once before.

"Many years ago, a General, by the name of Armstrong, developed a pathogen that almost wiped the serpents out. For a short time, the soldiers fought against the serpents but unfortunately the General had himself been probed by the serpents. That caused him to release a pathogen that was not ready for use. The plague that was produced not only killed most of the serpents but it mutated and destroyed most of humankind. Only tiny pockets of human survivors lived through the plague and now memory of what happened is almost gone. We are one of the only survivors that managed to escape both the plague and the serpents. The only other exception would be the Hopi Indians who have always lived in isolation and apparently have some kind of defense against the serpents' influence. Then of course, there are the ranches to the north and east. They operate like tiny kingdoms or feudal states that have absolute control over their territory. We know little of them because they refuse contact with all other people."

"So, you cannot ask the tribes to the north and west for any help?"

"They refuse any invitations to talk. The truth of the matter is we were hoping that perhaps we could use you to find out what they are up to. We need you to find answers for us. The real question is, would you be willing to find answers for us?"

Charlie and I looked at each other and decided to discuss the situation with each other. After a day, I answered her question. "We will work with you if we can, but we do not want to hurt the people who live in Serpiente, we are not going to go there to destroy or kill anyone."

"That is exactly the answer we were looking for," Wilkerson says. "We do not want to kill the people who live there either, we want to rescue them from the serpents before the serpents become too powerful and decide they don't need the humans anymore. But before we can turn you lose, we need to train you, so you can understand exactly what you are dealing with. Only then, can you be of any use to us and only then, can you defend yourselves against the influence of the serpents. Are you willing to go to school for a few weeks in order to learn what you need?"

Charlie and I again looked at each other. We were terrified with the new insights that we had acquired and were intimidated by the whole idea of going to Serpiente. I was in particular intimidated and sad. The girl that was the object of my dreams, could very well be the evilest person on the planet.

Computer Simulations of an Invasive Species

School started early the next day after a night of washing themselves in a shower that had both hot and cold running water that poured down on us, followed by a night's rest on comfortable beds like the ones we had seen only in deserted houses of the ancient ones. The first thing that the scientists did was to place an amulet around both our necks, which seemed to not do anything as far as we could tell. Now the serpents could not find us, we had disappeared. We were taken to a small section of a much larger building where a small assortment of tools, including a large computer was stored on a table top. A gruff looking, balding man walked in and introduced himself.

"My name is James," the old man said.

"Do you have a last name," asked Charlie?

"Yes, answered the man. My full name is, as far as you are concerned, Professor James. James is my last name. You two can just call me Professor, Dr. James, or simply say; yes sir. That last one is the one I really prefer. Anytime I am talking you should be taking notes or at least listening very carefully. Do not talk when I'm talking and if you have a question, raise your hand. Do we have an understanding?"

"Yes sir," answered Charlie who was wondering just what we had gotten ourselves into.

"I am a computer simulation specialist. It is my job to make predictions based upon programming a computer with as many variables as I possibly can. Then I run the program to see what all the possible outcomes are. That and teaching young people how to be productive citizens here at the labs. It will not be necessary for you to learn everything. Only what you need to escape the manipulation of the serpents. Normally we use virtual reality programs to instruct people in basic knowledge, however, we do not have the time for your programming. So, I am going to instruct you directly beginning with history."

Dr. James turned on the computer, typing on a keyboard, until a written message appeared on the large screen.

Charlie asked him again, "What exactly is a computer simulation?"

"Well again, I do computer simulations for the entire planet. A simulation tells us how things turn out if a variable is introduced. For example, I will take an ecosystem and introduce a foreign species and see what happens years later. When it comes to the plant kingdom, things are very straight forward and predictable. Simulations involving predators are far more difficult. It is the computer simulations that involve humans that are the most difficult. We program in all the pertinent information, which can take days to do, then we run the program forward and see what happens. But let's see what you can do for me."

"Mr. Chato, would you read this please?"

"First of all, Dr. James, my name is Chato Williams. Williams is my last name and Chato is my first name. Secondly, I can easily read what is on that screen."

"Prove it," Dr. James retorted.

"The brown dog jumped over the fence into the pool of water."

"Try this one," says Dr. James, as he changed the words on the screen.

"Naturally the Texans were grievously disappointed at the utter failure of their grand filibustering expedition, and loud in their threats of vengeance for what they chose to regard as the treachery and barbarity of the New Mexicans."

"Good," Dr. James says, "Now what does it mean?"

"Well, for some reason a group of people known as the Texans were upset because they felt that the New Mexicans had treated them badly."

"Very good," Dr. James exclaimed then went through the same procedure with Charlie discovering that Charlie could read as well as myself, which pleased him immensely. Finally, he asked us where we had learned to read, and we explained that it was important for everyone in our families to be able to read so we could pass on knowledge to our children.

"I think that there is hope here," Dr. James says. "We can provide you with what you need and you can teach yourselves what you need to know. But for now, I just want you to listen to what I have to say, we are going to have some interesting conversations, but in the evenings, I expect you to either read or take part in a virtual reality program. You can teach yourselves about a whole world of things."

We settled down with a cup of tea to drink and Dr. James began talking. "The history books that we have in our libraries that the old ones used are wrong. The version of history that the old ones learned in their schools were heavily revised to favor our own nation's agenda while hiding its crimes and in so doing fostered an unrealistic sense of false patriotism which was used to manipulate everyone's allegiance to a corporate entity masquerading as their government. In every country where people lived, this process occurred, in effect, they were lying to themselves. Only the most rudimentary facts of history are important. You will not be expected to learn dates or even significant names. They don't matter anymore. First of all, you need to understand that serpents have been involved in human affairs since humans first migrated into North America, some fifteen to twenty thousand years ago. We don't know exactly when the first humans came to this place but we suspect that early people came at different times from all over the old world."

"The Old World?" I asked.

Dr. James brought up a diagram of the earth with the continents on it. "We think the first humans who lived around here came from Europe and Siberia, mostly Siberia. The Indians who constructed all those old ruins, hundreds or even thousands of years before the plague hit are Native Indians who migrated here down the western coastline and then into the interior of the continent from other parts of the world, basically a place called Siberia. Later, a vast wave of people who are our ancestors migrated into this area and drove many of the original inhabitants out. But that was fairly recent. The important thing for you to understand is that the serpents were dropped off near what was Salt Lake City" He brought up a map showing Salt Lake City, then panned out to show all of what was Utah, then the entire country labeled as America. He then showed us where Los Alamos National Laboratories was. We studied the flickering map carefully to determine where we were in relationship to the Rio Grande River and the place called Serpiente.

Dr. James continued, "The serpents originated somewhere north of here, dropped off in what is called Utah and then they traveled in reverse of the humans well before our ancestors came to this continent. Certainly, before the plague hit, they were all over the planet. Lesson one that you need to learn is just what Dr. Wilkerson said; the serpents live off the life energy that humans lose as they die. As a species we have been farmed, cultivated and taught to kill each other for their use. By the way, we have lost all contact with what is known as the Old World. Now, we don't know if there are survivors there at all, but I suspect that there are, just like there are survivors here. Anyway, there doesn't seem to be any organized groups there that can communicate with us."

Charlie scratched his head, obviously, he was already a little confused as to the purpose of the conversation.

Dr. James continued, "So far, we humans have also been a plague on this earth. Even without the serpent's intervention, we humans are invasive creatures, it is in our nature. We tend to populate an area until all the resources are gone and then move to the next area. Just before the plague hit, the population of the earth had grown so large that there wasn't anywhere left to plunder and as a result we began to war against each other in longer and more bitter wars. We couldn't simply plunder an area and then move on. In the Old World, where the resources had disappeared long ago, the overpopulation of humans created intense regional wars whereas here in the New World there were less depleted resources which slowed the inevitable wars, but by the time of the plague it was already happening here. Actually, at the time that the plague hit we were well on our way to causing one of the greatest extinctions of life on this planet even if the plague had not happened."

This time I asked, "Extinction?"

Dr. James continued. "We are aware of several mass extinctions which have occurred on this planet before humans. I don't know what you boys know about the history of the earth but it is millions of years old and life has been developing slowly until something happens which causes a massive die off. Then life has to start all over again with only a few survivors. Humans were well on their way to creating a sixth mass extinction when they released the plague that destroyed their very civilization, and now it is on a pace to occur all over again."

I seemed to cut his conversation off when I said, "We are aware of this. The Hopi Shaman told us how there had been several extinctions of life on this planet. The last one was the plague that killed most of the humans on this planet."

"Well, I certainly understand their point of view, and we certainly can emphasize with the Hopi point of view, but we have scientific evidence of six massive extinctions on this planet, times when nearly all life, not just human life disappeared from the face of the earth. The Cambrian Age extinction occurred millions of years ago and no one knows exactly why it occurred. This was followed by the biggest one which was after the Permian Age when almost all life was exterminated on this planet. During that time, the oceans turned a sickly purple in color and the skies were more green than blue. The oceans became so acidic that most life in it disappeared as well as most life on the continents. During the ages of dinosaurs there were several small extinctions that caused life to change dramatically ending with the extinction of the dinosaurs which were finally eliminated by disease and an asteroid impact ending the Cretaceous Age. After the dinosaurs died out, millions of years passed until humans evolved. They spread out over the entire planet and within recent history they dominated the entire planet changing the very chemistry of the planet. Before the plague was released against the serpents, which actually killed off most humans, humans managed to almost destroy this planet by the excessive burning of fossil fuels."

I raised my hand as instructed, "What are fossils and what are fuels?"

Dr. James answered, "In nature, fossil fuels are either coal, which is a compacted plant matter which has been compressed and then changed into a rock like material that burns. It produces tremendous amount of carbon dioxide when it is burned and the ancients used it as a cheap way to produce electricity which powered things in people's houses. Then there is petroleum, which is a black liquid which is pumped out of the ground. It is the remains of tiny animals and plants that lived under oceans, millions of years ago. The black liquid is distilled, that is taken apart, down to its essential components, and it is used for many things. Mainly the ancient ones used it for driving around in their cars and trucks which ignited small amounts of the liquid called gasoline with huge volumes of oxygen that produced more huge volumes of carbon dioxide. The important component was the gasoline which was portable and fairly easy to produce. All the machines that the ancients rode around in were powered by that liquid. Using fossil fuels, they managed to put so much of the carbon dioxide into the air that it started the rise in acidity of the planet as had been done during the Permian age. The carbon dioxide gas was produced as a result of burning the fossil fuels which powered their economy. Furthermore, the entire human species living in all its communities known as nations, based their economy upon the concept of constant growth which produced constant profits for a select few individuals. Humans were using every resource the planet had to offer, in time, the entire system would have come tumbling down, collapsing upon itself. But it didn't happen. Human life was at the apex of its existence just before the pandemic."

I didn't quite know what he was driving at but I certainly wanted to learn more. Dr. James then brought up something on the computer screen. "Here read this," he suggested. "You have much to learn, so let's go all the way back to Thursday May nineteenth during the year two thousand eleven this appeared on the Internet."

The article was entitled, "No Where on Earth, 78% of Arctic Sea Ice Melted Since 1979."

I began reading it. 'Nowhere on earth is global warming more rapid and more shocking than in the Arctic. The most rapid and the most shocking change has been the disappearance of the Arctic sea ice. The polar bears have been forced to swim over a hundred miles to land. Walruses have been beached by the thousands in late summer in northern Alaska because ice has retreated for hundreds of miles toward the pole.' I noticed that the remainder of the article was complicated data charts and graphs.

Dr. James continued talking. "They refused to accept the scientific facts and buried their heads in everything from religion to politics. There were too many greedy people who thought that wealth would protect them, no matter what. After all, all they had to do was stay under air conditioners and pay others to do what needed to be done outdoors. But the earth couldn't deal with the extra carbon dioxide without heating up, it became like a greenhouse, like where we grow our food in winter."

"It sounds like when we prepared meat and vegetables by putting them inside of the old cars. The heat would dry the food out," I said.

"Yes," Dr. James exclaimed. "Imagine if the entire earth just kept getting hotter. The rise in temperature of the planet by only a few degrees caused the climate to dramatically change. But all we could do about it was to argue among ourselves. Storms became more intense. For a while, the summers became hotter and the winters became colder. Instead of the usual mild fluctuations in weather, the climate began to swing back and forth dramatically. Fall and spring seasons were filled with terrible droughts and tremendous rain in other areas. Storms such as tornados and hurricanes became more prevalent and dangerous. Winter could be mostly warm days leading up to the middle of winter, then suddenly very strong and fast moving storms would dump record snows. Snow was followed by flooding from the melt water. Summers would be spent sitting at home under the air conditioner. It would be far too hot to work outdoors. If left to our own devices, we humans may have managed to destroy the entire planet. According to the computer simulations we have run that assume the pandemic had not occurred; we humans would have become extinct anyway."

"By extinct, I assume you mean, all humans die out and disappear from the earth?"

"Absolutely," he answered. "That is exactly what I mean. With only a few degrees of heating and assuming the same amount of carbon dioxide was released into the atmosphere, the planet would cook off its seabed gas hydrates and when that occurs, the entire planet would undergo a runaway greenhouse effect, and everything would die; except for the simplest of living things such as bacteria."

Fossil Fuels

"Instead, we killed the real cause of the release of carbon dioxide into the atmosphere. We killed the culprit who had released all that excess carbon dioxide, well, we killed nearly all of them. The pandemic killed off all but a tiny few of the organisms who were changing the chemistry of this planet. The planet then slowly corrected itself, but you understand that if the pandemic had not occurred, no one would have lived anyway."

At that point, we had a better idea what he was talking about. I asked him if the liquid that burns was still being used, here at Los Alamos.

"Oh, heavens no," he laughed. "For the most part, we use photoelectric cells that collect energy from the sun and then we store that energy in batteries. Over a century ago, we figured out how to make a very good battery, the device we use to store electricity. We learned to make batteries that are far more powerful and would hold a charge far longer, than the batteries that were being used by the pre-pandemic humans. It is energy from the sun that powers everything we have here at Los Alamos."

Charlie asked, "Why were the people before the pandemic so determined to continue using fossil fuels if they understood how bad it was?"

Dr. James, with his shoulders now visibly slumping, answered, "Because of greed and corruption, it seems that making money was all they were concerned with. They also all believed that they would be taken care of by their God. You see, currency or money is a source of power, but they seemed to pursue it to their own destruction. They were caught up in keeping an ever-expanding economy which required more and more consumption of resources, resources that someone else always possessed. The end had already started to occur during the years of the pandemic. Here in this country we stood by and watched as millions of people died in other countries. America was always blessed by having plenty of food to consume. People in this country ate well, right up to the actual pandemic, however in much of the rest of the world, people simply starved to death in endless wars, wars that we could have done something about, but we were arrogant, lazy and greedy. We allowed agents and spies who were eagerly working for the government to create wars. Instead of representing America by planting good will through education and diplomacy, our agents were making huge profits by selling weapons to other nations or tribes who were at war. Sometimes they sold weapons to both sides of a conflict. It made those agents rich and everyone else desperately poor. Afterwards, even when a temporary truce was achieved, the war zone would be mined for renewable resources. Under a temporary truce, much could be gained by profits made off of the labor of the desperate people who lived there. Under extreme circumstances, people can be made to work very hard, just for a chance to live.

"By the way, did you know that wars produce immense quantities of carbon dioxide gas?"

Studying the blank look on our faces, he started to change what he was talking about, but couldn't until he had completed his point. "Petroleum does have its uses, I suppose, but the ancient humans could have used other energy sources that were not nearly so destructive. Take liquid hydrogen for example, they could have used it instead, producing no carbon dioxide, but they chose instead to do things the easy, most profitable way despite the warnings from scientist."

"By the way, it is recess time."

"Recess time?" I asked

"Yes, I expect you to take a break, every once in a while. Take a walk or get something to eat. Visit with some of the other scientists that are close to your age. Just be back here in, he looked at the clock on the wall, in fourteen more minutes."

We had no idea how long a minute was so we watched the clock on the wall for a few moments then left to find a bathroom. When we returned, Dr. James immediately started in on another long discussion.

Human History

"History is the cumulative written facts about what has occurred and has been recorded by humans. During the last ten thousand years; this history of mankind can be summed up as an expression of warfare. The sum total of all of history is far more about the wars that have been waged than about creative inventions and accomplishments mankind has been able to accomplish. The very basis of our societies is capitalism, an economic system in which investment in and ownership are the means of production, distribution, and exchange of wealth made and maintained chiefly by private individuals or corporations. From the earliest times on, capitalism quickly became a form of warfare, a warfare conducted but without obvious bloodletting.

"Phoenicians, an Old Word people, for example, came from the desert sands to the coast of what became Lebanon where the lands were forested with cedar and cyprus trees which were used for boatbuilding. They traded those cedar trees to people in Egypt who had no trees that could be used for building beams in their houses and more importantly, they had no trees that could be used to construct the keels of large boats. Cedar wood is a sweet smelling and relatively soft wood, making it easily worked into a number of shapes, yet it is very strong and resists rot. The wood was traded for a variety of goods and services of which Egypt had a surplus, such as metals, of which Lebanon had very little. In only a short time a relationship developed between Egypt and the early Phoenicians, which was based upon mutual needs but not particularly mutual security.

"In time, the relationship grew as the Phoenicians changed from desert dwellers to become a sea faring people who built their own ships, ships built with keels and sails that made transporting goods across the Mediterranean easy. As they learned how to sail those ships their sphere of influence grew and they found themselves not only trading cedar wood but also purple dyed cloth as well as a multitude of goods obtained from new allies. These goods were traded for enormous profits. Although they themselves were not particularly artistic, they traded with many other peoples who specialized in highly artistic and beautiful goods. Trading allowed them to obtain highly prized items which they could not create.

"They, and many other ancient peoples used armies to protect those profits until just recently. As the serpents manipulated the people, wars raged throughout the world. Then, humans reached a tilting point where all life could easily have died, the plague then ravaged the earth, in a strange sort of way it saved humans from completely exterminating ourselves. The serpents brought it all on but it was human nature to engage in war over resources."

Dr. James stopped talking for a few seconds reflecting upon what he was saying. "We are much like the serpents themselves; parasites. It is now up to us all to find a different way of living on this planet so that we can learn to live with all the other creatures that live here on our planet rather than using them for our own means."

Both Charlie and I were confused. What did all this history have to do with our current dilemma with serpents and dreams?

Dr. James seeing our blank faces turned to us and said "Let me share a story with you."

While scratching his head, Dr. James started another explanation. "Here in America it all started with the Moche, a tribe of Native Americans who were one of the first to be subdued into committing blood sacrifices. For years, archeologist, those scientist that study ancient people, were perplexed by the amazing evidence of blood sacrifice. At first, they thought the evidence pointed to an entire culture which was trying to appease the wild fluctuations of weather caused by a condition known as El Nino.

"El Nino caused extremely heavy rain patterns that eroded their mud structures and destroyed their farmlands. That is what was thought for many years, that the people committed blood sacrifices, to appease the weather gods and bring calm to their society. It was, of course, only a pretext that the serpents used to inspire them to make blood sacrifices. The cultural remains of the people always show a king being delivered the blood of the sacrificed victims by another character who was thought to be a bird like creature. We now think that the bird like creature was a serpent that had changed its form to resemble a shaman. Virtually all the pottery and wall drawings have a representation of a serpent on them, but for years, the connection was not made in the minds of the archeologist. Now we know that the serpents were Quetzalcoatl and Kukulkan. They are the royalty, the leaders of the serpent clan who orchestrated what the humans did for them back then, as well as now."

"So, what you are saying is, that it was the serpents that caused the early Moche humans to learn war?" I asked.

"Well, let's just say that there is little evidence for warfare and blood sacrifice on this continent before the Moche civilization and afterwards there is strong evidence that the early people were all involved in it in one way or another. The serpents are creatures who love all human warfare and blood sacrifice. The thing is, after a few centuries of warfare the human culture just seemed to take it for granted that the way to solve disagreements between themselves would always be solved by warfare."

"Since those days, based upon the history we have saved, modern warfare was almost entirely brought on by resource depletion. Not enough land, not enough energy in the form of oil, and always too many people. Again, we are an invasive creature. We humans call it exploration, manifest destiny, you name it. As a species, we tend to always want more and need more. We are never satisfied with just living comfortably, we have to explore and conquer. The pattern has been the same now for some ten thousand years. The only difference is, we now know the serpents were often instigating or manipulating us into that pattern of existence for their own sake. You see, the serpents are also invasive creatures, which is why they were isolated on this planet in the first place."

I asked Dr. James a profound question. "What would humans be like without the influence and meddling of the serpents?"

He answered, "I don't know. Personally, I think it is in our nature to conquer and kill everything around us, to the point of our own extinction. In time, we may have started to conquer and use other worlds that exist out in space. But there are those who imagine a whole different world here on earth. There is only one other people who live like natural humans were meant to be, and they are a good example."

"Who is that," asked Charlie?

"The people you met on the way here, the Hopi."

We learned that by engaging in conversations with our teacher, Mr. James, we were actually learning something that was important. Charlie and I enjoyed the sessions as well as all the other amenities that the gentle scientists at Los Alamos National Laboratories allowed us. Charlie and I immediately began to gain weight. We were invited to eat with everyone in the main dining hall which served about fifty people at a time. Each time we sat down to eat, someone, different would come over, make introductions, and ask if they could eat with us. It was a most pleasant way to get to know everyone. They seemed to all make a point of sharing some time with us. They were evidentially as curious about us, as we were about them; particularly, the one young lady who flew the dragonflies. She made a point to sit across from Charlie. We learned that most of them had never been beyond the fence. They wanted to hear stories from beyond the electric fence.

How Los Alamos Worked

We were amazed at the technology that was available to us. Particularly the virtual reality programs that made you feel like you were in another world. We stayed at Los Alamos National Laboratories for six weeks absorbing as much knowledge as we possibly could. We also learned the practical side of what it takes to operate a scientific community. The facility seemed to grow all the food they needed by using huge greenhouses in the winter. During the summer, they grew crops as far away as the Rio Grande River and areas north into fields below the Puye Cliff Ruins. It was an easily defended area, particularly with the technology they had at their disposal. No other tribe dared mess with them. The Painted People had not discovered them yet.

We learned new things in many ways, for example with the computers that Charlie and I saw after we were first captured. At one time, the computers were connected to an invisible web that circled the entire earth. People could communicate and share ideas throughout the world but now the limit of the communication was to the fences that surrounded the laboratories. The scientists did have, however, a wealth of information stored in those computers. They had access to a vast library of information, books and articles the humans had created. As we learned to use the devices, we discovered a wealth of information about the history of this world. It was all informative, but we found very little information about serpents. According to the information we found on the machines, it seemed that throughout all of history they were present but apparently had little impact on humans except on their imaginations. We, of course, knew better. The serpents had made a profound impact on human civilization and the only peoples who were aware of it were the Native Americans like the Navajo and Hopi who had dealt with them personally. It made us wonder, how had the Hopi escaped the influence of the serpents? The Hopi people seemed innocuous to the serpents, but how?

We found a small amount of information about the Anderson families' dealings with the serpents and then a wealth of information all marked top secret and classified. I thought to myself, that at this point, there was no one to keep the secrets from. What we really learned about, with a little directing by Dr. James and occasionally by Dr. Wilkerson herself, was about human nature.

During the years leading up to the plague, the world had been divided into those who had access to resources and those who didn't. National boundaries had meant very little. It was a very overpopulated world. The problem could be seen on a graph that we found.

Back when people were first entering the New World, there were only a few million people in the entire world. Back then, people depended upon each other for survival and they welcomed strangers among them when they met them. Then as people settled down to cultivate the land they developed small communities which in time grew into empires. For the most part, they lived in peace with one another but eventually they all turned to war.

The population of the Old World grew until finally they had stripped the resources from the land and they grew hungry. Then, the New World was discovered and the surplus people who had no future left the Old world for the New World. For a time, the original people who lived in the new world, sometimes referred to as Indians, fought with the invaders from the Old World. They won many of the battles but lost the war due to the fact that the invaders had better technology and immunity to diseases they brought with them.

In only a short time, the New World was as populated as the Old World. Because the people who lived in the New World had more resources at their disposal they soon became the most powerful nation on the planet but fear of the lesser nations of the world caused them to live in a police state with constant wars being fought around the world. The lesser nations were extremely poor and those countries that at one time could be seen on a map, dissolved into feudal gangs based upon such things as race, religion and access to resources.

Overpopulation by humans along with diminishing resources appears to have been the main cause of war. The serpents simply used our own invasive nature against us. They exacerbated the problems, making warfare far more likely, deadly, and of course the serpents relished in the deaths.

It took several weeks of intense instruction from Dr. James before Charlie and I began to understand exactly what he was talking about. Before now, we truly had no idea what had happened to our world. The more we studied, the angrier we became as we learned how the serpents had used humans for their own diabolical purposes. We also began to understand the nature of humans and it scared us.

Dragonflies

Because of the body mass we were acquiring, we began to look more like young men than boys. When not in school with Dr. James, we used our time to learn more about how Los Alamos Laboratories worked. We began to cherish our spare time and helped out in the agricultural buildings that grew food for the colony. It also allowed time for Angie Wilkerson to develop a game plan, as to how she could use us. She wanted to know what the serpents had planned for not only the scientist of Los Alamos, but also the humans who lived in Serpiente, as well as the entire human race.

During the last two days at Los Alamos National Laboratories, questions began to circulate as to what route we should take. Pamela, who was the young lady who flew the dragonflies, and had become close friends with Charlie, became very busy with her tiny dragonflies flying them first down the mountain then over the Rio Grande River which was all programmed as the source of orientation for the devices. They then flew south to places where modern humans had been seen and documented. Each one would go to a specific area, search for the signatures of living humans, document them and transmit that information immediately back to the labs. The dragonflies would then return to the labs, like bees returning to a hive. Unfortunately, sometimes they didn't make it all the way back to the lab and they would plummet to the ground and die, eventually corroding into a useless mass about the size and likeness of a small stone. They had served their purpose.

Charlie and I watched in amazement as a computer screen lit up, a computer screen that covered the entire wall. First Pamela would bring up a topographical map with blinking dots that represented the location of a dragonfly. Then she would click on to one that was nearing a target area, then after a few key strokes, a perfect square insert frame would appear, showing what the drone was seeing. The dragonfly was preprogrammed to fly a preprogrammed pattern over the area and report what it saw. It reported a perfect view but could produce an image in many modes such as a thermal or UV image.

The human viewer on the other end had complete control over the device, but always preferred to leave it on automatic, doing its prearranged task. Even at the labs, it took an experienced person to be able to integrate the computers in order to free fly the devices, unless something strange happened, such as having your dragonfly being swallowed by a large bird. But then it was always unfortunate for the bird. The heads would seemingly explode or the entire bird would explode from the insides out. Either way, it was a mess; the tiny dragonfly was never recovered from such an encounter. Charlie watched Pamela and Pamela and I watched the images produced on the screen.

Preparations for a Journey to Serpiente

*A*s we reached the end of our stay at Los Alamos we were offered rifles with scopes mounted on them, much like the ones we had first seen at the gate, but we turned them down. Too much noise, they would give away our position far too easily and besides we knew little about them. We were outfitted instead, with bows made from a milky white glass that was many times more powerful than anything that we could make from wood. Our quivers were filled with perfect arrows, much like the ones I found embedded in the rear of my sea kayak. Finally, we were given new tomahawks, fire starter kits, and our old pots and pans we had assembled at Chaco. We were also provided with what was apparently the best in backpacks and sleeping bags and tarps. But first we wanted to scout about. Explaining that we actually wanted to see where we were going.

Were we all part of an elaborate science experiment? The laboratory scientists, including Dr. Angie Wilkerson, had run out of possible reasons to suspect that Charlie and I were anyone other than who we said we were. They were as curious about us as we were about them. They were mystified as to why I had been summoned by the serpents of Serpiente. They were also stymied as to how the serpents had found me in the first place. Alaska is a long way from New

Mexico. All proposed theories concluded with the serpents; even dragonflies couldn't have visited me so far away.

We now knew, thanks to our numerous visits to the dragonfly map room, exactly where we were, in relationship to the Rio Grande River that flowed north and south through what at one time had been the state of New Mexico. Finding Serpiente would not be a problem at all. Actually, getting to Serpiente and surviving our arriving there could be another thing altogether.

After analyzing the data provided by the dragonflies, we decided we had a choice of two routes to take, both of them with flaws. One, we could back track and circle around to the southwest, crossing over to the Rio Grande River. We could stay on the west side of the river and walk all the way to Serpiente. The route involved a long walk back into the desert to escape the steep and treacherous side canyons that flowed away from the main caldera of Jemez Volcano. The problem was, it would also take us deep into the territory of the Painted People.

Or, we could go back out the main gate and stay on the main trail that the farmers used in the summertime to tend crops down along the river. We had a decision to make but like most decisions, they tended to take care of themselves. After reaching the river, we could easily cross over, above where the bridge at Ottawa used to be. Unfortunately, the bridge was no longer there. It had washed away after tremendous water flows. We were already dreading another river crossing even though the water should be low and warm by now. We decided we could then turn south, following the ancient roadways, and follow it all the way to Albuquerque and beyond to Serpiente. We did not know if the Painted People could or would cross the river. We suspected that they could not swim but the Rio Grande River in fall is a very shallow and calm river that should allow anyone to find places to easily walk across. Besides, we were well aware that there were several bridges across the river.

Before we could leave, the dragonfly reports showed a sharp increase in individuals located in the same country that Charlie and I had recently walked through, up the flanks of the mountain where Los Alamos was hidden. Needless to say, that made our route on the east side of the river the obvious route to take.

Preparations of the Painted People

Something was happening in the land of the Painted People, as if they were building up to a war campaign. The technicians and Pamela had no idea why the Painted People were congregating in the mountains; just that they were there, gathering in small groups just to the south of Los Alamos. We delayed our departure to see what was going to happen. The painted people, after several days of preparation, were following the ancient Route 4, a road that intersected with the same road and trail that Charlie and I had followed. In only a short while they would come to the electric fence that separated Los Alamos from the rest of the world.

We watched the whole spectacle of men walking in single file. The scientists flew the dragonfly as close as they dared. The main warrior was obviously a determined woman. Her entire body was covered with colorful illustrations of dragons, human skulls, ravens and other birds and an assortment of minor illustrations that appeared to be old. All the skin illustrations were outlined in wide black geometric designs leaving all other space white in order to make the designs stand out. She was armed to the teeth with hand axes and a bow and a quiver full of arrows. The warrior swatted the air without looking at what was making the buzzing sound the dragonflies were making. Finally, she stopped, which caused everyone behind her to stop, and she looked around for something that was bothering her. The dragonflies were backed off to keep them safe. They knew what would happen if one of them got to close to a warrior. It would be destroyed.

Just below the gate, the warriors stopped and prepared to attack the fence. But this time they had a different plan. One of the warriors took out a huge tool known as a bolt cutter and reached up to cut the wire. After the sparks cleared and the warrior hit the ground, two more warriors attempted to cut through the wire. The results were the same, now there appeared to be three dead warriors.

"I'm glad those wire cutters are not insulated," Pamela said. "If they ever figure out what they are doing wrong they might get inside the fence."

"What happens then?" Charlie asked.

"Oh, we simply shoot them dead. They could never actually get close to one of our buildings. They are using Stone Age weapons and we have automatic rifles that would mow them down. We don't really want to do anything to hurt them; we just want their experience here to be so unpleasant that they never come back." In a few seconds, several more of the warriors had placed a large log in front of the fence and rammed a long pole under the fence. Smoke began to form almost immediately as the wood on the pole began to burn. Then two more warriors managed to receive sharp shocks and they gave up on leveraging the fence up. It was all over in a minute with the warriors making a fast retreat about a mile back down the trail, leaving their stunned comrades behind. In a few minutes, the three warriors were sitting up, rubbing their heads. As soon as they saw the soldiers from the facility they started to crawl away but they were quickly shackled and led back to the main gate where they went through a procedure similar to the one Charlie and I had experienced upon our arrival.

Unlike us, the three warriors were covered with a black hood and dragged into the building where the box was. They were unceremoniously dumped on the floor and the hoods removed. Angie Wilkerson seemed to appear behind us and observed, "Watch them; they cannot communicate with the serpent now. They are lost."

The three warriors wandered over to the walls and began kicking them, each time receiving a sharp jolt of electricity which dropped them onto the floor. Within a few minutes, they were just sitting in the middle of the metal box, crying like small children. Angie said, "They will not know anything. We will blindfold them again and drop them off in the forest where they can find their way home. Unfortunately, as soon as the other warriors see them they will be killed and eaten. It seems that as soon as the warriors lose communication with the serpent, they are finished. The dragonflies reported exactly what Angie Wilkerson had predicted would happen; she had seen it all happen before.

Scouting for the Departure

Everyone agreed that we would likely run into some kind of warriors on either side of the river. After all, there were major cities there in the process of being looted. The scientists had found no trace of living humans and few other creatures beyond the watermelon mountain, to the east. But in the city of

Albuquerque, the dragonflies had found heat signatures of living people who were active there. The dragonflies could confirm the location of several of them. The only one that was actively observed walking across a street; looked like a wild man, like I had seen while kayaking. The creature was certainly not one of the Painted People. But there were bound to be others, hidden away in places where a heat signature would not show. No one knew exactly what we would find there. On the maps was a large road, Route 25 that we would find south of a town labeled Santa Fe. It would funnel us directly into Albuquerque. If we survived Albuquerque, we had only a relatively short distance to get to Serpiente.

After many weeks of instruction, Charlie and I were, as spies, finally allowed to be escorted out of the facility to the edge of the canyon rim that overlooked the Rio Grande River. While moving along we passed through a tiny town called White Rock. We didn't even have to walk there. We rode there in the bed of a truck that was powered by electrical batteries. The caravan of trucks silently but surely took us to the edge of the canyon, where there were ancient houses right up to the edge of the rim. The houses had provided homes for the scientists who had long ago worked at Los Alamos. From there we could see the Rio Grande River flowing over tumultuous rapids at the bottom of a deep canyon. It reminded me of a smaller Grand Canyon but it cut through black volcanic rocks including layers of white volcanic ash giving the canyon its name despite the preponderances of black lava.

One of the scientists, a young man by the name of Jerold O'Malley, suggested that the easiest way to get to Serpiente would be by using small battery powered motorcycles that would noiselessly carry us and all our gear. We could drive the motorcycles all night long, and charge them the next day with solar panels that we would unroll on the ground. We wondered how we would get the cycles across a river if there was no bridge or what would happen if the weather became overcast. Another scientist, an athletic young lady by the name of Jackie Martin, suggested we use small open boats called canoes. She brought up several images of people using them on a computer screen. We would, for the most part, be completely invisible until we ran into others on the river. If we could manage the rapids in White Rock Canyon, and be willing to portage around what remained of Cochiti Lake, the journey from there down would be on a river in flat country. But then we would also have to deal with existing logjams, and old bridges with massive amounts of brush piled against the great beams that held the bridge in place.

Dragonfly had not reported any humans living on the river. The boats could carry us to within a few kilometers of our destination. We were seriously intrigued with that idea but ruled it out. Our experiences on the big river called the Colorado, was still on our minds. We understood rivers, they were where the wildlife lives, and there is cover. But thoughts of floating down the river in small boats were immediately dismissed. We would be sitting ducks on the river. We knew we would walk the entire way, except for the short drop off down to the river.

The caravan of vehicles drove back through what was the town of White Rock then it drove over to a lookout where we could see the entire valley below us. The ancient road dropped down in a series of switchbacks that we would need to cross to get to the river far below. We could see distant red mesas covered with juniper and cedar and black volcanic mesas close to the other side of the river. We could also see traces of an ancient road winding up the other side through a small side canyon then disappearing. I had been up that road many times with the help of Pamela operating the computers that ran the dragonflies. She had long ago given us free reign to explore with the extraordinary devices. The bridge that crossed the river appeared to have been pushed over, by some titanic force coming down the canyon. The blocks of cement with the great metal girders were sticking up in the air at an acute angle, but the actual roadway, had fallen into the river. Downriver, from where we would cross the river, the water flowed around great slabs of the derelict bridge, forming a vicious rapid.

Returning to the facility we spent the evening in the cafeteria, saying good-byes and being given a thousand last minute instructions. Charlie disappeared with Pamela but was quickly discovered and redirected back to the party. Early the next day, we were again loaded onto the metallic trucks with the seats in the back, and driven all the way down the mountain to the bridge.

The river was deep, fast and dangerous around the old bridge. After riding on the truck a distance up the river, we passed an old adobe house that was in ruin with a roof that had long ago collapsed. We followed the riverbank until we found a good rock shoal that extended far out in the river. From there we would have to take off our packs and push them ahead of us as we swam to the other side. It was not far but the water was flowing so fast at the outside of a long curve in the river, it pushed us downriver very fast. It seemed like a long time before a sweeper appeared just above the bad rapids formed by the collapsed bridge, a large tree that had fallen into the main channel. It was collecting debris that floated down the river and in moments it was going to collect us. With the force of the river pushing us, it took us an hour, just to get our packs with the gear tied to it, through the branches of the tree and over to the dry bank. Now exhausted, cold, and wet, our journey would begin.

It felt good to be on our own again, even if we knew that our every movement was being monitored back at Sandia Labs. Walking down the other side of the bank of the river we walked through huge thickets of burrs that stuck to us every time we brushed up against them. We were glad the scientists at Los Alamos had provided us with camouflaged clothes which protected us. Beyond the bridge, we followed the road we had seen on the computer screen up into the dry desert. Deciding that it would be difficult to hide if we ran across warriors, we decided to cross overland though the small forested hills and side canyons that drained into the larger river. We had a general idea of where Santa Fe was and decided not to venture into the city. Instead we followed the animal trials around the foothills and took a long loop back to the river.

We had become very acquainted with the majestic canyon that the river flowed down thanks to Pamela and the dragonflies. Where the river empties out of White Rock Canyon, it entered a small basin where a lake used to be and a washed-out road ended. The water had long ago washed a portion of the dam away, scouring away a small canyon below, through what was once an ancient settlement but now was nothing but remnants of adobe walls.

We planned on following the left bank of the river into Albuquerque. Large roadways were available to us, but there were vast sections of them that were open and without water, besides a determined group of warriors could easily run us down, if they spotted us. We knew walking along the river would be far more difficult, but it would also be much safer away from the settlements and roads. The river would provide both water and food. Without the sewage from thousands of ancient communities dumping crap in the water, the fast-moving river water, had become safe to drink again.

The river flowed down a serpentine channel with a huge forest of cottonwood trees on either side. On the left bank where we were, the river was contained by a raised roadway, which was itself supporting a community of new trees. Then, there was also a man-made channel which was full of water, then flatland and finally sandy hills beyond. We watched for views of the mountain so we knew where we were, but we came to a large lake where the water was backed all the way back to the edge of the mesa. We suspected that a bridge had been impacted with brush and trees forming the lake. We backtracked to the nearest crossing of the canal, and we left the river. In this logical place, it was obvious that others had walked into or out of, the same trap. We hadn't seen any sign on the overgrown road, but here in this sandy soil, were the imprints that many persons had made, walking up the hill in loose gravel to a trail further up.

After we climbed up the hill and crossed a distance of soft sandy hills, we could see we were at the foot of a long open rise up to the roadway that sliced though Albuquerque. We had a dramatic view of 'slice of watermelon mountain' having recently learned it was known as *'Sandia'* or watermelon, in an ancient language. After a short walk, we found ourselves at the edge of the vast ruined city of Albuquerque. We now returned to the roadway we had avoided earlier and after climbing up a tall structure, we could see far to the south in the city. We could see a plume of smoke from a large fire. We had seen a few errant fires, a fire logically burning from something in nature such as lightning, but we needed to know, was it manmade smoke or something else?

We encountered signs of human activity immediately as we entered the north of the city. Someone had driven a vehicle out to the edge of northern Albuquerque, and then returned into the city. The tracks were very old but undeniably there. We dropped off the main road and camped, not starting a fire this night. Camping between houses that evening I had an epiphany. Looking to the east we could see a majestic mountain which appeared to be a slice of fruit. On the top rim of the mountain was a verdant green forest growing out of a thick layer of creamy white looking rocks. The majority of the base of the mountain was made of a red rock that glistened in the setting evening sun which made it appear to turn red as the sky turned red.

The ancient city of Albuquerque appeared to have grown from the river all the way up to the base of the mountain. In places, it appeared that houses had been built into the actual foothills of the mountain. It was larger than most cities we had ventured through since we had left the ocean and it seemed to be in better shape than most. In the dry desert air, objects made of wood lasted longer, but things made of such materials as plastic, decomposed faster.

Again, stopping every once in a while, and climbing to a high vantage point, we determined that there were several bridges that crossed the Rio Grande River, and they were still intact but showed signs of gigantic floods that had occurred sometime in the past. We hiked into the northern end of the city, well below the main road along houses that were now ruins, not a single living human could be found. We had actually expected to find a few survivors but all we found alive was an occasional dog or coyote which had taken to living in the houses. We climbed to the top of one of the structures to escape dealing with dogs and discovered the plume of smoke was still lifting into the sky, white smoke; the kind of smoke from burning wood around a campfire. It was still a mystery to both of us as to what had created the smoke we were seeing, but we suspected Painted warriors.

In the areas of the city where houses were located and people had once lived in them, there was little evidence of looting. Charlie and I found all the canned food and water we needed. But in the areas of the town where businesses had been, there was ample evidence of looting. Store doors had been broken into and obviously, things had been removed. Coming to a large flat store we recognized as a food market, we stepped inside to see what we could find. The entire contents of what had at one time been a supermarket, was long ago stripped of everything. Someone had been stripping the stores for anything edible or useful.

More perplexing to us was the discovery of tire tracks leading up to one of the stores. Someone had driven one of the machines that the ancients used, right up to the front of the store and loaded it with contents from the store. What we found interesting was that the store sold the rubber tires that went on the wheels of the ancient machines. Under a thick layer of dust, the store still had many tires in it, tires that did not fit the vehicles someone had been driving.

We could find no living people; the city was just far too large to find anyone. There were only the decomposing bones of the ancient humans scattered about and in disarray. Seldom did we see a complete skeleton. I was having serious thoughts about what I was doing. After all, my entire journey was based upon a vision; a dream quest. But now it was as if the fate of the entire human race depended upon Charlie and me. I had second thoughts. Now that I was wearing the amulet, I had not had any visions. My imagination began to create scenarios. Maybe we would find Serpiente to be just another ruin. I decided we would search the area called Serpiente and if we found nothing, Charlie would return to Los Alamos and continue his relationship with the computer technician named Pamela. I could go back to San Francisco, reclaim Charlie's kayak and return to Alaska. If I had to, I could build another one. At least in Alaska there was a family that would appreciate knowing that they could leave their frozen prison. I thought about the red warrior I had run into early on my voyage. Would he still be there? Would I be able to slip past him on the return trip or would I be required to go into mortal combat with him? Paddling against the river current would slow me down making me more of a target. Rather hopefully, I wondered if Charlie might decide to go with me, but after all, he knew there were no available women in Alaska as far as I knew. It had taken me three years to get to this place called Albuquerque by the ancients, and then there was Pamela, it would take far more than friendship for Charlie to consider returning with me.

Maps

While cleaning out our packs, Charlie discovered something in his back pack that was hidden inside a zippered pouch sown into the pads of the backpack. He discovered a flat package inside a plastic bag. Taking the contents out of the bag, we found the nearest table and laid it out flat, discovering that it actually was a packet of several map images, all of them exactly one meter square. Someone had provided us with maps, knowing that sooner or later Charlie would discover them, and who knows? We could possibly use them. The brightly colored maps were made from dragonfly images of our route and destination. We took our time, studying each one. The first map was of the entire area we were likely to walk through. The image was further enhanced with things like the river and other waterways highlighted in blue; and ancient roads which were enhanced, as Charlie and I would expect then to be on an ancient roadmap.

The next map was actually two maps, side by side, both showing much closer views of the river directly below Los Alamos where the broken bridge could clearly be seen with the river making a slow curve to the edge of the map. To the north on the map, was the river, almost to the ancient town of Espanola. We discovered that just above where we had crossed the rock shoal and then swam, the river became very wide. It would have been easy to wade across the river there. We also noticed a small road that would have allowed us to walk down to the bridge, avoiding a walk through all the burr fields. The other half of the map was the upper end of White Rock Canyon, with escape trails marked in red on it. Known routes for a lost person who desperately needed to return to the rim of the canyon and the sanctuary of the laboratory were well marked.

Charlie looked at me while again grinning and said, "Someone must have been worried that we might be washed down the river."

Well, I couldn't imagine what he was talking about. Certainly, all I had ever seen them do was look at each other. Around us, Pamela, the scientist, was always a professional but very friendly. She was the technical director, the one who knew how to perform the duties of spying, which is what dragonflies do. It wasn't her fault that she was playful, willing to take chances, loved by everyone and a stunning beauty. Charlie had said nothing to me. She was a scientist, doing her job. But Pamela was far more. Charlie and she must have found some time together.

There was another side by side of Santa Fe and a larger view of Route 25 all the way down to the upper edge of Albuquerque. The next image was a full-page map of the city of Albuquerque. The next image was not a map; it was a numbered series of images called photographs, taken by dragonflies, taken from fifty to a hundred feet high. The first image showed a maintained fence followed with green fields and in the far distance was a settlement made up of rock houses with metal roofs, where many people lived; a view of the community of Serpiente.

The next image was a wide-angle view of the small settlement of houses with very large buildings in the distance. The third image showed what appeared to be a street in front of the large buildings. We could make out a blacksmith shop as well as what appeared to be a garage for keeping machines. People were walking about and a moving vehicle similar to the one we had ridden in at Los Alamos Laboratories, with occupants appeared to be moving down the street. The fourth image showed a small peach orchid with a large ranch house in the middle of it. A large path was clearly visible through the trees to a large porch, where tiny pixels did their best to represent an image of humans. The sprawling ranch house was well maintained, with a roof that was made of metal. The last image showed the front porch where three young ladies and two men all appeared to be talking, all of them dressed in work clothes. But one girl stood out, she was strikingly beautiful.

I froze when I realized who I was looking at. I had seen her many times in my visions. I was looking at the first real evidence that what I was doing was not madness. It took some time, conducting digital research, but Pamela was able to pick up an exact image of the girl I had described, to her. For a minute, I really didn't quite know what to say to Charlie. Our lives were getting very complicated. The last map was another collage of images. The largest image was of the cafeteria with everyone we knew, and the other half was several views of Pamela in different poses. In each pose, the look on Pamela's face was that of a teasing young girl. Now I was certain that our lives were going to get really complicated.

Charley says, "Look, I know what you are going to say, but I have had visions too, I feel compelled to get to the end of this adventure with you. Pamela can wait, but I have to be honest with you. She told me to look for something in that backpack. I knew something would be there all the time." Again, Charley started grinning and says, "She is very special to me."

The maps all appeared to have been immersed in a liquid plastic, making them waterproof then pressed. Unfolded they took up a lot of space, but folded up with all the air burped out, they assumed their original shape which was easily stuffed back into the thin plastic bag which was also burped, sealed, and returned to Charlie's backpack.

We were in a quandary as to how we were going to actually get inside of Serpiente. The maps showed a direct approach from the north, but in my vision, Charley and I had approached the ranch house from the south, through the sandstone canyon. We had many questions. Would we be killed before we could discover why the serpent entered our dreams? Would the people of Serpiente kill us before the serpent could intervene? Would we simply be tortured and then eaten?

Exploring Albuquerque

Whenever exploring a city, one has to be constantly on guard for the unknown. It is a perfect place to set up an ambush. An ambush however, would require foreknowledge. It is also a good place to disappear. One or two individuals would be incredibly hard to spot, however in a direct confrontation with warriors it is a deadly environment. In a deserted city, there would need to be an accidental encounter where suddenly we notice warriors, or worse they could see us first. Finally, we stopped at a large building which appeared to be built on a small hill. Towering well above the rest of the buildings was a large bell tower. We decided that it might make a perfect place to camp where no one could reach us without climbing the stairs. The tall structure turned out to be a church. Built on high ground, it offered us views of the business district which was up toward the mountain, and the entire valley, with the river flowing through it. The city extended on the other side of the river for as far as we could see to the horizon. To the flat hills to the far west were three small volcanic cones.

We ate corned beef on hard little crackers which the scientists had given to us, along with pear halves in light syrup. I preferred the sweet liquid of the pear halves in light syrup. It did not make me feel a sick like the ancient one's peaches in heavy syrup had done. I was learning that my stomach was a servant to my mouth, and I liked to eat. In my youth, my body still allowed me to eat the ancients' canned food. But I knew I couldn't live long, eating that stuff, it was tasteless and had lost most of its nourishment. Fortunately, the scientist at Los Alamos had stocked our packs with freshly canned food that was light to carry and nourishing.

We watched the sun set behind the volcanic features of Albuquerque's west mesa, and settled down to just sitting and watching for movement anywhere in the city. We saw nothing moving within the city but to our surprise, straight down the road that was in front of the building we had taken refuge in, we could see a tiny fire in the distance. It wasn't actually next to the river; the fire seemed to have been built some distance inside of the city. My first thought was that maybe it was a place where the ancient ones would bring their children to play. Now it was a large overgrown opening with mature trees between the buildings, located close to the cottonwood forest that grew along the river. The fire grew as the night darkened. Looking carefully, we could see a flickering of the light, as if someone was walking in front of the fire. But it had to be a huge fire, a fire saying, "We are here, and we don't care if you know it."

We decided to leave our packs in the tower, taking only our weapons with us. We were dreading what we would find, suspecting Painted warriors who could cause us serious delays at best and death at worst. It would take us some time to slip past three blocks of buildings that served as some kind of business for the people who traveled in the rusty cars that were everywhere. We walked where there was the most cover, always looking over our shoulders.

It was late at night and there was no moon out, which helped us to find a place where we could spy on the fire keepers. The fire had burned down to coals and all around the fire were Painted Warriors, all of them seemingly asleep. Then, in unison they seemed to all stand up, get into a circle around the fire and as men and women sang for them, they danced in an endless circle until they began dropping out from exhaustion. Then they were released again. There didn't appear to be any hostages, only the men and women who serviced the warriors and little in the way of food, at least there didn't appear to be any human food. The warriors were being punished by the serpent for not getting under the fence. The serpent knew what would happen when the warriors touched the fence, but it wanted to test both his warriors and the defenses that it suspected where behind the fence. The serpent knew that a simple electric fence was certainly not enough to protect the multitude of people thought to be inside the fence. What it did not know about was dragonflies and the natural ingenuity of the scientist, at Los Alamos.

We returned to our tower arriving, just as the sky over Slice of Watermelon Mountain was becoming light. We climbed back up the stairs setting traps for anyone who would venture up the stairs after us, and after searching for any movement and seeing none, we settled down on the floor of the tower and fell fast asleep. It offered us a place where we were as far from the ground as we could get, if the dogs smelled us and followed us here, we would hear them coming long before they could reach us and we would be ready for them anyway. I was quite good, distracting the dog's teeth with a tomahawk and then sliding a long thin knife into the dog, just above the shoulders. The blade cut down the inside of the ribs, through every organ that ribs are supposed to protect. If the blade hits the heart, it is all over in an instant. I wondered how well the technique would work with a bear. But today, we drifted off into a deep sleep.

That afternoon, Charlie came over and touched my shoulder, "You have to see this," he said with blank look on his face. Getting up, I came to a stop when I realized that I was looking at a form, sitting on one of the four chairs that littered the tower floor.

Two wiry hands slipped the hood off the head exposing an elderly human woman, her brown eyes watched our every move but she didn't say anything. She seemed harmless, but we were astonished at her presence. How and when did she get inside the tower with us?

We learned that she lived here in the church, where she was waiting for us when we returned from spying on the Painted People. We never noticed her sitting in the dark, motionless. She had watched over us as we slept, the entire day. We were unaware of her until Charley got up to relieve himself, walking in the early morning light he crossed to the other side of the tower which was just a few feet away, then while peeing over the wall onto the roof below, Charlie turned his head to the side and realized that someone was sitting in the chair. Cutting his pee short, he then ran over to wake me.

After many starts and stops we began speaking to each other in English, a language she had not heard in thirty-five years. She had lived here in this church ever since she was a young girl, totally alone. Somehow, after an altercation of some kind, her people had hidden her away then vanished. She found herself living in the kitchen of the old church. Sleeping under the cabinet that was used to serve food, she had stocked her tiny world with water and food, just in case an uninvited guest came along. Charlie and I remembered that we had not explored the old building. Walking past the rows of pews we had taken to the room where a long series of stairs lead directly to the tower. The old lady now became animated, pacing back and forth looking over the edge of the wall, each time, she pointed in the direction of the Painted People we had seen the day before. It was obvious that she was terrified of the Painted People. We wondered what her experiences with them had been.

Remembering what Angie Wilkerson had said, that the Painted People had appeared about twenty years ago, I asked her, how long have the Painted People been coming to Albuquerque?

She answered in a tiny voice, "Jesse, my name is Jesse. The painted creatures you saw last night started coming to the park here in Albuquerque about four years ago. They do some of their ceremonies just down the road there, where they feel safe. Like you, I spied on them long enough to understand their cruelty. At first, I was mesmerized at what I was seeing; geometric designs covering the bodies of both the male and female warriors. I saw personally what they do to humans they catch. I watched while they abused captive humans and then ate them. But what they did was ungodly, they are demonic. They look like human beings underneath all that body paint, but I think something controls them, something horrible that we cannot see It is not in the nature of humans to act that way."

We explained to her what we knew of the serpents who had taken control of this part of the country. It didn't help. Her home was being invaded by creatures who only wanted to harm her. She quietly explained that we should be concerned, as the warriors would occasionally walk into the city looking for food, arms, and any humans who they might accidentally encounter.

We further explained our problem to her; we had to somehow find a way past the Painted People without them ever seeing us.

She answered, "I can help you get as far as the business district, beyond that, I have not ventured in years, I stay close to this church but I now worry because the Painted People are so close." She, like Charlie and I, was afraid of accidentally encountering the warriors, unfortunately everyone had to leave the confines of the camp to hunt, find food, find water, to bathe, to take care of bodily functions.

That evening her point was proven correct. Up the street came a female painted warrior along with two undecorated men who were scouting. They walked up the center of the street, showing no fear or intimidation as to what they might come upon, walking about fifty feet apart. We carefully watched them from the tower underneath a device that Jesse had made of a metal frame and old cloth. The cloth had slits whereby we could look through them. From the street, it would appear as fallen plaster, we could watch the warriors without having to duck our heads, every time one of them looked our way. They never saw us but we knew they would return later, carrying sacks with cans of food, freshly killed animals usually consisting of dogs or rabbits, or anything else they could find to eat including the fresh meat of humans which they relished. During ceremonies, the Painted tribe sent out several warriors and men who in groups of three would always stay within sight of each other for mutual cover, and hunt for anything edible. Then the warriors returned to camp and shared their spoils. Charlie and I sat and discussed a document we had read while at Los Alamos, 'Dragonfly Report: The Painted People.'

Dragonfly Report

Los Alamos National Laboratories was in a quandary, an impasse. They had accomplished little as the world around them stagnated into constant warfare. Outside of Los Alamos, the surviving people had either locked themselves away on feudal ranches far to the north and east, or hid themselves away in isolation. The report concluded that many survivors who had hidden themselves away had been discovered and either killed by the warrior bands or were absorbed and controlled by the serpents. There were questions regarding those small populations who lived hidden away in isolated homesteads covering the entire area to the north and east. The scientists at Los Alamos had released the two newcomers to learn more about what the Painted People and the people they once knew who lived in Serpiente, were they up to? The scientists were also concerned, about a change in serpent technology and tactics with the surrounding peoples. Too much time had passed without any communications with other humans, therefore an experiment was being conducted, am dot was Charlie and me.

A dragonfly report is the final product of intelligence gathered by spyware housed at the Los Alamos National Laboratories. Dragonflies are programmed to journey to a specific location such as a limb in a tall tree overlooking a combatant's camp. Once the dragonfly gains a branch it wraps a wire around the branch which holds it in place as it watches. It can watch for many weeks after it has attached itself and finally when the batteries no longer work, or cannot recharge, due to a lack of sunlight, it self-ignites, destroying the delicate computer chip which directs its operations.

All of the images of the dragonflies are transmitted simultaneously to Los Alamos Laboratories where they are evaluated by computer programs which eliminate uninteresting or uneventful data. Actionable scenes are watched and analyzed by human technicians, many of them the same people who were on that map that Charlie had. All data is analyzed and a situation report is made. The purpose was to understand and defeat any forces that wish to do harm to the scientists and facilities of Los Alamos National Laboratories.

Dragonfly Analysis
of
Proximity and Surveillance Report
on
The Painted People: Mesa Verde and Jemez Locations

The people controlled by the Painted People are living somewhat like the ancient Ancestral Puebloans or Anasazi, who during the last millennium lived in this part of what is known as north central New Mexico. Dragonfly first discovered the Painted Warriors, by thermal imaging of the Mancos canyon which flows into the San Juan River. They are currently living in Mesa Verde, in a deep canyon where the ancient people lived before the European invasion. During the first three years, the dragonflies observed them living there, they usually raided to the north like the Red Face had always done.

Then during the last two years, dragonfly detected and documented a new structure, looking like a star with readouts, a fort is being built. New cabins are being constructed and old ones being reconstructed directly at the sight of the ancient pueblo of Jemez. A small stream actually flows through a metal grate through a portion of the enclosure, solving any question of water needs. A growing adobe and rock structure would soon enclose the central plaza with a large fire pit at the center. Great Mounds of firewood are stacked for some future use. In time, the Painted People will have a wall built completely around them that will defeat any foot solder. With the readouts, any soldier approaching the wall will be in a kill zone, solving a defensive problem that was first solved in Medieval Europe. Castles worked well with foot armies but poorly after the invention of gunpowder. Why are the Painted People so carefully building a wall to protect themselves? Speculation is they are building it to protect themselves using the fort as a home base, to launch attacks against Los Alamos Laboratories.

During the winter time, the Painted Warriors returned to their ancestral homes located in Mesa Verde with only a few of the older people watching over the new construction. It was estimated that they would completely rebuild the new site before the serpent would go there. Somewhere, a small but highly motivated army provides the security for the serpent. The serpent is perfectly capable of fighting for its 'self but always lets the humans do its bidding instead. Living in an alien world with millions of microbes, the serpent would never risk getting hurt, whereas humans are totally expendable.

The new structure is being constructed by three warriors and two dozen workers, both men and women. They appear to be moving to an ancient place strategically located just down the mountain on State Route 4 from Los Alamos. It is also strategically located for the serpents' needs and if necessary, they could escape the structure following many routes. The warriors had easy access to all the large cities with their resources in the Rio Grande Valley, and if necessary, a direct route back to Mesa Verde.

Recently the Painted People were quietly moving a skeleton crew to Jemez Pueblo, a family at a time with a warrior providing protection for each family. This movement started only a year ago after what we hypothecate was a decision of the serpent, out of his curiosity to redirect his efforts to understand the scientists who live here on top of Jemez Mountain. We scientists as a whole appear to be a mystery to the serpent. They lived invisibly, in huge glass and metal structures, and when the Los

Alamos workers journey down to the river to work in the fields or to do work on the buildings, the serpent could not probe their minds. Because of their amulets, humans here do not allow the serpents to enter their dreams, to learn about them, to control them which must bother the serpent. The serpent, in the form of a raven, would watch the workers using machines to till the fields. To the perplexed serpent, there seemed to be nothing there yet it could watch as the workers tended their crops then always returned to the buildings inside the fence.

This always frustrated the serpent known as Tikal. By nature, the creature is envious, jealous, and cruel. It is hypothecated that Tikal sees everything as a possible threat to his serpent superiority, his royalty; particularly when it comes to humans, the most dangerous creature on this planet, except for the possible exception of cats. Tikal appeared to be challenged by the idea of raiding Los Alamos. It was because of his pride; he couldn't allow human creatures to escape his control, not in the center of his territory, and Tikal desired the possibilities the practical technology that is available at the Los Alamos Laboratories. Certainly, Tikal may have assumed that if it could assume control over the technology, it could shorten the time it would take for the serpent clan to return to the stars. Tikal knew that it would take a long time for that to happen but he certainly would long for that day, as all the serpents did. But for now, the humans who live at Los Alamos are an enigma to Tikal; he can no longer be satisfied in raiding to the far north like the Red Face People, now he is considering attacking Los Alamos.

Mesa Verde

The majority of the report was based upon information gathered from the Painted People while they lived in Mesa Verde. We wondered if the people now living in Jemez would want to return to Mesa Verde where they lived well. In Mesa Verde, the serpent lived in a cliff dwelling home that had been occupied by humans for thousands of years. Just like the ancient Anasazi, royalty moved into the cliff houses and the actual tribe lived on the flat mesa that was above the cliffs. They looted the towns of Cortez and Durango, bringing in many windows as well as salvaged galvanized metals, which were fitted into the natural rock openings. Now sealed in, with a metal stove with flue pipes, brought all the way from Cortez, the entire structure stayed cozy during the coldest of winter nights. The serpent was the living thermostat that dictated the temperature, which the workers maintained. Curled up in the sun with a pane of glass between it and a cold breeze, the serpent was very comfortable, but during the wintertime and at night, a fire had to be maintained.

The ancient rocks the building was built into always radiated heat back in the wintertime and stayed naturally cool during the summertime, when the sun was much higher in the sky. According to our thermal records, they actually preferred to remain just a little cooler than we would have expected for an alien serpent. We assumed that it would prefer a higher temperature. They actually lived in an environment that stayed right at 76 degrees, year around.

All the men of the tribe were responsible for wood gathering, and hunting small game which was always shared with the royalty, if they happened to capture a hostage, the hostage was also turned over to the warriors. The warriors would terrify and torture, each of the hostages, one at a time. After the warriors were done playing with the victims, the workers who waited on the royalty prepared the food; usually roasting it on a great fire pit. Large amounts of carrots, onions and potatoes were laid on top of the coals then one live human was added on top of the vegetables, and the entire mass covered and sealed with a sheet of metal. Death was horrible but fast, and certainly celebrated. Large amounts of food would be cooked and eaten by the warriors and the workers. Leftover food was then returned to the supporting families. In the final analysis, nothing was wasted. But of course, the humans who were captured certainly might have another point of view.

The warriors lived well, even during the long months of winter in rock shelters that they themselves had rebuilt into the south facing cliffs. Families lived in those shelters, with both sexes sharing responsibilities. Women worked with women, and men tended to work with men, but not always. Sometimes it was the women who mixed mud and gathered stone to build structures that were warm in the winter and cool in the summer. Men would gather wood, or hunt for small game with the possibility of an occasional deer, or tend to the children. In the summertime, the men tended sheep and the women worked the summer fields of corn, chilies, and beans.

They shared work, but the women were considered the real masters of the tribe. It was a matriarchal system in which the most desirable and intelligent of the women would marry a male warrior and live in a much higher social class. She would be waited upon and always protected. The women willingly married the warriors, knowing she would forever be everybody's property. The sexual tensions the young warriors exhibited were taken care of by those women but were also enjoyed by the serpent. Recently, the royal females have begun decorating their bodies; they are the leaders; every square inch of skin is decorated with permanent ink. In Tikal's world, he was enjoying his human toys.

Unlike the Red Face serpent, Tsotzil, who hated females, Tikal seemed to enjoy the irony of the women being in control of his tribe of humans. The women naturally seemed in charge of the home fires. The women were the masters, the ones who kept the social life of the tribe coherent. They willingly worked, and worked hard. The men of the tribe who were not warriors also worked as the women did, however they also assisted the warriors, and could be a force themselves, they were usually well armed, but nothing like the warriors, nor did they wear any sign of body paint. They simply looked like a people who worked and lived to support the warrior class of people. They lived in fear. They had good reason to be afraid. They worked hard because they were afraid of the consequences of not working hard. They were a people who were in direct service to Tikal the serpent, and human flesh provided a great deal of the protein the warriors consumed in the winter time. There was no such thing as old Painted People, the oldest of them being in their forties. Everyone wanted to prove his or her worth; they did not want to wind up on the dinner table. Sometimes a warrior would simply walk up to an older worker and simply dispatch him or her with a knife under the ribs. Directly to the heart; it just happens, then others come and take the body to the food preparation area.

Early in the springtime, the very nature of the warriors change, they leave the rock shelters becoming more a warlike group as they prepare for another season of raiding. Early in the spring of the year, a ceremony occurs deep inside one of the great circular kivas that line the courtyard, and a yearly cycle starts again. Three or four new warriors and brides for them; the best the tribe could offer, would arrive and be presented to Tikal for his inspection. Each young person would be inspected up close. Perhaps one of them might become a warrior but not likely. The serpent enjoyed direct control over a few humans, usually about eighteen to twenty warriors who were treated like royalty by the rest of the tribe. But they had to earn that position, and constantly fight to maintain it. They were the samurai who defended the community, and raided others.

The women did much more than provide sex; they were the doctors and nurses that minded the bodies of broken and hurt warriors. Warriors got hurt in a number of ways, but seldom during warfare. Warfare happened far too fast for the victims to defend themselves. Occasionally a warrior was killed but they were never captured. Warriors were programmed to fight to the death. Despite that, there were warriors who returned with great wounds that required a reasonable length of time to heal; those that didn't heal, or lost a limb due to gangrene were simply eaten.

The warrior's eyes are a living extension into the mind of the serpent. If the serpent wanted to, it could see and feel everything the warrior was seeing or feeling. But the serpent could also make the pain of a forced walk go away, or reward the pleasure center in the warrior's head for a good raid. During the long sessions when the warriors are tattooed they felt pleasure, rather than pain from the needle that injected the ink used by the artist who illustrated the warriors. More powerful than any drug, the serpent rewarded the successful warriors, manipulating the pleasure centers of their brains. The serpent experienced the world through his warriors and the warriors experienced the world through the serpent's desires.

In another kiva, the oldest warriors plotted ideas and made plans for the summertime raids; always presented to the serpent for approval. During the summertime, the warriors and families spread out over the entire region, living in tiny structures scattered though out their land. They are forced to constantly follow the local game moving from herd to herd until the summer sets in. The Painted People have done this long enough to know of many perfect places to live and to have ceremonial gatherings.

By an unknown means, the individual warriors are contacted and instructed to meet in a special place. Usually this is a bowl in a large canyon where they are absolutely hidden. A place where there is a large area for ceremonial purposes, with plenty of wood and natural game. They also prefer places where the ancients met, where they can loot canned food and anything else they could use. After spending some time going in different directions, they all met at a place that was apparently prearranged. The high school football stadium, the park in Albuquerque, the canyon pool below Serpiente, somehow, they all know where to meet and in time they all arrive at a ceremonial camp. They camp there for several days, then split up. After a while they all meet at another camp, all at the same time. They stay there until the local resources are depleted then move to another. Moving about, they always travel in groups of three, which makes detecting them difficult.

Before the pandemics that killed most of humanity as well as the serpents, the serpents preyed upon all humans, everyone. Now they have changed. Some serpents have learned to manipulate and use the humans to provide work, as well as provide pleasure for them. The serpents are evolving their strategies.

Los Lunas

As long as Charlie, Jesse and I stayed deathly quiet, we were safe. Even if the warriors wandered into the church all they would see is rows of empty chairs, it would appear as a poor place to loot anything. The following night, there was no fire. The tribe of Painted People had moved to the north along the same trails that we had just traveled down. If we had begun our journey only a couple of days later, we undoubtedly would have walked right into them. Survival depended as much on luck as on skill and ability. We had been very lucky so far.

Jesse declined our offer to take her with us. She had lived in her church sanctuary far too long and would never leave it despite the proximity of the Painted Peoples' ceremonial camp. We said our goodbyes and hiked south finding the bridge that the Painted People had walked over. At one time or another, a large flood had carried great trees and deposited them on top of the bridge making crossing a challenge. We decided that since it was the route taken by the warriors we would continue walking, even though we knew of a better place to cross. Finally, at the very southern end of Albuquerque, the road dropped behind huge flat-topped volcanic mesas, and then crossed the river. We came upon a giant bridge that carried a major road over it, that crossed to the distant volcanic mesas where we would venture deeper into the unknown. This road had been well traveled by someone traveling in vehicles, probably right up to the front door of Serpiente.

We dismissed any thoughts of the Painted People. Fortunately for us they were busy dealing with another attempt to conquer the electric fence that surrounded the Los Alamos facility. The serpents had decided to travel all the way to Espanola and cross the river there. This time, they would try it from the other side, like a serpent, looking for a weakness. They would arrive at the main gate this time and try a different way to get inside.

Charlie and I, instead of following the larger and traveled road dropped down and turned south again to a Route 448 which we followed. Here, there was plenty of cover, game and water. Two days later we came to a place that was marked Los Lunas on the road sign. Coming to a street intersection, we could see that going one way would take us to the river and the other way was our route to Serpiente. We were drawn to the river, after stopping to look in several buildings that appeared to have been completely cleaned out. Shortly we discovered a perfect place to camp under a span of a collapsed bridge. The river had recently dropped leaving a huge sandy beach that was perpetually in the shade of the remaining bridge. I wondered why they even needed a bridge there. I could easily wade across the entire river there but then I realized that the heavy machines the ancients used would have bogged down in the mud.

We settled into our normal routine duties, basically waiting for the pack of dogs to show up. We would need to kill a couple of them, then cook and eat one of them for dinner but no dogs showed up. Only a single black raven that landed on a tree branch showed up. It appeared to watch us intently, studying us, waiting for both of us to settle down on our leather pads we put down before we put our bedding down. I watched the bird as intently as the bird appeared to watch us. Then unexpectedly, we both watched as the raven finally flew down within a few yards of us on the sandy beach. It walked around with its wings spread in case it needed to make a fast escape but when neither of us moved, it came closer. As the raven came to within a dozen feet of us, to our astonishment it transformed into a large black snake. The snake rose up and undulated back and forth a couple of times, then dropped to the ground and began to move away. As it did, the snake appeared to vanish, right in front of us, leaving both of us speechless. It was one thing to see something like that in a dream; it was another thing altogether to see it in broad daylight. Again, for the second time since the voyage began, I was convinced that what we were doing was the right thing. My original dream was real and as for Charlie, he didn't know what to believe. He wasn't scared, just mystified. He thought to himself, "Just what kind of magic was that?"

Preparing for Serpiente

We stayed under the bridge for a couple of days, resting and equipping ourselves. We had long ago discovered that there were a multitude of features that had been incorporated into our back packs. The metal pipes that carried the weight of the pack, had black plastic covers. Actually, they were the eyes of a camera that could look around just like a flying dragonfly. Besides the maps, we found tiny cameras, locaters, and listening devices. The scientist' must have been laughing at us while we were asleep, in the tower with Jesse looking over us.

According to the map we had, the one most direct way into the canyon lands known as Serpiente was to walk directly west, following an ancient road over a small river, the Rio Puerco River, and then turn south following something that was marked only as a dotted line. We surmised that even in the ancient times, the road there was only a gravel or dirt road and that it went past a small mountain marked Ladron Peak on the map and then turned slightly west where a tiny community of humans had once lived. In a strange way, it all made sense to us. It was an isolated community but then we had traveled through many isolated communities and never found anything but skeletons of the ancient ones. Again, I thought about the few people I had seen, the red warrior, the footprint, the Hopi, the scientists at Los Alamos, the elderly lady, and of course Charlie. Charlie was the only person I had ever seen that had a logical reason for surviving the plague. But here in this country, most places seemed isolated to us, but what made Serpiente so special? I could only wonder. After turning off the small overgrown blacktop road we discovered the unmistakable tracks of ancient cars or trucks. This puzzled us. Where did they get the fuel that powered them?

That evening, Charlie and I had fitful dreams about snakes that transform into ravens and back. But they were only dreams and obviously not visions. I did however, also dream about the girl in my previous dreams, even though it was only glimpses of her, like a regular dream. Since I started wearing the owl amulet, she must have assumed I had died. Upon awaking the following day, I was determined now, more than ever, to find her.

After roasting two cottontail rabbits for breakfast, we put on leather clothing and handmade moccasins, tying large feathers in our hair that shaded our faces. We packed up all the clothes that the scientists had provided us, hid the back packs inside a place marked Huning Mercantile, and headed west. We expected to gingerly walk over a partially collapsed bridge that turned out to be instead, well maintained and well-traveled. We traveled only another mile or so until we headed south again. In the sandy hills and arroyos, the vehicle tracks also turned south following an ancient road where many years ago, someone had driven a heavy earth moving machine into a gully and it was still there, covered with sand and rusting. Yet there were fresh tracks here where we were. Other than that, all we could see were game trails but clearly to the south we could see the one great mountain peak marked on the maps as Ladron Peak. We would follow the tracks and aim for a camp on the mountain, then search from there.

A day later, we dropped down the flanks of Ladron Mountain and found the old road again and decided to stay on it until we were within sight of the community, instead we came to the remains of a high fence with a huge locked gate that had been built directly across the road. There were many faded "keep out" signs and evidence that someone had stopped to open and then reclose the locks to the gate. We knew we could climb over the gate but I wasn't sure that was the route I wanted to take. In the far distance, we could see what appeared to be large fields that were currently under cultivation. Beyond that was a cottonwood forest that appeared to follow a stream bed out of a small sandstone canyon. We could see different types of trees growing around a small community. It all seemed very familiar to Charlie and me, thanks to Pamela and the Dragonfly imaging crew. Yet I was in a quandary. In the vision, Charlie and I had walked down the canyon to the south, well behind Serpiente. Should we circle around and come in from behind as in the vision? Or go climbing over the fence and just walk in? We wondered if the fence was only a front and that once out of sight, it would disappear.

We decided to follow the fence, and skirt around our problem. We would see where it would take us. To our surprise, it only seemed to be a better made fence as we walked. Inside the fence was clearly the reason why, we could see cow patties scattered across the pastures. It was a working ranch. We walked another two miles until we could see what appeared to be a village nestled in the distant cottonwood trees. The buildings appeared just like I had seen in my vision. They looked like the homes of the old ones who had lived here years before the plague. But there were doors and windows as well as large structures with glistening panels attached to the metal roofs. We then noticed what appeared to be a young warrior walking out to a large lake of water that had an earthen dam holding the water in place. We hid behind some scrub brush as we watched the man toss a bucketful of something into the water. Evidently the large pond had fish in it because we could see them eagerly splashing around as they ate the contents of the bucket. We found it entertaining at first but then realized that something was moving behind us. We turned to discover four men on horses, armed with bows and arrows riding toward us. For the first time since I had left Alaska, I was truly worried.

Part 5

Serpiente, New Mexico

The most beautiful experience we can have is the mysterious — the fundamental emotion which stands at the cradle of true art and true science.

—Albert Einstein

An Introduction to Serpiente

The four men approached us with arrows mounted in their bows ready to shoot but they didn't, instead the leader made motions with his bow for us to raise our hands which we did. I thought that they were strange looking people. They looked somewhat like the Eskimo people I had seen in photographs while in Alaska or like the Hopi people we had encountered earlier. Finally, one of them said something to the others in a language I had never heard before. Then one of them walked over to us and asked in perfect English, which one of you is Chato?

I was mystified as to how the stranger could possibly know my name and I stepped forward. The warrior said, "There is someone here who has been waiting for quite some time to meet you."

I almost passed out when I heard my name. I had so many questions to ask I could hardly restrain myself but instead simply handed the bow and arrows over and followed him into a new world. We walked past fields being worked by humans who were cutting down weeds from the rows of soil with hoes. They were growing all manner of food, some of which we recognized and some we didn't. There were several large structures that stuck up into the sky like the one where we found the horses that had blades of metal that turned in the wind causing water to pour from pipes that fed the rows of crops. Charlie and I marveled at the ingenuity but we knew that they were tools that the ancient people had invented long ago.

Finally, we entered a large plaza surrounded by rock buildings that were carefully built with the stones fitting perfectly into place. Almost naked children ran around playing with toy bows and arrows as well as small carts that were used to haul things around. The children were taking turns pulling other children around in them. We realized what had laid the tracks down as we passed two trucks, one with a large tank in the back of it that was apparently used for hauling something from town. Then we came to a large structure that clearly looked familiar. I was seeing the same house that had appeared in my Alaskan dream. The excitement of the newcomers caused all the people to come out of their houses so they could see the new strangers. We had not seen so many people since we had left Los Alamos. Even Charlie was amazed that so many people were alive and prospering. There were almost as many people here, as at Los Alamos laboratories. We were directed to a small structure that had one of the wind machines above it and ordered to step inside. Inside were several young ladies who stared at us intently and giggled. The mysterious warrior looked at the two of us, pinched his nose and said, "See those tubs over there?"

Charlie and I looked at two large white tubs that were overflowing with water, the excess water being channeled down the road we had just walked up and into a field where large melons were growing. "The warrior then says, "Take off all your cloths, and get into the water."

"Why," Charlie asked, unable to understand why they could possibly want us to get into the tubs of water.

Laughing, the warrior looked intently at us and says, "Well maybe we want to cook you in them, but then, maybe you just stink and we would like you to smell better before you meet royalty." As that was being said, three young girls stepped up to each of us and began disrobing us. Embarrassed, we resisted for a moment but then realized that our resistance was futile. I noticed that the tiny amulets were carefully placed with our other cloths. Evidently the girls thought they were just ornaments. After a moment or two we gave up, disrobed and stepped into the water. It was cold but crystal clear. Next the young girls began to scrub us using cloth with a soap made from a yucca plant; removing every bit of the grease, charcoal, sweat and dirt we had accumulated over the last few days. One of the girls then carefully took a pair of knives that had been fashioned together and cut the hair from both of our heads, leaving me with my natural brown hair and Charlie with his natural red hair showing. Using sharp knives and soap, they scraped the stubbly whiskers away from our faces. Once clean, we were given towels to dry ourselves with and a set of clothes that seemed to fit better than any we had ever worn before. We had never used buttons before and it took one of the young ladies to show us how to use them. At almost twenty years of age and clean now for the first time in some time, I looked at a mirror that was hanging on the wall. I didn't recognize the person I saw in the reflection. We wanted to put the amulets back around our necks when we thought that no one was watching but never had the chance. Instead the girls gathered up our old clothes for us putting the amulets inside the bag they were carrying them in.

We were escorted to the main house where we could smell food being prepared. Having not eaten anything since the day before, we were ravenous. The warrior who introduced himself as Jim opened the door for us and showed us to a large table that had at least twenty chairs setting around it. The cold air that was inside was intoxicating. I asked where the cold air was coming from. Jim answered me, "From the air conditioner," whatever that was. It seemed a little mysterious to Charlie and me but then we had experienced cool air at Los Alamos. We had no way of knowing that the house had a motor that was turned on every evening during the summer so the house could be cooled. Inside the house more men and women sat, waiting while food was being brought in.

"Sit here," Jim said as he pointed to a couple of chairs.

I was curious about the strange implements that sat next to each empty plate. They appeared to be a spoon, fork and knife. I had not seen implements like them since our days at Los Alamos and now I carried a fork and spoon with me. Finally, two young girls walked into the room and sat down across from Charlie and me. One, a raven-haired beauty with dark eyes and the other girl was the girl that I had seen in my visions. She seemed very human to me. I had expected a girl who might have reptilian characteristics. But instead she was ravishingly beautiful with long blond hair that trailed down to the middle of her back and brilliant cracked glass blue eyes similar to Charlie's but even more beautiful. She had applied something to her lips which made them slightly red in color and above her eyes were tiny sparkles from something she had applied there. She wore a blue blouse that accentuated her eyes and a pure white skirt. The outfit amply showed off a perfect figure. I could not say anything nor move a muscle. I just stared in disbelief.

The girl that I had dreamed of offered her hand as Charlie had done once, and said, "Hello, my name is Penny Anderson. I was named after my great-great grandmother. What is your name?" It was obvious that she already knew my name but was trying to be gracious.

I was slow to answer but I finally answered. "My name is Chato Williams. I was named after a character in a book about Indians that my family in Alaska has."

"I didn't know that you were named after an Indian," says Charlie, "You never told me."

"You never asked," I replied.

One of the young girls who had scraped the dirt and grease off of us began piling a spoonful of enchiladas, then beans, and finally salad on our plates, along with a tortilla. Everyone began eating but Charlie and me. After a couple of bites Penny reached over and picked up a spoonful of enchilada and stuck some of the red food in my mouth. I was more than surprised. The food tasted great and I was actually eating with the same girl I had dreamed about. I had a thousand questions to ask but I knew we would have to wait until after dinner, besides Charlie and I were starving.

Penny looked at me and laughed, "I know, you are full of questions, we can go out on the patio after we eat and I'll try to answer them."

"How did you know I had questions?" I asked, knowing that it would be obvious that we were bursting at the seams with questions.

She answered me, "I could see the pictures in your mind." Everyone at the table giggled or laughed at that point. Since she was finished eating her tiny meal she said, "I would love to see what it was like to paddle in the ocean in a sea kayak like you and Charlie did!"

Charlie and I were both dumbfounded. "How could she have known about the sea kayaks?"

A Walk in the Patio

After eating three plates of food, far more than anyone had recently eaten there before, Penny flashed her eyes at me and whispered, "Would you like to take a walk in the patio? I will try and answer some of your questions such as how I knew about you and why you were brought here."

"I was brought here?" I asked. "I thought I was looking for a girl that I saw in a dream.

"That's true, but my friends placed that dream in your mind."

"I don't understand."

"Let's go for a walk," suggested the girl named Penny. So, I followed her out the door to the patio where it was just like I had dreamed. The patio was a production area where all manner of pottery was being made.

"This is where I work," said Penny. We sat down on a bench and for the next two hours we talked about what had brought us together.

"Dr. Hartsell was the one who first discovered evidence of a plague and fled here with our family to escape it. It was she who first placed a phone call to the Anderson household about the deadly abilities of the pathogen. The family had barricaded the road into the ranch as soon as they got the news. We are all descendants of that small group of people who lived here many generations ago. Let me show you." We walked back into the house where Charlie had already made friends with Juanita, the raven-haired beauty who was Penny's friend. On the mantle of the fireplace were framed yellowed photographs of the original Penny along with her little girl Jenna Brook who turned out to be Penny's great grandmother, along with Corey and Hidalgo who was with a beautiful lady; Jill Thompson as well as Ken, June, and Manuel Ortega and his family. "Everyone here is descendants of those people."

"So, the serpents killed all those people?" I asked.

"No, none of these people were killed by the serpents. Everyone in this tiny village can trace their family back to these people, for example, the fellow that captured you is named Jim Hidalgo. He is a direct descendant of Hidalgo and Jill Thompson which is why he has blue eyes. Throughout history, ninety nine percent of all human deaths that are not natural or accidental; are caused by humans killing each other, serpents make up less than one percent of one percent of human deaths. Sure, they caused deaths, they even enjoy gaining life energy from the deaths of humans, but it was ultimately the humans, particularly one, who is responsible for the death of the humans who lived in all those empty cities, a shaman by the name of General Armstrong."

Changing the subject, I asked, "How did you find me in Alaska and how did you plant that dream in my mind?"

"After the plague hit, most serpents and humans died, but not all. A few surviving serpents who had been isolated migrated back here to Serpiente where they had been before. Here, they felt safe with our ancestors and they befriended us, even teaching us how to communicate with them by sharing pictures in our minds. We humans are not as good as the serpents are at sharing images but we are learning."

Penny Anderson then got quiet for a moment. "You want to know the truth, don't you?

"It would be helpful," I answered.

She continued, "There are many young warriors here that I could marry but I have a problem.

"What is your problem," I asked?

"It has become obvious that I will never find a mate here."

"I don't understand," I entered the conversation, "There are men all over this country that are available, why would you need someone you had never met who lives as far away as Alaska?"

"My spies found you there."

"You mean your serpent spies."

"That is correct, my serpent spies. They found you in Alaska. They could read your mind long before they ever actually saw you. You were a bear hunter and provider for your tribe, but there was no one there for you to mate with. They looked into your mind and found that you were a good person, but more importantly they also looked into your very chromosomes and genetic material."

I had no idea what she was talking about. Dr. James had failed to educate us in biology. "Yes, there are people here, she was reading my thoughts, however I don't love any of them and there is something called inbreeding. People are not supposed to marry those that are biologically related to them, and besides, you have special qualities that make you very different. You are far more intelligent than most humans, did you know that?"

I didn't know what to say, I merely made a 'no' gesture by rocking my head back and forth.

She put her hands on her hips and said, "That is why they brought you to me."

I had to ask, "Am I a captive here?"

"Not at all. You can leave any time you want, but I truly expect you to stay. You didn't paddle a thousand miles, and walk across a thousand miles of country that is mostly desert, just to turn around and leave. Your curiosity will not allow you to go."

Hearing a note of agitation in her voice, I changed the subject a little, "So you truly are the girl of my dreams?"

Penny, who was now blushing, took my hand and whispered, "I don't know about that, but you are certainly the man of my dreams." We held each other, looked into each other's eyes and finally I kissed the girl from my dreams, I already knew I was deeply in lust, I wasn't yet sure about love.

She changed the subject in an interesting way, "So when are Charlie and you going back to Alaska? I suspect that you want to rescue your family?"

"Rescue my family," I asked incredulously?

"Yes, they have run out of the things that make life bearable there. In time, if we don't rescue them or at least let them know they can leave the tiny valley they live in they will eventually die. It is a human condition. The serpents have the same problem. There was so few of them left, they changed their entire life view. Instead of using humans to gain life energy they have decided to partner with us humans. They feel that if they can work with us this terrible war between us will not be the death of us all. This time," Penny returned to her subject, "Your Alaskan family is afraid of leaving the small valley they live in, aren't they?"

I had to admit that it was true; the Williams' Community had lived in fear of the plague all these years.

It suddenly occurred to me, that she was answering questions that I had not asked yet. "Let's get back to basics, first of all, how do you know what I am thinking?"

She calmly answered "The serpents shared their gift of mind reading with we humans many generations ago." Then changing the topic again, "Your family is terrified that you are dead, particularly since they have not heard from you for three years now and they are starving. We really need to rescue them and add them to the human gene pool."

I was a little uncomfortable with the scientific terms I was hearing but Penny says to me, "I understand your concerns, you do not understand how I can read your mind, how I communicate with serpents, and certainly you think that the serpents cannot be trusted. In time, you will conquer your fears and they will go away, but I won't. I will be at your side all the way to Alaska and for the rest of your life if you want me to."

For some reason, I thought back to the huge fields of berries that grew along the Alaskan river. Wouldn't the women love to be able to pick in those fields?

"Yes, they would love the freedom, you see, no one lives in the entire region. Not till one goes all the way out to the coast on that river can living humans be found, like the red warrior you encountered, the women would love picking berries out of those fields." Penny looked at me knowing that I should be impressed. I was, but I was also scared and worried.

How would we get there?" I asked.

"Easy. We can just drive there."

I was mystified by that statement. "How do you make those machines go?"

"Actually, it is easy, we drive up to one of the places that the old ones used to fill up their trucks and run a hollow tube down into their underground tanks, pump up the gasoline, put it into the truck and barrels, and go on. We could actually drive nearly all the way there. Maybe all the way to that Bed and Breakfast that your family is so scared of. But I warn you, we may not make it all the way. Many of the bridges that were used to cross rivers may be down and I'm sure we will need tools like chain saws to remove trees that have grown or fallen across the roads. It could take us a while but there is no reason why a group of us couldn't drive all the way to that Bed and Breakfast your family is so scared of. Besides, you do understand we will be sending out scouts ahead of us."

"Scouts?" I asked out loud.

"Yes, my friend, the serpent Teotihuacan will venture with us, flying ahead of us and reporting the best routes for me. He is the serpent you saw while camping under the bridge a couple of days ago."

"I still don't understand. Why would the serpents want to do us any favors?"

Penny smiled a minute, and then looked at me right in the eyes, "Because some day, our descendants are going to help them return to the stars."

I looked up into a blue sky that would soon become sprinkled with stars as evening set in. "Why would they want to go to the stars?"

Penny frowned for just a second then says, "It is the one thing that they have always wanted to do, to return to the stars. They have a personal grudge against the star people who left them here thousands of years ago. They don't want to hurt the star people, they couldn't even if they wanted too, but they do want to confront them."

I thought about the situation for a minute without saying anything, Penny, who was reading my mind says, "Yes, the serpents have a human condition that we call pride, but it is not revenge that the serpents want. You see, serpents change over long periods of time just like people do."

I finally got the courage to ask, "Why don't the serpents simply inform my family for us? Why do we need to drive all the way back to Alaska if they can fly there?" For the first time since I had met her, she frowned just a little.

"I assumed you would be thrilled to be able to inform your family that they can leave Alaska."

"I am." I paused just a moment then asked, "Do you want me to return to Alaska or do the serpents want me to return to Alaska?" The question obviously hit a sensitive spot.

"Chato, I have lived here on this ranch my entire life. I have never been beyond Albuquerque and I want to see what is out there."

I thought to myself that it seemed like a logical answer. But I still wondered.

We walked around the old ranch house for some time looking at the large ceramic pots that Penny made. They were her contribution to the work around the ranch. Even the queen had to pitch in and contribute. It was starting to get late, the sun had already dropped behind the mesa to the west and the cloudless sky was just starting to darken.

Penny says, "We really should go back inside the ranch house. We can finish our discussion tomorrow. I'll show you where you and Charlie can sleep tonight. I'm certain that I can answer all your questions in time."

Feeling as if I had been a little rough with her, I pulled her over to me and said, "I do hope that tomorrow brings us closer together. I simply have too many unanswered questions about what I am doing here. Perhaps tomorrow will bring those answers but one thing is for sure."

"What is that," asked Penny?

"I certainly am falling in love with you. I can feel it in every fiber of my body. I feel like I have known you all my life and now that I can actually see and touch you, I may never be the same again."

We kissed again in the deepening dark of the evening and then turned and walked back into the ranch house. There Juanita took Charlie and me down a short corridor past several doors on one side and bookshelves on the other then opened a door with two small beds inside. She pointed out where the bathroom was, pointed to the stack of freshly laundered cloths on an end table, showed us how to operate the electric light and turned and gave Charlie a kiss on the cheek before disappearing down the hall. It was obvious that Charlie had also found someone interesting. What would Pamela think?

We lay in bed that night talking quietly about our experiences, not quite understanding what had happened. Our encounter with the people of Serpiente, was not at all like we thought it would be. Everyone was very polite to us, treating us like royalty. We fell into a hard sleep that night feeling safe and content for the first time in a long time, just Charlie, me, and Teotihuacan who was curled up at the foot of my bed, and who was listening to every word we said and thought.

Revealing the Amulets

We awoke the next day refreshed and invigorated having had no visions during the night and, in fact, we could not even remember dreaming during the night. We redressed in the clothes that we were given and then looked into their cloths sack where we found the cleaned amulets that were still there. Obviously, the young ladies who cleaned our clothes had no idea what they were. This pleased both of us for we felt safer with the amulets on, particularly after the weeks of being warned never to take them off by the scientists. Walking into the living part of the ranch which was also a large eating area we discovered both Juanita and Penny sitting at the table drinking a hot dark beverage. They had been kidding each other like all girls in love tend to do but as soon as we walked into the room the climate changed. They turned and simply starred at us.

Charlie was the first to ask, "Is something wrong?"

"I don't know," answered Penny. "There is something different about both of you."

"No," I stammered. "It is just Charlie and me, we are the same people who came here yesterday." I was attempting to keep everything on a friendly basis.

"No there is something different about you," Penny exclaimed. "I cannot tell what you are..." The words trailed off as she realized that now she didn't really want us to know that she was trying to read our minds.

"Is the word you are leaving off possibly the word, thinking?" I asked.

Charlie says, "We have decided that it is not fair. You can read our minds but we cannot read your minds, nor do we expect to be able to for a considerable time."

"Just a moment," Penny left the room then returned a few minutes later and sat down at the chair she had been in. She picked up her coffee, took a sip and then asked, "Are you two wearing amulets?"

Charlie playfully responded, "Amulets?"

Penny was clearly frustrated; it was becoming an intense moment.

Charlie continued, "Yes, they are tiny owl shaped ceramic things that some of us humans wear around our necks just like the one that your great-great grandmother wore."

Charlie's statement completely flummoxed Penny who actually turned a shade red.

"Well, yes, but how could you have possibly known that!"

We knew we could not hide the amulet anymore and reached inside our shirts and pulled them out. Juanita and Penny had never seen one before but knew how they worked. They would no longer be able to read our thoughts or enter into our dreams at night as long as he wore the amulets.

"Where in the world did you get that thing? I thought that there was only one that was given to my great grandmother many decades ago. It was turned over to the scientific community for study and we never saw it again. We thought that it was lost"

I explained that the people at Los Alamos Laboratories had given them for us to wear. In fact, I told her the entire story of how the scientists had spent years duplicating the device in order to protect themselves from the serpents.

"But why would you want to be protected from the serpents," Penny asked. "They are our protectors. Just look around this place, do you really think we would have all that we have without their assistance?"

"Actually, I think people are perfectly capable of creating things without the serpents' help. In fact, I suspect that we as a species would be very advanced without them at all."

Penny was now getting angry. She huffed, "Words like that are blasphemous, and I don't want you to ever talk like that again."

With that said there was an obvious division between us that would demand mending. I was not sure what to say but was relieved when she didn't demand that Charlie and I remove our amulets. Actually, the whole idea of Penny not asking us to remove them intrigued me. Maybe there was hope of a relationship after all. One thing I was certain about, I couldn't live with a girl who could read every thought I ever had. She had to respect my privacy and the most private thing in the world to me was my mind.

Finally, Charlie asked Juanita how they lived in a world where everyone could read everyone's mind?

"Actually, we don't," she answered. "We have to focus on one person at a time and they must be close to us and most importantly be willing to let us enter their minds. It has to be that way. Imagine if you could listen in on what everyone around you was saying. It would drive you crazy just trying to sort out all the different voices you would be hearing. The most interesting thing I have learned from the serpents is how to think in their hieroglyphic style. It is interesting but hard for me. Personally, I prefer to just talk to people like humans have always done. However, it is the only way that we can communicate with the serpents."

"How do you talk to the serpents?" Charlie asked Juanita.

"It is difficult for me to talk to the serpents; however, Penny is far better at it than I am." Everyone looked at Penny who by now had regained her composure and was thinking what to say as a response.

"Well, I grew up speaking a serpent language that was taught to me as a child. It is as natural for me to speak in serpent as it is to speak in human. There are other languages spoken around here too." As she tried in vain to redirect the conversation. She spoke of both Navajo and Spanish which was still being used by many of the people of Serpiente, but everyone generally spoke in English as it was known by all."

It was Charlie who asked the most important question of all. "Can we talk to you without the serpents hearing everything we are saying?"

"Serpents can only read your mind if they are in close proximity and if they are trying to. Take for example the serpent that shared your bedroom with you two last night. Teotihuacan could certainly read your minds"

With that revelation, both Charlie and me grimaced trying to remember everything they said to each other or even thought about. All they could remember thinking about as they went to sleep was having relations with the two girls. In this case, young love as well as lust had saved our lives.

Charlie brought the obvious question back, "How can we know when we can speak to you, without a serpent listening in on our conversation?"

Penny answered, "You can't, unless you are some distance from them. They roam the ranch on some days but most of the time they stay to themselves well up the canyon from here. They have a nest there and actually prefer to be left alone."

Charlie who was rubbing his chin where he used to have a beard asked, "How do you know they are close to you here?"

"We don't see them if that is what you are talking about. However, we can tell they are here by the mental pictures they share with us. In other words, we have a serpentine language that appears in our heads. We simply do what they ask us to do and we don't bother them. It is probably a good thing that you did not wear the amulets last night. They would know that something was up and would never have trusted you with them on. You would have died in your bed from a venomous bite and never have seen the serpent that was biting you. I will explain to them that you are wearing the amulet. They will then leave you alone."

Exploring Serpiente

We spent the day exploring the ranch, first on foot and later on horses. We were amazed at the wonderful things that were being done there. We were particularly impressed by the large structures with metal roofs and solar panels on them. Each one was a world into itself. Inside of one, all kinds of machine work were being done. Engines droned, powered by a gasoline engine that turned lathes which turned metal into every imaginable shape. In another large building, there were rows of vegetables that were being grown to provide food through the cold months of winter. In another large building a truck was dangling from an overhead hoist which allowed workers to install a new motor transmission. Of no particular interest at the time, was a large building where chickens were being raised. I could not imagine how they could use so many chickens in a community even as large as Serpiente. But then, Serpiente was no longer a ranch; it was a small community with over fifty buildings, most of them homes in which a growing population lived.

Outside and for miles around, fields grew all manner crops that would be processed into food to feed not only the humans but also the large array of farm animals such as chickens, hogs and cows. Penny suggested that they take a short ride up the serpentine canyons behind the old ranch house. Everyone agreed, and so we loaded up a picnic lunch and headed up the canyon, in reverse of what I had dreamed about.

As we followed what was now a well-worn trail, I asked, "We are not going to run into a nest of serpents are we?"

"No, they are well up the canyon. But if you want an adventure and don't mind a little hiking I could like to take you to a special place."

After a few miles of riding through typical canyon country down a well-worn road we dismounted from our horses and tied them off. Then we started up another foot trail to the rim of the canyon and down the other side until we came to a large pool of crystal clear water. The same pool that Corey and another Penny had discovered many years ago. We were famished so we ate our sandwiches then Penny surprised us all.

"Juanita and I are going for a swim." We had never dreamed that we would find ourselves swimming and naturally had not come prepared. "That's all right," Penny says. "We didn't bring swimsuits either." As that was said, Penny and Juanita slipped out of their clothes and dived into the cool but certainly not cold water. Charlie and I just stood there watching the whole spectacle for a few minutes not quite knowing what to do but with a little prodding from the girls we threw off our clothes and dived in after them. It was a joyous occasion splashing water on each other and rough housing in the water but as the afternoon waned we knew it would take some time to get back to the ranch house. It would be almost dark before we reached the bottom of the canyon.

Just as we came to the opening of the canyon I suddenly decided to ride my horse up a short trail where I could see for miles. Penny called for me to stop but I rode up to the crest of the hill anyway. There I could see the lights from another immense building far away on what at one time had been the Luna property. Returning to the group the first thing I asked was what was being done in that building.

"Oh, that building is off limits to all of us. The workmen are constructing something for the serpents and we are not allowed to visit it. They are afraid that one of us might get hurt there." Charlie and I looked at each other but didn't say anything.

The next few days very little happened. Charlie and I spent the day introducing ourselves to people and making ourselves useful. We found that the people were extremely friendly and seemed grateful when Charlie and I helped them with their chores. Everything seemed absolutely normal except we noticed, everyday a group of the men would load themselves into a pickup truck and disappear, making the drive that lead them to the large structure that was off limits. Everyone we talked to seemed to have no knowledge of what kind of work was being done there and when I approached one of the men who I had seen leaving to work there, I learned nothing.

"Oh, we are just building another machine shop in order to keep the tractors and trucks running around here," was the workman's reply. "The area is off limits to everyone here, because of all the heavy equipment that is there."

Being young boys, Charlie and I suggested returning to the pool where we stayed until the following afternoon exploring in the steps of Corey and the original Penny many years ago. We were amazed at the petroglyphs that were there and Penny even pointed out a Mayan petroglyph that she could read. It was the official seal of a Mayan chieftain who had at one time visited the place and in effect, it said; "Copal was here." Charlie and I were intrigued by the place with the small ruins that still made perfect camping spots and the waterfall that plummeted into the huge pool of water. We both were getting serious with the two girls and were doing all we could do to navigate them into separate quarters or at least ends of the pool. Finally, just when we thought we were about to get somewhere, Penny asked me to look up at the hill where we had come down. There were twenty or so young children along with an older man and women who stood starring down at us. Down the hill trail they came disrobing at the edge of the pool and diving in to join us.

By this time, we realized that in this community nudity was simply normal. We had to reconsider what we were doing with the girls. Perhaps the girls were not being suggestive at all when they removed their clothes, and went in the water. That was the way everyone here did it, including the elderly couple who had escorted the children.

I was having fun watching the predictable water fights that broke out between the children. Like all kids, they loved to sneak away to the swimming hole and play. After a while, I swam over to the elderly man who sat waist deep along the edge of the pool watching the children. I started up a conversation with him. The elderly man, who was of Navajo decent, seemed very amicable about getting to talk to the new people, he rarely, if ever got to speak to outsiders. We talked of Alaska, and the trip Charlie and I had taken to get here, including descriptions of the Red People we had to deal with. He seemed to have no knowledge of the Red People. We talked about the Hopis which he apparently knew a little about and the work that was being done in the fields and many other topics until I asked him about the children. Then the elderly gentleman became saddened by the turn in the conversation.

"There should be many more children in Serpiente," he said in a matter of fact way. "Many children die at childbirth. They are born unable to breathe and sometimes they have tiny heads. They die and we don't know why. Sometimes even healthy children just seem to die."

I couldn't understand what I was hearing.

"We have many children born here in Serpiente. Most of the people I know produced many children but most of them die."

"Wait a minute," I exclaimed. "You mean that during your years, children have been dying, one by one, and no one knows why?"

The old man appeared to be truly sad but now was worried about the ramifications of his replies. Suddenly he stood up and yelled for the children to put on their clothes, it was time to leave.

"Wait a minute," I pleaded, "All I want to know is what happens to the children who die here." The old man started to walk away but turned and answered, "It has been something that has happened around here for so long that no one says anything about it anymore. It is a mystery. We just have more children. I really can't tell you anything more. I don't know." At that, the old man and women started up and over the trail where there were wagons waiting that would take them down the canyon. I was deep in thought. Had the people here just come to except that many of the children would die? All kinds of thoughts entered my mind. Perhaps the serpents expected a sacrifice of children. Certainly, the population of Serpiente was growing, even if children were disappearing but how could they all simply be quiet about it? Then it dawned upon me that maybe, just maybe, the old man had been far braver than he had realized. Maybe the truth bothered him too and because of his advanced years, he wasn't afraid to expose the problem. Then the truth dawned upon me, after really looking at the children. The children were victims of inbreeding. Many of them exhibited classic symptoms of genetic problems for which I had no name to attach.

We talked of the serpents. The old man could identify three serpents, Quetzalcoatl and Kukulcan, the king and queen, and Teotihuacan, the serpent's emissary.

Teotihuacan is the serpent that we have to deal with. Quetzalcoatl and Kukulcan rarely visit us. They are serpent royalty who deal with humans through Teotihuacan.

Charlie and I got together and I mentioned to him, "Have you noticed something around here that seems strange."

"What?" Charlie asked. "The only thing that is strange around here is twenty naked kids and two naked old people."

I explained, "Well, the old man talks about Teotihuacan, Quetzalcoatl and Kukalcan. They only know of three serpents around here. There is no mention or knowledge of Tikal and the Painted People or Tsotzil and the Red Face People. Evidently, because of the serpent royalty that lives here, everyone is living under a truce."

"Perhaps," Charlie reflected, "They are unaware of the Red Face and Painted People. After all, Penny and Juanita have said nothing about them. We need to be careful of what we say and learn more."

The Luna Project

After almost four weeks since we had arrived in Serpiente, we finally got the opportunity we had been waiting for. Most of the people who lived at the ranch house proper had traveled into what was left of Albuquerque in order to haul away goods such as coffee and sugar from the stores wherever it could be found in bulk. They also took a large truck with a tank on the back in order to siphon gasoline from one of the large storage tanks they had discovered. It would take them until the following day so that night we made plans to sneak out and discover what was being built in the large building that was off limits.

As soon as it was dark we climbed out of the window that allowed light into our room. We were at the last structure and easily found ourselves following the trail up to the mouth of the canyon. Then following the same trail, I had discovered, we climbed over the rim of the canyon and into the sagebrush flats that separated the old Luna property from the ranch house. It was actually considerably closer this way than by following the old dirt road which crossed numerous arroyos and the wet stream of Serpiente Canyon which was flowing with a few inches of water. Water that at one time simply disappeared into the sand but now was impounded by a lined lake where fish were raised. We were following the same trail that John Luna had ridden over many times on his favorite horse in a different age. None the less, it was an arduous hike, up and down deep arroyos where water flowed after flash floods. Well before morning we finally came to within a hundred yards of the building.

The exterior of the building had small lights that illuminated the grounds around the entire place making anyone or anything that approached it highly visible. There appeared to be only one way in. We thought it strange that the building was roughly triangular shaped and the roof was different than the other roofs we had seen in Serpiente. There were no solar panels on the flat structure, it appeared to not be a roof at all but rather some kind of fabric like a large tent that kept rain out but was easily removed. The solar panels we were so used to seeing on top of the buildings were set up in a field alongside, taking up a large area. At the door sat a single man who was obviously extremely bored and sleepy.

"Why would they need a guard here?" Charlie whispered.

"I don't know, but it's obvious we can't look inside as long as he is there." Then after watching for only a few more minutes the man got out of his seat and disappeared inside the building.

"This is our chance," I said.

We quickly ran over to the door which had fortunately been left ajar and looked in. At first, we had no idea what we were looking at. A huge gleaming metallic object in the basic shape of a triangle sat on massive wooden scaffolds. The machine had no wheels and had a large opening in the top where it was still being constructed. Charlie and I returned to the trail, out of sight and walked fast for some time before we stopped to talk.

"What in the world is it?" asked Charlie.

I answered him, "I don't know, but if it is what I think it is, we may have a serious problem on our hands."

"Okay, what do you think it is?" Charlie asked.

"Well, when I was a kid living in Alaska we had some books and a lot of old magazines that we used to read over and over. One of those books was called *War of the Worlds* and it showed a picture of a large alien craft that flew through space. There were also pictures of similar flying machines on the computers back at Los Alamos. I think we are looking at a spaceship, a machine that can take people, or maybe in this case, serpents to the stars."

Mercury

The following day the caravan from Albuquerque arrived back in Serpiente. Charlie and I helped them unload three truck-loads of looted goods. The stores in Albuquerque had been long ago stripped of usable goods but the warehouses that supplied those stores had been sealed from looting since the time of the pathogen. Given time and the right tools, the workmen from Serpiente went right through the walls of the warehouses. Now they were able to systematically remove loads of goods out of the stores and then seal them off afterwards just in case other humans showed up. There was also a truck loaded with a large tank of fuel that was siphoned into another holding tank. But the last truck to be unloaded appeared to be something that was going to go to the mysterious building that was being used to construct an alien ship. Charlie finally was able to get a look inside of the back of the covered truck, what he found mystified him. It contained two round cans that were sealed. Looking around him and discovering no one watching he climbed into the bed of the truck under a makeshift cloth shell which kept water out and broke the seal of one of the containers. To his surprise, he found them filled with a metallic silver liquid, what was known in another time as mercury. As Charlie started to climb back out of the truck he found himself face to face with Jim Hidalgo and three large men, the same men that traveled to the Luna property every day.

"You and your friend Chato need to come with us," Jim, the leader told him. We were marched up to the ranch house and told to sit down at the kitchen table where a small group of people were gathering including Penney and Juanita. Jim started the conversation, "We have been very kind to both of you but you have broken the basic laws of our community. We had hoped that you would join our community and maybe even decide to mate with Penny and Juanita. Our serpent friends have explained that we need genetic variation to have a healthy population here." He looked straight into my eyes and said, "That is the only reason you were summoned here. The serpents discovered that of all the people left on earth you had the right genetic makeup to suit our needs. You are very intelligent but it is more than that. Without your genes, the effects of inbreeding will become worse. In fact, it has already started to become a major problem with some of our children. We have lost many children, but your actions have complicated what we are doing here."

Charlie asked, "Exactly what have we done to complicate what you are doing here?"

"We know that you are wearing amulets that have been supplied to you from the people who live on the mountain north of here. We really didn't care. There is very little that we want to know about your private thoughts but we know you snuck out of the house and discovered what we are doing on the Luna property. Do you really think that wearing those amulets could keep the serpents from following you and reporting it to us? They watched your every move and then we found Charlie examining the contents of the truck."

"Well, you are hauling some kind of metallic liquid you found in Albuquerque, what possible use could it have for you?" Charlie asked.

Jim was obviously getting angry at the question. He answered, "The liquid provides a gyroscope in which an antigravity pod is installed. It is what powers the spaceship. Now do you understand?"

He knew that we had no idea what he was talking about and he seemed to be bragging about his own knowledge of the project. "You are restricted to the ranch house. If you leave the ranch house you must be escorted by one of us. If you break that simple rule you will both be forced to provide genetic material and then be killed. It is your choice, mate with the girls and live in comfort here at the ranch house or die!"

Everyone got out of their chairs and left the ranch house, leaving behind Penny, Juanita, and two angry young men. Now that my purpose in being 'summoned' to the community of Serpiente was clearly understood, I immediately began to reevaluate my purpose for being here. I was saddened by the thought that I had truly found the girl of my dreams and that we could create a new life for ourselves, but now, I realized that my entire purpose was to provide genetic material. I couldn't stomach it.

Espanola

The serpent Tikal was determined to learn the secrets of Los Alamos Laboratories. He was aware of what Teotihuacan was developing in Serpiente and he knew of the spaceship that was being built there but he also knew that it would be impossible to fly without computer technology. Even a serpent could not fly a spaceship without the aid of artificial intelligence. The artificial intelligence did far more than plotting a course and actually flying the ship. The weight of the ship rested on the force produced by an antigravity pod that negated gravity. Theoretically, the greater the gravity that pulls on the ship, the greater the force it could exert in the opposite direction. Gravity turned upon itself, which is why those particular types of spaceships seem to flitter about like butterflies. With the force of the entire earth's gravity pushing them, rather than pulling them, the combined matter that makes up the earth would exert considerable gravity.

When gravity is inverted as aboard a spaceship, it becomes very powerful, and it can turn on a dime while in sub-orbit. Once in space, the ship was very powerful. The ship was not pushed along, rather it was pulled by the force of a faraway gravity source. Only a tiny force was required to actually pull the weightless ship through space. Gravity itself is a weak force that only works when there is enough mass to allow mutual attraction, as on a small planet. The spaceship travels while increasing in speed until mid-point is reached, then the ship would flip over and the same device worked as a break. The energy output of the gyroscopic mercury produced an excess of energy which would power the ship through empty space regardless.

Artificial intelligence is what controls the gyroscopic mercury. Once set to spinning, it spins at an incredible rate, providing the gyroscopic effects that allow the ship to balance itself, it was an easily maintained and self-contained reaction. Tikal knew perfectly well that a ship was being built in Serpiente, his friend Teotihuacan had told him all about it. Tikal also knew that it was extremely difficult to navigate a spaceship and achieve orbit before the mercury gyroscope was safe to operate at full capacity. Once in space, after it reached a critical spin, the energy it produced was far greater than what it took to get it spinning. It would spin until it reached a frequency, like a large bell ringing. Then as the spin increased, physics would change inside the spinning mass. Enormous amounts of energy could be generated. But Tikal was pretty sure it all had to be activated while in space, where there was no background gravity which would warp the spin causing a catastrophic explosion. That background gravity could only be negated and controlled, in fact the entire process had to be controlled by artificial intelligence. There was only one place on the planet that now possessed access to the kind of artificial intelligence that was required; Los Alamos.

He had thought about the possibilities of leaving earth many times, Tikal would think about the possibilities that the galaxy could provide him. There were many life forms he could dominate. But it all seemed impossible to Tikal. It would take a herculean effort here on earth just to teach the local humans how to construct such a spaceship. He realized that there is always one more highly technical project that would have to be done. Then his mind would drift back to his imprisonment on this planet called earth.

But Tikal also enjoyed being who he was. He was the magic that held his tribe together. His warriors were an artistic impression of himself. He directed the artisans who illustrated the men and women who became warriors and offered them pleasure while the inking was going on.

After staying in Albuquerque, Tikal made a point to win his warriors back to him. The last evening was a sexual ceremony. Next to the fire, they all danced themselves into frenzy, then spending much of the evening mating and exchanging partners. Tikal manipulated the pleasure centers of each warrior's brain into ecstasy. With all the designs moving and interlocking, they appeared like a nest of serpents themselves. The serpent was always crawling among them. Then, with nightfall, they all fell into a healing sound sleep induced by the serpent.

When they awoke, the warriors finished off any remaining food and then without saying anything, they began to disperse in groups of three. Within an hour, they had all left in a northern route, forming a wide line of warriors. They would trap and find as much food as they needed that way, few animals could escape the warriors' arrows. But mostly, by splitting up, if they were attacked, only three of them engaged in a fight. Usually that was more than enough. The rest would, by using stealth, remain invisible from possible Los Alamos Spies. Tikal imagined warriors from Los Alamos watching the entire Rio Grande Valley from the high rim rocks.

Tikal rightfully suspected that there were many people who actually lived in the laboratories, far more than the small groups of workers who tended the fields along the west side of the river. That many people meant a high degree of sophistication. Tikal wondered what kind of artificial intelligence might be there. He visualized a honeycomb of people living there with tunnels or caverns reaching far below the surface. Most of Los Alamos was underground, he rightly hypothesized.

It was nothing for Tikal to metamorphose into a raven and cross the river, but for his warriors, it was another thing altogether. Tikal, as well as all serpents, held a personal aversion to swimming. Swimming brought their body temperature down to dangerous levels, or to put it politely, swimming hurt and the serpents avoided it at all cost. Therefore, his warriors never learned to swim and reflecting their master, they avoided all contact with water except to drink. They all came together in Espanola, meeting in a deathly quiet camp, forty or so people, and twenty warriors. They took refuge in a building that was actually a large vacant grocery store, the display racks had long ago been removed by someone, probably one of the ancient ones. The warriors arrived and within an hour or two, everyone was accounted for. A search of the community revealed many homes that had never been looted and they helped themselves, stealing from the dead.

Scouts were sent out and within a few hours, they learned that the bridge that crossed over to the west bank was there, but it was completely covered with hundreds of dead trees, brush and sections of many destroyed houses. The river flowed through the whole mess that was impacted against the bridge. They spread out, in groups of three and camped.

Working independently, Tikal's warriors and workers, found all manner of tools that could help them solve the problem with the bridge and fence. This time Tikal was serious. Not just testing. He wanted to achieve real results, but the real problem was the fence. Searching through the farm store they found what they were seeking, bolt cutters with rubber handles. This time, the fence would not be able to bite back.

Tikal was concerned about the time it would take to clear a trail through the brush. He was sure that the humans from Los Alamos would spot the work being done and compromise the entire mission. He also thought about simply sending a single warrior down, maybe one of the females, and let her set the wood ablaze. But Tikal was worried about the consequences. What if the bridge itself caught fire? The black stuff that the ancients used to make roads out of would melt and then probably burn. Would the bridge even be passable after a great fire? What would happen when the people of Los Alamos saw a huge plume of smoke which would be created, and certainly be visible from Los Alamos. Tikal also considered, and then produced a serpentine smile, realizing a fire could slow the warriors from Los Alamos, if they were chasing them.

After a couple of days, one of the men who had come along, came forward with an idea. He had been hunting along the river and had found a wide place in the river that would allow them a crossing. He had himself, already walked all the way to the other side and back. If the warriors could overcome their fear of being washed down the river, they could easily cross and avoid all the complications with the bridge. Tikal thought it would be a good idea. They could cross the river at night and wait until the workers showed up the next day to attack. The main problem was not letting the workers escape and return to the rim in their vehicles.

At first, it worked exactly as Tikal thought it would. The workers, twelve men and two women who prepared a lunch for the workers, had driven the fifteen-minute drive to the river in three electric trucks, unloaded garden tools and settled into getting rid of the small weeds that had spouted around the base of the much larger food producing plants. Today they were working on chilies and cantaloupes, but at noon, the two women called the workers back to the trucks where they had prepared a lunch for the men. They were aware of the Painted people, on the other side of the river, but didn't fear an attack because of the river.

Suddenly a volley of arrows came down on them, impaling two of the agricultural workers. Once immobilized, they were quickly chopped to pieces by the Painted warriors. The remaining workers fled to the safety of the vehicles which protected them from flying projectiles, but would be of no use if the trucks were actually caught by the warriors. The twelve of them that were still alive put their electric trucks into gear and headed back up the road. Two of the trucks escaped with four occupants in each one, however the last one was momentarily captured by the painted warriors before it could get back on the main road. Four warriors were killed as the workers took out automatic arms and shot anyone who got close to the truck.

Dragonfly and the scientists at Los Alamos knew the tribe had come together in Espanola, but they calculated the warriors could not get across the river from that side, without actually getting in the river. No one at the laboratories would have guessed the warriors could cross the river. It would be the first time it had ever occurred as far as they knew. The scientists watched in horror as the attack took place and quickly prepared for the eventual encounter that would surely occur at the fence.

It took almost two hours for the warriors to climb up the road to the top of the rim. Once there they stopped for a minute to rest while one warrior walked over to the fence and using a pair of bolt cutters with rubber covered handles, started cutting through the wire. It snapped and lots of sparks flew but the warrior was able to actually cut a large opening through the chain link metal. Within only a few minutes they were standing outside a glass door looking in at the freighted people inside. A different warrior, a female wearing nothing but moccasins on her feet, with a large sledge hammer walked up to the door and started a long swing to burst through the glass, but she was stung on the side of the neck. They had experienced many bee and wasp stings before; therefore, she thought little of it. But, the warrior hesitated, before she could really swing at the door she dropped the sledge hammer, leaning against the handle to the consternation of the remaining fifteen warriors. She stumbled forward a little and fell down where she collapsed into unconsciousness. Within a few minutes the entire troop of warriors found themselves swatting at the tiny insects, but the insects won. Within three minutes all of them were sound asleep.

The doors of the building then opened and several well-armed soldiers walked out and put the warriors into handcuffs and leg irons. Then workers with stretchers came out and loaded the unconscious warriors on them delivering them to the confines of the box.

The only ambiguity was the appearance of a raven that flew into the building while the door was opened, and disappeared inside, a raven that was actually the serpent, Tikal.

Tikal had sacrificed his best warriors just to gain entry into the mysterious complex. The warriors were of no consequence to him, they were easily replaced, but now he had to gain control over the scientists who lived there and he was experiencing trouble right away. He could not find a single mind which he could read.

Pamela's Dilemma

Pamela had kept track of the Painted warriors ever since they had attempted to attack the fence on the other side of the compound. They had failed miserably but then regrouped at the park in Albuquerque. She had also watched every move Charlie and I had made; wanting to warn us of several possible encounters. Instead she never gave away the fact that we were being monitored. She had giggled while we had been watched over by an elderly human lady. But more importantly, she had watched as the Painted People held a ceremonial meeting where despite all the dancing they had also done a lot of talking about Los Alamos. The serpent, Tikal clearly made his warriors aware of his plans. The warriors could see the images in their minds. They knew exactly what to do.

The problem was, Pamela had no idea what Tikal was planning. They had followed the warriors, using thermal imaging all the way to Espanola where the scientist knew the warriors would run into a dead end with the bridges. The warriors could have continued traveling north to the tiny communities that were located along the Rio Grande River, until they could find an intact bridge, but Tikal had no idea how far north they would have to venture before they discovered a passable bridge. It would take much time and effort and he wasn't sure that there was a way across further north so he sent out a trio of spies to discover the facts for him. The only practical way they could cross the river was by actually getting in the river, and that had never happened in all of the history of the Painted people. Like their serpent master, they feared the river. The scientists suspected that they would continue going north until they found an intact bridge, but this time they were in for a surprise.

After the assemblage in Espanola they were distracted from what was occurring in Serpiente because of the impending attack on Los Alamos. When the attack actually occurred, all resources were focused upon the Painted warriors. The agricultural workers were totally surprised by the river crossing, but everyone was much more amazed that the warriors had figured out the secret of the fence. Fortunately, the tiny dragonflies delivered up sixteen warriors.

The Painted warriors were kept in the metal box that was designed to hold them. After losing contact with Tikal, the warriors milled around for a while then attacked the door. Each time they struck it they received an electrical shock. The scientists then turned on the electricity to the floor, and watched as the warriors hopped around for an hour or so trying to climb on each other to escape the floor.

Finally, after they were totally exhausted, the electricity was mercifully turned off and the door was opened and one at a time they were removed from the box. Two guards would escort each struggling warrior to the infirmary and the warrior was put under anesthesia, each warrior was then surgically implanted with an owl amulet, just under the cranium, next to the brain. It was a form of trepanning but a very well done procedure. Experiencing total amnesia, when they awoke, it was to whole new world. They were allowed to eat, and then were taken care of for one day. Then they were escorted to the opposite site of the compound and released outside of the fence. They would then wonder off, helpless, in complete isolation from Tikal. They could no longer wage war. Not having a serpent to tell them what to do, and without the support and hard work of an army of humans in the tribe, many would die during the next winter. It was a cruel end for the Painted warriors; however, it was far less cruel than what they would have done to any hostage.

When Pamela finally got back to watching Charlie and me, she had lost us. Then two days later, she saw Charley and me walking around Serpiente with the dark-haired and blond girl. Pamela felt very real pangs of jealousy as she watched us on her computer screen but Pamela was very professional, she wouldn't let her private affair with Charley come between her and her professionalism.

Tikal found a large metal cabinet with a small electric motor in the back of it which was mounted to the wall. The motor put out just enough warmth to keep Tikal comfortable. Curling up around the motor, invisible to all the humans, Tikal contemplated his situation. He was more than a little mystified. He was now trapped and could not understand how it was possible for the humans to have acquired the ability to completely block his probes, but as he scouted around the buildings, he realized that the scientists were extremely gifted, particularly when it came to such things as artificial intelligence, and Tikal realized that they were using the technology the ancient ones had passed down to them, but they had improved it significantly in two hundred years.

The humans at Los Alamos were unaware of Tikal as he explored every aspect of the community. He had become ravenous until he found a large room where hundreds of mice were being raised, part of a medical research project. He helped himself to several of them so he wouldn't need to return for a long while. But the following day, when the mice were counted, the missing mice became a problem. Nobody could explain it.

Angie Wilkerson finally called for a general assembly of all the laboratory personnel and made an important announcement to the combined group who was there. "Let me get right to the point. We here at Los Alamos Laboratories, have recently come under attack. As you all know, some of our beloved soldiers and workers have lost their lives recently as a result of an attack by the Painted Warriors. They put forth an extraordinary amount of work and preparation for their attack upon us, and we are all thinking that we defeated them. But we didn't." Everyone got very quiet when she said that.

"Let me show you something," With a wave of her hand, a large section of the wall turned into an image of an outside door. Everyone knew it was the same door they had brought the Painted warriors through. Everyone watched as litter after litter of people carried the bizarre and colorful creatures into the building where they were put into the box. Then, there was a tiny flash of black that punctured the air above the heads of the soldiers, who apparently didn't notice it. Nobody noticed it until the computer ran a self-check and found the object.

Angie froze the frame with the palm of her hand then calmly took two fingers and enlarged the flash of black over and over until a large raven could plainly be seen, with its wings tucked back and under as a diving bird does.

"Let me ask a question to all of you, has anyone here seen a raven flying around this or any other building?"

Everyone looked around at each other but not a single person acknowledged that they had seen anything unusual. Angie pointed up at the eye of the raven, "What you see there is a serpent, probably Tikal, the leader of the Painted Warriors. After he entered, he morphed into a serpent shape and probably disappeared somewhere into the plumbing. We need to use thermos imaging sensors and find him. As soon as we find him, we seal off that area and send for our friends in herpetology. I feel certain that they can deal with a serpent in whatever form it takes. As soon as we find it, it goes into the box. Remember, as long as you wear the amulets it cannot harm you unless you have a direct physical confrontation with it. A direct confrontation with a serpent could be extremely dangerous. They can strike, and are extremely venomous. The main thing I want to say to you is use common sense around these creatures; you will be dealing with a highly intelligent creature, but it can be handled just like any biological creature."

The air conditioning was turned as low as possible and a search begin. Technicians systematically searched each connecting hallway and building.

A few hours later, one of the scientists found a refrigerator that was close to the original entrance. The sensor, when slid behind the unit, observed up close revealed a serpentine shape at 76 degrees curled up around a motor that normally put out a temperature of 86 degrees. The herpetologists, true to their natural ability to use the tools of their trade, enclosed the serpent, Tikal in a glass box with a lid.

He was taken directly to the box, where he was dropped off in the middle of it and released.

Tikal was furious; he had never been taken hostage before. He crawled out of his glass box and explored the walls, never touching them. He could sense the flow of electricity that was invisible to most. Tikal knew if he touched it, it would hurt. He returned to the glass box in the center of the room, for the first time in his existence he was completely at the mercy of others. He would need to contemplate how to conquer his conquerors and Angie Wilkerson wondered how she would conquer Tikal.

After a full week of searching for evidence of other attacks and finding nothing, Pamela was able to return her Dragonfly's attention to Serpiente and the whereabouts of Charlie and me. She was obviously in love with Charlie but she knew he would have to play along to get to the bottom of what was occurring at Serpiente. Pamela also knew that sometime in the future she would have a reckoning with Charlie. It was one thing for him to spy for the scientists; it was another thing for him to have relations with a dark-haired beauty.

Teotihuacan's Dilemma

Teotihuacan was aware of the terrible defeat of Tikal, he was also sure that Quetzalcoatl and Kukulcan knew of Tikal's defeat. Even Tsotzil became aware of the defeat which satisfied him as he was always jealous of Tikal. But even an enemy like Tikal was still a serpent and Tsotzil and the Red Face warriors could be enlisted to rescue Tikal.

Teotihuacan was worried. He knew if Quetzalcoatl or Kukulcan discovered his duplicity as serpent emissary, they might kill him. But Kukulcan was pregnant with a dozen new serpents that would greatly expand the royal domain. In a short while, there would be replacements for all of the remaining serpents.

The serpent royalty was each a world unto itself. Quetzalcoatl and Kukulcan were determined to work with the humans whom they had enlisted in order to escape earth. The plan had been working now for two hundred years, ever since the great pandemic; and they felt like it was their only hope of escaping the bounds of earth's gravity. The serpents had even recognized and found a solution to the human queen's genetic problems. Her offspring would all be born deformed without the genes present in Chatos' DNA. Teotihuacan had even instructed Tsotzil to release Charlie and Chato, but they had disappeared before the serpent Tsotzil could intervene. All contact with Charlie and Chato was lost and they were presumed dead. Teotihuacan was, for a while in great trouble until one day the ranch workers found the two boys just outside the settlement of Serpiente, much to his relief.

Teotihuacan's situation was extremely precarious. He had condoned the return to earlier methods of dealing with humans when it came to Tsotzil and Tikal knowing that if Quetzalcoatl and Kukulcan found out they would be extremely displeased. He too enjoyed the release of energy from the sacrificed humans, but he also knew that cooperating with the humans was their only chance of escape. Humans were the only creatures that could do the complicated mechanical construction required to build a spaceship. He had hoped to keep the actions of the Painted People a secret from Quetzalcoatl and Kukulcan until it didn't really matter anymore. Now he would be called to the royal court and be required to account for his actions.

The Captive Tikal

Angie Wilkerson calmly slipped into a pair of rubber soled shoes and walked onto the floor of the box. Tikal nervously watched her get to within a dozen feet of him and Angie angrily shouted, "All right Tikal, you have managed to get yourself captured and your tribe is now in complete disarray. Without you to tell them what to do they are utterly helpless, frankly I doubt if any of your warriors will last the next winter. They are like children alone in the world. They have taken off in all directions and can no longer be controlled by you or any other serpent. But you and I have a reckoning to deal with. It is not just the people here at Los Alamos that you want, you want something else. What is it?"

Tikal arose out of his glass box thinking of getting just a little closer to Angie Wilkerson before delivering a strike. He would sink his fangs into her calf and that would be the end of this pesky human, it never dawned on him that the floor would be electrified, after all, how could the human be in there with him? He brought his head up almost half the length of his body before he let it drop down to the floor. Instantly he was writhing in pain from the shock that set his entire body into convulsions. Using a probe, just like the herpetologists used, Wilkerson carefully picked the serpent up then set it back into the glass box. It took several minutes for the shock to wear off and for Tikal to regain his senses. Then Angie Wilkerson asked the same question, "What is it that you want of us?"

Tikal of course had no way of communicating with her because of the amulet she wore. She gained the attention of Tikal and slipped the amulet off of her neck and held it away from her body. Tikal understood the gesture and entered her mind.

Again, Angie asked, "What do you want of us?

Tikal answered her, "To die!"

"No, there is much more you want," Angie says. "I suspect that you want to capture our technology and use it against us or for some other diabolical reason."

Angie Wilkerson placed the amulet back over her head and says, "You stay in here and think about your predicament for a while. Maybe when you are hungry enough we can do some useful communicating." With that said she retreated to the door of the box and wouldn't return until the mice had been digested and all their useful energy had been expended. She also lowered the temperature in the box to sixty degrees, very cool, particularly for a serpent. Tikal would require spending energy just to maintain a bearable body temperature.

Penny's Discovery

Penny and I walked up to the picnic area that had provided cook outs for over two hundred years. Sitting there on wooden chairs built from cottonwood limbs and wood planking to allow a comfortable chair, I decided to confront Penny with details of serpent culture that she seemed to be unaware of. But on this occasion, I held her close and actually held the amulet over Penny's head, which she objected to, however by talking as sweet as I could and using a lie I thought that I could get through to her. "You don't want everyone to know what we are talking about when it comes to love, particularly when it comes to solving certain genetic difficulties?" I reasoned with her.

She seemed to relax as I held the tiny amulet in my hand over her head. I had also brought a bottle of local wine if all else failed. At least for the first time since I had arrived we could talk in private. I spoke about many sweet things to her, going for short trips, teaching me to make ceramics, about love making. She seemed content with her head resting on my arm. Finally, I got around to the real subject.

I asked, "Do you mind if I ask you a couple of questions about the serpents?"

"Sure, go ahead."

"Why are the serpents leading tribes of vicious warriors who are preying on other human beings? Why do they eat the humans they capture?"

Penny's eyes flashed anger but instead of leaving mad, she wanted to hear more. I told her all about our experiences with the Red Face People, and the Painted People. She listened for more than an hour in a state of disbelief. Finally, Penny's eyes welled up with tears.

"I suppose that you will never want to be with a creature such as me again?"

I quickly responded, "That is a wrong assumption. You truly are the girl of my dreams, and I would certainly want to marry you, however, we need to resolve the serpent problem before we can have our own lives where we can be free of the serpents."

"Why would I want to be free of the serpents," Penny asked, showing her frustration, "This is their home as well as ours. They have lived among us for hundreds of years. They visit me in my dreams and share images."

"Yes, I have also experienced visions, but I am not serpent. I wear the amulet. Besides, you need to know, there are actually a few thousand-people living out there, all descendants of the first survivors of the plague; the people in Serpiente are not the only ones that survived the pandemic."

Penny seemed in agreement to at least talk some more about it, but her feelings were obviously hurt. She just couldn't understand it. It would take several afternoons sitting under the cottonwood trees before I could explain everything to her. I discovered she had been unaware of Tsotzil and Tikal, and of what they were doing. She only knew of the three serpents of Serpiente. Teotihuacan was the serpent she had always had dealings with. It all seemed like a lie to her. She had been so enamored by her relationship with the serpents that she couldn't believe she had been deceived. She had to find out for herself.

She confronted Teotihuacan.

"What can you tell me about two serpents who do not live here in Serpiente?"

Teotihuacan swung his long neck back at the question, fearing the repercussions of the answers. He knew if the knowledge of human genocide was exposed, he would have to answer to Quetzalcoatl and Kukulcan. But at this time in serpent culture and history, the serpent royalty was dealing with a long and difficult pregnancy. Kukulcan was nearing the limit to her birthing years and she was the only female.

Teotihuacan had always represented the serpents when dealing with humans. But recently, all matters of state were turned over to the Teotihuacan, they left everything to him.

Teotihuacan explained, "They are following the same procedure in their lands as we are doing here, that is, we are all attempting to create a meaningful state of peace between our species, so we can all be better off."

Penny pointedly asked again, "What can you tell me about the two serpents that do not live here?"

Teotihuacan was at an impasse, making the decision all serpents would naturally make, he lied and made up a story about Tikal and Tsotzil to tell Penny.

"Tsotzil is the leader of the Red Face People. They live alone in western Arizona and live like the ancient people who lived there more than a thousand years before the people who caused the great pandemic. They are an agrarian people who live in their own world, unaware that there are others, like us. You need to realize that it was Quetzalcoatl and Kukulcan's idea to split up the serpents to better our chances of survival. After all, we are the only remains of a vast empire of serpents that lived here before the great pandemic. Back then, the five of us were very isolated from the nest; we survived by staying hidden away. That is why we separated, not only for us but for the good of the humans as well."

Causally Penny asked, "Why are they known as the Red Face People?"

Teotihuacan answered, "They wear three stripes of red ochre, it is a way for them to maintain a cultural cohesiveness, rather than living apart. Trust me; they are a harmless people who are blissfully unaware of other people around them."

"And of Tikal," Penny asked?

Teotihuacan was in a quandary. How could Penny have known the serpent's name? He thought Penny was totally unaware of what was beyond Serpiente, and for the most part, he was correct.

Intervention of the Helicopter

It had taken a week for things to settle down in Los Alamos after the discovery of Tikal, wrapped around a refrigerator motor. Tikal had refused to communicate with the scientists. He felt he should have easily been able to conquer them once inside the Laboratories; instead it had been a trap. Put into isolation and unable to communicate with his fellow serpents, for all practical purposes to the other serpents he had died. Tikal was informed that he would receive one mouse a month. With the cold environment he was living in, and being unable to communicate in any way, Tikal would at times wish he had died, however, there was still hope that the scientists would make a mistake and he would escape.

Angie Wilkerson and her fellow scientists who governed Los Alamos were at an impasse. Pamela had lost all ability to communicate with Charlie and me, and could only get glimpses of us as we walked from one building to another. The dragonflies were unknown to the people of Serpiente, however they had limitations. They could spy but they could not communicate to others. Nor did the dragonflies have the capacity to carry anything but electronic information and it was doubted that Serpiente had access to computer technology. The technicians did however have many forms of hover craft called drones that could deliver a message and Angie Wilkerson wanted to make a statement.

One of the two Apache helicopters that had been packed away for the last eighty years was unpacked and made ready to fly. The pilot found himself in a box flying an imaginary helicopter desperately relearning a skill that had long ago been forgotten. The difference was, now they had a computer assisted pilot program that took over well before the pilot was about to make a fatal mistake. Actually, a child could have flown the machine.

At high noon, most of the residents of Serpiente were amazed when a large machine flew over their homes stopping just out of range of any small arms that could be fired at them. Hovering in space above the buildings, a small object was dropped out of the door and after a fall of some one hundred feet, it exploded making a loud concussive noise but was in itself harmless. Then out of the door of the chopper a small box was dropped with a parachute that allowed it to drop into the center of the community where it was picked up and rushed to the ranch house where Penny, Juanita, Charlie and I, and of course Teotihuacan waited.

Inside the box, called a brief case, was a bound document directed to the leadership of Serpiente. It described in detail the attack of Tikal and his warriors, as well as photographs of Tikal while he was in a visible form as well as several photographs of Painted warriors who were sedated before amulets were implanted next to their brains. Penny and Juanita had never seen people who looked so bizarre but could certainly guess what their function was; to wage war against other humans for the sake of the serpents. Finally, a map was provided showing a route up the west side of the Rio Grande River which would direct them to the front gate of Los Alamos where they would be received. The last paragraph offered a truce for the meeting with guarantees that the delegation from Serpiente would be guaranteed safe passage.

An ultimatum was also issued. Either Serpiente needed to meet and agree to some kind of truce whereby the warlike actions of the serpents would cease, or a state of war would exist between Los Alamos and the communities ruled by serpents, including Serpiente.

A War with Los Alamos?

Teotihuacan was confronted by the information in the documents and decided to go on the offensive, before he gave away too many facts. He asked Penny, "What do you know of Tikal?"

Penny, knowing the facts would come out eventually answered him, "I know that he is a captive of the scientists who live at Los Alamos."

The unusual and unexpected statement caused Teotihuacan to drop low, placing his head in a defensive posture. His skin flashed colors up and down, he was embarrassed.

Penny continued, "I know that he sacrificed all his human warriors in a dim-witted attack on the scientists! I know that you have deceived me, and probably Quetzalcoatl and Kukulcan as well. There was supposed to be a truce with the humans so they could live and prosper, but Tsotzil and Tikal instead went back to the old ways of dealing with my people. They enslaved them, turning them into ruthless killers, all to provide Tikal with pleasure. What did they do with their hostages?"

Finally, after a few seconds had passed for dramatic effect, Penny asked the serpent, "What did they eat at their ceremonials?"

Teotihuacan was taken aback. Finally, he answered, "Many years ago I lost all control over Tzotzil and Tikal. They seemed to hold me in contempt. They are not part of us anymore and have not been for many years. The best I could do was to arrange to have Serpiente off limits to attacks. Whenever a dominant species is conquered by another, there is complete breakdown of the conquered culture. It is only through consideration, that humans are allowed to live at all. Conquered species tend to do better when they are directed and controlled. We serpents are only doing what is in our nature. There are winners and losers but sometimes a compromise must be made. That is what has happened between the serpents and the fine citizens at Serpiente."

Penny, for the first time in her life realized how deeply she had been lied to.

Finally, Teotihuacan says, "You are part serpent yourself. If the Kukulcan finds she cannot carry the serpents within her, they will be transferred to you to give live birth for her."

This was a lie but Teotihuacan thought placing the idea into Penny's head might give him some leverage.

The thought caused Penny to feel a revulsion she had never experienced before. Now instead of being royalty, she had been delegated to being a human incubator.

Charlie and Penny studied the documents carefully and sure enough, the story I had been sharing with Penny about the serpents, was now believed. A council was held inside of the ranch house with the same men who had earlier captured Charlie and me, led by Jim Hidalgo. Teotihuacan was not invited even though he knew what was being spoken about.

Penny started, "We do not want a war with Los Alamos, they have been our friends for hundreds of years and certainly we have little hope in defeating them if war is inevitable. Besides, war would not solve the problem of Tsotzil nor would it solve the problem of the other serpents." Penny as well as the other residents of Serpiente decided that they would accept the invitation to venture to Los Alamos. Teotihuacan would have nothing to do with any peace gestures.

Early in the morning three gasoline powered trucks, loaded with extra gas, soldiers armed with bows and arrows, and Penny, Charlie and I left the tiny community of Serpiente. Juanita stayed at home knowing that her presence might cause a problem after Charlie took her aside and revealed his relationship with Pamela.

Peace Council

*I*t took the entire day to get to the gates of Los Alamos. The route required several stops in order to remove small trees that had grown through the asphalt making passage difficult. Just as the sun was going down we appeared at the gates of Los Alamos. There was not a single person in sight behind the fence. Then the gate magically opened as it had done before, and we drove the three trucks into the parking lot that still contained a few rusty cars that ancient scientists had driven.

A single elderly lady walked out of the building and raised her hand in a gesture of palms out, with no weapons. She then returned inside the building and the group from Serpiente followed her after putting away all of their weapons. We were escorted into the conference center and offered a place to sit; it was hardly a sign of war. Then about a hundred top scientists that represented all areas of study casually walked into the hall and draped themselves over the aging plastic seats. Angie Wilkerson walked up to the podium and slipped on the glove that ran the computer images she would be sharing with the guests.

Charlie and I sat on each side of Penny, comforting her. Jim and the rest of the warriors we had brought along just sat in amazement, saying nothing. Everyone was served glasses of juice and plates that were piled with fresh fruit. Most of the scientists accepted but none of the guest from Serpiente would touch or eat anything. Then the lights were dimmed and Angie began to speak.

"First of all, my name is Angie Wilkerson, the great, great, granddaughter of Jim Wilkerson who used to be close friends of the Anderson family that lived in Serpiente. There was a time when we were the closest of allies, the best of friends. I would like to take this opportunity to renew that friendship. But first I need to share some images with you. We also request that after I show them to you, we discuss the ramifications of what we are looking at." She causally held her hand up and the entire ceiling behind her came to life instantly. As if a computer screen had been magically created, an image forty feet high and sixty feet long appeared, with an image of the park in Albuquerque.

The screen then came to life as the dragonfly flew over the Painted Warriors camp. The image stopped as the dragonfly attached itself to a tree branch and then it watched the camp. The image showed the warriors going around and around in endless circles around a large fire, then the image changed and the warriors were then copulating in a circle around the fire and with a small amount of image manipulation, the serpent Tikal appeared, crawling over them all. There was audible gasp from the nervous scientists who were not used to dealing with such sights.

"There is more going on here than what you see. We suspect that the serpent is manipulating the humans for its needs. The serpent appears to be absorbing something. Let's go to the next images."

The next images showed a Red Face ceremony where two women were tortured, cooked and then eaten.

Tears were now flowing down Penny's cheeks prompting Pamela to hand her a small white towel which she graciously accepted. Jim stood up and asked if they could now have some of the juice. The situation was instantly taken care of by Pamela. Before the Navajo called Jim sat down he says, "I hope you all realize that we have never seen any of what you have shown us, we were unaware of it. How do we know that what you are showing us is real?"

Angie calmly answered his question while the house lights came back on.

"Yes, it is true that we could have changed what you are seeing on that image a pixel at a time, however I assure you. What you have seen is very real, and it has occurred many times all over this region. There are two serpents that we know of that are terrorizing this whole land. They control the tribes of humans called the Painted People and the Red Face People, and they have been stealing humans from settlements throughout the west. They are cruel masters who only live for their own personal needs. Furthermore, the members of their tribes are no more than slaves to the serpents."

Again, Jim stood up and said, "We live in Serpiente and never bother anyone. We cannot be responsible for what happens outside of Serpiente, and you still have not produced one shred of evidence that what you are showing us is real."

Angie answered firmly, "We felt that you might feel that way, but my story is not over, I can show you the entire attack of Los Alamos, right down to the capture of Tikal."

Jim replied warily, "Show us one shred of real evidence and we will continue watching your show, otherwise we have little to talk about."

Angie Wilkerson took off her tiny electronic glove and signaled for Pamela to go get something. Everyone talked among themselves for a moment when a female Painted warrior was lead to the center of the room. A sheet was removed revealing an athletic woman. The completely naked woman was covered in striking geometric designs. Her hair was grown straight up forming a Mohawk giving the impression that she was very tall which she was anyway. Pamela wrapped the warrior back up and directed her to sit in a chair which she obediently did, her bizarre head poking up above the sheet. Then two more men entered the room carrying a large clear box, then after another moment, two other men arrived with Tikal, one metal snake grip tight around his neck and one half ways down his body. He was placed in the clear box with ventilation holes and the lid latched.

The men from Serpiente all stood up as the serpent called Tikal was brought in, sitting down with chagrined looks on their faces. Penny started to cry once more but after looking at me for a moment I could tell she was deeply troubled and increasingly becoming emotional. All I could do was hold her hand.

Angie Wilkerson took command of the presentation again, "Please allow me to document what occurred during the attack and how we captured Tikal." That series of images, illustrating and documenting Tikal flying through the door, followed by his capture, took about twenty minutes. Each surviving warrior had been photographed from different angles, which captured the geometric design they wore. Using the computer, images were mixed together and the image of the warriors dancing around a fire was generated. The geometric patterns worked together to form an optical illusion of a large serpent moving in circles. It truly was a serpentine creation done on the backs of humans.

Angie brought up the lights again and walked over to the table in front of the delegation from Serpiente, and says, "So what do you have to say?" She leaned back in the chair waiting for an answer.

Finally, Jim stood up one more time and answered, "We didn't know, Teotihuacan never conveyed any images of what was really going on. Please, I hope you do not hold us personally responsible for what those serpents were doing. Are we your captives?"

This brought out another murmur from the crowd who knew the unspoken answer.

Angie looked up for a moment then replied, "You are an honored guest, and we consider you allies and are begging for your help. Simply put, we as a people do not want to live under the control of serpents. We are scientists and the last thing in the world we would do is consider you captives. You may leave at any time you wish; however, I believe if you are humans at all your natural curiously will demand that you help us get to the bottom of this. We will do what we have to do, with or without your help. But one thing we know, the serpents will use you for their purposes and then abandon you. Someday you will need to join us, perhaps we will create something like the United States of America, you represent the state of Serpiente and we represent the state of Los Alamos. There are more human communities out there as well but as long as the serpents and people such as the Red Face use terror as a tactic, humans will never be part of a greater United States. Everyone lives in fear of each other. Apparently even the serpents live in fear of each other."

Jim interjected, "We are all slaves to the serpents, but look at you, don't they affect you too, living here in fear, inside of these huge buildings, but never leaving?"

"Well," Angie responded, "If it were not for the marauding bands of warriors out there, we might enjoy traveling all over. But, we do not need to. We have a program called Dragonfly. It can take us anywhere we want to go. If you would like to see what I'm talking about, I would be delighted to show you some time."

Jim, who didn't stand this time before he spoke, asked, "Would you give us an example?"

Pamela walked over and slipped the glove over her hand and after going through a few operations showed Serpiente from one of the windmills that provided water for the gardens, and livestock. Two operations more and a young man and Juanita appeared on the ranch poach. They were obviously in an impassioned embrace. Both Pamela and Penny looked at Charlie who only grinned.

Penny then stood up and addressed the audience, "We have been deceived by the serpent Teotihuacan. He knew what Tsotzil and Tikal were doing. But he consciously concealed their crimes, even their existence. It was a sin of omission. He deceived us, by not saying anything."

"We humans from Serpiente have lived in peace with the serpents all these years. We are a peaceful people who are proud of our accomplishments. We are not under their control; I don't think we are anyway. However, we do communicate with them through a hieroglyphic language much like what was discovered in South America, where the Mayans used it. It is a strange language that took us several generations to master. Yet we were deceived. How can we help you?"

Angie answered, "For a start, can you tell me what is on Tikal's mind? He certainly has been unhappy since he was captured. Even I can tell that."

Tikal

Tikal was returned to the box. Everyone else was given a grand tour of the facility, fed a good dinner, and assigned to sleeping areas. The real action was taking place in Pamela's apartment. By now it was common knowledge that Pamela and Charlie were hopelessly in love. Penny and I found a room off the cafeteria lounge for some privacy. We talked into the night, and it wasn't about serpents.

Just as Angie Wilkerson had done, Penny slipped on a pair of rubber shoes and stepped into the box. Tikal rose up from the floor of the glass box and watched every move that Penny made. This time he tested the floor before spilling out on it. Discovering it was electrified, he pulled himself back into the non-conducting glass box which had become his cell. He could only wait and see what this human wanted.

Tikal was amazed and perplexed when he felt his mind being probed. He knew little of the humans at Serpiente, certainly he had no idea that they could communicate with the serpents, and Teotihuacan had said nothing to either Tsotzil or Tikal about the interactions with the humans of Serpiente. Tikal and Tsotzil had rejected the human truce breaking away from Quetzalcoatl and Kukulcan. Thinking that they would be destined to live here on this planet forever, they went back to enjoying what was available to them. They had created their own warrior class and returned to the old ways of manipulating the humans as always. They were hopelessly addicted to the life energy released at the death of higher life forms.

Penny started her questions with a statement, "I want you to understand that I intend to share what I learn from you with the humans who live here at Los Alamos. Is that understood?"

The first symbol that formed in her mind was the glyph for Teotihuacan. It was all Teotihuacan's idea.

"No, it was not Teotihuacan that enslaved those people to provide you with hostages that you could torture and have served up as food."

"So," Tikal answered, "They are a completely different species than us. Don't you do the same thing to many species here on earth, don't you eat them, even organisms that feel pain. Don't you absorb the life energy from those creatures?"

Penny thought about it for a second, and then answered, "Perhaps we humans are somewhat like you serpents, but only in that we require nourishment. We do not torture our food before we eat it. We do not enjoy killing others, even animals."

The serpent says, "Serpents are scary for you but you humans look scary for us serpents. You should always try to see yourself from the eyes of others. Given time you would be just like us even if we had never been condemned to live here on earth. Your history is replete with humans who resort to cruelty and perversion. Your people are just as deadly as we are, but we are right up front about it."

Penny answered thoughtfully, "It is true that we as a species are an invasive species, we have taken over the earth, however, we strive to live in peace and over time we have changed our ways. Why is that not possible for you?"

"Because it is in our nature to conquer and use the life forms around us, it is what we have done for millions of years."

Penny asked, "If Quetzalcoatl and Kukulcan can change their ways in order to work with the humans why can't you and Tsotzil change your ways?"

Tikal answered, "Quetzalcoatl and Kukulcan need the humans to build a spacecraft that can take us off of this planet. Tsotzil and I thought it would be impossible for the humans to help us, but after I learned about the technology here at Los Alamos I felt there could be a chance that you humans could actually pull it off. It would take the computing power that is stored here at Los Alamos to control the mercury induction reaction that is required. Without that computing power, we are doomed to stay here on earth forever, with it we have a chance."

"Did it ever occur to you that all you really had to do was make peace, and the humans might help you?"

"The only way humans have ever helped us is by giving up their life energy which we absorbed."

Penny countered his thought with, "Perhaps it is time for you serpents to give up your life energy for us humans. Perhaps it is time for you to die, or make a real truce with the humans. Maybe we can help you leave this planet, heaven knows, maybe we would be better off without you serpents who manipulate us into killing each other for your amusement."

Tikal mulled over his position and then answered, "Kukulcan will soon give birth to more serpents, and then our position will be much stronger. In the long run, we will conquer you again."

"Why do you feel that you must conquer us humans," Penny asked?

"Because it is in our nature," he answered.

With that, Penny turned on her heels and left the box to report her findings to Wilkerson.

The Rescue

The delegation from Serpiente was escorted to the gates, but this time, Penny stayed behind. Only Jim, a direct descendant of Hidalgo and Jill Thompson, and the other men would return home. Penny felt that she could accomplish more by staying at Los Alamos, besides we had made plans. Unfortunately, our plans would need to wait. I had major problems that needed to be solved. First of all, thoughts of my family and what they had suffered through was foremost in my mind. We decided to meet with Angie Wilkerson and discuss the situation with her.

Angie quickly proposed a solution to our problem, "We need to conduct a little research in regards to fuel sources; however, I know of no reason why you two, along with a pilot couldn't fly in one of the two Helicopters that was stored at the facility. One was out of mothballs and ready to use anyway, however, it has a limited fuel supply."

There was a stipulation that we would return for a showdown with the serpents, particularly Teotihuacan. There was also a problem with Tsotzil that needed to be solved and ultimately the serpents as a group would either need capturing, killing or removal from this planet.

Angie agreed that because it was late in the fall, my family should be rescued before they had to face another long winter. After a stopover at a military installation in what was Idaho, where they acquired fuel, the helicopter continued all the way to Williams' Creek in Alaska setting down in the middle of a pasture directly in front of the cabins.

At first, no one appeared to be living there but as I exited the helicopter and walked toward the cabins, five people appeared who slowly walked out into the clearing after the helicopter's blades slowed down. The rest of the people living there were too weak to walk. They appeared slowly at first, leaning on walking sticks and terrified, but when they recognized me they began to all came out as fast as they could move, including both of my parents. Everyone was thin despite it being the end of summer when much food should have been available, they were starving and obviously in dire need of food.

After we hugged each other and introductions were made everyone settled into one of the cabins while the air turned cold and a few snow flurries occurred, the first of the season. Everyone had given up on acquiring meat. Everyone was grey and had given up hope figuring that this was to be the end of the world for them. After I explained that they could leave Williams' Creek Community, that the pandemic had been over for some time, they wanted to leave. Of course, carrying them out in the helicopter would be impossible. I had an idea. Revving up the helicopter we took the short trip back to the Bed and Breakfast on the other side of the lake. There we found canned goods and loaded the helicopter with all that we could carry safely. On the way back, I spotted three deer grazing on the last of the grass that wasn't covered up with the rapidly melting snow. After we returned to the community, everyone ate the first food they had consumed in a week and I returned to my old role as the meat provider for the community. Using one of the weapons carried on the helicopter I shot and brought back a large deer which would hold them over until they could get out of the impending deep snow that occurs in Williams' Creek and make the hike out to the lake.

Everyone decided that since the chopper couldn't carry us out, they would walk out and settle into the Bed and Breakfast where they could survive the winter much easier. There were still canned goods there. At one time, it had been a store that served a wide area. They could always fish in the lake and the wildlife had not experienced people there making hunting much easier. We left a rifle and a box of ammunition as insurance against hunger. After much discussion, as to where food could be acquired, including the large amounts of berries, grapes and other food producing plants located below the dam, the Williams' Creek Community immediately moved to the lake where they could survive much easier. Penny, who everyone had been unable to believe was a real person was perceived by all as the most beautiful girl in the world. She and I along with the pilot then returned to Idaho, where we could acquire enough fuel to make the trip back to Los Alamos. It had taken me three years to make the journey to Serpiente; it would take us only a few hours, with another stop for fuel, to return to Los Alamos.

We agreed to return to Williams' Creek as soon as possible to retrieve all of the survivors but we would not be able to help them further for some time. The situation with the serpents was never discussed. The Williams' Creek Community had far too much to worry about already.

Part 6

The Arrival of Viracocha

*Scientist know we must protect species because they
are working parts of our life-support system.*
—Paul Ehrlich

Extinction is the rule. Survival is the exception.
—Carl Sagan

Extinction

Millions of years ago, Viracocha's home was a beautiful blue planet, orbiting a distant star. But as the planet's interior radiation decayed, the planets interior cooled and became solidified. This caused the planet to lose its ability to produce a magnetic field, a magnetic field that blocked all manner of radiation that came from their sun and space. After attempting various solutions to the problem, such as coating surfaces in a thin layer of gold foil, his ancestors simply moved to the next inner planet. A planet not as comfortable as their original home but closer to the sun and lived there for several million years but as with all planets, it's radioactivity in the core of the planet soon diminished and again, the planet lost its magnetic field and became unlivable. Viracocha's ancestors considered migrating to the planet closest to their sun in an attempt to live but by then, the star it orbited suddenly began to expand outward producing an intense stellar output. His planet was eventually cooked by the ever-expanding sun. Eventually, on its way to supernova, the massive star enveloped most of the solar system.

Only a tiny few of Viracocha's people escaped into space, becoming more and more dependent upon technology for survival. They always kept their biological basis, reproducing artificially every few thousand years. But then, all this had occurred many thousands of years ago. In time, the survivors became almost pure technology that searched the universe for other life forms and seeded promising planets with life. But, what Viracocha did more than anything else was to seek out knowledge which was stored in the computer circuits of his library.

Viracocha was a living technology, the essence of the original sixteen beings who escaped from the mother planet before it burned up. They escaped into space where they managed to imprint their collective knowledge and con-sciences onto computer chips, constantly reincarnating into better, more efficient microchips which after many generations produced creatures that seemed like magic to even the most advanced civilizations they encountered throughout the universe.

Viracocha was one of the original sixteen survivors. After his home planet died, he took it upon himself to spread life throughout the galaxy known as the Milky Way. Aboard the spherical library, Viracocha's avatars raised living things not for personal consumption but rather to produce biological packages used to seed likely planets. Small balls of genetic material would be coated with a ceramic coating then simply dropped on the surface of a planet. Often Viracocha would simply fly around the planet, making a slow drop of the ceramic devices, letting them fall through the atmosphere. Being made of ceramic, most of them survived until impact occurred. Some of them died, leaving a curious geode looking object in the soil. But in some cases, the packet landed in a favorable environment allowing life to start. In time, whole new civilizations grew from them.

Viracocha was unique even among his peers. He was incredibly intelligent and strong yet had noble intentions. Quetzalcoatl, Kukulcan as well as Viracocha are not really proper names; they are titles, titles signifying royalty. The librarian and diplomat went by the name Viracocha as his father had and his father for hundreds of generations, each lasting several thousand years. Through genetic engineering he could replicate himself and in time a new Viracocha would appear. He would on occasion think back to his youth and his biological mother and what it was like to survive as a terrestrial creature. He missed his biological mother. As one of the sixteen survivors, she involved herself in diplomatic responsibilities throughout the galaxy.

Viracocha's library home was massive enough to produce a weak, natural gravity field; just enough to stimulate bacterial growth in the sections of the ship engaged in microbial and photosynthetic farming. The power that was generated to actually power the ship was located at the very center of the sphere. It was a plasma ball, powered by a simple nuclear reaction held in place by a magnetically contained shell all controlled by the system computer. The self-generating plasma ball provided a primary source of energy, the same energy found throughout the universe. It was the same source of energy that powered natural stars, where hydrogen fused to create helium, releasing tremendous amounts of energy. The tiny, computer-controlled star generated enormous amounts of power that could, if necessary, be focused on faraway targets. If necessary, the sphere could easily obliterate a distant planet, or blanket a quadrant of space occupied by malevolent alien creatures. Although it was the primary source of energy in Viracocha's home, it was only one, of many, power sources the ship used.

Fortunately, Viracocha had never been required to use those powers in war, leaving him very content in his position in the world. Most civilizations grew until the indigenous population rose and then failed as their populations over-taxed the carrying capacities of their planets. The majority of the surviving civilizations lived on the edge of survival as all natural creatures do, in a delicate balance. But there were other reasons that civilizations fell. Often, they warred among themselves until they achieved the ability to commit mutual suicide. A few died after realizing that they were not alone in the universe and indeed were only back county cultures, they lost their incentive to advance.

Some civilizations recognized the danger they created for themselves and survived to become interstellar forces, living in harmony with the thousands of other civilizations that exist, but a few arose and became monsters to deal with. However, there was only one planet that Viracocha truly dreaded to deal with, the planet that provided a home for the serpents. The serpent culture had long ago escaped their native planet and was spreading to several solar systems across the galaxy causing serious concern for Viracocha. Even his home, the giant golden sphere known as a library, had at one time been infested with the serpents.

Inside the library where Viracocha lived, he simply plugged himself into the circuitry of the ship and was instantly aware of everything. The entire ship became the essence of Viracocha yet the real essence of what was Viracocha, was not contained in biological material, but rather biological material connected to computer chips that made up his exoskeleton. He, and his kind had long ago become pure technology and every detail of what was happening inside the shell of the massive moon was available to him. He could remain motionless for many earth years, yet direct the operations of the artificial moon. His home was the entire interior of the ship but much more, he was aware of everything that happened for a light year around him. He held complete control, using remote sensory, which allowed him to make decisions. The ship actually ran like a well-tuned clock, in perfect synchronism to the universe. The library incorporated avatars that did all the physical work such as caring for the genetic material that had been collected and was being farmed along the outer shell of the ship. The library engaged in growing genetic material which was used to seed planets orbiting the stars, following one of his personal prime directives, to seed life throughout the stars. It was a dangerous job. But of course, he did far more than that, he enjoyed actively helping struggling civilizations. His mind, now supported by the library's infinite computing power, was free to follow his interests. But for now, Viracocha's exoskeleton held his essence in its computer circuitry.

Viracocha lived in his exoskeleton which provided him with all his biological needs as well as giving him great powers. No known projectile could penetrate the suit nor damage the wearer due to kinetic, electrical or laser energy. The tiny invisible field that the suit generated would cause any projectile to simply bounce off harmlessly, including biological creatures such as microbes. But what was even more important about the exoskeleton was that to the average earthling, it appeared to be nothing but regular clothing. Even his face, hid behind a golden mask, took on the appearance of a human with a long flowing beard, but he knew that if an earthling actually gazed upon his real face they would run away in terror.

The current Viracocha did not necessarily enjoy interstellar travel; leaving his library in one of the triangular spaceships still required weeks to travel to earth, even at the speed of light. Sometimes it took many earth months to reach a destination and Viracocha did not relish being away from his duties or the security of the library. His avatars took over all his duties but sometimes the time delay caused unforeseen problems in communication. It had been two hundred and forty earth years since the last time he had boarded an interstellar spaceship and he himself had never actually traveled to the planet called Earth. His father however, had been there many times while he was alive and his father's memories of earth were imprinted on his son's memory chips.

Long before the ages of Ice occurred, Viracocha's father had visited this planet, but all evidence of his visits had been lost. Earth was struck by a small asteroid which caused the poles to shift and global flooding occurred which destroyed entire continents. Many civilizations such as the one known as Atlantis simply vanished. Viracocha assumed that all human life was lost, that as a species, humans would never recover. Viracocha was not perfect, and this time he was wrong. It was sometime during this time he also discovered serpents hiding inside his triangular scout ship and disposed of them in North America. He honestly thought that it was an innocuous decision he had made. But in reality, there were survivors who would begin the arduous process of starting human civilization all over.

In time, his father made contact with those people and traveled around the planet studying the impact the serpents had made on them. What he discovered was that the serpents that he had released on earth had naturally incorporated the humans into their food chain. The serpents had learned to manipulate the local societies into providing them with the energy released upon death. There had been some hope that the humans on earth would be able to resist the serpent's manipulations but as the ancient diplomat suspected, the humans were defenseless against the stealthy creatures that had millions of years of evolution on them. He had to solve a paradox. He was responsible for this. He also knew that destroying them would be against the universal laws that he lived by, yet they were expanding their influence throughout the planet and undoubtedly in time, they would escape earth and expand their influence into nearby solar systems.

Viracocha's father had attempted to help the humans by teaching them many new skills such as moving stones which could be used to construct megalithic buildings and helping them develop rudimentary forms of writing that would speed up the transfer of information among them. He wanted to improve upon the evolution and learning of the humans in hope that at some point, they would be able to defend themselves against the serpents. But as he traveled around the world, he realized that the serpents were manipulating and teaching the humans also. Simply helping the humans learn to deal with the serpents was futile.

First of all, the serpents were invisible to the humans. Most humans never knew that they were being manipulated. He had hopes that if the humans couldn't conquer the serpents, perhaps the newly evolving humans would learn to live with the serpents, but all reports lead to the same conclusion; that the serpents had changed the natural evolution of life on the planet and the humans were defenseless against the serpents. The humans were farmed for the energy the serpents were addicted to.

Viracocha knew that long ago there was evidence that at one time, many of the creatures who lived on earth were on their way to becoming creatures that were self-aware and intelligent. Thousands of years before the present there were creatures known as Neanderthals that actually had larger brains than humans and who in time, if left alone would have evolved into a modern race of civilized creatures. And there were many others, tiny creatures who lived on islands and even bipedal creatures who settled in what would become eastern Europe that were just as likely to evolve as the humans who finally lived there. Even the lower apes showed promise of eventually becoming intelligent creatures. Certainly, it was obvious that baby chimpanzees, for example, were more intelligent than baby humans. But as humans continued to grow they surpassed the intelligent actions of other creatures and ruled them. Humans had grown into a species that had very little respect for other creatures, even creatures on their own planet. They even created belief systems that excused their dominance and use of other creatures. The humans had caused mass extinctions of many species on their own planet and it was understood that if they journeyed into space they would treat the species they found there even worse than the ones on their own planet. Viracocha was worried that humans might require extermination as well as the serpents.

The librarian felt responsible for what had happened on earth. Earth could have been a perfect jail for the serpents if humans had never appeared, but now they were manipulating the humans for their own diabolical needs. It was in their nature. In the realm of ranking intelligent creatures, the librarians had encountered in the galaxy who were self-aware, humans ranked low on the evolutionary scale. But humans showed promise and they had the right to evolve by their own means. Of course, the serpents had simply taken over that process by teaching them war and sacrifice for their own purposes. The natural abilities of the humans to evolve into a positive species, was being ruined by the serpents.

Viracocha had an ultimatum to deliver to the earthlings. The earthlings needed to understand that they themselves had evolved to be parasitic creatures much like the serpents. Before the humans could make decisions about other creatures they needed to understand their own nature; that is, what it is to be a human in a community of other creatures that occupy this tiny portion of the galaxy.

Troubled Planet

Extinctions of life on planet earth were natural. It had occurred many times before in the geological past but it had always occurred due to natural causes such as acidification of the oceans, dramatic climate change, and even plate tectonics. When a continent existed in isolation from other land masses, life there evolved in its own way. When that continent touched other land masses the mixing of species always caused mass extinctions. Some species were winners and some were losers. Intelligent life would slowly evolve again, perhaps this time the survivors would be more benign but the normal way was toward more warlike creatures.

Natural creatures living in the wild live on the edge of existence. They live meal to meal, always dependent upon a chance encounter with other creatures that they can eat. It is a give and take situation whereby all creatures live in a balance with others. They developed several mechanisms to allow them to survive usually involving the production of many offspring. Deer for example produce offspring almost every year and were plentiful even at the apex of human population growth. Creatures like elephants on the other hand have a two-year gestation period, producing only one calf at a time. They reproduce so slowly that only through extreme cooperation by the humans could they survive. Earlier species of animals did not make it. It took only a few mastodons and mammoths to be killed before the viability of the species died. Early humans did not kill all of them, only enough to tip the balance of nature and soon they became extinct.

Humans caused a great extinction of life on planet earth due to their prolific breeding, weapons and arrogance. Then they themselves almost became extinct due to the plague that was released to kill the serpents. Now they were starting to reproduce and populate the world again but this time, they were being directed by the serpents who had motives all of their own. Given time, the entire planet would be used by the serpents to farm the creatures used to feed the humans who are themselves being farmed to provide energy for the serpents. In the end, Viracocha knew that if he could not change this, the serpents would subjugate all earthly creatures for their own use and he was leery of what would become of the humans themselves. He also felt a certain dread, a suspicion, that in time the serpents might cooperate with the humans in escaping earth. Both species could become a danger to the galaxy.

Viracocha and Chimalma, the serpent's ambassador arrived over the planet after several weeks of travel and Viracocha was impatient to get on the job. While in route he had studied the history of the planet and in particular the interactions of his father who had spent several earth years among the natives teaching them. He was surprised at what he discovered from his scans of the planet. Geologically there had been an increasing amount of volcanism and plate movement. Climate change had occurred but seemed to be in the process of self-correcting. High levels of carbon dioxide were recorded but the source of the gas was now gone. Winters were colder and summers hotter than when his father had journeyed to earth. There had also been massive die offs of creatures that had at one time lived on earth and at first, he was puzzled as to what had caused the extinctions. The answer became apparent when he discovered the obvious humanization of the planet. There was evidence that at one time there had been humans everywhere, consuming fossil fuels as a basis for their economies, which had raised the levels of carbon dioxide to dangerous levels. He wondered why they had not used other forms of energy that were not as dangerous to the health of the entire planet.

From his records, he knew that the carrying capacity of the planet was only a few billion humans. He had seen it happen on other planets. When the population of an organism reached a critical level, there was a population collapse followed by an increase in warfare among the survivors until equilibrium was reached. Now the people had vanished, and the levels of gases were dropping. The only energy traces were where at one time nuclear energy plants and storage facilities had once been. Connected to power grids in deserted cities, they had at one time powered the cities. Despite the fact that they no longer generated energy they still had concentrated amounts of radioactive materials in them. They were now death traps for all creatures to avoid.

The roads that connected the cities were now overgrown with shrubs and trees and the buildings themselves were completely derelict. The other creatures that were considered food animals by the humans had now made a comeback, particularly in the oceans. The oceans literally teemed with fish and all manner of organisms that lived there. Terrestrial life had not fared as well. An ecological equilibrium had occurred when the herbivores such as deer and cows experienced population explosions only to diminish again as carnivore populations increased. It was the way nature operated; predator and prey playing a balancing act.

Viracocha examined continent after continent finding no trace of organized human life. He could find evidence of living humans but could find only traces of them scattered far apart until he crossed over what would be known as North America. He was surprised to find organized human society there. He found evidence of two electrical grids that were operating. One he discovered on top of a large volcanic plateau and another, much smaller one, a few units of space toward the equator. Upon closer inspection, he discovered many tiny units where humans were all living in a crude state of existence. Although there were many other individual places where humans seemed to be living, they existed without any power generation at all.

The one thing that truly was obvious was that the larger facility showed no signs of the presence of serpents whereas the smaller facility was actually occupied by three serpents that seemed to be living among the humans. Viracocha wondered what had happened to the populations of serpents whom he assumed lived everywhere. From his on-board computer, he requested the names of the two facilities. The larger one was called Los Alamos Scientific Laboratories, the other, where traces of serpents could be detected, was known as Serpiente. How appropriate, he thought to himself. It puzzled him. How could a society exist on this planet with the influence of the serpents? Had they somehow conquered them? Were they immune to the mental manipulation of the serpents? Had the humans been conquered by the serpents and were they following the same pattern that had occurred over and over in human history or were the humans actually working with the serpents for some end that Viracocha couldn't understand? He decided to make his appearance at the larger settlement and attempt to discover how it had survived the population collapse, as well as determining if there was any influence by serpents.

The Trial of Planet Earth

Viracocha hovered above what was determined to be Los Alamos National Laboratories several earth hours, studying it. At one time the humans were on the verge of discovering how to generate electricity through nuclear fusion in the facility but all research into peaceful use of nuclear fusion had stopped when the population collapsed. Just as well, on other planets this had been a dangerous point in their development. On the one hand, it would have solved all of their energy problems and the humans could have actually increased their population; to a point. On the other hand, some civilizations had managed to destroy themselves with this discovery. It depended upon the nature of the creatures that lived there.

After several minutes of scanning the computers that were active at the site he was able to extrapolate exactly how to speak to the humans that lived there. His exoskeleton would then translate any language for him, besides it was an easy job for him to learn a language anyway. During his lifetime, he had learned hundreds of languages only to forget them as the planet site and sometimes the language itself changed. The mechanics were usually the same but the translator still made simple mistakes such as was it a white house or a house that is white. It didn't matter, after only a few hours of conversation the translation was perfect, particularly when the translator had access to computer files.

Viracocha allowed his triangular craft to descend, quickly at first from what appeared from the ground to be a tiny daytime star to an obvious craft with three small lights which were antigravity buffers and then he descended slowly, very slowly. He wanted to give the humans time to come to grips with the reality of what was going to happen. He also wanted to be able to pull away if his appearance frightened them too much and they tried to shoot him down. He knew that other visitors to earth had caused panic to ensue and he wanted to keep everything as calm as possible. At one thousand earth feet above open fields he dropped off harmless flares which would attract any ground to air missiles that might be fired at him. Nothing happened, so he descended to the surface.

After landing he waited to see if there was a response from the inhabitants. Before he descended, he had even hacked into the computers that were operating and put a simple message on every screen; "I come in peace." He waited another ten earth minutes to see what would happen and finally a single female stepped out of a large building and walked up to within fifty feet of the ship. A staircase slowly descended from the spacecraft and stopped within two inches of the surface and in another minute a door slowly rotated open exposing a mysterious dark corridor.

Angie Wilkerson nervously took ten more steps forward and then stopped with her palms facing the ship in a universal sign that she held no weapons. Then what appeared to be an extremely old man with long flowing grey hair which cascaded down to the middle of his shoulders appeared. He was wearing a hood and from underneath a hood was a head with a very high cranium. He appeared to be wearing a golden mask which hid all but his eyes. The mask was in the shape of a long flowing beard which was actually a device used to hide a multitude of devices, devices which allowed him to breathe the nitrogen and oxygen rich air which was mixed in almost the same ratio he was used to anyway. He had deep set, dark eyes which seemed to slant slightly downward which made him look like an ancient Chinese sage.

He also held his hands out with their palms out demonstrating that he had no visible weapons. He actually was armed and could have, with only a thought destroyed all that was around him, but that was not his intention. He flipped his hands with their long spindly fingers over in a gesture of 'what now'? He was pleasantly surprised when Angie Wilkerson, instead of running or prostrating herself on the ground, simply smiled and waved him over to her.

Viracocha was not sure what she meant by the gesture and paused for a second only to have the human female walk over to him and hold out a trembling hand which again confused Viracocha for a second. Then realizing how foolish he was, he reached out and clasped her hand, then he followed her inside the large building from which she had appeared.

Angie Wilkerson could not keep her eyes off of Viracocha. She realized that every detail of his exoskeleton was actually a complicated machine. Unlike the pre-scientific people in the distant past who encountered Viracocha, the closer she looked the more she realized that every centimeter of Viracocha was covered with intricate devices, each a marvelous device containing ever more intricate devices. The more she looked the more she realized that she indeed was dealing with an extremely advanced creature. She thought, for just a moment, about the amulet. She realized the similarity. Was the amulet something this creature had left on earth long ago?

A large group of curious, if not scared, people gathered inside the metal building. After a few minutes, scientists from several buildings streamed into the building used for assemblies not knowing what to expect. Viracocha sat down at the head of a large oval table but he faced Angie Wilkerson rather than facing the crowd of onlookers. Angie was not sure what to say to him. After all, she had never spoken to an alien other than the serpents before, as far as she knew.

"Do you understand what I am saying?" Angie asked.

Viracocha blinked his eyes and then slowly answered, "I am fluent in thousands of languages. We can learn the language of a society that uses electronic devices in only a few seconds if given the information in those computers. Without them, it takes about thirty earth minutes to fully be able to communicate. This planet has been contacting and speaking to us for many years."

Angie knew what he was talking about. Every time one of the pre-pandemic humans broadcast a radio or television show, an electronic signal carried into the depths of space where undoubtedly, they were listened to by any advanced society that had the facility or desire to listen. People on far away planets could easily be wondering if all people on earth were like the programs "I Love Lucy" or "Gilligan's Island." They probably found it confusing when Matt Dillon of the "Gun Smoke" show, rode around on a large beast of burden using crude hand cannons to defend himself and yet could broadcast his adventures into space.

"Actually, I'm sure you have been noticing visits from other worlds but they seldom make actual contact with the people who live here. You may not be aware of it, but at one time your planet was actually fought over by alien entities. It is recorded in your most ancient of records from a place called India. They warred for some time until one group won the battle that was fought in the sky above. They would have completely dominated your infant planet except for one thing."

"What was that," Angie asked?

"The serpents, they invaded the alien force and found their way back to their home planet of origin. From then on, all outsiders have avoided actual contact with this planet. They fear the serpents."

"So at least at one time in our distant history the serpents actually did us a favor?" Angie responded.

"That is correct," Viracocha replied with a slight smile. "No outside force would attempt to conquer you and risk encounters with the serpents. The serpents are too stealthy, it is too easy for them to stow away on an invader's spaceship. They certainly had little trouble stowing away on my spacecraft which is how they got here in the first place. If they do not want to be detected, they are almost diabolical in their abilities to hide among others. We disposed of them on this planet well before the rise of you humans. If we had known how your culture would develop we would never have left them here. They are, of course, the hardest species to communicate with. They are a species who communicates with each other telepathically."

"So that is how they communicate," Angie said, realizing the import of what Viracocha was saying. The sarcasm in her voice caused Viracocha to pause a minute.

"What exactly do you know of the serpents?" he asked.

"I know enough to know that they have manipulated we humans for thousands of years. We have learned to keep them out of Los Alamos by using electrical fences which emit a force field."

"Don't they change shape and simply fly in?"

"They do, but they cannot manipulate our minds when they try. They gave up trying a long time ago."

For the first time in a long time, Viracocha was confused. He couldn't imagine a mere human who could withstand the manipulations of the serpents. "How do you keep them from entering your dreams?"

Angie looked at him for a minute then reached inside the lapel of her blouse and pulled out a tiny owl shaped ornament. Viracocha looked at it in astonishment, then looked around the large room as everyone reached inside their shirts and pulled out tiny amulets. Finally, he reached down to his own chest and lifted his beard up to expose an amulet just like everyone else was wearing. "We seem to be kindred spirits." he responded.

Angie explained that they spent years in the development and duplication of the amulet. It had been a challenge because it powers itself by energy from the wearer. The field it generated was weak but just strong enough so that the serpents could not intrude upon the wearer. Viracocha was amazed that they had the technology to duplicate the amulet.

Angie and Viracocha spent the next several hours comparing notes about the history of humans and serpents. Viracocha spoke of earlier visits by the librarians going back to 25,630 BC. That was when the serpents had originally been cast off and sentenced to earth somewhere near present day Salt Lake City. It was the same date the Olmec civilization adopted as their beginning date of life on earth, probably a date borrowed from the serpents that quickly migrated around the world. Viracocha returned again in cycles of five thousand one hundred and twenty-six years until later in the earth year of 3114 BC he discovered that the serpents were actively farming the humans for their life energy.

The serpents had already set up a system, without the humans even being aware of it, that satisfied the needs of the serpents and even drew upon the natural creativeness of the humans. In effect, humans changed from a hunting society to an agricultural society and the first cities and cultures appeared. The changes made farming of the humans even easier for the serpents.

On earlier visits, there were few humans who lived and those that did appear seemed to be inconsequential. Viracocha had planned to return again in the year 2012 AD but discovered that the world had dramatically changed due to the natural evolution of humans. Emissaries had visited the earth but did not make contact because they feared their appearance would cause upheaval in the complex societies that were now populating the earth and of course they wanted to avoid another encounter with the serpents. Viracocha had assumed that massive earth upheavals and war among the humans would naturally occur but instead, shortly after their date of return, the pathogen that the shaman who wore stars on his shoulders had been developed and was released. The planet went through a new cycle of destruction and creation just as the wisest humans had predicted; particularly the Mayans who had been absorbed into modern culture and the Hopi who were well aware of these cycles, all based upon the librarian's calendar. Viracocha's father had told the ancient Mayans, "We will return." Only when we did, we found an entirely different planet than we expected.

This was the first planet that Viracocha knew of that had been able to resist the serpents at all. Everywhere else that the serpents had invaded, the local creatures had struggled for many centuries and then finally succumbed to the serpents. They were then farmed for the energy they released upon death. In some cases, all had died or committed suicide. In many cases, the entire ecology of the planet broke down and everything died including the serpents who then starved to death. As with all parasites, they are harmful to their host, as well as to themselves.

Manifest Destiny

After several hours of frank discussion about human evolution, technology, and of course the serpents, Viracocha let the truth about his visit out. He was obviously concerned about the serpents. Now the serpents seemed to have changed their game plan and he feared that they were using the humans in order to regain entry back into space. The evidence for human space exploration was still circling the planet in geosynchronous orbits. There were numerous satellites and even a space station with the skeletal remains of humans in it to attest to the progress the humans had made before the pathogen hit. The unfortunate and sad astronauts had starved to death being unable to return to earth after the pathogen struck. Everything still functioned, except for the humans. Viracocha knew that it would take very little time for the humans to regain the technology for space travel. Particularly if assisted by the serpents. If the humans actually enabled the serpents to journey into space the results could be disastrous for creatures all over this portion of the galaxy. Viracocha certainly knew that the serpents would, and could change the way they interacted with humans for a while, but in the finale analysis, they would always return to their basic nature. Serpents are invasive parasitic creatures.

Viracocha found himself in a quandary as what to do about the serpent problem. His own personal prime directive forbade him from interfering with other cultures. He knew how to destroy the serpents in numerous ways, yet the ethics he had lived by his entire life, stopped him from carrying out such an action. Furthermore, he knew that he couldn't share his technology with other cultures such as the humans and allow them to carry out the deed, although the thought had crossed his mind. All he could actually do, is lay out the problem to the humans and allow them to solve the problem on their own. He could also teach them things that might improve their own culture as long as it didn't involve teaching them to build weapons of war, particularly if the weapons were directed toward the serpents. In his thinking, all life is precious, even serpents although he wondered about this own wisdom in regards to this.

Viracocha did not trust the humans. They had lived among the serpents and learned war all too well. In time, they would have the ability to become parasites themselves, invading other planets and harvesting the resources there. They even had a name for it, manifest destiny. Humans could justify any action they wanted because of a number of reasons, such as resource depletion, or fear of invasion. Perhaps it was an unfortunate dogma of their religions, or perhaps it was simple fear, or simply in their nature.

Viracocha, after many hours of talking to the humans who stared at him spellbound, grew tired. Even with the assist of his exoskeleton he tired after a while. Returning to his triangular ship the staircase magically reappeared again and the door rotated open. After promising to return he decided to return to geosynchronous orbit where he would be safe and he could rest. Being almost eight hundred years old, he was starting to slow down. Returning into space, he was considering how he would investigate the happenings in Serpiente, without anyone there knowing of his presence. He could certainly use the ships sensors but he knew that what he could learn would be limited. Certainly, he could not determine communications that took place between the serpents, nor could he determine what was going on in Serpiente other than to do a count of the organisms that were there. All living creatures, including the serpents, produce a heat signature that can be read from above. But all that tells you is that an organism is there. It would not tell Viracocha what the organism was doing or thinking.

The Nature of Serpents

Angie Wilkerson fully understood the problem. She had, however been unaware that the serpents in Serpiente, were using the local humans to assist them. She tried to think about such a relationship whereby serpents would actively enlist humans to help them; as Viracocha had said, to help them return to the stars. Certainly, the serpents knew far more about interstellar travel and such things as antigravity than the humans would or even could know. But then, many of the greatest discoveries in science were not achieved through years of arduous research but rather as serendipitous luck. The scientist has an epiphany and the next thing you know gravity becomes a law, or energy equals the mass times the speed of light squared. She wondered if it had not all happened once before on earth, after all, science never could explain how megalithic structures all over the world were built. In her mind, she pictured Tiahuanaco in South America. The precision cut blocks of rock were at one time moved by a force greater than can be achieved by humans, no matter how many humans are pulling on a rope. Blocks of stone in other locations made the precision cut blocks at Tiahuanaco seem like toys in comparison. But those megalithic structures had been built and the only logical conclusion was that some kind of antigravity force had been applied. Surely if an antigravity device can move a large rock, here on earth, it can lift a spaceship into the stars. Perhaps the solution was right in front of them and humans simply couldn't see it. Perhaps it had nothing to do with antigravity; it was something humans had not even imagined yet. Perhaps characters like Viracocha had been very helpful in the distant past but appeared to be hesitant to now share technologies on earth. After all, humans were very good at retrofitting technology and of course, they had become acclimated to serpentine ways. Many humans were now themselves, serpentine in nature.

Then there was the problem with the nature of serpents. They were parasites who live off of a host. Angie naturally assumed that young healthy humans would release far more life energy than an older person would. Just like in young bean sprouts, the cellular activity and particularly the mitochondrial activity was far more intense in a young spout compared to an older plant. The life force produced by young cells would be far more enjoyable to the serpents than older cells. Were children being born in Serpiente just to be sacrificed for the pleasure of the serpents? She made a bet to herself that whenever any human in Serpiente became extra baggage they would mysteriously die, releasing their life energy for the serpents no matter what the age of the human. She wondered if the humans in Serpiente were aware of their precarious position in the realm of things. She had no idea to what extent the serpents and humans were able to communicate with each other. In fact, she could not imagine a working relationship with serpents at all. It was not in the nature of humans to allow a parasite to live among them. Nor was it in the nature of the serpents, not to farm the humans. But the facts spoke for themselves, perhaps some of the serpents had truly changed the way they worked with humans and decided to take them in as partners in order to return to the stars.

Viracocha did discover one bit of information, but it wasn't new, some serpents had established themselves in human communities, subjugating the humans and changing their brain chemistry to have them search for victims. Wilkerson knew that beyond the fences there were headhunters who would spend all their days doing nothing more than causing havoc among other humans. Called by such names as Red Face and Painted Warriors, each tiny tribe of humans would search for victims for the serpents. The serpents would then reward the warriors by activating their pleasure centers. Those people had already digressed into a sub form of humanity. They no longer had morals against the most basic human qualities such as cannibalism, and murder, the serpents had a steady supply of humans releasing energy to them.

The Solution

Wilkerson and Viracocha held a general assembly, open for all scientists who wanted to provide input into possible solutions to the serpent dilemma. Several solutions were proposed and submitted, but the most commonly proposed solution was to use the technology available such as dragonfly, to simply kill all organisms that were currently involved or under the influence of the serpents. A count was made of those organisms; including the humans that lived in Serpientes, there was several hundred of them already documented in this area alone. But undoubtedly there were pockets of humans all over the world and possibly other serpents who were manipulating them. Separated by great distances they were thought to be unaware of each other, but it was assumed that many serpents had migrated around the planet. Destroying the serpents here would solve the problem locally but what about, for example, the dragons in China? The following day Viracocha returned to the assembly hall.

Viracocha made clear the enormity of the problem he was dealing with. If the humans helped the serpents return to space, it would create an enormous problem on many worlds. Once serpents escaped earth and journeyed into space, they would seek out planets where they could conquer and colonize. In time, they would control all planets where there were advanced civilizations. The entire galaxy could, in time, become infected with serpents.

Viracocha was aware that in Serpiente a spaceship was being built. A spaceship that was almost an exact copy of the one he was currently using. The technology to control the mercury induction gyroscope was unavailable to the serpents and people of Serpiente, however, it was certainly available in Los Alamos. The serpent known as Tikal understood this, and it was feared that it would only be a matter of time, until a mistake could be made. In time, somehow the serpents might conquer Los Alamos.

Viracocha as well as everyone at Los Alamos understood that the technology should never be shared with the serpents and so everyone was brain storming a solution to the problem. Most solutions were like the one the captain of the guard proposed. "Why don't we just take one of those helicopters and load it with armaments? Using thermal imaging, they would be sitting ducks, easy to kill."

Viracocha countered the argument with, "The simplest solution is simply to exterminate all invasive creatures on this planet including humans, then we don't need to worry about an invasion into the galaxy. As humans, you have learned too much. You are more like the serpents than you realize."

Realizing the import of what Viracocha was implying, Angie Wilkerson interjected, "Surely there is a simple way of solving this problem without killing everyone, including the humans."

Viracocha rubbed his long beard, and frowned. "Actually, the purpose of our meetings is to determine if there is a way not to kill anything. The purpose of this meeting is to solve a problem, in what at one time, was called a humane method, a way without having to resort to killing; do we have any other suggestions?"

Penny, who was playing with the amulet that was hanging around her neck, was the one who directed the conversation in a positive way. "Tell me more about this amulet. Can the effect it produces be enlarged? The scientist here at Los Alamos seem to have solved the problem by surgically implanting these devices in the Painted Warriors, can it be made to protect a larger area, say an entire planet?"

Angie Wilkerson answered thoughtfully, "Yes, it should be very possible to create a device that could shield a large area, even the entire planet. A few satellites could blanket the entire planet. However, we have lost the infrastructure to build a machine that could place them into space. Besides, if we develop the technology to return to space, won't the serpents use it to escape earth?"

Penny continued her point, "Well, think about it. If the serpents cannot read our thoughts or enter our minds it would make them just another species of snake. They could defend themselves but they couldn't manipulate us."

Viracocha entered the conversation again. "I am pleased with your line of thinking. What all of you need to realize is that serpents are certainly not the only creatures in this galaxy that you need to worry about; there are many creatures who have achieved interstellar flight out there that are quite war-like. They are themselves parasites and follow a policy of manifest destiny. That is, they feel it is their right to continually expand their influence at the cost of other species. Unfortunately, you humans follow that same line of thinking. You do it here on earth and undoubtedly you would do it on other worlds in space."

Angie Wilkerson spoke up at that thought, "I'm afraid Viracocha is correct about us. We are a species who always want to explore and learn new things. Before the plague hit the earth, we were on the verge of exploring deep space. We wanted to discover other life forms. What is never spoken about is the fact that we wanted to exploit other life forms to our advantage. I'm afraid Viracocha is absolutely correct about us!"

Viracocha reentered the conversation with a statement. "Actually, by placing the working mechanisms of the amulets into space above this planet we would accomplish far more than just making the serpents unable to enter your thoughts and dreams. It would act like a beacon to other aggressive species out there that serpents are alive and living here on this planet. They would avoid it like the plague it is. They fear the serpents, as well as any creature and in the end, the serpents would protect the earth from them."

Angie Wilkerson says, "So if we can build satellites that function as the amulets do, Viracocha will you deliver them to orbit in space?"

All Viracocha said was, "Agreed, however I will need to clear it first, with the ambassador from the serpent planet."

Penny asked, "You mean you brought a serpent with you?"

"Well, yes and no," he answered. "I will present to you the Serpent Ambassador. You will need to judge her for yourself. I have already summoned the ambassador and she and will be here shortly."

A few minutes later the door to the conference room opened and an elderly lady entered the gathering of scientist and emissaries. She appeared to be extremely old, clothed in black clothes with a dark veil completely hiding her face. She slowly walked to the center of the stage being careful to balance her steps with a walking cane shaped like a serpent. She finally stopped in front of Penny, appearing to stare at her then she says;

"You look exactly like the Penny Anderson I met several generations ago."

Penny was confused. "I do not understand what you mean. Did you meet my great-great grandmother whom I am named after?"

"Yes, she was a very unusual human who had experienced an encounter with my serpent. She was an impudent and arrogant young girl who had bad manners, or so it first appeared to me. But you see, she was dead tired, scared, and was trying to sleep. I had disturbed her. After a moment aboard the bus, she moved over and appeared to sleep but she wasn't really asleep. She was curious about me and of course she seemed to be scared of my cane. It would have bitten her in an instant if I directed it to. It was interesting, watching her mind work which was in overdrive from the dreams and revelations she was experiencing. She couldn't understand those dreams she had experienced, it had been far too intense."

Everyone starred at her. She had been speaking slowly and coldly but her voice suddenly seemed to warm up. "She moved over to the window and pretended to sleep. I watched her and studied her. I could see the differences in her body warmth and of course her aura. I could see into her mind. She was so innocent, so scared, and just plain tired. She was helpless. But I also knew there was something very special about her, I could see that in the intense colors her mind emitted. I knew that a day would come when Penny Anderson would talk to serpents. I knew that she was the answer to the dilemma we face today and now her great-great grandchild is here to bring everything full circle."

Everyone pondered about what the serpent ambassador's discussion was leading too. Everyone had unanswered questions such as how could the ambassador possibly know what would happen hundreds of years into the future. But in a small community such as Los Alamos, everyone knew, deep in their memories the details of recent history with the Anderson family at Serpiente. The scientists were certainly aware that the serpent ambassador had special abilities that they were just beginning to realize and understand. They couldn't fathom how the ambassador could possibly influence history across several generations but she certainly appeared to be doing so. Everyone wondered, what were her motives?

The ambassador slowly bent her body over, leaning in to Penny, and whispered, "Serpents aren't supposed to have feelings, but they do. That is why we let your great-great-grandmother live. She could have died in her dreams but I realized that she was important to us all. That is why we found her in the first place. This single human being who creates such interesting colors, because we didn't kill that young lady so many years ago, all of you are here today, her descendants.

You see, we decided to do what is not in serpent character. We decided to change the natural flow of history and allowed the girl to live rather than dispose of her. History would have turned out very different if Penny Anderson had mysteriously died on a bus somewhere between San Jon and Tucumcari, New Mexico. That is one reason why I am serpent ambassador. As you may know, serpents use a collective conscience when talking to each other. I however, think for myself and directed my wishes to the serpent. That is why I am the ambassador and why I represent them. Having lived among them for many generations I may appear to you as a serpent but believe me I am an individual."

Penny interjected, "We have lived with the serpents for many years now and I certainly have had no trouble communicating with them. They are like humans in that some of them are truthful, some of them tell lies, and some of them fail to expose those lies. But if you agree to speak the truth to us we will speak the truth to you."

The Ambassador seemed to ponder what Penny was saying then said, "You humans as a species have little to brag about. It is in your nature to form communities that consume every living thing around you."

Penny countered her argument with, "Get real now. We are mostly farmers in the community of Serpiente. We encourage life."

"That is true," says the serpent ambassador. "You encourage life so you can consume it. You use the life energy of all creatures around you for your own nourishment. Again, you are as ruthless as the serpents." She turned to address the collection of scientists.

"Thousands of years ago, serpents were doomed to live on this planet as a punishment. It is true that they secreted away on Viracocha's spaceship. It is the only way for them to travel for they cannot build their own spaceships without the help of other creatures. It is how they have always traveled from one place in the universe to another. Then they were discovered. From our point of view, we were unjustly forced to deal with an alien world. We only did what was necessary for our survival. It is in the serpent's nature to conquer and use resources just as you humans do. You are also an invasive, parasitic species. All serpents require is a fat warm rat now and then, but you are omnivores, you will eat anything."

Everyone strained to hear and understand what the ambassador was saying. Some of them grimaced at the thought of eating a live rat. Angie Wilkerson entered the conversation with, "Well that is not exactly true. It has become clear to us that the serpents are addicted to the energy they receive upon the death of living creatures, particularly us humans. Your demands are far beyond simple nourishment. Your species is addicted to the energy released upon our death and that energy is far more important to your species than food. Furthermore, your species enjoys the torment and fear which is encountered upon death. We humans are too large for you to swallow; however, you relish our deaths. The energy we release at death is a drug to you. It is not a nourishment, it is an addiction fulfilled only by the death energy you crave."

The ambassador seemed to get upset with Wilkerson's point.

Wanting to break the tension, Penny asked, "May I see your face? I am not used to talking to someone I cannot see."

The ambassador slowly lifted her veil to expose what appeared to be a beautiful young girl. Everyone gazed at her in relief but within a moment the face morphed into a hideous serpentine face with glowing red eyes. As her face changed her cane became animated, turning into a classic serpent. Then turning and facing the somewhat terrorized scientists she hissed, "You see me now as the ambassador for the serpents. I will never allow you to destroy them. They now consider themselves as rightful owners of this planet. We have a right to your life energy just as you have a right to the energy you receive when consuming food. I forbid their destruction. I demand that any harm you intend to do to the serpents must also happen to the humans. We demand equality, if the serpents are to be eliminated, then so too must the humans. As ambassador for the serpents, it is my consideration that the best solution is for Viracocha and myself to return to space and allow a natural solution to occur on this planet. We demand it, this is my ultimatum."

The serpent that had crawled around the stage in a show of defiance changed into the shape of a raven and flew around the assembly room. After two turns it returned to the ambassador and then as if by magic returned to her side and became a cane again.

Angie Wilkerson stepped forward and whispered to Viracocha, "Exactly what kind of a hideous creature are we dealing with? What does she mean by her ultimatum?"

"Her name is Chimalma, she is my mother. It is her job to attend the serpent ambassador which you assumed was her cane but is actually a royal serpent from the serpent homeland and she is deadly serious about her ultimatum."

Viracocha turned to Penny and asked, "Will you explain to Chimalma what we have discussed as a possible solution to this problem?"

Penny Anderson explained in detail the idea of placing satellites in orbit which would mimic what the amulets did. Afterword, several seconds passed in absolute silence as everyone watched the face of Chimalma slowly returning to looking like a young girl. Chimalma then simply hissed, "We agree. However, if we detect duplicity in your actions we will not honor the agreement, all of you will die. Furthermore, the serpents would be given a place in which they will never be disturbed, a place where they can live in peace with no interference from humans. However, I warn you, if given the opportunity to escape into space they will. As a species, I suspect that in time, you will want to explore space on your own, just as you have done before, and the serpents will be there with you."

She then turned on her heels and started her short walk back to the door which would lead her to the triangular spaceship with her cane in hand. But she stopped in front of Penny and again leaning over into her, she said, "It is in the nature of all humans to want to explore, to conquer and consume. In time your species will again attempt to leave this planet and explore space. If you do, you had better have the technology to deal with the serpents. Again, I warn you, the serpents will be there with you." Having said this, she again continued her walk to the door. This time she seemed to have no difficulty walking at all.

Viracocha says, "What she says is true. When I studied, the space station your early astronauts built, my scan found the remains of three humans and one serpent there. My bet is, no one on the station was aware of its presence."

A few days later, Viracocha released a series of satellites in geosynchronous orbit that circled the planet and acted just as the smaller amulets did. Now there was telepathic communication between serpents, as long as they remained in a subterranean place. But there would be no communication between humans and serpents and humans no longer needed to wear the amulets in order to avoid the serpents. The serpents would be dangerous to any alien species that attempted to conquer earth but would live in peace with the humans. Alien species were warned against the presence of the serpents by the satellites electronic communication; literally a warning sign that says, "Warning! There are serpents on this planet."

The serpents built another nest deep in the canyons of Serpiente where they would never be bothered. Tikal was released in Serpiente but driven away. After losing contact with their warriors who provided them with everything such as warmth and life energy, both Tikal and Tsotzil soon died. Teotihuacan was allowed to continue living with the clan, but his duties as emissary for the serpent clan become obsolete; all of his powers were taken away. He was directed to document what had happened for future generations.

Kukulcan gave birth to twelve baby serpents that are living in the nest.

Quetzalcoatl instructed them to never leave the confines of the canyon.

Both the Red Face and the Painted warriors suddenly found themselves without direction. Free from the influence of the serpents they suffered at first but eventually some survived and began living a peaceful life. After a time, they became productive members of their societies. The Red Face men kept their three painted stripes on their faces but they began to treat their women with respect rather than keeping their misogynous ways. They had no choice, the women demanded it. They faced starvation unless they changed their ways. The painted warriors never used skin illustrations again but continued their matriarchal society. Both tribes returned to farming and ranching eventually making friends with human tribes to the north who overcame their fear of them. In time, they acquired horses for use on their ranches.

Charlie and Pamela married and lived in Los Alamos. Pamela continued her work as a dragonfly technician and Charlie decided he could be most helpful as an agricultural worker. His proposals included the use of the water from the Rio Grande River which would provide water for large ponds which would be used to raise fish.

Penny and I, are now living in Serpiente and are expecting our first child. A child who will be raised as a human, rather than a serpent surrogate. Several volunteers from Los Alamos also moved to Serpiente where they found mates. The problems associated with inbreeding in Serpiente have disappeared. Penny and I also act as emissaries to represent Serpiente in the newly formed government. Our goal is to communicate with the ranchers and settlers who live throughout the land. We have decided to create a United States of America. Without the influence of the serpents that would have done everything possible to disrupt the process. Everywhere we meet people who wish to join and live in peace in a mutually beneficial union. No wars are occurring on planet earth for the first time in many millennia. Humanity has been offered a second chance and will be safe from alien invaders as long as we leave the serpents alone and use technology to implement serpent free exploration of space. For now, we have decided to stay on our home planet, Earth.

Déjà vu

The Greyhound bus slowly made its way through the streets of Tucumcari, New Mexico. Penny had been fast asleep despite the lateness in the day. It was not like her to sleep in late but after the dreams she had experienced the previous night she was feeling as if she had been up for days. Immediately she looked over to the seat next to her and discovered that the veiled lady with the serpent cane had disappeared leaving her wondering how in the world she could have left a moving bus without Penny being aware of it. She had a dull headache, was confused and her head was swimming with the memories of visions that had overcome her during her sleep. As the bus rumbled into the bus terminal it took all she could muster just to get out of her seat.

Walking into the station she searched for the mysterious lady who had kept her company since the last stop in a tiny town during the night but the mysterious lady had completely vanished. She went into the lady's room to take care of her business expecting to see the mysterious lady in there but again, the lady had truly disappeared. Penny took time to wash her face and brush her hair before walking back out to the bus where she settled into the same seat she had occupied for the last sixteen hundred miles.

Passengers continued to board until finally a large man who looked strangely familiar to her sat down next to her. He was obviously a Native American but dressed in working cloths. Penny was overcome by a feeling that this had all happened before. Despite her obvious familiarity with the Native American from her dream, she had reservations about sharing her seat with him. She turned and looked down the rows of seats and seeing that they were all occupied by passengers, she turned around and discovered that the Indian had propped his feet up blocking any plans of an exit.

"Excuse me!" she said. "I've come nearly the whole way from Tennessee with this seat to myself."

Penny was perplexed; not wanting to look arrogant and say something really rude, but she sure didn't like being boxed in. Only this time it was the memory of her dream that was blocking her. She decided to pretend to be indifferent to the Indian by looking out the window. This way she could collect and sort out her thoughts but soon she couldn't help but glance at him every few minutes. He was dressed roughly, in old jeans with cowboy boots that looked completely worn out. But from his waist up he appeared to have on a new plaid shirt. He was wearing no Indian jewelry, rare among Indians who carry much of their wealth in the form of turquoise and silver jewelry. His black hair was cut short like a business man, allowing Penny to think that maybe he wasn't entirely wild. Never the less, Penny was a little nervous, having never been around an Indian before, not even the local Cherokee Indians that were indigenous to East Tennessee. As the bus continued down the interstate, flashes of memories from her revelation continued to play with her mind.

After a quick stop in Cuervo, New Mexico, Penny awoke as the bus pulled into Santa Rosa. It was lunch and bathroom time, and a chance for her to change seats. But just as she started to leave, the Indian glanced over and said, "Penny Anderson?"

In amazement she replied, "Yes?"

"When you come back I have to talk to you about your uncle," he said. Blankly she stared back at him wondering what to say. How did he know her name? How did he know her uncle? Something was terribly strange about what was happening. She knew in her heart that this had all happened before. He finally stood up and allowed her to gently ease past him. Penny was confused. It seemed as if she had already done all of this before, an experience known as déjà vu.

Away to the restrooms she ran, then realized that she was starving. Unfortunately, by the time she had arrived in Santa Rosa, she was for all practical purposes dead broke, having used up all but two quarters from her stash of lunch money, saving these to make phone calls.

Inside the bright bus counter the smell of hamburgers being grilled made her stomach growl, having not eaten for two days. She also noticed the mysterious Indian, casually eating a hamburger while watching the tourists pick at the trinkets in the curio shop adjoining the lunch counter.

She stood behind him trying to figure the man out while flashes of the intense dream she had experienced continued to bother here. Then he turned, without looking back at her and quietly signaled with two upturned fingers to come and join him. He then pointed to the empty chair next to him, just as if he knew that she had been watching him.

Penny was totally perplexed. Somehow, he knew her name and the fact that her uncle lived in Serpiente. It was as if she had known this man for years but he seemed so mysterious. Penny quickly dismissed the thought, knowing that she had never actually met him before. Now that she really had a good look at him, he really didn't look as old as her first impression had given her, perhaps five years older. He was just weathered, as if he had spent a lot of time outdoors.

Deciding to confront him, Penny walked up to him in front of the many people eating in the café and blurted out, "How did you know my name, and what do you know about my uncle?"

He casually glanced up and stuffed another French fry into his mouth. After a few chews and a slow swallow, he said, "June received a phone call from your mother. After searching everywhere, she finally ran into your friend from the high school who gave you the ride to Knoxville. She explained to your mother what had actually happened which caused a confrontation with Turner. Your mother found out what was really going on and called the police and had him arrested. Since then, we have been watching for you to show up. My truck is in Albuquerque at the bus stop. I'm supposed to, maybe," he said hesitantly with a frown on his face, "give you a ride out to the ranch house."

Penny stared at him, not saying anything. She had heard this conversation before only it was in a dream.

"Okay." The Native American continued, "Your uncle, Ken Anderson sent me, but we have a problem. There are some things, funny things happening out at the ranch, and so he sent me here to talk you out of coming out to Serpiente. By the way, my name is *Naalyehe Ya Sidahi*." He looked over at Penny who had a look of astonishment on her face and he followed his name with; "That is my birth name, which most people have no idea how to pronounce or what it means. By the way, it means one who is a trader but all my friends just call me Hidalgo, like the horse or the county in southern New Mexico. I've been called Hidalgo ever since I was a little kid growing up on the reservation, the name just stuck to me." Looking at his reflection in the lunch counter he said slowly, "I don't know how I got that name. Its the name I've been called all my life." And with a flip of his wrist he ordered the waitress over.

Penny now was completely confused. She appeared to be reliving the craziest dream she had ever had. But how could that be? Like all dreams, she was already starting to forget some of the important details despite the vividness of the visions she had had. But every move she made seemed to involve her reliving a memory. Perhaps it was more than just a dream. She wondered if she had experienced a premonition. Perhaps her life was preordained but how was that possible? All she knew was that she was experiencing a road map to her future but that meant that someone or something was in control. Obviously, something or someone was directing her to a future that based upon her revelations was going to be very mysterious but she was willing to embrace that future. Deep in her heart, she decided she was ready for the challenge.

Readers Guide

1. Evidence for the presence of serpents are found on every continent, throughout all of history. Many Native American Cultures such as the Navajo believe in creatures known as skin walkers, shapeshifters or serpents. Do serpents represent a metaphorical side of human nature or are they real creatures?

2. What kind of research is currently occurring in respect to biological weapons? Has the United States ever conducted biological weapon research on its own citizens?

3. What is a genetic bottleneck? Is there scientific evidence that it has occurred before? Why did the author discuss previous bottlenecks?

4. The families at Williams Creek were terrified of contact with outsiders and they were dependent upon Chato for their mutual survival? Yet they agreed to let him go? What would you have said if you lived there?

5. As Chato made his journey to the Pacific Ocean he encountered a warrior. What did that tell him about the pandemic?

6. Why do geological changes occur on this planet? Where does the heat from volcanoes come from?

7. What items would be of use to a survivor after two hundred years of human depopulation? Would the canned food be eatable?

8. Why did Chato and Charlie avoid using guns which would certainly still function?

9. Why did Chato and Charlie search for traces of contemporary travelers as they paddled down the coast?

10. Why did the Red Face Warriors not venture into the coastal areas of America?

11. It was in the nature of the serpent Tsozil to degenerate and disregard women. Why do you think this was in his nature? Is this also a human characteristic?

12. Why did the Red Face Warriors covet horses so much?

13. After capture by the Red Face Warriors, would Chato and Charlie have been killed if Tsozil would have appeared, before their escape? Why or why not?

14. The Colorado River was a perfect escape route for Chato and Charlie. The Red Face Warriors avoided water, except for drinking, at all cost. Why?

15. As far back into history as archeologist have explored, humans have placed objects such as food and flowers on graves. Why?

16. Why were the Hopi willing to help Chato and Charlie?

17. What outdoor survival skills were used by Chato and Charlie as they hiked through the desert?

18. Why did the scientists at Los Alamos Laboratories avoid using fossil fuels? What inventions enabled them to survive after the pandemic? Are devices such as these currently available, and if so, why are they not used?

19. Why were the Painted Warriors mostly women? Why were their bodies tattooed into geometric designs?

20. Why were the descendants to Penny Anderson, as well as the people of Serpiente, unaware of what Tzotzil and Tikal were doing?

21. Did Chimalma trick the serpents into a solution? Whose side was she really working for?

22. Considering the modern political climate of the world, are there real people that are analogous to the characters in this novel?

23. Why did the author return to the beginning of the Serpent Trilogy? Why did Penny experience a Déjà vu? Do you think her future was preordained by Chimalma?

24. Did Chimalma know what was going to happen? Did Chimalma do, what she did, for the humans, or was she only thinking of her diplomatic responsibilities to the serpents?

25. Was Chimalma a shaman?

www.ingramcontent.com/pod-product-compliance
Lightning Source LLC
Chambersburg PA
CBHW030648020726
47493CB00006B/1930